THE
UNWILLING

ALSO BY JOHN HART

The Hush

Redemption Road

Iron House

The Last Child

Down River

The King of Lies

THE
UNWILLING

John Hart

ST. MARTIN'S PRESS

NEW YORK

First published in the United States by St. Martin's Press, an imprint of St. Martin's Publishing Group

www.stmartins.com

Designed by Omar Chapa

Library of Congress Cataloging-in-Publication Data

Names: Hart, John, 1965– author.
Title: The unwilling / John Hart.
Description: First edition. | New York : St. Martin's Press, 2021.
Identifiers: LCCN 2019058395 | ISBN 9781250167729 (hardcover) |
ISBN 9781250167736 (ebook)
Subjects: GSAFD: Suspense fiction. | Mystery fiction.
Classification: LCC PS3608.A78575 U59 2021 | DDC 813/.6—dc23
LC record available at https://lccn.loc.gov/2019058395

Our books may be purchased in bulk for promotional, educational, or business use. Please contact your local bookseller or the Macmillan Corporate and Premium Sales Department at 1-800-221-7945, extension 5442, or by email at MacmillanSpecialMarkets@macmillan.com.

First Edition: 2021

10 9 8 7 6 5 4 3 2 1

For Tommy Dobson, an admirable man

ACKNOWLEDGMENTS

It's a strange thing, the genesis of a novel. Some ideas stick. Others don't. Years ago, I read the story of Hugh Thompson, Jr., a helicopter pilot serving in Vietnam who, along with his Hiller OH-23 Raven Crew, was instrumental in stopping what's come to be known as the My Lai massacre. If you're unfamiliar with his story, you might want to check it out—an act of exceptional heroism backlit by what most consider the worst atrocity of the entire conflict. Having been too young to serve in Vietnam, I would never presume to write a story of that actual war, but the idea of this man's unflinching courage—both physical and moral—has been with me for a very long time. My first acknowledgment, then, is to Hugh Thompson, Jr., and those who flew with him, Glenn Andreotta and Lawrence Colburn, heroes in the best sense of the word and the inspiration for one of the finest characters I may have ever written.

That being said, this is not a novel about the Vietnam War, but of an American city in 1972, of young men who served and died, and of the boys who grew to manhood in fear of the draft. It's also a story of courage and sacrifice, of families and girlfriends and the sad, hard truth that acts of horrible violence are not relegated to war alone. Writing such a novel takes a lot of support, and I'd like to thank my family for all they do to help, not just my wife, Katie, and my daughters, Saylor and Sophie, but all of my family, fine people who keep me sane and make life a joy.

After seven books my editor, Pete Wolverton, remains a rock of encouragement and sound advice. Hannah O'Grady works at his side and has also been a blessing. I do love a beautiful book, so thanks, as well, to the production team of Vincent Stanley and Ken Silver, to Omar Chapa, who designed the book, and to Mike Storrings and Young Lim, who designed a lovely jacket. Only a writer knows how easy it is to embarrass oneself in print, so thanks to Sara Ensey, my copy editor, and to Ryan Jenkins, who proofed the manuscript—your work allows me to hold my head up in public. And because I write for a living it matters that the reading public knows about the book, so a huge shout-out to all the pros at St. Martin's who work hard to spread the word. I'm looking at you, Jeff Dodes, Paul Hochman, and Joe Brosnan, marketing gurus that you are; and at my wonderful publicists, Tracey Guest, Sarah Bonamino, and Rebecca Lang. I wouldn't be where I am without your efforts and expertise. That sentiment applies, as well, to the Macmillan sales force. Thank you all for what you do.

I have also been blessed with the kind of top-down support about which every author dreams, not just for one book or two, but for my career to date. This is book seven with the same publishing house, and it's hard to walk such a long road without the intangibles that matter, things like vision, patience, and faith. For that I thank the shot callers at Macmillan: John Sargent, Don Weisberg, Sally Richardson, Jennifer Enderlin, Andy Martin, and Lisa Senz. You've made a lot of calls that went my way, and for that I am grateful. Thanks, also, to my agency, ICM, and to Esther Newberg, my agent, who does what she does, and does it well.

I do owe a brief word to the City of Charlotte and those who call it home. For the story to work I needed to make the city a bit larger than it was in 1972, also a bit dirtier and more violent. Apologies for that, but hey, it's fiction. I must also thank Laura and Maurice Hull, fine friends who did a kind thing. I mean, seriously—what other novelists get their books plastered on a race car? Finally, I'd like to thank all the people here and abroad who've read my books and spread the word. I wouldn't be here without you.

We the unwilling, led by the unqualified to kill the unfortunate, die for the ungrateful.

—*Unknown Soldier*

1

Daniel Reed knew many things about ex-cops, and one of those things was that not all the *cop* died when a man quit or took early medical or got fired for smoking weed. Four years of pushing a bus station mop, and he still felt that burn beneath his collar, the prickle of skin that drew his eyes up from the slop bucket and busted tile.

He considered the young people first. They sprawled on a bench, drunk and loud, but that wasn't the problem. The families and the hippies came next, then the old men and the pregnant woman and the soldiers in uniform. Beyond the glass, the two fifteen from Raleigh idled in the bay as a dozen people waited for suitcases, old Mac sweating in the heat as he hauled them out and lined them up. Daniel had known a thousand days like it, small-city South in a country tired of war. Inevitably, his eyes found the pretty girl in the yellow dress. She was eighteen, maybe, with a shabby suitcase and leather shoes starting to split. He'd watched her, on and off, for an hour: the small walks from one wall to the next, little turns, the tilted head. At the moment, she stood unmoving, lips slightly parted.

Following her gaze, Daniel spotted the young man in a dim recess leading to the bay. Angular and lean, he stopped five feet from the double doors and stood long enough to study the people in the room. Daniel's first thought was, *Vietnam,* and not long from the war. Something about the way he stood, the awareness. When he stepped into the light, Daniel got a better look at the Zeppelin T-shirt, the cheekbones, the belt made of black leather, turquoise, and tarnished silver. Faded jeans brushed the tops of old boots; and when he walked past, he smelled like diesel and whiskey and tobacco. "Detective," he said; but Daniel looked away, ashamed that he was old and stoned and not a cop anymore. He waited until a swinging door flashed sunlight into the room, then asked the ticketing agent if he could please use the phone. She handed it over, and he dialed the station from long memory, requesting a detective by name.

"Just a moment, please."

Silence rolled onto the line, and Daniel watched the young man cross against traffic, breaking into a jog as he hit the final lane and a truck blew past. In the bright sunlight, he was a blade of a man: the waist, the shoulders, the angle of his jaw. He looked back once and slipped dark glasses across his eyes.

Shit, the old cop thought.

Just . . . shit.

Detective French took the call at a phone on his partner's desk. "French," he said, and listened. "That seems unlikely." He listened some more, then thanked the caller and hung up.

"Everything okay?"

French glanced at the familiar lines of his partner's face. He and Ken Burklow went back twenty years, and had few secrets between them. One was about to come out. "Jason's back in town. That was Reed, at the bus station."

"Reed's a burnout."

"Not so burned out he wouldn't know my oldest son."

Burklow leaned back in his chair, hard-faced and unhappy. "I thought Jason was still in prison."

"Halfway house in Raleigh. Seven weeks now."

"And you didn't think to tell me he was out?"

"I need to call my wife." French dialed the phone and watched emotions play across his partner's face. Sadness. Worry. Anger. "She's not answering."

"Would he go to the house?"

"Not after the way things ended."

"You can't be sure of that."

"He wouldn't do that to his mother. Not after the last time."

"You say that, but come on. Vietnam. Prison. Who knows what he'll do. You've heard the stories."

French scrubbed a palm across his face, and sighed unhappily.

Twenty-nine confirmed kills . . .

That was the story: twenty-nine in his first year.

Dialing a few more numbers, he asked his questions and hung up. "She's not at the neighbor's house or with either of her best friends."

"What about Gibby, then? If Jason's not going home . . ."

The sentence trailed off, and French thought of Gibson, his youngest son. "Gibby's in school. He should be fine."

"Uh-uh. Senior Skip."

French did the math, and realized that his partner was right. Senior Skip Day had been tradition since the first year of the draft. Last three Fridays before final exams, the seniors cut school and went to the quarry south of town. Teachers looked away and so did the cops. Gibby would be there, and he *should be,* they all should. That was the thing about childhood and endings and war in some foreign fucking jungle.

"I'll check the quarry." Burklow stood. "That way you can look for your wife, and let her know Jason's in town. Give her time, you know. Get her ready."

"I should handle this myself."

"Don't be stupid." Burklow shrugged into a coat, and checked his weapon. "Not even Superman can be in two places at once."

William French was no genius, and was smart enough to know as much. He was steady and solid, a determined man who'd become a better cop than he had a right to be. It was the same with his marriage. Gabrielle was out of his league on the day they'd met, and still there on the day they'd married. He'd asked her once how someone who'd studied litera-ture at Vanderbilt and lit up every room she entered could possibly settle for a college dropout three years into a job that might get him killed.

She'd kissed his cheek, put a hand on his heart, and said, "Don't ever ask me that again." Three sons and thirty years later, she was still a gift—his whole life—but she'd lost one son already.

Now this . . .

He parked in front of their house, and thought, as he often did, how empty it felt. That, too, was about the war. They'd buried their oldest son, then watched his twin brother return from the same conflict only to spiral into violence, drugs, and prison. In that regard, Vietnam had killed two of their three boys, Robert with a bullet to the heart, and his brother more insidiously. Jason never talked about the things he'd done in the service of his country, but Burklow had a friend at the Department of Defense. He refused to provide details, but said once that there was *war* and there was *WAR*, and that Jason had fought the latter kind.

"Gabrielle?"

The silence inside was familiar from all the years of mourning, a large house with parts of its soul carved away. Nearing the bedroom, French heard running water, and stopped where the bathroom door hung open an inch.

"Sweetheart?"

She was in the tub and in the dark, but he could see her silhouette against the tile.

"Don't turn on the light."

He took his hand from the switch, wondering if she'd known or merely guessed. As his eyes adjusted, he saw more of her shape. Water rose to the curve of her breasts, and her arms were wrapped across her shins.

Without turning, she said, "Is he the reason you're here?"

"What do you mean?"

Her head tilted, then, and a glint showed in one of her eyes. "You haven't come home midafternoon since we were newlyweds. I'm asking if Jason is the reason you're here."

French sighed unhappily. "Who told you he's back?"

"Marion called. She saw him at the square. His hair was longer, but she knew him. She said he was pale, that prison cost him twenty pounds."

"I'm going to handle this, Gabrielle. I promise."

"Gibby will want to see him, to spend time—"

"I won't allow that."

"How will you stop it?"

"Gabrielle—"

"He's dangerous, Bill. He's a danger to our son. Don't you see that? Can't you feel it?"

French sighed again, and knelt by the tub. Gabrielle had tried to make room in her heart for the man Jason had become, but Jason had not made it easy for her. Heroin. Prison. The effect he had on Gibby. Before Jason's conviction, all Gibby had wanted was to trail in his brother's shadow, to know about the Marine Corps and war, and whether he, too, should go to Vietnam. "Listen," he said. "I just wanted to tell you in person that Jason was back, to promise you that I'll keep Gibson safe."

"You think I'm silly, don't you? A silly, overprotective woman."

"I promise you I don't."

"If you were a mother, you'd understand."

"Jason would never hurt his brother."

"Not intentionally. Not with malice."

She left the rest unspoken, but he understood the deeper fears, her worries about corruption, deception, dangerous ideas.

"Gibby's not in school," she said. "Did you know that?"

"It's a skip day. He'll be at the quarry with his friends. Ken is already looking for him."

"What if Jason finds him first?"

French looked away from the fear in his wife's eyes. Gibby was her world, and Jason was a destroyer of worlds. "I'll go, too," he said. "I'll find him."

"You do that. You bring him home."

French stood, but didn't leave. He pushed his hands into his pockets, and looked down on the crown of her head and the curve of a dim, damp shoulder, bits of his wife on an apron of dark water. "Sooner or later Gibson will want to see his brother."

"Just make sure it's later."

"Jason was inside for two years and change. He did his time."

"Only Gibby matters. I'm sorry, Bill, but that's the truth."

"Won't you at least talk to him?"

"To Jason?"

"Yes."

"About what?" she asked. "Heroin?"

2

The quarry means different things to different people. For me, it's about the drop. They say it's a hundred and thirty feet from the top of the cliff to the top of the water, and from the water that feels about right: the granite rising, the gray sky above that. All that sameness makes the cliff seem small, and I know what people think, floating on their backs or looking out from the narrow shore across the quarry.

I could do that.

The more they drink, the more certain they become. It's only water, they say, just a dive. How hard can it be?

But then they make the climb.

The first good ledge is sixty feet up, and people do jump from it. A few might make it to the next good ledge. Call it eighty feet. Somehow that looks twice as high as the one right below it. Those who make it all the way up tend to lean out from the waist and look downward as if somehow the laws of physics might have changed on the way up.

Seventy miles an hour when you hit the water.

Four full seconds to get there.

From thirteen stories up, the water looks like plate steel, and people remember the stories they've heard: the kid who died back in '57, the ballplayer who hit wrong and drove a knee through his jaw, breaking it in four places and shattering every tooth on the right side. I've seen it a hundred times. The boys go pale, and their girlfriends say, *I take it back, don't do it.* I'm not the only who's jumped—a few others have, too—but only one person had the balls to dive, and that was my brother.

The dead one.

"Come on, man. If you're going to do it, do it already." The voice was behind me, my oldest friend. "You know Becky's watching."

I looked into the quarry and saw Becky Collins on an inner tube a hundred feet out from the cliff. She was as small as the rest, but no one else wore a white bikini. Her head rocked back, and I thought she might be laughing. The girl beside her might be laughing, too. Around them, a collection of rafts and tubes held half the senior class. The rest were on the far side of the quarry or in the woods or passed out in any of the cars that glinted in the distance like bits of colored glass.

"Are you making this dive or not?"

I looked away long enough to catch the gleam in Chance's eyes. He was a small kid, but would fight anybody; try for any girl. "Maybe she's looking at you," I said.

"I'm not dumb enough to jump off this rock."

I wondered what that said about me. I'd jumped seven times, but never made the dive, and everyone down there knew it. I'd sworn to do it before graduation, but that was two years ago, and I'd been angry when I'd said it. "Do you think I'm stupid?" I asked.

"I think you're a rock star."

"McCartney or Jagger?"

Chance offered up a devil's grin. "That depends on if you jump or dive."

I looked away from my friend, and thought about hitting wrong at seventy miles an hour. Beneath me, people began to chant.

"Dive, dive, dive . . ."

When my brother did it, it was a swan dive drawn against a high, pale sky, and I see it still in my dreams: the way he rose and hung, and then the long fall—no breath in my lungs—and how his hands came together an instant before he struck. Only three of us were there to see it, but word of it spread.

Robert French made the dive off Devil's Ledge . . .

Did you hear?

Can you believe it?

At the time, the world record cliff dive was only fifteen feet higher, some guy in Argentina. But this was Charlotte, North Carolina, a little place in 1967. That was five years ago, but on that day in this little city, my oldest brother became a god. People asked him why he did it and how and a thousand other questions, but only four of us knew the truth that mattered, and I dream of that part, too: the way light hit his face when it broke from the water, the eyes that looked brighter and more alive. *Let the Vietcong touch that,* he'd said; and that was the thing only a few of us knew.

Robert was going to Vietnam.

"I'm going to do it," I said.

"Bullshit."

"This time it happens."

"Go on, then."

"Becky Collins, right?"

"She'll love you forever."

I'd pictured the dive a thousand times, and it felt a lot like this: the wind in my face, the smell of heat and dust and distant rain. I rose to my toes, arms spread. "Give me a three count."

"Wait. What?"

"No talking, all right? This is hard enough as it is."

"Dude . . ."

"What?" I didn't look away from the drop.

"Dude. Seriously . . ."

Something in his voice was strange to me: a note of doubt or panic or fear. "What's the problem, Chance? We're here, right? Two weeks 'til graduation."

"Just jump, dude. Make it a jump."

"I'm sorry. What?"

"You know you can't actually do it, right? You can't make that dive." Chance looked embarrassed, turning his hands to show the palms. "I mean . . . come on. There's a pattern, right? You talk about it. You stand there. You never actually *dive*."

"But you egg me on. You tell me to do it."

"Because I've never once thought you were stupid enough to actually dive. It's thirteen stories."

"You think I'm afraid?"

"No."

"You don't think I can do it?"

"I think your brother's dead whether you do it or not."

The color drained from my face.

Chance didn't care. "Robert is gone, man. He won't see the dive or pat you on the back or say, *Welcome to the club.* He'll still be underground in that cemetery you hate. He'll still be a dead hero, and you'll still be a kid in high school."

Chance was earnest and worried—a strange combination. I looked away as catcalls rose up the cliff, and someone far below yelled, *Do it, you pussy!* I found Becky Collins, a slash of brown and white. She was shading her eyes; she wasn't yelling. "You think I'd die if I did it?"

"I know you would."

"Robert lived."

"Hand of God, Gibby. One in a million."

I watched Becky, thinking of God and luck and my dead brother. The Marine Corps said he took one in the heart, and that it killed him before he felt a thing. A painless death, they said, but I didn't buy it. "Two years ago I said I'd make the dive. I told everyone down there I'd do it."

"You mean *that* everyone?" Chance pointed at the water, where even more kids were yelling up the cliff's face. "You mean Bill Murphy, who told Becky to her face that you were a loser because your mom won't let you play football anymore? You mean his lame-ass brother? Fuck that guy, too. He blew spitballs at the back of your head for pretty much all of seventh grade. What about Jessica Parker or Diane Fairway? I asked them both out, and they laughed at me. They're not keen on you, either, by the way. They say you're too quiet and that you're distant and that you look too much like your dead brother. Listen, Gibs, you don't owe anyone down there a damn thing. That crowd there, those people . . ." He pointed down. "Empty heads and bullshit and vanity. They don't know you or want to know you. Maybe three are worth a crap, and they're the only ones *not* yelling at you to kill yourself."

I leaned out; saw jocks and stoners and pretty girls in mirrored shades. Most were laughing or smiling or yelling at me.

Do it . . .

Dive . . .

Dive, you chickenshit motherfucker . . .

They'd rafted up for the best view: a jigsaw of rubber and smooth skin and bits of bikini that looked like colored sails. I listened for a moment more, then studied the sky, the jagged rock, the far, familiar water. Last, I looked at Becky Collins, who, with a single friend, floated apart from the others. She was unmoving, one hand at her mouth, the other pressed across the heart. "You know something," I said. "I think maybe you're right."

"Really?"

"In part, yeah."

"What does that mean, *in part*?"

I disliked needless lies, so I shook my head, then turned from the edge, and started walking to the trail that would take us down. Chance followed, still worried.

"Dude, wait. What does that mean?"

I kept quiet, unwilling to share the conviction he'd put inside me. It was powerful and strange, and made me drunk with possibility.

Me alone, I thought.

Me alone when I dive . . .

It wasn't the first time Chance and I had walked the long trail down. We followed the slope east and then switchbacked through the trees, coming out a quarter mile later on the far side of the quarry, where people parked their cars. Walking to the edge of the field, we stood and looked down. Chance nudged me. "She's on the beach to your left."

"I wasn't looking for her."

"Yeah, right."

Becky saw me and waved. A squad of guys surrounded her, football players, mostly. One of them saw me looking, and spit on the cracked, granite ledge that passed for a beach.

Chance said, "Come on. Let's find a beer."

We turned for the trail that would take us to the water, but saw movement in a shaded place beneath the pines. A man was squatting with his back against the trunk, and his head shifted as he ground a cigarette into the dirt. "I caught your performance. Thought for a minute you might actually do it." He stood, and moved into the light: black hair and denim and prison-pale skin. "Hello, little brother."

Jason was five years older, but my size and shape. The same hair brushed the collar of his shirt. The same eyes stared out from a face that was similar in every way but the hard edges of it. "You're out," I said, and he shrugged. "What are you doing here?"

"Looking for you, believe it or not."

A pint bottle appeared from his back pocket. He unscrewed the cap and offered me a sip. When I shook my head, he shrugged and tipped the bottle back.

"You remember Chance," I said.

"Hello, little man." Chance bridled at the mocking tone, and Jason stood there looking unconcerned and dangerous and bored. "Why didn't you make the dive?" I shrugged stupidly, and Jason nodded as if he understood. "It was something to see, though, wasn't it?"

He was talking about the day our brother dove. Robert had been the kindest and my favorite. "Have you been home?" He shook his head. "You going?"

"After last time? I don't think so."

His grin, then, was the first truly familiar thing I'd seen. It had a sharp edge on one side, and the eye above it dipped in a quick wink. If Jason liked you, the wink said, *Life is good, I've got your back.* For others, it was different. Even in high school, grown men would back away from the wink and the grin, and that was before war and death and whatever devil Vietnam put inside my brother. He was calm at the moment, but that could change on a dime. Indian summer. Killing frost. Jason had both of those things inside, and they could trade places plenty fast.

He lit another cigarette, and I watched him do it, hating how much he looked like our dead brother. Were Robert here instead of Jason, he'd have wrapped me up, laughing. He'd have squeezed so hard I couldn't breathe, then he'd have pushed me back, mussed my hair, and said, *My*

God, look how you've grown. I often wondered if war had changed him as it changed Jason. Was he harder in those last days? Or was it Robert's goodness that got him killed in the end, some softness that my other brother lacked?

"What are you doing tomorrow?" Jason asked.

"I don't know. Hanging out, I guess."

"Let's do it together, the two of us. You have a car. I know some girls." He smiled around the cigarette, then pulled in smoke and streamed it through his nostrils. "Robert and I used to do that, you know. Back roads and cold beers, life before the war. What do you say? It could be like old times."

"What girls?" I asked.

"This guy." Jason hooked a thumb, and looked at Chance. "What does it matter, what girls? You don't trust me?"

"It's not that . . ."

I hesitated, and Jason's grin faded. "Don't say it's our mother."

"You know how she is."

"You're going to bail on a day with two fine women and your long-lost brother because it might upset our mother?"

"You're not around, man. You don't see how she gets."

"Let me guess. Demanding? Judgmental?"

"I'd call it overprotective."

Jason shook his head, and pulled hard on the bottle. "You don't think Robert would want us to be in each other's lives? You don't think that, deep down, even Dad thinks it's wrong, the way she keeps us apart? But hey, you know what? It's cool." He flicked the cigarette, and showed the brightest, coldest eyes I'd ever seen. "If you're not man enough . . ."

"Don't say that, Jason."

"Man enough. Grown enough."

"Screw you, dude."

He grinned again, and looked at the cliff. "If you were man enough, you'd have made the dive. You used to be a tough little nut. You remember that? How that felt?"

The bright eyes were a challenge, and I felt the same coldness in me. "Like you could make that dive," I said.

"Any day of the week."

"Not a chance in hell."

"Oh really?"

"Yeah, really."

"How about this, then? I make the dive now, and we go out tomorrow, you and me. Not only that, but you tell Mom what you're doing. You tell her all of it—me, the girls—you tell her all of it and see what she says."

I stared at the cliff, thinking of my mother. *Different kind of ledge. Different kind of dying.* "You understand what she's afraid of, right?"

"Course I do," Jason said. "She thinks you'll go to war because Robert did and I did, or that you'll decide it's cool to be like me, that maybe you'll get arrested or do drugs or, God forbid, screw a girl. I think mainly she's afraid you'll learn to think for yourself. Are you allowed to do that, little brother? Form opinions? Live your own life? Does she even know you're here?"

I didn't answer. I didn't have to.

"Here's the deal." Jason stepped closer and draped an arm across my shoulder. "I make the dive and we go out this Saturday. All day. The two of us." He squeezed my neck. "A brother should know his brother."

I studied those bright, cold eyes, and something twisted inside, like grease and old metal. Did he want to know me at all or was he just messing with me? I replayed his homecoming from war: the bitterness and unanswered questions, the family fights and all the ways he'd changed. How many days before the first arrest? How long before the heroin? I stepped away from what I saw in those eyes, and his arm fell to his side. "I don't want you dying because of me."

"A deal's a deal, little brother."

"I mean it," I said.

"I know you do."

He gave the grin and the wink, and looked so much like our dead brother it hurt. Kicking off his shoes, he shrugged off the shirt, and I saw all the places he'd been wounded in war, the bullet holes and burn marks and ragged scars. Beside me, Chance was small and tense and staring.

"Jesus Christ."

"Shut up, Chance."

Jason ignored my friend, and that felt about right. This was about us, alone. "Why are you doing this?" I asked.

"You know why."

"I really don't."

"Don't be stupid. You know *exactly* why." He pushed his cigarettes into my hand. "You keep those dry for me. I'm going to want one, after."

"Jason, listen . . ." I ran out of words.

He turned and started walking, and Chance gave a strange, small laugh. "No way, dude. No way he dives."

People stared as my brother moved out onto the stony beach, and I thought a few of the older guys recognized him. A couple of them nudged each other and whispered, but Jason looked neither left nor right. He made a shallow dive, and slid beneath the surface for a dozen beats. When he rose, it was into an easy crawl that took him out from shore.

"No way," Chance muttered. "There's no fucking way."

Across the quarry, Jason pulled himself onto the face of the cliff, and was pale against the rock. He made the ascent with effortless grace, and by the time he reached the top, word of his identity had spread along the beach. I saw it in the whispers.

Jason French.

Vietnam.

Prison.

A few eyes found me, but I ignored them. Becky Collins looked my way, but even that felt like the tail end of a nightmare. "He's going to do it," I said, and felt the moment as if I stood beside him. The same wind licked the stone, and the water, below, was cold, gray, and hard. The only difference was the silence as Jason spread his arms. No one spoke or called out, and I would swear, in years to come, that the wind stilled and even the birds fell quiet.

Please, God . . .

The prayer came in the instant of my certainty. I felt his breath as if it were my own, his toes as they took the weight. I knew the bend of his knees, the commitment, the moment his life was not his own.

"Sweet Jesus."

Chance spoke the words as my brother rose, and lint-colored sky spread between his feet and the stone. He hung on invisible strings, and looked as our brother had looked: the light on one side, the bow of his chest and arms. For that moment, he was pinned and perfect, then the weight of his shoulders took him down; and like that, I was thirteen again and choking; and I heard the same words, somewhere deep.

One Mississippi.

Two . . .

I counted as I had for Robert, and feared that a second brother would die. He was waiting too long, arms still spread as *Three Mississippi* sounded in my mind, and brought with it a terrible certainty.

He would hit wrong.

He would shatter.

But in the last moment his hands came together and, like the tip of a knife, split the surface to let my brother pass. He disappeared in black water, and I didn't breathe until I saw him again, his head above the surface, those long arms stroking for shore. Chance said something, but I was half-deaf from a sound like roaring wind.

It was blood in my ears, I thought.

Or maybe it was people cheering.

3

For the rest of the day I thought of my brother and his dive and the deal we'd struck. *Saturday. The two of us.* I didn't tell my mother at dinner that night, even though we ate in awkward silence, and she opened the door as if to invite the conversation. "Did I see Ken in the driveway?"

She watched her food as she asked the question. I met my father's eyes, but they offered no hint of his thoughts on the matter. "He came in behind me," I said.

That was true, but not the whole story. My father's partner had found me at the quarry, and insisted on following me home. He said, *I told your father I'd make sure,* and those were his final words. He didn't mention Jason or the kids he'd seen drinking or the guilty way I'd started at his sudden appearance. He'd watched Jason with those flat, cop eyes, then stared Chance down with the same unflinching distaste. *Shouldn't you be leaving, too?* In the driveway, he'd watched me to the house, then waited as my father pulled in behind us. I missed their conversation, but from the door, I'd seen my father glance my way with the same cop eyes.

"You weren't at school today," my mother said.

"I was at the quarry."

"Senior Skip Day is tradition, I know, but you're back in school on Monday. That means homework, papers, final exams. No slacking because the end is near."

"Yes, ma'am."

She forked a bite of salad, and that, too, was part of the dance. No mention of Robert or Jason or the war. I wasn't sure where her mind went in the silence between questions, but guessed it was the future or some other bright place.

My father knew the dance as well: keep it simple and light and surface. "Have you thought more about a summer job?"

"They want to hire me at the marina."

"Again?"

He was disappointed, but I liked the boats, the water, the smell of fuel. His frown deepened, but he couldn't really argue. I'd be at college in the fall. That meant deferment. He smiled stiffly, and my mother sipped wine.

For me, though, the dance wasn't working. "Did you know Jason is out of prison?"

The question fell like a bomb. My mother choked on her wine. My father said, "Son . . ."

"You should have told me."

The anger came unexpectedly and suddenly, and its cause was unclear. *How they managed my life? The things I'd felt as my brother fell?* Only the emotion was certain, this unfamiliar anger.

"Who told you?" my mother asked.

"I saw him. We spoke."

She dabbed a napkin at the corners of her mouth. "About me, I suppose?"

"We might have touched on that."

She smoothed the napkin in her lap, and looked away.

"You knew, of course. Didn't you? You knew that he was back."

"We thought it best to keep the two of you apart." Her gaze, that time, was direct and unapologetic. She sat calmly and straight, an elegant woman. "Shall we discuss the reasons?"

"Has anything changed since the last time we discussed reasons?"

"Not for me."

I turned to my father. "Dad?"

"Give us a chance to talk with him first. Okay? After prison. After all this time. Give us a chance to feel him out. We don't know his plans or why he's back."

"And when you know those things?"

"Then we'll see where we are."

I looked from one to the other. Nothing had changed. Nothing ever would. "May I be excused?"

My mother lifted her glass. "Do you have plans to see him again?"

"No," I lied.

"Talk to him by phone?"

"If he has a number, I don't know it."

She studied me with eyes that were as cool and bright as my brother's. "Are you still my good boy?"

"I try to be."

"Do you love me?"

"Of course."

"Are you angry?"

"Not anymore."

Another sip. The same eyes. "Clear your dishes."

I carried dishes to the kitchen, and took the back stairs to my room. Inside, I closed the door and tried to see the space as if it were not my own: the posters and old toys and plastic trophies. When my father knocked on the door, it was after nine.

"Come in."

He opened the door, surprised by the state of my room. The posters were down. Half the stuff I owned was boxed. "What's all this?"

I shrugged, and kept packing. "Just wanted a change."

He looked in one box and then another. "You giving this stuff away?"

"I guess."

"Your comic books?" He lifted a stack from a half-full box. "You've collected these since you were eight." I didn't respond. He put the comic books down and sat on the edge of the bed. "About your mother . . ."

"You don't need to explain."

"I'm happy to talk about it."

"She's afraid Jason will ruin my life. This is hardly news."

"It won't be forever, son."

"It's been years, Dad. Five years that she won't let me play sports or date girls. I can't go camping or hunting. She barely lets me leave the house."

"She let you have a car."

"Because I paid for it myself."

"She still allowed it."

"She did, yes, and it's the only thing she's done that's fair."

"None of this is fair, son. It's not fair that Robert died, or that Jason changed the way he did. It's not fair for your mother to worry so much, or for any of this to land on you. Just work with me. Stay away from Jason, at least for a little while."

"He's my brother."

"I know he is, but there are things about Jason you don't know."

"What? That he did drugs? That he killed people in the war?"

My father frowned and studied the floor, less certain than he used to be. "Three or four days, just a little while."

"You should have told me he was back."

"You're angry. I get it. I still need your promise."

"I can't give it to you."

"Not even for your mother's sake?"

"Not even for yours."

I stared at him, and he stared back; and in the end, that's where he left me: in a silence that spoke of fathers and sons and difficult truths. I couldn't turn my back on Jason, not after losing Robert.

I thought my father understood.

That maybe he approved.

French stopped ten feet from the door, and took a moment to remember his sons as they'd been before the war: Robert, with his easy smile and gracious nature, and Jason, who'd been sardonic and brilliant and occasionally cruel. From the beginning, Gibby's love for Robert had been the most obvious, but he'd been more like Jason than he chose to admit. He had the same insight and self-awareness, the same cutting wit. Gibby's heart, of course, was immense, and the only reason he'd yielded, for so many years, to his mother's insane demands. No girls. No sports.

"Damn it, Gabrielle."

Rationality played no part in her overprotective nature. Robert had been selected in the draft, with Jason being spared only because he'd been born two minutes after midnight, which made them twins with different birthdays. Gabrielle had wept on the day Robert left for Vietnam, and broken entirely at news of his death. He'd been the first and the favorite. Gabrielle would never admit such a truth, but her cries in the dark of that terrible night still haunted his memories.

It should have been Jason!

It should have been him!

He'd tried to stifle the words, but believed, to this day, that they'd carried through the house. How long after that before Jason enlisted?

Two days?

Three?

French sighed deeply, and his face was rough beneath his palms. Pushing away from the wall, he made his way to the master bedroom door and peered inside. Gabrielle was in the bed, on her side. Moving quietly past, he lifted his weapon and shield from the dresser.

"Are you going out?" She rolled over, a rustle in the sheets.

"Did I wake you? I'm sorry. Go back to sleep."

"Gibby's in bed?"

"Tucked in and safe."

"Where are you going?"

"A call," he said. "I might be a while."

"What time is it?"

"Not that late. Go back to bed."

He kissed her cheek, and she rolled again, showing the lift of a shoulder, a spill of hair. He felt bad about the lie, but had she known his intent, there would have been recrimination and tears; she would not have slept at all.

Outside, French slid behind the wheel, and followed a two-lane until he caught the state highway that would take him into Charlotte. As a city cop, he'd always felt guilty about life beyond the city line, but he was a father first, and city life had been trending down for years. It would be easy to blame the war, but the shift felt more fundamental than that. People didn't care like they used to. They locked their doors, and looked away on the street. There was less trust between neighbors, and no love for cops, either. It had been that way since the Kent State shootings, at least, since the race riots in New York and Wilmington, the uprisings at Attica, the bombing in Wisconsin. Even in a city as small as this—a half-million people—French had seen things he'd never imagined, not just the protests and riots but bra burnings and flag burnings, the explosion of homelessness and poverty and drugs. To jaded eyes, the problem was larger than broken families or loyalties or even broken cities. The country was wounded and hurting. Was *divided* too big a word?

Once across the city line, French worked his way past the subdivisions and commercial areas, then downtown, where buildings rose twenty and thirty stories, and people were out on the sidewalks. The restaurants were busy, so were the nightclubs and bars. The main drag was four-lane, and cars cruised it slowly before turning around to do it again. His interest was little more than passing, but eyes still found the cruiser as if *cop* were written on the side.

Deeper in the city, French slowed as he approached a half-mile stretch of abandoned factories built in the late 1800s. An experiment in city renewal had seen attempts at rehabilitation, but the longed-for influx of apartment and condo dwellers never materialized. The buildings now were mostly vacant. There were a few flophouses, some struggling artists, a bit of industrial storage. The building he wanted was on the last corner of the worst block, so he rolled in quietly, and got out of the car the same way. Darkness pooled between distant lights, and there was movement in that darkness, hints of glass and cigarettes where people huddled on loading bays and crumbled stoops.

"Anyone here seen Jimmy Hooks?" French showed the badge as he approached a group of men on a loading dock, their legs stretched out, backs against the brick. They saw the shield, but didn't care enough to hide the needle. "Hey. Jimmy Hooks. You seen him?" One of the junkies turned his head and gave a slow blink. French held out a ten-dollar bill. "First to tell me gets it."

"Oh, hey, man, I think I saw him . . ."

"Not you." French knew the guy, a proven liar. "You two. Jimmy Hooks. I'm not going to bust him. I just want to talk." He produced another five, and all three junkies pointed at an old factory across the street. "If you're lying, I'll be back. I'll take the money *and* your junk."

"Nah, man. No lies. Jimmy Hooks. Straight up."

French dropped the bills, and crossed the street, stepping over shattered glass and keeping his eyes on the door three stoops down. Two girls lingered there. *Hookers,* he thought. They saw him, and split. He let them go. Through the open door, he saw mattresses, old sofas, candle wax melted to the floor.

"Hey . . . mister cop."

That came from a junkie so skinny a good breeze might lift him up and float him away. He was on a sofa, barefoot and shirtless and half-gone.

"I'm looking for Jimmy Hooks."

The junkie pointed into a long, dark hall.

"Is he alone?"

"Shit, man . . ."

The junkie grinned a loose grin, and French thought, *No, not alone.* Following the hall, he found other rooms and other junkies. French was too jaded to feel much, but the spring inside wound a little tighter.

At the rear of the building, the hall bent right and ended at a steel door beneath a bare bulb. French palmed the revolver, and knocked twice. "Police. I'm looking for James Manning, goes by Jimmy Hooks." If this were a bust, French would have men behind him and at the back door and in the alley outside. Manning, though, had never been busted for dealing. He was too clever, too slick. "Let's go. Open up."

He pounded on the door until metal grated and a dead bolt slid open from the inside. The door opened to the length of its chain, and a sliver of face appeared, pale skin and a dark, disinterested eye.

"Warrant." It was not a question.

"Tell Jimmy it's Detective French, that I want to talk."

The head turned away. "Yo, it's like you said."

"So let the man in."

The door closed, and the chain scraped. When the door opened again, French saw James Manning in a leather chair with his hands behind his head and his legs crossed at the ankles. He was midforties, a local, a dropout. The men with him were a full mix of skin colors and ages. The room would be clean of drugs and weapons and cash. Those things would be in the building, but with other men, in other rooms.

"Detective French." Manning spread his hands in mock welcome. "I thought I might see you tonight."

"So you know he's back."

"Your son leaves a ripple larger than most, so yeah. I heard."

French stepped into the room. Five men, total. Only Manning was smiling. "Have you sold to him?"

"I don't understand the question."

"I want to know if he's using."

"Hey, the world is full of *wants*. I want. You want."

Two men slipped into French's blind spot; he noticed but didn't care. "Do you know where he is or not?" Manning showed both palms and a second smile that made French feel sick inside. He shouldn't have to do this. He should know where to find his own son. "You have a kid, right? A daughter?"

Manning stopped smiling. "Don't compare the two."

"I'm only saying . . ."

"Your son's a junkie. My daughter is eight."

"But as a father . . ."

"I don't give a shit about that."

"What, then?"

"Favors." Manning leaned forward in his seat. "I'll go first to show you how it works. I haven't sold to your son. That's a favor, and that's for free. I can tell you where he is, too, but it'll cost you."

"A favor in return."

"A *cop* favor."

French took a steadying breath. The men around him were bottom-feeders, the worst. He wanted to arrest them all or beat them until his hands bled. "I'm not asking for a kidney," he said. "The favor will be commensurate."

"That's a nice word."

"Where is he, Jimmy? I won't ask again. I walk and the favor walks with me."

Manning settled back in the chair. Three beats, and then five. "You know Charlie Spellman?" he asked, finally.

"Should I?"

"Two-bit dealer. Wannabe player. He has a house at Water Street and Tenth, one of those little rentals. Your boy crashes there."

"If the information's good, I'll owe you one."

"Yes, you will, Detective. One commensurate fucking favor."

French made his way down the filthy hall, ignoring the laughter that trailed him. He felt angry and unclean, and took those feelings all the way to Water Street and Tenth, a quiet intersection in a working-class neighborhood of small houses with small yards, of people good and bad. He'd known the area since his years as a uniformed rookie. Most calls were for domestic disturbances or vandalism or public drunkenness. There was little violent crime, almost never a homicide. Taking his time to study the houses near the intersection, he keyed the radio, and asked dispatch for the make and model of any vehicle owned by one Charlie Spellman. It didn't take long.

"Records show a 1969 Ford Maverick, license number LMR-719, registered to Charles Spellman, DOB 9/21/50."

"Thanks, Dispatch. Got it."

He found the Maverick in a narrow driveway, five houses up on the west side of the block. It had bald tires. Spots of primer dulled the paint. A flashlight through the glass showed trash on the floor but nothing illegal. Approaching the house, French saw movement through the curtains, heard music and laughter. He knocked, and a pretty girl opened the door. She wore bell-bottoms, a tube top, and blue eye shadow that glittered in the light. She was drunk, but friendly. Small freckles crossed the bridge of her nose.

"Hey, come on in. Booze is in the kitchen. Charlie's around here somewhere."

She turned, and left the door open, so he went inside. A dozen people filled the first room, and he saw more down the hall and in the adjacent room. Blue smoke hung in the air. Some of it was weed. Moving into the house, French caught a few unhappy looks, but ignored them. Everyone else was blissful and vague. A couple was making out on the stairs. A few girls were dancing in the corner as "Brown Eyed Girl" spun on the turntable.

In the narrow hall, he turned sideways to fit his large frame past a good-looking kid and a group of women in their twenties. "Jason French?" he asked the first one to catch his eyes, but she shook her head. At the end of the hall, he peered into the kitchen. Two beer kegs sat in tubs of ice, and open bottles ran the length of both counters. The men there were older, with mustaches and sideburns. "Anybody here seen Jason French?" No one answered, so French picked the one who looked most out of place and uncertain. "How about you? You know Jason French?"

The young man glanced at his friends. "Uh, upstairs, man. But he's not exactly looking for visitors."

"What room?"

"Uh . . ."

"Shut up, dude. We don't talk about Jason 'less Jason says."

After that, the group closed ranks, a common reaction. To certain men, Jason held a near godlike appeal. He'd enlisted to avenge a dead brother, done three tours, and kicked ass. He had the scars and attitude, the prison time, done clean. The aura of it still hung on Jason, but French was tired of it, all of it. He rolled back the edge of his jacket, exposing the shield, the holstered weapon. "I said, what room." After thirty years of cop, he was good at this kind of thing. He could deliver a beating; take a beating. It gave him confidence that went beyond the badge and gun. "Come on, boys, it's a simple question. No? No one? All right. That's fine, too. But I'm going upstairs to look for Jason, and if I find any of you boys behind me on the stairs or in the hall or anywhere else near me, I'll take it personally. Understand?"

He gave it a five count, then turned for the stairs. No one followed. On the second floor, he found a landing and four closed doors. Behind the first was a bathroom, empty. The second was a bedroom, and the door was locked. "Jason?"

He heard a stirring inside, then faintly, *Ah, shit* . . .

"Open up, son. I just want to talk."

"Now is not a good time."

"There never is with you."

"I said, fuck off."

"Right, then . . ."

French took the knob in one hand, put his shoulder on the door and felt the lock give. Cheap metal. Cheap door. Inside, a single lamp burned beneath a red cloth that softened the light and put shadows on the young woman's skin. She straddled Jason at the hips, riding him with a slow and steady roll. Her hands were raised behind her neck and linked beneath a spill of long, dark hair. Maybe she didn't hear the door give. Maybe she didn't care. "Tyra, baby. Hang on." Jason lifted his chin, and patted her hip. "Why don't you give us a minute?"

Sliding off the bed, she dressed with an utter lack of shame or embarrassment. French averted his eyes, but she took her time, moving around the room to collect bits of discarded clothing. Dressed at last, she kissed Jason long on the mouth, then brushed past French, and said, "Pig."

"Nice," he replied. "Thanks for that."

She gave him the finger, and he watched her go. On the bed, Jason was covered to the waist, the combat scars glinting in the reddish light. He reached for a pack of smokes, shook one out, and lit it. "Fresh out of prison, Dad. You couldn't give a man five minutes?"

"I doubt that's the first girl you've been with since prison."

Jason hooked a hand behind his head and blew smoke at his father. "What do you want?"

"You didn't tell us you were coming home."

"I didn't think you'd want to know." Anger. Distance. Another jet of smoke. "So what's with the drop-in? You heard about tomorrow?"

"What happens tomorrow?"

"Brothers doing brotherly things. I assumed you were here to stop it, Gibby being the favorite son and all, and Mom being such a flower."

"Please don't be disrespectful."

"It's the right word, isn't it? Flower. Snowflake. Ash in a sudden wind."

Jason made a gesture, as if sprinkling ash with his fingers. "Are you high?" French asked. "Are you using right now?"

"Does George Dickel count?"

Jason tipped up a bottle, and all the resentment showed on his face: the intrusion, the questions, the last years of his life.

"Gibby is not a favorite son. He's just young."

"Same age as Robert when he was drafted."

"That's different."

"It's not a bit different. And you know the tragedy of it all, the inside joke?" Another slug of whiskey. "Gibby was the toughest of us all, back in the day. Thirteen years old, and he could keep up with us both: hiking and dirt bikes, hunting, fighting. The kid was unflinching. And what is he now?" Jason pointed with the cigarette. "It's pitiful, what you've done to him."

"That is patently unfair."

Jason sighed as if suddenly bored. "What do you want, Dad? You want me to fuck off or leave town or stay away from my only brother? If that's it, then say it and leave. Nothing good will come of it, but at least we'll understand each other."

French struggled for a response, but was out of simple answers. He loved the boy, but didn't know him. "Tomorrow, then? Brotherly things?"

"Gibby was supposed to tell you."

French nodded. He had nothing else. "Bring him home safe, all right? Nothing stupid or dangerous or criminal."

"Roger that, Detective."

Jason drank again, and French wanted so much, just then. He wanted to slap the anger from his son, to pull him up and squeeze him so hard there'd be no question of favorites or history or love. He wanted to say, *You're my son, goddamn it, and I don't care what you've done or what you are or even that you hate me.* He wanted to hold his boy until his heart was flooded and the sun rose and his arms hurt. Instead, he nodded again and walked away.

4

I was awake when my father came home, and knew from long experience how clumsily he'd try to be quiet. With all the late nights and long cases, I'd expect him to know every loose floorboard in the house. He didn't. I heard a creak in the hall, and a rattle of ice as he stood for long seconds outside my door. When I was younger, he'd wake me up to talk, usually on the bad days when a case went sideways or someone particularly innocent was hurt or killed. He never talked about the details, but even at twelve or thirteen, I understood that he wanted to speak of normal things, to see his own children tucked away and safe. Nights like that came more often when Robert went to war, and ended abruptly when his body returned. Now it was like this: my father in the hall, the rattle of ice.

When he left, my thoughts returned to Jason and the cliff.

No hesitation.

He didn't even look.

Turning on a lamp, I opened a shoebox filled with pictures of Robert, some taken when he was a boy, and others he'd sent from Vietnam. I studied those the most on nights like this. He looked frightened in a few and, in others, mostly lost. Not everyone would see that, of course. They'd see the good looks, the half smile. But I'd known Robert better than most, better even than Jason. He'd taught me how to study hard and play hard, to find my place in the world. Every year, though, it was harder to remember him, so I looked more and more at the pictures. It's what I saw of him when I closed my eyes: Robert in the jungle and looking left, or standing

with other men by the edge of a burned field. Even the day he dove from
Devil's Ledge was blurring in my mind. I saw Jason instead, and felt the
pull of him, too. What did he want from me? Why was he home? I knew
what Robert would say, if I could ask him about tomorrow.

Live large, Gibby, but be smart.

You hear what I'm saying?

You feel me?

I stared at the darkness for a long time, then pulled on jeans, took a
cigarette from my mother's purse, and slipped outside to the porch. The
stars were pale, the air cool. I lit the smoke and felt something like a war
inside. *Be like Robert or Jason. Be a good son. A bad one.* I thought of
stealing whiskey, but did not.

I'd be drinking soon enough.

And lying, too, it seemed.

It happened on the same porch—nine in the morning, my father close
behind as I tried and failed to slip away unseen.

"Gibby, Gibby. Wait."

He tried to keep the cop off his face, but it was hard for him, trusting.
"Yeah, Dad?"

He was barefoot beneath jeans and a T-shirt. I'd been avoiding him.
"Where are you going?"

"Just out." A half lie.

"Back to the quarry?"

"I don't know yet."

"Hanging with Chance?"

"Yeah, maybe. I guess."

My father frowned, and looked at my car in the driveway. It was a
Mustang convertible, kind of old. I'd bought it used. It had a few dents,
the big engine.

"Listen," he said. "I spoke to Jason last night."

Shit . . .

"You did?"

"He told me about today." I expected more of the cop eyes, but that's
not how it was. The old man looked open and understanding, and . . .

I don't know . . . younger. "Your mother doesn't need to know about it, okay? Let's keep it between us."

I looked for the trap; didn't see it.

"I've been thinking about it, is all. He's the only brother you have left. Good or bad, that'll never change."

"But don't tell Mom?"

"Just be smart," he said. "You feel me?"

I nodded once, and there it was again.

The ghost of brother Robert.

Jason was hungover when I pulled to the curb. He sat with his boots crossed in the gutter and a bottle of beer pressed against his forehead.

"You're late."

I killed the engine, but didn't get out. The top was down, sun beating in. Jason took a long swallow, and got to his feet. The house behind him was small and littered with trash, his clothes as dark and worn as a country road. In spite of it all, Jason looked ready for anything, the smile ironic, the rest of him long and lean and coiled. He drained the bottle, tossed the empty, and hefted a cooler into the back seat. "You had breakfast?" I shook my head, and he opened the door. "All right, then. I'm buying." He named a place, and guided me across town to a diner that served a mix of soul food and Korean. "But the chicken and biscuits," he said. "You have no idea."

He was right about that. I didn't.

"Good, huh?" He took off the dark glasses, and his eyes were surprisingly clear.

"You come here a lot?" I asked.

He pointed at the cook behind the counter, a wiry black man with gray in his beard. "Nathaniel Washington," he said. "I knew his son in basic training. Darzell."

"Did he . . . you know. The war?"

"What? Die?" The same ironic smile. "He drives a cab downtown. Good guy. He introduced me to this place before we shipped out. Don't have much use for the Korean food, but the rest of it . . ."

He gestured, as if to take in the smell of chicken and collards, fatback and ham hocks. Spread out in the booth, he seemed relaxed. The quiet gaze. The easy smile. We finished breakfast and ordered sandwiches for the road. "Tell me about the girls," I said.

"Girls?"

"Yeah, you said—"

"Ah, the girls. Well, women, really. You been laid yet?"

I looked away, embarrassed. Girls were a mystery wrapped in sweetness and cruelty. They generally terrified me.

"Don't worry about it," he said. "These girls are nice. You'll like them."

After that, he watched the city beyond the glass. Shadows deepened in alleyways across the street, and bright light etched the pedestrians, the homeless, the big cars with chrome fenders. I was drawn by his lazy confidence, his stillness, the way he held his cigarette.

"What?"

He caught me watching, but I had no easy answer. People said we looked alike, but he was exotic to me. "How many people did you kill?"

It was not a fair question so early in the morning. He gave me a long look, neither upset nor giving.

"Not today, little brother."

My disappointment was hard to hide. Sex. Death. Experience. These were the things that made him a man and me something less.

"Listen," he said. "I get it. People talk. We're family . . ."

"I heard twenty-nine, just in your first year."

He shook his head, stubbed out the cigarette. Did that mean more than twenty-nine? Less?

"I need a drink." He rose as the old proprietor delivered a bag of food to the table. "Thanks, Nathaniel." Jason passed across a wad of bills without really counting them, then shouldered the door and led me into the heat. "You ready for a beer?"

"I'm driving."

"Nah, I got it." He circled the hood and slid behind the wheel. I waited a moment, then got in, too. "Bottle opener is in the cooler."

I looked around. No cops. No one seemed to care. Rooting through the ice, I found bottles of Michelob, and pulled out two, opening them and handing one over. Jason drained a third of it in a single pull, then eased onto the four-lane and turned east. I kept the bottle between my legs, sipping nervously when we hit gaps in traffic.

"Nice car," he said.

"Yeah?"

"Robert and I had to walk."

I looked for resentment, but didn't see it. I could have told him how I'd paid for it mowing lawns and fueling boats, but I didn't want to break the mood. His fingers filled the grooves on the wheel, and he whistled at the easy acceleration. In seconds, we were doing sixty in a forty-five, and he was smiling like a man fresh out of prison. He took us farther east and then north, bending around the city until we reached an expensive area filled with bright glass and trees and off-street parking.

"About these girls . . ." He pulled to the curb. "Don't let them scare you."

"I don't. What . . . ?"

"Ladies!"

Jason swung out of the car as two young women appeared from a nearby condo. I saw a blur of terry cloth and thin shirts and bare, smooth skin. They giggled down a flight of steps and met Jason on the sidewalk, each one rising on tiptoes to kiss his cheek. The shorter one leaned in as if whispering. "Is this him? He's cuter than you said. See, Sara. I told you."

Both were staring, both braless and tan. The blonde wore a headband with a turquoise stone in the center of her forehead. The shorter one with dark hair wore it feathered.

"All right," Jason said. "Ladies in the back. Little brother rides with me."

"Aww . . ."

"I'll share later. Now, come on. Load up."

He gestured at the car, and the young women piled in, the tall blonde speaking first, her voice soft and calm. "I'm Sara," she said. "This is Tyra." I responded as best I could, but was lost in a cloud of perfume and legs and the quick glimpse of a pale, curving breast.

"Oh my God, he's blushing. That is adorable." Tyra leaned over the seat, and I felt her breath on my neck. "What's your name?"

"Gibby."

"How old are you, Gibby?"

"He's eighteen," Jason said. "His birthday was last week."

"Oh my God. *So* adorable." Tyra squeezed my shoulders, laughing, but my eyes found Sara's. They were blue, shot with green, and they watched me from a calm, still place. "It's very nice to meet you, Gibby. Is this your car?" I stammered something, and she leaned forward, showing a second glimpse of the same pale skin. "It suits you, I think. The lines of it."

She leaned back after that, and looked away. I felt a flutter, an emptiness. Jason's knowing smile returned.

"All right, boys and girls." He fired the big engine. "Who's ready to party?"

The party started in the car and moved, over an hour's drive, to a gravel road that twisted through undeveloped forest at the southern shoreline of the state's largest lake. Sunlight slanted in, and water glinted beyond the trees. Pale dust rose behind the car as Jason took us farther from the neighborhoods and boat ramps and parks. The girls were on a second bottle of wine, talking a lot and asking questions that Jason apparently wanted me to answer. He rarely replied to any of them, choosing instead to smile or tip back a beer or say something like, *You know who has a funny story like that?*

Thing was, I *did* have funny stories. Whenever he said that and looked my way, I knew exactly what to say and how to say it. Maybe it was the beer, or maybe his confidence was contagious. Whatever the case, the girls responded. Tyra liked to laugh in a full-throated way, her lips as pink as the inside of a shell, her teeth as glistening and damp. Sara's responses were subdued but more gratifying. She'd touch my shoulder and lean close, her smile softer and intimate and small. As a spell, I wished it to remain unbroken. The streaming hair. The heat of her hand.

"Where are you taking us, anyway?"

Tyra raised her voice to ask the question, but Jason didn't respond. He turned right when the road forked, and bounced us down a weed-filled track that ended at a meadow filled with wildflowers. Beyond it, the lake stretched for miles, a spill of glass fringed by forest and hills and high, empty sky. When the car stopped, Tyra stood, pulling off her sunglasses. "Oh my God."

We got out of the car, the stillness remarkable in its perfection. "How'd you find this place?" I asked.

"It wasn't me. It was Robert."

I took a few steps into the meadow. Flowers carpeted the earth, a thousand colors, a thousand shades. Wind made jewels of light at the water's edge. "Why didn't you ever bring me here?" I asked.

Jason moved beside me and pressed a fresh bottle into my hand. "I didn't know about it."

"How is that possible?"

"Robert didn't bring me, either. Not until he left for the war."

"What do you mean?"

"He came home right before he shipped out. Remember?"

"Of course."

"He brought me here before that last dinner, just the two of us. The sun was setting. It was cold. He said he found this place when he was sixteen, and wanted me to know about it, just in case. Beyond that, he didn't say much. We had a beer and watched the sun go down. He was scared, I think."

"Why did he keep it a secret?"

"We were twins, right. That meant we shared most everything, whether we wanted to or not. Birthdays. Clothes. Even girlfriends got us confused. I think he liked having this place for himself, alone. Do you blame him?"

It was a fair question, given the beauty and the stillness. I wondered who owned it, but only for a moment. My thoughts turned to Robert. It was easy to see him here all those years ago, alone or with a special girl. It hurt that he'd brought Jason and not me, but they *had* been twins. I forgot that sometimes.

I'd forgotten the girls, too.

"Who wants to go for a swim?" Suddenly Tyra was beside us, one hand on Jason's arm. "How about you, big boy?"

She shrugged off her top, laughing. The shorts followed, and she was naked, running through the flowers. I'd never seen tan lines on a naked girl, never seen a naked girl at all.

"Hold this."

Jason pushed a beer at me, and sauntered into the field. He took his time, and Tyra enjoyed it. She turned and feigned shyness, then splashed waist-deep into the water, covering her breasts as Jason disrobed with a slow dignity I could only imagine in myself. He was marked by war and prison-pale, but muscular and confident and steady. I didn't think I could be jealous of Jason, but suddenly was.

"They've been together a few times." Sara appeared beside me, her eyes on Jason, but on Tyra, too. They met in deeper water, kissed once and long, then stroked out from shore, splashing each other, laughing. "We don't have to swim," she said. "Come on. I found a shady spot."

I didn't know if I was relieved or disappointed. She took my hand in an almost careless way and led me to a bald spot beneath a weeping willow where someone had long ago placed Adirondack chairs, the wood of them silvered and smooth. Sara sat me down, then put a hand on each leg, leaned in, and kissed me lightly.

"I thought we'd just get that out of the way." When she drew back, her lips were slightly parted, the smile in her eyes alone. She took the chair beside me, but left fingertips on my leg, a proprietary touch that delighted me. "Tell me about Gibby French."

"What do you want to know?"

"Have you ever been with a girl?"

I answered honestly, but the day was like that. "No. Not really."

"But you've had girlfriends?"

"Nothing serious."

"That's good. I like that." She sipped wine, and her profile was flawless.

"How about you?" I asked.

"Men, yes. Relationships, no." She showed the blue-green eyes. "Does that shock you?"

I shook my head—a lie—and tried to match her frankness with my own. "How old are you?"

"Twenty-seven."

"What do you do for fun?"

"This is a good start."

Her hand moved on my leg, but absently. Her eyes had drifted shut, and a half smile played on her lips. I stole a glance at the length of her legs, the thin shirt, and the small, perfect breasts. It lasted a second or two before I looked away, ashamed of myself. I didn't know what to do or say, and Sara knew as much.

"Just breathe, Gibby French. It's a lovely, lovely day."

It *was* a lovely day. We spoke of things large and small. We drank and laughed, and once, midsentence, she kissed me again. It was longer that time, and certain and real. Afterward, we watched Jason and Tyra swim, looking away only as they emerged from the lake to make a secret place deep in the flowers. For a moment, then, it was awkward, but Sara didn't care for awkwardness. She stood with the grace I'd come to expect, then settled onto my lap, her palms warm on my face as she kissed me. It was a woman's kiss, and different from the ones I'd known from girls at school. There was no fumbling or self-consciousness or doubt. She made a shadowed place of her hair—a private world—and in that world she made the rules, too. She pressed hard and drew back, a giver and a tease. She put my hand inside her shirt and squeezed, her fingers over mine as time, for me at least, folded and stretched.

"I see that you two are getting along."

It was my brother, and he was close. Sara pulled away, but slowly. She squeezed my hand with hers, and then withdrew. "He's nice," she said. "I like him."

"I thought you might."

She turned in my lap, settling a shoulder against my chest, and resting there. At the water's edge, Tyra was getting dressed. She saw us looking, and waved. "Nice swim?" I asked.

Jason called over his shoulder. "Tyra, baby? Nice swim?"

"The best!"

She came through the flowers, grinning. Jason pulled her tight, and lifted an eyebrow. "Anybody hungry?"

Hours later, we were back in the car, yellow light in the trees, the sky above impossibly blue. Jason took us back to hard pavement and the world beyond the trees, driving in a pattern that made little sense to me: north and then east and then north again. I'd never seen this part of the state before, the miles of forest and farmland, the worn pavement and small towns, like beads on a string. I rode in the back with Sara, who watched the world much as I did, silently and content, her eyes hidden behind round glasses with rose-colored lenses. She had a hand at her throat, another on my leg. In front, Tyra was the talker.

"Where are you taking us?"

Jason lifted his wide shoulders. "Just driving."

"Can you go faster?"

Jason accelerated, blowing dust off the blacktop and litter off the verge. "Fast enough?"

"Only if you kiss me, too."

He kissed her well, one eye on the road. When the kiss broke, Tyra laughed wildly and pushed her arms above the windshield, into the rush of hot air. "Faster!" Jason nudged the gas, and the car leaped forward again. Eighty-five. Ninety-five. "Yes! Yes!" The speed energized her. She bounced twice on the leather seat, finished the wine, and slipstreamed the bottle. It shattered on the road behind us—a starburst—and when I looked at Sara, she raised her own narrow shoulder.

"It's just Tyra."

The day soured a little after that. I didn't care about Tyra one way or another, but Sara's easy attitude cheapened her a little.

"We need more booze!"

Tyra shouted over the roar of wind, and Jason high-fived her open hand. Twenty minutes later, we stopped on the main block of a narrow downtown street, angling in where piebald tarmac met the façade of a run-down ABC store Jason claimed to have shopped in once.

"Won't take a minute."

"What town is this?" I asked.

It was a dusty place made of two-lane roads and blinking lights and low buildings. I saw kids on bikes, old men, a tractor at a feedstore.

"Does it matter?" Jason asked.

It didn't matter to the girls. They spoke across the seat as Jason disappeared inside, and I watched him through the glass. At the feedstore, the tractor started up, pulled onto a side street, and disappeared. I smelled pollen, pine resin, and hot pavement. Sara tucked a strand of hair behind an ear, and I saw the pulse at her throat, the flush of her cheek.

"Gibby, hey. I'm talking to you."

My eyes shifted up from Sara's skin. Tyra was leaning over the seat, a cigarette between two fingers. Lipstick made a rim on the filter. Virginia Slims. Menthol. "I'm sorry. What did you say?"

She rose up on her knees and leaned farther over the seat. "Is it true what they say about your brother?"

"Tyra, this is uncool . . ."

"Zip it, Sara. I'm talking to Gibby." Sara tried again to turn the conversation, but a strange, hungry glint had kindled in Tyra's eyes. She leaned even closer, the seat back in her ribs. "They say he killed a lot of people."

"Do they?" I asked.

"In the war, they say. Maybe even in prison."

"I don't really know about that."

"But you're brothers, right?"

"Tyra . . ."

"It's hot, Sara. Okay. The scars. The stories. I know you see it."

"I don't think it's hot at all. If it's true, it's sad. If it's not true, then you're being really stupid."

"Oh, like you wouldn't screw him."

Sara took off the glasses and showed me her eyes. "I'm sorry, Gibby. She gets stubborn when she's drunk." She looked back to Tyra. "Stubborn and ridiculous."

"You're ridiculous."

"Drop it, Tyra."

"Fine. Whatever."

Tyra spun around and slumped in the seat, reaching for the radio and moving it up the dial, passing John Denver and the Hollies before settling on Eric Clapton and turning it up. I wasn't surprised by her feelings for my brother. I'd seen similar things in one form or another. Fascination. Loathing. Jason understood the effect, but paid little attention. He kept the dark glasses on, kept the silence.

Back at the car, he picked up on the tension. "What?"

He slid into the driver's seat, and Tyra shook her head, arms crossed. Sara tried to smooth it over. "Party slows down without you. That's all."

"Well, I'm back." He rustled around in a paper bag. "No wine, but I got these." He handed a pint of vodka to Sara and another to Tyra, who twisted off the top and took a pull.

Sara touched her friend on the shoulder. "We all good now?"

Tyra drank again, and spoke to Jason. "Let's drive, all right?"

Jason did as he was asked, backing away from the curb and making a slow roll through the little town. The kids watched us pass, and so did the old men. In the empty lanes beyond, the day was just as clear and bright, but the mood had shifted. Tyra sulked and drank. She put her hand in Jason's lap, and looked at Sara as if offering a challenge no one understood or cared about.

"Here." Sara passed the bottle, but I had little use for straight vodka. "You sure?" she asked.

"Yeah, I'm good."

She took the bottle back, drank small sips, and trailed a hand in the hot, hard air. After that, no one really spoke. The radio played. The sun beat down. I watched the countryside, liking how large certain trees grew when they stood alone in empty fields. Around four o'clock, we came to a crossroads and a right turn that took us deeper into the countryside. Jason took his first pull on the bottle, gesturing at pine forest, shimmer, and sandy verge. "This is the edge of the sandhills. Another hour or so, then we turn back west. Everybody happy?"

Strangely, I was, and it was only in part because of Sara. Her hand was back on my leg, yes, but Jason was being very cool, and Tyra had settled into the kind of quiet resentment that was easy to ignore. I thought the day had found its second breath, that everyone was good.

I was wrong about that.

The first sign came when Tyra took another giant pull on the bottle, and Jason said, "You might want to slow down."

She took another swallow instead, turning the radio louder.

"Do you mind?" I asked. "They're new speakers."

She turned them even louder. Jason studied her from the corner of his eye, then said to me, "I'll buy you new ones if she blows them."

"Damn right." Tyra said it loudly, and turned her face to the wind.

After that, Jason took us south. At first, we had the road to ourselves, but we passed a pickup, an old sedan. They fell away, far behind, and the car was steady at seventy miles an hour when we crested a small hill and saw the bus a mile or two ahead. We dropped off the slope, and heat devils shimmered far out on the blacktop. Beyond the distortion, the bus seemed half-real and half-mirage, a white shape that floated above the road and solidified as Jason took us up to seventy-five and then eighty, the road perfectly straight as it cut through a world of wind and sunlight and scrub. The bus swelled as we raced up behind it, and I could feel the speed building.

"Shit."

Jason's foot came off the gas as we closed the gap. The car fell back, fifty yards behind the bus, then a hundred. "What's wrong?" I asked.

"Nothing," he said. "Reflex."

I looked from my brother to the bus, and understood, at least a little. Tall, black letters stretched across the back of the bus.

LANESWORTH PRISON

INMATE TRANSFER

I saw the windows next: the wire mesh in steel frames. I saw the prisoners, too.

"You good?" I asked.

"Yeah, man. No problem."

It was the first time I'd known anything about prison to affect my brother. At trial, he'd been calm and cool, even as the verdict came down, guilty. He'd looked at me for a slow moment, then held out his hands for the bailiffs and their cuffs. I'd visited prison once, and he'd been sanguine then, too. *You're too young for this,* he'd said. *I'll see you in a couple years.* It was a rule of childhood that Jason was unlike the rest of us, and it was strange, now, to see him so human.

"What's the problem, pretty boy? Let's go."

Tyra was impatient and drunk and speed-addicted. She moved to the music, half-dancing. Jason frowned, but accelerated until the gap closed and I could see the bus better. It was half-full, maybe fifteen inmates, their clothing as black and white as the bus. We hung on their tail for a full minute, and no one but me noticed that Jason was sweating. Tyra was lost in the music, and then suddenly not.

"Whoa, hey! Convicts!"

She sounded callous and cruel, the kind of voyeur that would watch a good friend fail, and smile on the inside. Maybe that was unfair, but it bothered me to see such ugliness in such a beautiful woman.

From the rear of the bus, two men stared at us through dirty glass. Tyra clapped and grinned, bouncing where she sat. "Pull up beside them! Pull up!" Jason moved on automatic, his right hand tight on the wheel. "Yeah, like that. Right alongside them." He eased into the left lane, and Tyra turned in her seat to watch the bus slide up beside us. We were alone on the road—us, the bus, and a second lake of shimmer, far out in the flatness. "Not too fast," Tyra said. "Right there."

"This is not cool."

Jason spoke quietly, and Tyra ignored him. Men were watching now, their fingers curled in the mesh. Tyra rose to her knees, her left hand on the top edge of the windshield as she waved and mocked them, pushing out her breasts and blowing kisses.

"Tyra . . ."

Jason spoke in that same lost tone. His eyes were locked on the road ahead, as if no part of him could bear to look right. He was paler now than when I'd seen him yesterday.

"Jason, just go around." I leaned forward.

Tyra's hand found his shoulder. "Don't you fucking move."

His hesitation lasted a few seconds, but that's all it took. Tyra lifted her top, exposing herself and laughing. Her breasts were large and pale, but I watched the convicts instead. If she'd meant to give pleasure, she'd failed. The faces I saw were angry or bitter or sad. Only one man smiled, and it was the kind of smile I hoped to never see again.

"Tyra, that's enough." I turned to Sara for help, but she was looking away, her head shaking in small movements. In the bus, men began to stand, seven or eight crossing from the other side, their fingers, too, in the mesh.

Tyra said, "Watch this."

She touched herself below the waist, grinding her hips, her breasts still exposed. A prisoner beat on the mesh; another did the same. Behind them, a guard was moving down the aisle, pushing, shouting. Men began to yell, most of them on their feet. The guard pulled a prisoner from the window, then another. A third prisoner pushed back, and the bus swerved across the dotted line, forcing Jason onto the road's edge, tires in the gravel as the car shimmied, straightened. I said, "Jesus, Tyra!" But she was excited, oblivious. Another guard appeared, his baton rising and falling. It was a riot, a beatdown. Blood flecked the glass. "Jason, let's go!"

My voice seemed to penetrate at last. Jason made no sudden move, but took his foot from the gas and let the car coast. The bus pulled away, and I saw movement in the back—a convict, the smiling one. He stared at Tyra, then licked the glass. She didn't see it happen. She dropped into the seat, adjusting her top. "That was hilarious." The car slowed further, wind noise dropping. No one responded to the comment, and she looked around, surprised. "What? Come on. Did you see those guys?"

Jason steered the car onto the verge and stopped. "That was stupid, Tyra."

"Oh, stop it."

"Stupid and fucked up and cruel."

"Jesus. Why are you being such a baby?"

"I need a minute."

Getting out, Jason walked along the road for thirty feet or so, then stood with his hands in his pockets, staring at the horizon and the last far, faint twinkle of sunlight on glass.

"You guys wait here."

I said it with rare authority, and followed the dusty road to where it met my brother's boots. He turned at the sound of my steps, then closed his eyes and tilted his face toward the sun. "Sorry about that," he said.

"You okay?"

"I don't know. Maybe."

It was not the answer I expected—too honest and, again, too human. "That was bullshit, man. Tyra knows you did time."

"Maybe she forgot," he said.

"Maybe she doesn't care."

Jason lifted his shoulders, noncommittal. Far away, the bus glinted once more, then disappeared. It was quiet on the road. He was still paler than usual.

"You want to tell me what's going on?"

"It's like a slow bleed, is all."

I wasn't sure what he meant. Prison, I supposed. The memories. He put a hand on my shoulder; faked a smile. "Did you have fun today?"

"Until Tyra. You know."

"Tyra. Yeah." He looked at the car, and we saw the same things: Tyra impatient and flushed, Sara in the back. "I might have to do something about that."

"You want me to drive?"

"Nah."

"Home, then?"

"Sure, yeah. Why not? But you ride up front with me."

Tyra didn't like it. No one cared. She collapsed into the back seat like an angry child, drank herself into a sullen stupor, and slapped Jason's hand when he tried to get her out of the car. "Sara?" he said.

"Tyra. We're home. Let's go."

She blinked at the condos, the trees, the setting sun on clean glass. "I can do it myself."

She made it to the door without looking back, then stumbled inside. For an instant, I was alone with Sara, but the mood was gone for her, too. She kissed my cheek, said, "Bye for now," and walked up the same stairs.

That night in bed, I tried to hold on to the good parts: the meadow, the taste of Sara's mouth. I played the day like a tape, but the tape kept breaking. I saw the beatdown on the bus, the batons that rose and fell and slung blood like red paint. That was the loop, over and over: Tyra half-naked and teasing, Jason strangely frozen. I saw all those men—the lust and rage—but in my dreams, the loop tightened and drew smaller. I saw one face, a single man. He stood at the back of the bus, damp-eyed and staring; and that's what I remembered when I woke.

His tongue on filthy glass.

That terrible, awful smile.

5

It took a long time for things to settle on the bus, and that made sense. The guards liked beatings; prisoners liked a riot. A guard went down. Clubs rose and fell, blood all over the floor. One prisoner stayed clear of it; he always stayed clear. Part of that was choice, and part was his age. After seventy-three hard years on God's good earth, he was too withered and thin for most convicts to care about or even notice. Fifty-two years. That's how long he'd been inside. Half a century for the rape and murder of twin sisters all the way back in 1920. If he closed his eyes, he could still see the day it happened, the narrow girls on a red-dirt road, all that emptiness and time, the wildflowers they'd tucked behind their ears.

But that was then . . .

Watching the violence on the bus, the old prisoner kept his back to the window, and ran the odds in his head. Four guards and a driver. Seventeen other convicts. The convicts were chained, but chains could be weapons. Point in fact: Justin Youngblood, a guard in his fourth year. Three men had him down, a chain between his jaws, teeth cracking as he screamed.

The old prisoner thought: *Sixty-forty, guards.*

But the bus was steady on the road now, the driver in control of himself, radio close to his mouth as he shouted to make himself heard. "Highway 23! Six miles west of the crossroads! Request immediate assistance!"

A mesh wall kept the driver safe. No keys on this side.

Eighty-twenty, then.

He heard it like he saw it. Shinbones. Faces. Kneecaps.

That was the thing about batons.

When the last convict was beaten into bloody submission, the old prisoner looked again for the car, but didn't see it. He remembered the faces, though, and every gesture. If he lived to a hundred, he would know the girls, and the men, too. That was his thing. He never forgot a face or an injury or a reason for anger. The way she'd exposed herself, taunting. He'd dream of the brunette for whatever years he had left alive. Dark fantasies. Violent ones.

But it was the car's driver who really mattered, and the old prisoner pictured him as he had been in those final seconds: the sweat and over-pale skin, his hands on the wheel, and how he'd barely moved. He'd been an inmate at Lanesworth, the old man remembered, and there was a prisoner there, now, who'd pay dearly for a description of what had just happened. He'd want the nuance of every moment. *How was the light? Tell me about the road, the wind, the grass on the edge of the road.* He'd ask about the girls and the younger man, but only as reflections of the driver. The old prisoner could deliver all of that: the clothes they wore and how each had behaved, the hair colors and skin tones and breast size. The younger man was only a boy, but the prisoner at Lanesworth would want those details as well. In the end, though, it would come back to the driver. *How did he seem? How did he look?* Before it was over, they'd talk about the car. That was the rubber on the road; and the old prisoner would play the old games. He'd hold out for money and special favors, but in the end, he'd give it all. Letters and numbers came easily, too.

XRQ-741.

That was the plate.

6

The next day passed in a blur. I cut grass, spread mulch, joked with the old man. He didn't ask about my day with Jason, but at times I caught him staring at me as if some vision might appear in the air between us. Monday was a school day like any other, but people wanted to talk about Jason, the dive, the darker stories. I ignored it all as best I could. That worked for everyone but Chance.

"Do you think he *wants* to die?"

We were in the courtyard at school. Bagged lunches. A group of girls close by. "The hell are you talking about, Chance?"

"The way he dove, man. Like he didn't think about it, like he didn't even care. They say war can mess a man up. Dark places, you know."

I bit into a sandwich, chewing slowly. "I don't think that's it."

"But four seconds, man. Christ. It's like it took forever, like he was hanging there and then, *bam*! I thought that was it. I really did."

I didn't want to talk about Jason, not even with Chance. "Let's drop it, okay? He made the dive. I didn't. So what?"

"Hey, man. Chill."

"I'm chill."

"You know my cousin saw him last night at the Carriage Room. He was mixing it up with some scary dudes."

"What do you mean?"

"Bikers, I heard."

"Get out."

Chance tipped back a Coke. "Hells Angels, maybe. There was a fight or something. People got hurt."

"My dad didn't say anything."

"Bikers, dude. It's not like they'd run to the cops."

I didn't buy it. Chance's stories were usually bullshit. *Charlotte Booker got naked at a party. Mike Aslow slept with Buddy's mom.* That's how his mind ran.

"Whoa, hey. Red alert." He nudged my ribs, whispering. "Becky Collins. Three o'clock."

Becky emerged from the covered walkway that led past the cafeteria and to the gym. She wore a denim skirt and white vinyl boots that rose to her knees. Crossing the courtyard, she headed straight for us; and when she stopped, my eyes were down. I saw the way she bent a single knee, the safety pin holding up the zipper of her left boot.

"Gibby," she said. "Chance."

She held books cross-armed against her chest. Calculus. European history. It was easy to forget how smart she was. People focused on the hair, the legs, the cornflower eyes.

"Hi, Becky."

She frowned as I looked up. "I waited for you at the quarry," she said. "After your brother dove. Why didn't you talk to me?"

Because I chickened out on the dive . . .

Because you were with other guys . . .

I mumbled some kind of answer, but it didn't satisfy her. Beside me, Chance was grinning into the back of his hand.

"You've been ignoring me here, too."

"Um . . ."

"Are you ever going to ask me out?"

"Um. What?"

It seemed *mumble* was my new language. She tapped a foot, and made things very direct. "We've been dancing around this for a while now, but the year's almost over. Are you going to ask me out or not?"

I glanced at Chance, but he was no help. Becky was a cheerleader, the homecoming queen. People said she was going to Princeton, though she denied it. "Are you serious?" I asked. "You want to go out with me?"

"I'm here, aren't I? We're talking."

I looked to Chance for help. Nothing. "Will you go out with me?"

"Was that so hard?" She offered a satisfied smile, and held out a slip of paper for me to take. "I'll be getting ready at Dana White's house. That's the address. Saturday at seven o'clock."

"Um . . ."

"I'll see you then."

She turned in a swirl of motion and color. I stared at the paper in my hand. "What just happened?"

Chance laughed out loud. "Dude, you got *told* what to do."

"I think you're right."

"Wuss."

"Yeah, but it's a date with Becky Collins."

Suddenly, I was grinning, too.

"You know what that's all about, don't you?" Chance pointed at the slip of paper. "The pickup at Dana White's house? Becky doesn't want you to see where she lives."

"Come on."

"Have you ever seen her parents? Her parents' car?"

"She rides the bus."

"There's a reason for that."

"You're off your gourd."

"Truth, man. I'll show you."

We did it after school. I wasn't eager, but Chance was like a bulldog when he got a notion in his teeth. He guided me so far out in the county it felt like a different school district. When I balked a second time, he told me to shut up and drive the damn car. He said his insistence was due to my lack of faith, but Chance had his own jealousies and insecurities.

"This is the street. Turn here."

He meant a narrow street between a muffler shop and a weed-choked lot. I made the turn and stopped the car. The street ran off between small houses and trailers and dirt yards. A few houses missed bits of siding, and I saw a tuft of insulation that hung from one and spilled, like a tongue, into the yard. I thought of Becky's confidence, her satisfied smile when I'd asked her out.

"Why are you stopping?" Chance asked.

"This is far enough."

"Three more blocks. You can almost see it." Three blocks in, it was worse: a burned-out house, another with boarded windows. "Dude, come on. This is why we're here."

"No. I'm sorry." I shook my head, then turned across the narrow street and drove us out. Chance craned to look behind us, then sat low in the seat, arms crossed. On the four-lane, I finally spoke. "You made your point, okay? It's a shitty street. She's poor."

"Hey, man, drive away. Ignore the deeper truths."

"You're mad at me?"

"I want you to know what you're getting into."

"I don't care if she's poor."

"You should."

"Why?"

"Stop the car."

"What? Why?"

"Just stop the car. Look at me."

I pulled off the road and stopped on a wide spot that was half-gravel and half–red dirt. A rickety table stood in the shade of a locust tree beside a hand-painted sign that advertised produce for sale on weekends. I imagined corn and peaches and carrots, an old couple in an old truck. "Why should it matter to me if Becky Collins is poor?"

"Because she's already being dishonest with you. If she does it again, you should understand the reasons."

"You're being ridiculous."

"Say it goes five dates, or even ten? She won't introduce you to her parents. Trust me on that. She won't let you pick her up or take her home, either. And she'll have some big old buttons, too, and you'd better know 'em so you don't push 'em by accident. Clothes and shoes, for instance. If they're nice, they're borrowed, so be careful with compliments. Think twice about expensive restaurants, too. Same thing with birthday gifts, Christmas presents. Not too expensive. She won't be able to do the same . . ."

"Wait a minute. Wait." I held up a hand. "You're trying to help her?"

"Of course I am, you dumb shit. She's a good girl. You're my best friend."

I sat for a moment in stunned silence, thinking at last of the poverty in which Chance had been mired for his entire life. Father long gone, his mother worked three jobs, the best of which was running a cash register at the local drugstore. Chance's house was as bad as any on the street we'd just left, and I knew for a fact I was the only friend who'd been there.

Ever.

"Hey, man. I'm sorry. I should have trusted you."

"Just don't screw it up, okay?"

Back on the road, I thought about Chance's worn clothing, his single pair of blown-out sneakers. He acted as if dressing that way was a choice. He'd been doing it so well and for so long that I'd forgotten it was an act. Chance brought his lunch in a brown bag. At school, he didn't even buy milk. "You want to come over?" I asked.

"With your mom around? No thanks."

The comment could be taken two ways. My father earned a cop's salary, but my mother came from money, and it showed. The nice house. The fine clothes. We decorated for Christmas, and did it in style. Chance combed the local woods for a tree that was green and the right shape. I usually helped him drag it home and set it up. "You want to do something else? Pinball, maybe? They have a new machine at the Gulf station on Innes."

"Nah. Take me home."

It was one of those days now. Talk of poverty had invited in everything else that was real, and that included graduation, the future, Vietnam. Twelve days from graduation, and the draft was out there, and waiting. As if to reinforce the thought, we passed a billboard five miles down:

HAVE YOU REGISTERED FOR THE SELECTIVE SERVICE?
IT'S THE LAW!

They wanted our names, addresses, the best way to fill the ranks. And it wasn't my brothers alone who'd made it real. We both had friends who'd gone and died. "How did it feel to sign those papers?"

I asked it to make conversation, but Chance averted his eyes. "I haven't done it yet."

I opened my mouth and closed it. Once a man turned eighteen, the law allowed thirty days to sign up. I still had time, but Chance's birthday was three months before mine. "Are you serious?" I asked.

"It's a bullshit law."

"But still a law."

"It's a bullshit war."

It occurred to me then that we'd not spoken of Vietnam in months, and I realized now that the reticence had come from Chance. If I raised the subject, he laughed it off. If I pushed, he deflected in some other way. I'd been so caught up in my own frustrations, I'd not thought twice about it. But my best friend had just revealed more in two short sentences than he had in three long months.

A bullshit law . . .

A bullshit war . . .

I wanted to push, but knew at a look he wouldn't have it. The silence continued until I stopped at his house: a dingy cube with a blue tarp on the roof, where it leaked around the chimney. "You want me to come in?" I asked.

"I told Mom I'd clean the kitchen."

"I can help if you want."

"Nah, I'm good." Chance climbed out and closed the door. "Don't forget what I said about Becky Collins. You might not see the chip on her shoulder, but it's there and it's big."

"I'll remember."

"Tomorrow, then."

"See you at school."

I watched him into the house, but stayed on the street for another moment. Was it possible my best friend was afraid to register for the draft? I couldn't see it. Some kind of conscientious objector? Protests against the war were on the streets and in the news, but those were hippies and cowards and people in big cities.

What happened when someone like Chance broke the law?

Would they come looking for my friend?

Like Chance, I had little desire to go home. Instead, I pointed the car at the city line. I couldn't remember the exact house where I'd collected Jason the other day, but I remembered the intersection: Water Street and Tenth. When I got there, a couple guys were in the front yard throwing a football back and forth. They were older with long hair, lit cigarettes, and T-shirts with the sleeves cut away. I parked the car, followed a cracked sidewalk, and waited until one looked at me. "Hey. I'm looking for my brother."

"Who's that?"

"Jason."

"In the back."

I said thanks, and ducked my head so the football wouldn't take it off. Inside, I followed the sound of clanking metal to another open door and a small porch on the back of the house. Jason was there, shirtless in faded jeans. He was doing curls with a heavy bar and thick plates. When he saw me, he lifted his chin.

"What's up, little brother? You need something?"

"Hey, it's cool. Finish your set."

He worked through the rest of his set, and veins popped in his arms, no fat anywhere. What I saw most clearly was the bruising. It ran on the left side of his face, and on his ribs, too, seven or eight places, each the size of a fist. He lowered the bar, then whipped a shirt off the rail and shrugged it on, speaking as he did. "What are you doing here?"

I pointed at his ribs. "I heard about the fight."

"What, this?"

"Bikers, I heard."

"A few, maybe. Who told you?" Jason flipped the lid on a Styrofoam cooler and dug around for a Budweiser. "Chance, right? I saw his cousin there. Weasel-looking little sucker."

"He said it was pretty hard-core."

"Is that right?"

He handed me a beer. I opened it. "What was it about?"

"The fight?" He shrugged. "Tyra, I guess."

"How so?"

"She's a shameless flirt. And she gets ideas." There was a lie in there somewhere, or at least some evasion. "It doesn't matter," he said. "I'm done with her, anyway. You seen Sara?"

A sudden flush embarrassed me. Sara was a fantasy, a schoolboy's dream. "Not since the day."

"You should follow up on that. She's a good girl, and not like Tyra."

"I don't know. Maybe."

"So, why are you here?"

He leaned on the rail, and it was strange to see cop eyes in a convict's face. I tried to find the best answer: that I didn't want to go home, that maybe it *was* about Sara. Deep down, though, it was about being brothers. "Bored, I guess."

"You should try prison sometime."

He drained the can and crumpled it; and I tried to understand why things felt so different from the last time. He was aloof, impatient. He scratched at an arm, and I thought, *Shit, is he using?*

"So, uh. You want me to . . . you know?" I hooked a thumb at the hall leading through the house.

"Yeah, man. It's not really the best day. Maybe this weekend."

"We could catch a movie. Maybe shoot some hoop."

"Let's talk about it later, yeah?"

He came off the railing, and I looked again at the bruises, the torn skin. There was more to say, but I never found the time to say it. We heard a racing engine, then the squeal of rubber as something fast and loose took the corner five houses down. The engine screamed louder, and metal scraped metal. Voices from the front yard: *The fuck, man? Watch it! Watch it!* The crash that followed was louder and close, and extreme for the silence that followed. Seconds later, a voice carried the length of the hall.

"Jason, yo! You better get out here!" I followed my brother through the house. A man with the same voice said, "Yo, it's your girl."

Jason stepped onto bare dirt, but stopped before reaching the wrecked car. It was a Mercedes two-seater, sideways in the yard, with paint stripped from the fenders and the front end pinned against a tree. Tyra was half out of the front door, both hands in the dirt as the engine ticked, and a shattered turn signal flashed *orange*.

"Tyra, Jesus. You okay?"

Jason moved to the car, and helped her up. She wore a white skirt and a teal tank top. Her knees were skinned, a trickle of blood at the hairline. She stumbled, and Jason caught her, the top of her head tucked beneath his chin. She could barely stand. She leaned into him, kissed his neck long and slow, then said, "Get your convict hands off me." Pushing him away, she pulled an arm free, and stumbled again. Mascara smeared the skin beneath her eyes. Her words slurred. "You don't get to touch me. Not 'til I get what I came for."

"Tyra. Come on. Take it easy."

"You don't get to break up with me. Not you . . ."

"Tyra . . ."

"Not some two-bit, pasty-white, deadbeat, convict-looking son of a bitch."

"Come on. Sit down."

"I said don't touch me!"

She swung at him, and he danced back, light as any boxer on *Wide World of Sports.* Around us, people stood in the street and in other yards. A sign was down at the corner; cars along the curb were damaged. I sidled up behind my brother. "Can I do anything?"

"She's just high."

I didn't know if that meant weed or something harder. She was glassy and loose, her skin splotched, her skirt hiked up on the left side. Noticing the bystanders, she said, "The hell are you looking at?"

Jason tried again. "Tyra?"

"Do you know what this man is? What he does?" She stumbled closer, waving a finger. "He kills dreams! He fucks women and he kills dreams!"

"All right, Tyra. That's enough."

"What do you think about that?"

She waved the same finger, and someone behind me said, "This is messed up, man."

Tyra half-turned but, in the end, cared only for Jason. "Why did you do it? I mean . . ." She cupped his shoulder, all the animosity gone. "I mean you and me. Come on." She trailed her fingers down his chest. Jason backed away, but she followed, staring at his mouth, his chin. "You didn't mean it, did you? Not really. Just tell me that. Just say you'll screw me like you used to." She kissed him, but he didn't kiss her back. She pressed her hips on his, and her hands danced. "What's the matter, baby? Nobody works like we do." Her fingers twined in his hair, but he caught her wrists, looking away from the confusion and hurt in her eyes. "Don't say it again, baby. Please don't . . ."

"We're finished. I told you."

"We can't be."

"I'll say it for the last time." He released her wrists, and kept his hands up. "It's over. We're done."

"Why? Because you say so?"

"Yes."

"You?" Fury in her voice. "You—you fucking asshole?" She moved forward, all eyes and angry edges. Even the bystanders stepped back. "So give me what I came for."

"I don't know what that is."

"An apology, you arrogant prick."

"Fine, I'm sorry."

"Oh no, more than that. Spell it out so everyone here knows. Tell them what happened! Tell them what you really are!"

For an instant, I thought Jason would do the gentle thing, and elaborate in whatever manner it took to calm her down. He'd say something, I thought, anything; but Jason was not that kind of man. I saw the coldness glint in his eyes, as sudden and sure as sun on glass; and Tyra must have seen it, too. She made a wordless sound of pure rage, then lunged for him, fingers clawed. He danced away again, but she followed at a stumble, swung for his face. But Jason was no kind of runner. He caught the wrist, twisted her where she stood, and pushed her away. Her foot caught a root; she sprawled in the dirt.

"You bastard." She said it softly, tears on her face. "You fucker."

Jason turned to the men at the house. "Somebody call her a cab, all right?"

"Don't do me any favors." Tyra found her feet, and scrubbed at her eyes, smearing the mascara. "You don't do favors, do you?"

"I want you to wait for the cab," Jason said.

"Screw you."

She weaved across the yard, and fell into the ruined Mercedes. I said, "Tyra, don't be stupid." But she'd already turned the key. "Jason, do something." She got the car started, but he showed the same pitiless stare. Tyra gave him the finger, as wheels spit out grass and dirt, and she slammed into another car. "Jason, come on . . ."

"Fine. All right."

He crossed the yard as she struggled with the gearshift, metal grinding. "Gibby's right, Tyra. Let me have the keys."

He was ten feet away when she bent for something on the floor, and reappeared with a gun in her hand. "You stay away from me." The gun was small and silver. Jason acted as if it wasn't there. "I'll pull the trigger. I'll do it."

She pointed the gun at his chest, but was spilling tears that cut tracks in the mascara, and turned back at the corners of her mouth. People were moving, ducking for cover. Only Jason was calm. "You shouldn't have the keys *or* that gun."

"You don't love me. You don't get a say."

"I'm trying to help you, Tyra."

"Stay back." She worked the clutch, the stick. The car lurched, and metal scraped. She forced a different gear; rolled forward and stopped. For an instant more, Jason was pinned on the barrel of that small, slick gun. "It would have been easy," she said. "You could have said yes."

"Maybe."

"Don't follow me."

"I wouldn't dream of it."

It was the wrong answer, I thought, fuel on a burning fire. The look on her face was terrible as she struggled to contain whatever emotion burned hottest. Fury. Want. Need. The tension stretched until she tossed the pistol on the seat beside her, and rocked the little car off the curb. She looked back only once—another tortured gaze—then she gave my brother the finger, and gunned it.

7

I didn't tell anyone what happened between Jason and Tyra, but thought about it all night and even when I woke. I'd never seen such raw emotion in a woman or a man so cool in the face of it. Tyra's volatility was beyond question, yet in two short encounters, she'd bared everything a woman could bare—body and soul—and I was frustrated at how small I felt afterward, how my own life felt made of expectation, stillness, and pent-up frustration.

I wondered what Robert would say about that.

And what Jason was doing.

After school, I drove by the house on Water and Tenth, but no one there had seen Jason since the dustup with Tyra. They didn't know where he'd gone or when he was coming back. "What about Tyra?" I asked.

"That crazy bitch?"

No one had seen her, either, so I left them on the sofa, and felt my way to the condo Sara and Tyra shared across town. I didn't know if I wanted to see Sara or not, but hoped for some kind of epiphany. Parked on the street, though, nothing came. Her door was closed, the windows blank. I tried to imagine arousing the kind of passion I'd seen in Tyra, the qualities it would take in a man to generate so much desire and rage. I couldn't get there, couldn't even imagine it. I chewed on that, disheartened, then remembered Becky Collins and how she'd pressed that slip of paper into my hand.

Saturday night.

Seven o'clock.

On the way home, I took the top down, turned up the radio. At dinner, I spoke when addressed, used my manners, and ate everything on my plate. The quiet was no less oppressive, but I thought of Becky and Saturday night. I doubted she'd kiss me, but that was all right. We'd talk, and get to know each other.

I thought I had time.

I was wrong.

The trouble came first in hints, and started with my father. He stopped me after dinner, and took me into his office, a narrow room jumbled with files and boxes and books. Family photos covered one wall, awards and citations the other. "I don't want your mother hearing this." He closed the door, and looked hesitant. I'd seen my father angry, perplexed, and disappointed, but this reticence was strange to me. He twisted his fingers, and had trouble meeting my eyes. "Have you seen your brother?" he finally asked.

"Not for a few days."

"No phone calls? Nothing?"

"What's going on?"

He moved to the window, and peered into a dark night broken by streetlamps on the road. He stood there for a bit, then turned as if he'd reached some kind of decision. "Sit down, son." We sat in flanking chairs. He leaned close. "I think Jason might be in trouble. They're just rumors at this point, but cop rumors. You understand the difference?"

"No."

"Okay. Fair. How should I say this? Your brother's name has come up in, uh . . . recent investigations."

"Drugs?"

"Why would you ask that?"

"His history, I guess."

"Has he been doing drugs?"

"I don't know."

"Would you tell me if you did?" He studied my face as if looking for a secret door. "How about his location? If you knew where he was, would you tell me that?"

"I want to know what's going on."

"I can't discuss that."

"Hey, *you* brought me in here."

"To ask if you'd seen him. To warn you. Jason might be a lost cause. You're not."

"Jason is *not* a lost cause."

"I'm not asking you to rat him out or to stop seeing him. If he's in trouble, I can help him. If he gets in touch, tell him that."

"You could tell him yourself if you hadn't chased him out of our lives."

"Complications, son. We've discussed this."

"Will he be okay? The cops, I mean."

"If I can help him," he said. "If I can find him in time."

He touched my shoulder, nodding as he spoke. Neither of us knew the world was ending.

8

The same darkness pressing down on Gibby's house deepened the sky above Lanesworth State Prison Farm, forty-five miles east. If anything, the night sky there was blacker, unspoiled as it was by streetlights or traffic or civilization of any kind. First opened in 1871, the walls at Lanesworth were three feet thick, the windows little more than barred slits in the stone. Situated at the end of a four-mile private road, the prison filled an empty corner of a rural county; and though it had not worked as an actual prison farm in over forty years, the signs of its original intent could still be seen in the ditch lines and fallow fields and new-growth forest. Before nature had retaken so much of it, men had suffered in the cold, died in the heat. The chain gangs were long gone, but the prison still sprawled across eighteen thousand acres of lowland and scrub. Built to house a thousand men, it held twice that number now. A few inmates were classified as *moderate offenders, potentially dangerous,* but most were the worst the state could offer. Killers. Drug dealers. Serial rapists.

In a subbasement beneath death row was a string of cells that stayed warm when others were cold, and cool when others were hot. In one such cell, a killer stood beside a bed, but it was not his bed, and not his cell. He didn't like the man whose cell it was, but nothing at Lanesworth was about *like.*

In a corner of the same cell stood a man known as Prisoner X—or just, X. That wasn't his name, but people called him that. They thought it was short for *Axel,* his true name, or because he'd killed ten men, and eaten parts of them. Others said that he'd killed his wife for infidelity, but only after he'd emasculated her lover, then cut Xs into his eyes. X had been an inmate for so long that people didn't really care anymore. He was part of the prison, like the steel and concrete and stone.

"Higher, please. Your left hand." X gestured, and the man by the bed complied. Shirtless in prison jeans, he stood with both hands up and fisted. "Excellent. Perfect."

The man by the bed was only two inches taller than X, but wide and rawboned and forty pounds heavier. Raised hard in the Georgia mountains, he'd run away young and grown up a thief and a killer, a bare-knuckle, fight-for-cash brawler on the streets of Atlanta. He'd been inside for less than five weeks, but every guard told the same story, that the kid could take a beating, spit blood, and come back for more, that he was a serious, determined, no-bullshit kind of fighter.

"Don't move," X said. "You're moving." X was not a great painter, but he wasn't bad, either. He made a few more strokes with the brush, then said, "It's strange. I know."

"It's a freak show, is what it is."

The kid talked tough, but the doubt was in his eyes. He'd heard the stories. He was, *in fact,* having his portrait painted in a subbasement beneath death row. X enjoyed the young man's doubt, but didn't let the pleasure show. That would be weakness, and X despised weakness in all its forms. After a final stroke, he turned the painting so the young man could see it, a hyper-contextualized impression of violence and its aftermath: the broken stance, the bruising, and the blood. "You understand what comes next?"

"They told me, yeah."

"Good."

X put down the painting and stripped off his shirt, revealing a narrow torso corded with muscle. Even at forty-nine, there was nothing soft, not anywhere.

"I'm not afraid of you," the young man said. "I think the stories are only stories."

X smiled, but it was not a nice smile. Backing through the open door, he moved from the cell to a narrow corridor that ran the length of a half-dozen other cells, all devoid of prisoners. The corridor ceiling was twenty feet high, the light fixtures rusted where old water stains discolored the concrete and stone. A guard sat near a metal door, but knew better than to watch.

Trailing X from the cell, the young man said, "Why me?"

"Was it four men you killed, or five?"

"Six. Bare-handed."

"Is that not reason enough?"

"I don't fight for the fun of it."

"For what, then?"

"Cash money. Or if someone needs killing."

"And today?"

"They say the warden is in your pocket. That you own the guards, too."

"You fear retaliation."

"Yeah, well. Busting up random convicts is one thing . . ."

He left the thought unfinished, so X pulled a sheaf of cash from his pocket, counted out some bills, and dropped them on the floor. "A thousand dollars for the fight. That's a hundred a minute for the next ten minutes of your life."

The young man stared at the money like a dog would stare at meat. "I'll take your money, old man, but you're not going to last any ten minutes."

He stooped for the bills, then came with his chin tucked and the big fists up. He thought the fight was a joke, that X was used up and stupid-crazy, an old man with half the reach. In a different life, he might have been right, but X, in motion, was a marriage of power and speed that few in the world could match. He worked the right eye first—four hard jabs—then bloodied the mouth, the nose; cracked a rib on the left side.

That was the first nine seconds.

X slipped out of reach, then came back for the face, two lefts and right, then a roundhouse kick that cut cables in the big man's knees. X danced away a second time, not yet breathing hard. He saw the fear then, the understanding.

What if they were true?

The stories . . .

X smiled as that fear opened like a flower. The big man saw it, and hated it. "You paid me to fight, so *fucking* fight."

He came harder that time, and X bled, too. It's why he'd picked the big man in the first place.

All those kills.

That *readiness.*

X made it last the full ten minutes, but the fight was never close. X got hurt; the big man got ruined. By the ten-minute mark, he was bent at the waist and half-blind, too bloody and broken to lift his hands. He looked once at the guard, and X felt the first real distaste. "He can't help you."

"Do it if you're going to do it."

The man's face was a mask of blood, one eye ruined for life, the right shoulder out of its socket. The rage was still there, though; he could go longer. But what was the point?

"Guard. We're finished here."

The guard kept his eyes down, but knew from long experience what to do. He got the big man up and out, and never looked at X.

When they were gone, X went into a second cell, washed blood from his hands and face, then taped up the cuts.

Bored again, he wandered the cells he kept like a suite of rooms: one for the wine, another for his art. Everyone knew he was rich, of course. Years ago, he'd been in the news all the time: the jets and mansions, the models and call girls and socialite girlfriends. Of course, the stories changed after his arrest: profiles on the family fortune, the long list of famous friends and political connections. An inmate had asked once how much money X really had, intending to leverage that information with violence of his own. He'd have considered it an easy thing: a rich man, new to prison. But X was unlike other rich men, so he'd given that inmate a long smile and a silent count, three full seconds before he'd torn the esophagus from his throat, and flushed it down a prison toilet. Since then, there'd been so few questions.

"Ah, well . . ."

He had his privacy and his comforts. For the privilege, he gave the warden an unholy amount of money each and every year, plus a solemn, cross-his-heart vow that the warden's wife would not be gang-raped ever again.

Not on a Sunday morning.

Not with the kids watching.

It was late that same night that something broke the steady routine of X's life. "Excuse me. Um . . . sir?" The guard was a large man, and apologetic.

"What is it?"

"Someone has been asking to see you. Francis Willamette. A prisoner. We didn't want to bother you, but he's been asking for a few days now, very insistent. We . . . um . . . we took a vote. The guards, I mean."

X lit a cigarette, and leaned back. Six guards served on his regular detail, but he had other guards in other pockets. "What does Mr. Willamette want?"

"He says it's about Jason French. It's . . . um . . . it's why we voted *yes*."

"Then I suppose you should bring Mr. Willamette down."

The guard backed from the cell, and hurried away. When footsteps sounded in the stairwell, the same guard said, "Third cell. You can go on down."

"Are you certain? He's not . . . you know?"

"He's expecting you. You'll be fine."

When Willamette appeared, the same doubts seemed to fill every line in his face. X had met the old man once before. He'd claimed to be a chess player, but managed to embarrass himself in three moves. He'd lost weight in the years since they'd played that single game, and the skin was loose on his bones. One hand clutched at the cell door, and he held on to the bar as if he'd fall without it. X took in the sunken eyes, the brown teeth. "You claim to have seen Jason French?"

"Three days ago, yes, sir. On the road, um, I was on the prison bus."

"Why should I believe you?"

"Because I can describe him in perfect detail, the car he was in, and the people with him, how he froze the moment he realized the bus was from Lanesworth. My memory's photographic. Any detail you ask for."

"Assuming all of that is true, why should I care?"

The old man was cunning enough to hide his satisfaction, but the glint in his eyes was pure greed. "We both know that you do."

X stared for long seconds, his entire being dangerously still. He'd never cared about the stories that circulated in the general population, not who he'd killed or why he'd done it, or what really went down in the subbasement under death row. True or false, such stories were irrelevant. X stayed above them. But this, however, this presumption to know *anything* about X's wants or needs or preferences . . .

The old man understood the shift in X's eyes. "Hey, buddy, hey now. No judgment." He spread his fingers, showing the seamed palms. "We all have our kinks. You. Me. It's just that I'm too old to play games. Fifty-two years inside. I know you see the logic."

X studied the old man's face. The lips. The damp eyes. "So you can tell me about Jason French. What would you want from me in exchange?"

The old man took a breath, and named his price. Money. Pornography. Two days with a girlish inmate he'd seen once in the yard.

X shook his head dismissively. "Descriptions of an isolated encounter. A few flowery words."

"I can tell you how to find him."

X blinked, a hard thump in his chest. "Go on."

"I know the car, the license plate. From there, it should be easy. Anyone on the outside could track him down."

X tried to conceal his emotions, but the old prisoner knew better. A smile split his face as he said, "There's one other thing," then drew back a chair, and sat as if he owned the place. "There was a girl in the car, a brunette . . ."

When Willamette was finished and gone, X paced the empty hall, debating the pros and cons of the bargain he'd made. He didn't care about the brunette in the car, or the girlish inmate on cellblock C—let Willamette have his fun. But some time ago X had given Jason certain assurances—promises, actually—and while most people mattered little to X, Jason was not *most people*. That made the debate more like a war of attrition.

A full hour, pacing.

One more staring at a stain on the ceiling.

In the end, though, X knew exactly what he'd known at the moment of Willamette's proposal: there could be no real debate.

"Guard!" He raised his voice, suddenly impatient. "I want Reece, and I want him here now."

Reece lived on the other side of Charlotte. His arrival took time. When it finally happened, the same guard led him down the corridor. "Your appellate lawyer is here."

X had no appellate lawyer—he'd never leave prison alive—but he did enjoy the small fictions. "Wait upstairs."

The guard turned and left. Behind him, Reece appeared as he always had: narrow-shouldered and thin, with a wisp of beard on a face that could be forty-five or sixty-five. Deep lines cut the corners of his mouth, and his skin had a chalky cast that X associated with a great-grandfather he'd known as a boy. That's where any impression of agedness ended. Reece was as vicious and quick as any predator X could imagine. Over seventeen years, he'd earned enough money from X to buy mansions and fund a dozen retirements. There was no affection between them, but X knew what Reece could do, the things he *liked* to do. Of every fixer X had on the outside, Reece was the one he trusted most. Even so, X could not hide his frustration. "It's not like you to be late."

"I was out when the call came in. I left as soon as I got the message."

"What time is it now?"

"Three a.m. I'm sorry. I truly would have been here sooner."

"It's fine. I've been impatient." X accepted the excuse, nodding. "Any problems out there that I should know about?"

"Smooth as glass." Reece slid his palm across an imaginary pane. He meant payoffs, threats, the parolee whose car they'd burned as a reminder to keep his mouth shut. "What do you need from me now?"

X told Reece what he'd learned from Willamette: the prison bus, the car, the people in the car.

"You're sure it was Jason French?"

"Willamette was convincing."

"You want me to find him?"

"Finding Jason is only the start." X explained what else he wanted.

He offered specifics, and Reece took a few moments to play it out in his mind. "Why does Willamette care about this girl?"

"Why does anyone care?"

"She's brunette?"

"Young. Attractive."

"I'm glad you called me for this."

"I thought of no one but you." That was true. Reece had certain desires that made him predictable. Supporting those desires made him dependable in a way that money alone never could.

"How soon?" Reece asked.

"As soon as possible."

Reece removed a pen and pad, all business. "Can you confirm the plate number for me?"

X gave him the number again. "Sixty-six Mustang, maroon with whitewall tires and minor rust on two fenders."

Reece jotted down the license number. "Give me her full description."

X described the brunette as Willamette had. Facial features. Skin tone. Height and build. "He puts her age at twenty-seven."

"What about the blonde?"

"Just the brunette."

Reece looked at his watch, and frowned. "The sun will be up in a few hours. Give me a couple days."

"Today," X said. "Today would be better."

Reece found the car easily enough—with X's resources at his disposal, there was never a question—but it didn't belong to the girl. The kid who owned it was a good-looking kid, but that was no surprise, either. He looked like Jason French. Following him from one place to another made Reece sick to his stomach: the hair and the suntan, the strong arm, hooked in the open window. Reece had no illusions about his hatred of people like Jason and his little brother. The world came to people like that, and Reece had to take what he wanted. In high school, he'd heard every insult.

Hey, little man . . .

Hey, pencil-dick . . .

The pencil-dick thing had been tough.

Gym class, communal showers . . .

One girl, in particular, had teased Reece mercilessly. Jessica Bruce. She'd been his first.

The memory was fond enough to stir a host of others.

Jessica . . .

Allison . . .

That Asian girl at McDonald's . . .

The cashier who'd rolled her eyes when Reece asked for her number . . .

It helped time pass, but the boy didn't make Reece's job any easier. He went to school, hung out with some other kid. He bought candy, played pinball, did normal stuff that did not involve a five-foot-three, pale-breasted brunette, aged approximately twenty-seven. A moment's interest rose around dusk when the kid drove into the city, and parked where expensive condos met an immaculate street. Reece watched him approach a door, hesitate, and then leave before ringing the bell. The moment felt significant, but Reece wasn't convinced until he followed the kid home, then returned alone. Nothing about the condo said *teenage kid*. Too much money. Too much style. Curtains were drawn inside, but Reece waited as people came home from work, and streetlights snapped on. For three hours, he watched the cars, the foot traffic, the condominium.

He smoked a cigarette.

He was used to waiting.

At midnight, a van rolled up, and a tall, broad-shouldered hippie got out on the other side, flipping long hair as he walked to the passenger door. Reece wanted to hurt him on principle, but what mattered was the girl who spilled out when the hippie opened her door. She stumbled, laughing. The hippie caught her, and held her against the van, kissing her with one hand on a breast and the other up her skirt. She pushed him away, but didn't mean it. He kissed her again, and groped her again, then half-carried her up the steps, where they fumbled with keys and each other, but managed the door, and went inside. Reece frowned, but was happy.

The girl was five-three, brunette, and every bit of twenty-seven years.

She was also very pretty.

That was a bonus.

9

Tyra slept late, woke to the sound of rain, and used both hands to hold her skull together. Curtains made a gray square in the dimness, and she imagined cool, wet rain, the patter of it on her face. It didn't help. Curling into a ball, Tyra tried to stitch together the pieces of her night. She'd argued with Sara—nothing new—then stormed out, angry. That was early. *Then what?* Happy hour at the Tiki Lounge? That seemed right. Then pizza at Shakey's, down the block, and ladies' night at some club downtown. She remembered an empty dance floor, a seriously hot bartender, and some old guy making a play from the stool beside her. She had visions of cab rides and other dance floors and other bars. Eventually, she remembered the dude.

"Oh shit, the dude . . ."

That's what she'd called him. He had a name, but it was something vanilla like Alex or Winston or Brad. He'd introduced himself with a name and a drink, and she'd said, *Thanks, dude.* He'd been tall—she remembered that—a tall guy with Jesus hair, a silk shirt, and something like a bearskin rug on his chest. After four tequila shots, Tyra had run fingers through that rug, and said, *Dude . . .* Later, there'd been dancing and kissing, a blur of streetlights from a van with shag carpet on the dash. It was a dude's van. She remembered saying it. *Dude, this is a dude's van.* She'd said the same word when he pumped up Jimi Hendrix, and when he lit a joint, and when he ran off the road trying to make the turn for Dairy Queen. It seemed the word had been her language last night. She'd laughed it, and said it soft, and panted it twice when he went downtown, her fingers curled in all that hair. *Dude, dude . . .*

But the dude was gone, and Tyra wasn't sad about it. Out of bed, she drew the curtain and looked out at gray rain, a gray sky. She already wanted a drink.

No, she decided. *Not today.*

Pulling clothes from a pile on the floor, Tyra crept from the room. Her favorite diner was only two blocks down, but it felt like miles. Even after coffee, eggs, and cheese grits, she still felt less than human. But the rain had dwindled. The sun was trying.

She still couldn't handle Sara.

A movie made better sense. That was another six blocks, but she made it in time for the early show, stopping at the posters to consider the choices.

THE GODFATHER

DELIVERANCE

She went for the second because Burt Reynolds looked *good.* When it was over, she bought candy and a Coke, and watched the other movie, too. It was cool inside. It was dark. Even so, it took two drinks at a local bistro before she was ready to try again with Sara. She was being so unfair! Tyra was trying to make her life a better thing.

Almost no drugs . . .

Less drinking, kind of . . .

She'd even considered calling the cops about the parked cars she'd hit. How many was it? Five? Six? Hell, she could have hit fifty. She could have killed someone.

Shit . . .

She dropped money on the bar.

Sara was right to be angry.

Telling herself that she was ready at last, Tyra aimed for the condo, but ended up walking four or five times around her own block, unready to go inside. It was dusk when she finally stopped and looked up at the light in Sara's window. The shade was drawn, but she was there.

"Okay," she said. "One more try."

She kept her nerve all the way to Sara's door. "Sara? Sweetheart? I know you're in there."

"Go away, Tyra."

She knocked harder for a full minute. Eventually, she beat on the door. "For God's sake, Sara, I'm trying to apologize. Open the door. Come on . . ." She stopped pounding, and spread her fingers on the wood. "Why won't you talk to me?"

Not everyone would understand her need, but Sara was the gauge by which Tyra measured all the ways she'd screwed up in life: the bad boyfriends, the failed jobs. A silent treatment like this had only happened once before, when Tyra went beyond doing drugs, and tried to make a living selling them. She remembered the arguments, the screaming.

Your parents are rich. Ask them for the money!

But how could Tyra explain the debts? The kinds of people she owed? Her father owned his own business; he was a deacon of the church. Bad enough she'd dropped out of college . . .

"Do I need to beg, Sara? Is that what you want? I'll beg. I swear I will."

"You wouldn't beg me if your life depended on it. You're too proud and stubborn and spoiled."

Tyra covered her mouth, choking down an unexpected sob as the dead bolt turned, and a crack appeared with Sara's face behind it.

"You could have killed someone, you know."

"I do know that, sweetheart. I promise I do."

Sara opened the door all the way. She wore pajamas, an old robe. "Are you sober now?"

"Of course I am. I mean, two glasses of wine . . ." Tyra held her thumb and finger an inch apart. She wanted a smile, a hint of a smile. A smile meant forgiveness. Forgiveness meant she wouldn't lose her only friend.

"I've seen you do some stupid shit, Tyra . . ."

"I know you have."

"That biker last year. Kiting those checks. The heroin . . ."

"All in the past. I swear." Tyra held up a hand and crossed her heart. Sara softened, but looked tired. That was on Tyra, too. "I'm a bad room-mate, I know. I spend too much. I party. I keep you up."

"You're not *bad*," Sara said. "It's just that you have horrible judgment, no limits, and no consideration for others."

"Let me make it up to you."

"How?"

"Doughnuts. Krispy Kreme."

"Well, if it's Krispy Kreme . . ."

The smile appeared at last, and Tyra clapped with joy. "Yes! It's a plan! We can stay up late, watch TV, whatever you want."

"No drinking, though."

"Cross my heart." Tyra made another *X* on her chest. "Twenty minutes, yeah? I need to shower. I'm gross."

"I'll make tea."

Tyra skipped to her room, and thought she might cry a little. She showered, then pulled on the flared jeans, the T-shirt with no bra. In the kitchen, Sara gave her a hug, and made it a good, tight one. "You know I love you. You just make bad choices."

"Not after today. Hand to God. A new start." A tear slipped out; Tyra didn't fight it. "I'll be right back with doughnuts."

"Bring a dozen," Sara said.

"A dozen. Check."

"And get some for yourself."

Sara blew a kiss, and Tyra left with the lightest step she'd had in days. In the night air, she actually laughed. "Get some for yourself . . ."

Fumbling with the keys, Tyra made it to the driveway. The Mercedes was too wrecked to be an option, so she slid behind the wheel of Sara's Beetle, a little Volkswagen with pale cream paint and red, vinyl seats. Tyra locked the door and started the car, then saw the joint when she turned on the lights. It was only half a joint, maybe a third, the end of it blackened where Sara had crushed it against the bottom of the ashtray sometime days or weeks before. Tyra peered guiltily through the glass.

Only the doughnuts . . .

That lasted to the store and halfway back. The break came at a red light where pavement made a cross on the face of the city. It would be nice, she thought.

Get high . . .

Eat some doughnuts . . .

The light turned green, but there was no traffic, so Tyra kept her foot on the clutch, thinking about it.

It's just a joint, right, not even a whole one . . .

The light turned again before she lit it.

"Ah . . . shit, yes."

Smoke rolled out, and her head went back. She took another toke and drove with the windows down, finishing the joint in six blocks, then stopping at a gas station for chewing gum and eye drops. The cashier rang her up but did it slowly, his eyes on her face, her chest. "Anything else?"

"Camel Straights."

"That's it?"

Tyra paid the man, then made a peace sign, and pushed the door with her ass, liking how he watched, liking the buzz. From there, the drive was groovy. She didn't care about Jason French—the fucker—her job, or her parents. Traffic thickened, but the music was good, and warm air brushed her face. By the time she reached the neighborhood, she was tapping the wheel and singing with the radio. On the final block, she slowed, too high and happy to notice the parked car or the men inside it. In the driveway, she got out of the Volkswagen, already practicing.

Am I high? Of course I'm not high . . .

Come on, Sara. Don't be silly . . .

"Excuse me, miss?" A man's voice broke Tyra's concentration. He stood to the side of the driveway, looking apologetic in khakis, a button-down, and a bow tie. He said, "I'm sorry to bother you." And Tyra thought: *Sweet old man, somebody's husband.*

"Yes?"

He stepped onto the driveway. "Would you be good enough to look at a photograph for me?"

"I don't understand."

"It will take but a moment."

The situation was strange, but the weed had been pretty strong. She thought, *Okay, whatever . . .* The photograph he showed her was small, but the streetlamp was close and bright enough.

"That's Jason French." Her mouth hardened into lines of sudden suspicion. "Did he send you? You can tell that son of a bitch he had his chance. Tell him he's an asshole and he can go fuck himself. You can tell him that from me."

"And you are . . . ?"

"Tyra. Don't pretend you don't know."

The small man nodded once, ignoring the anger, pocketing the photo. "Earlier, I saw a blond woman enter your condominium. Is she your roommate?"

Tyra squinted, confused by the questions and the fuzz in her head. "I don't understand. What . . . ?"

"Five-seven. Slender."

Tyra started to nod, but something was off with the old man and his *moment,* and not because of the pot. His eyes didn't match the clothing—they were too knowing—and he wasn't that old, either, just seamed at the eyes, the corners of his mouth. "I'm going inside, now. My friend is waiting."

"Sara, yes. She's lovely. Really, truly . . . lovely."

"How do you know her name?"

He shrugged, and Tyra stepped back, suddenly afraid. "Don't come near me."

"I won't take a step."

"Mister, I will scream."

Showing small teeth, the man gestured with his right hand. "If you will look behind you."

Tyra turned, and saw a second man, a giant with a wide face and shaggy hair. Behind him, the street was empty, and he knew it, too. The grin. The bright eyes. She thought, *Mistake, misunderstanding.*

The smaller man nodded as if sympathetic. "It's best if you don't fight."

Tyra glanced at Sara's window, so close. She wanted to run, but her feet were heavy. *Like a dream,* she thought; but the night was no dream. The big man said, "Hey, lady," then hit her so fast and hard she went down on the concrete, a pain in her head as if something inside had broken. She tried to crawl, but hands caught her, and lifted her, and pushed her into the back seat of Sara's car, down onto the floorboards. Even then, she could see the same window. It was Sara's bedroom, the pretty one with pink walls and views into the park across the street. She stretched out a hand as someone outside said, "Follow me. Keep it slow. And here, you'll need this."

The car rocked as the big man climbed in, turned in his seat, and pointed a Polaroid camera. "Hold still." There was a flash, a whirring sound. Still stretching for that far, high window, Tyra said her roommate's name. "No talking. I don't like talking."

The little engine started, and he turned on the headlights. Tyra said Sara's name again. She tried to scream it, but the big man twisted again, and found her throat with his hand. Tyra tried to fight, but he was strong and her fingers weak. They scraped an arm. Darkness flickered.

She opened her mouth, but had no air.

The darkness came again.

The darkness stayed.

10

The boy was not a bad boy. Anyone who knew him would agree. He was inquisitive but scattered, the kind of child who might forget he was in a baseball game, and wander out of right field to look for crawdads in the creek. That had happened once. Seventh grade. Last year. Granted, he did catch the largest crayfish anyone at school had ever seen—even the biology teacher agreed—but they still lost the game on a two-run pop fly straight down the right baseline. The coach had spoken to him about it afterward, explaining in his quiet, patient way that the team was a machine, that every boy had a job. The other boys were not wrong, he'd said, to be upset. Winning mattered. So did teamwork. Nods had followed; so had sincere apologies and promises it would never happen again. The coach had smiled in that same, soft way, then sent the boy out to his mother, thinking as so many did.

The boy was a good boy.

Just not very bright.

On this particular morning, the boy was not at his usual stop when the big yellow bus rolled up and opened its doors. He'd left the house at 7:15 but turned left instead of right. That wasn't a mistake—he *did* know left from right—but older boys had told him about an abandoned construction site where they'd been finding arrowheads in a patch of churned dirt. The boy liked arrowheads—most every boy did—but for him, it went deeper. His grandfather had been full Cherokee, descended in a straight line from the Eastern Band of the Cherokee Nation, those not forced to walk the Trail of Tears all the way back in 1838. He was dead now, but the boy remembered his lessons.

Pride of people.

Pride of place.

Arrowheads and spearpoints were to be preserved and treasured, not traded like comic books and baseball cards. And he was good at finding them. When they'd built the baseball field, for instance. Or that time the river dropped. They rarely lay flat—that was the key. Inexperienced hunters looked for the telltale shape, as if they'd been placed on purpose the day before. The boy knew better than that. He looked for the edges, the points, the small bits raised above the dirt. After heavy rainfall was a good time to look, especially in plowed fields and new subdivisions. He didn't know how old the construction site was or why it had been abandoned, and didn't care, either.

Turning off the roadside, the boy cut the corner where his neighborhood ended and a four-lane stretched off as far as he could see. The construction site was on the other side and two miles down, a building seven stories tall and incomplete, just the frame, the elevator shafts, the cinder block stairwells. The spot, they'd said, was behind it where a hilltop had been cut down and spread out to fill a gully. When the boy arrived, he stopped where a chain-link fence paralleled the road. Cars sped past, but no one noticed or cared or slowed. Squeezing through a half-open gate, he followed the construction road, his eyes on the red-dirt verge. The boy liked corner-notched arrowpoints the best, but loved the basal-notched and the stemmed almost as much. Even a leaf-cut or a simple triangle made his heart skip a beat. He'd found a flint knife once, and a Clovis point as long as his hand.

Ax-heads. Grinding stones. Scrapers.

Anything was possible.

Because of that, the boy kept his eyes down, and sensed the building more than saw it: a dark mass, rising ahead. He paid no attention until its shadow touched his feet, and he saw caulk guns and soda cans and dropped rivets. Stepping onto cool concrete, he peered up through a spiderweb of beams and cable. Moving deeper, his shoes scraped in the grit, his hands on the concrete, the rusted steel. He circled a stairwell, and saw the blood first.

After that, he saw the girl.

Detective French got the call at home. "Ken," he said. "Good morning."

"Not so much." There was crackle on the line, a radio patch. "You know the empty construction site on the edge of Highway 16? The developer who went bust last year?"

"A hotel, right?"

"Was supposed to be, yeah."

"What about it?"

"I need you here."

"Why?"

"Body. Female. It's bad."

"Hang on, hang on. Shit." French trapped the phone between his ear and shoulder. He was making eggs. They were burning. "All right, Ken. Sorry. Tell me what's happening."

Burklow started with the boy.

French flashed his shield at the gate, drove into the old construction site, and saw a dark shape that evolved into a small kid with his knees drawn up, and his chin pressed into the bones of his chest as if he might never look up again. Exiting the car, French looked at the building, then back at the boy, taking in the sneakers, the T-shirt, the blown-out jeans.

"You okay, son?" The boy didn't look up or speak. "I'm a cop, okay? I'm here to take care of you." Still nothing, not even his eyes. Thirty yards away, Burklow stepped from the structure, and waved. French said, "Wait here. I'll be right back." Facing his partner, it was hard to hide the anger. "That boy should be with an adult. His parents. An officer. Someone."

"Not yet."

"Why not?" Burklow looked away, and French caught all the signals. "It's really that bad?"

"Have you had breakfast yet? 'Cause it's like that."

"Jesus. Okay. The boy called it in?"

"Kid stumbled into traffic, and a motorist almost took him out. Older woman. Grandmother. She got him out of the street and flagged down a patrol car. New guy. Dobson, I think. That's him at the gate."

"It's a school day. It's early. The kid's what? Twelve?"

"Maybe. Maybe younger."

"What's he doing out here?"

"He's not really talking."

"No name?"

"Not yet."

French looked around at the weeds and dirt, the windblown litter. "It's pretty quiet out here, Ken."

"I need you to see it first. I *need* that."

French frowned as a pit opened deep inside. Burklow's opinion mattered more than most, but rules existed for a reason. There should be other personnel on-site: detectives, technicians, chain of command. Ken had behaved like this only once before, and that crime scene had been so disturbing, they'd kept most of it from the papers, even from the victim's family. "All right, partner. I'll take your lead for now. Give me a second with the kid."

French crossed to where the boy sat. Even standing, he could smell the child's sweat; see dust in the creases of his skin. "How're you doing, kid?" He knelt beside him. "Can you tell me your name?"

Nothing.

Silence.

"That's fine. I run quiet, too. How about what happened? Can we talk about that? Or maybe why you were here?"

Still nothing.

Burklow was watching, shaking his head.

"Would you like to sit in my car? Air-conditioning. Cop stuff. It's pretty cool."

The boy shrugged

Progress.

French got the boy up and into the car. He showed him the radio, the spare cuffs, the shotgun locked to the dash. "Listen, son. I need to go inside . . ." The boy shook his head, terrified. "You're safe here. Promise. All that . . ." He gestured at the building. "Whatever you saw, whatever is in there—it's my problem, now. Okay? Not yours. Not ever again." The boy looked away, trying not to cry. "You wait here." French patted him on the knee. "We'll talk more when I come back."

The boy watched him go. Burklow was waiting at the superstructure, and French followed him into the shadows.

"Watch the vomit."

French stepped over it. "The boy's?"

"Mine."

That one-word response spoke volumes. Ken was a twenty-year murder cop. He'd fought in Korea. Moving more deeply into the structure, he angled left at an elevator shaft. "That's where we're going. North stairwell."

The stairwell shaft rose the full seven stories. Beyond it, red earth and scrub stretched to a distant tree line. Rounding a final corner, French saw blood on the floor, reddish black, mostly dry. Above it, the woman hung from chains tossed over a steel beam. His gaze went to the torn wrists first, and then the cloudy eyes. After that, he soaked it up like a sponge: the way she'd been tortured and ruined and cut. He tried to stay level, but Burklow was right.

It was bad.

French had to walk away. When he had himself under control, he returned to the scene and studied the body from top to bottom, shying from none of it, not the blood or the excisions, not the organs and bones, the bits of marbled flesh.

Burklow kept his distance. "Can you imagine the kid? Finding her like this?"

French circled the body. Silver tape had been twisted around the victim's head to bind her mouth and keep her quiet. Parts of her had been opened up, and parts removed. Her toes grazed the floor, and he saw drag lines in the blood. The way she'd fought. The way she'd swung. "White female. Mid- to late twenties." French sought comfort in the routine; couldn't find it. "Jesus, Ken. I've never seen anything like this. Not ever, not even close."

"I tried to count the cuts while I waited for you. I stopped at ninety-seven. That's when I got to the, uh, the . . ." Burklow pointed at the raw patches where her breasts had been cut away. "You think she was alive when that happened?"

"Possibly."

French pulled on rubber gloves, and moved blood-crusted hair from the woman's face. One eye was swollen closed, the nostrils black with blood. He studied cheekbones, the good eye. Something about the face was familiar.

"You okay, Bill?"

"Um . . ."

"What is it?"

"I was just, uh . . ." French shook his head as if to hide a sudden sickness. He pointed, but had no idea if Burklow was looking or not. "She chewed through the tape. No wedding ring. No other jewelry. Any sign of her clothing?"

"Not yet."

French stepped away from the body, more than shaken. Undone. "Check for me, will you?"

"Bill, you don't look so great."

"Search for the clothing, okay? I need a minute here."

"Yeah. Course. Whatever you say."

Burklow lurched into the shadows, and French took the most difficult breath of his life as a cop. He counted to ten, then lifted the woman's head a second time.

He knew the face; he'd met her.

A week ago she was screwing his son.

Twenty minutes later, the place was crawling with cops, technicians, pathologists. Directing their movements, French appeared to be in perfect control; but deep down, he warred with himself.

Tyra . . .

That was her name.

"Do we have ID on the victim?"

French turned in the hot sun. He'd not heard the footsteps. "Captain, I'm sorry. Say again?"

"Do we have a name yet? An address? Did you find a wallet? A driver's license?"

David Martin stepped closer. As a homicide captain, he was competent, fair, and smart. Generally, French liked him. Not now. "No, sir. No ID."

"What about the kid who found her?"

The captain was a clear-eyed, narrow man in his early fifties. French looked past him. The kid was still in the car. "He's pretty shut down. I'll try him again in a bit."

The captain nodded, already distracted. "This'll be a media shit storm. You know that."

"Yes, sir."

"So let's keep it tight. You and Burklow, the medical examiner and me." He pointed at other detectives. "Martinez. Smith. We're the only ones who've seen the body, right?"

"The boy . . ."

"Of course, the boy."

"And Dobson, I think. He looked pretty green when I showed up."

"Right. First responder. Shit. I don't know if we can keep this wrapped."

French dipped his head at the structure. "Don't forget the photographer, the fingerprint techs, the boy's parents, when we find them."

"I want time. Talk to your people. Give me what you can."

"Yes, sir."

"Jesus, Bill . . ." The captain's composure failed as he mopped sweat from his face. "As a father, what do you do with this?"

"I say a silent prayer and thank God for my sons."

"I have girls."

"The twins, I know."

"Have you ever seen anything like that?" He wasn't looking for an answer, so French didn't give him one. "You know how long I've had this job? Too long, maybe."

"You'll be fine."

"But you've got this, right? I can leave it with you?"

"Absolutely."

"Good man. Thank you." The captain gathered himself, buttoning his jacket. "If you need me, I'll be at the high school, then at the station."

"The high school?"

"I think I'll give my girls a hug."

"Good idea."

"Oh, and Bill . . ."

"Yeah?"

"Call me when you identify the victim. She'll have family and friends. Someone somewhere is worried."

"Soon as we have a name." French watched the captain nod, and slide into his car. Inside, the war raged on.

Her name is Tyra . . .

She's been with my son . . .

When French returned to his car, the kid's color was better. "Mind if I sit with you for a while?" He slid behind the wheel. "I'm sorry you had to wait. It's kind of crazy out there."

"I've been watching."

"Ah, he talks." French kept it light because the boy still looked as thin as glass. "Remember what I told you before? You're safe here. The bad people are gone."

"Yes, sir."

"What's your name?"

"Samuel."

"Do you live nearby, Samuel?"

The boy gave an address. French knew it.

"I know I'm supposed to be in school . . ."

"Don't worry about that. You're not in trouble. My name is Bill."

The boy held out a small hand, and they shook. He looked like Gibby at the same age: the thin shoulders, the same solemn eyes. "Do your parents know where you are?" The boy shook his head. "Will you tell me their names?"

"It's just my mother."

"Your mother, then."

"Kate."

"Kate. Good. Thank you, Samuel. Will you tell me why you came here this morning?"

"Some older boys said I might find arrowheads."

"Did you find any?"

He shook his head, eyes filling. "I found . . ."

"It's okay, Samuel."

"I found . . . I found . . ."

"You're okay, son. Breathe." French squeezed the narrow shoulders. "In and out. That's a boy."

When the kid stopped crying, he told a simple story. He'd wanted one thing and found another. When he finished talking, French put him in a car with a female officer who had kids of her own. It was a good fit. He saw it in the boy's eyes.

After that, they cut the body down.

It took bolt cutters and three men with strong stomachs. When she was bagged and in the van, French called the medical examiner into a shady place by a different stairwell. Malcolm Frye was a small man with coffee skin and salt in his hair. He was good at his job. The two of them went back at least a decade. "What can you tell me?" French asked.

Frye pulled off latex gloves, his eyes as doleful as the kid's. "Where should I start?"

"Cause of death?"

He shook his head, and used a handkerchief to polish wire-rimmed glasses. "I doubt any single cut killed her. Preliminarily, I'd say shock, cumulative trauma, massive blood loss."

"Was she alive for all of it?"

"Probably."

"Jesus."

"It was precision work designed to keep her breathing and conscious. No damaged organs or nicked arteries. Whoever did this to her had training."

"Surgical?"

"Not to that degree, but training. Paramedic, maybe. A corpsman. A med school dropout."

"How long, do you think?"

"Once they subdued her and strung her up?" He lifted his shoulders, weary. "Long enough to chew through her own tongue."

The ME settled the glasses back on his face, and French studied him more closely. "You okay, Doc?"

"I'm a black man in the South, Detective. What's not to like about a good lynching?" The bitterness came out; he couldn't help it.

"Listen, I'm sorry this one landed on you. If you want, we can get a different examiner."

"No, no." He waved off the suggestion. "Forget I said that."

"Forgotten."

"What else can I do for you?"

"Can you be more specific on timing? When it happened? How long she lived? This early in the case, even a guess would be helpful."

"I can't speak to her abduction, but she suffered for a long time, make no mistake. Inflicting that kind of damage would have taken hours. Methodical work. Careful work. Then there's the underlying psychopathy."

"Meaning?"

"That he probably enjoyed it. I doubt he rushed."

French closed his eyes, but could not unsee the flayed skin, the exposed organs. Were there a theme to the crime, it would be that people, in their expressions of cruelty, could be endlessly inventive. "Anything else you can tell me?"

"Not before the autopsy. Speaking of which . . ." He gestured at the van, the body inside.

"Hang on one second, Doc."

Burklow was moving in their direction. When he arrived, he nodded at the ME, but spoke to French. "We've been working from the inside out. No sign of her clothes or personal belongings. No usable footprints or tire tracks, but the chain out front is cut. Looks like they came right up the main drive."

"Pretty brazen."

"Dark of night. Light traffic. We did find this." He brandished a clear, plastic evidence bag.

"Is that what I think it is?"

Burklow handed over the bag. It contained a crumpled package made of foil and white paper. "We found two more empty packages like this one."

"Looks fresh."

"I'd say it's brand-new."

"Oh, the sick bastard . . ."

"I know. I'm sorry."

French walked away, and studied the sky as if it were the last clean thing in the world. The ME looked a question, so Burklow explained. "Polaroid film," he said. "The son of a bitch took pictures."

It was still early when French left the crime scene. He tried to stay, but couldn't focus, couldn't *lead*.

"What do you mean you're leaving? Where are you going?"

"I can't talk about it, Ken."

"We still have work to do. Uniforms are canvassing. We haven't identified the body. The hell's wrong with you?"

French shook his head; kept walking. He'd buried thoughts of his son, but Jason was out there. So was an explanation.

Please, God . . .

"Bill, stop walking away from me. I'm talking to you."

Burklow trailed him to the car, two steps back. French found his keys. "Just wrap the scene, Ken. Whatever it takes. Remind everyone to keep this quiet. I'll meet you at the station later."

"The station? Our next stop should be the medical examiner's office. He'll have her on the table by now."

"Fine, I'll meet you there."

"Bill. What the hell?"

"Step away, Ken."

"Not without an explanation."

"I mean it. Step away." He put a palm on his partner's chest, and pushed hard enough to make him stumble back. He wanted to apologize, but was in a river of guilt, and drowning.

Her name is Tyra . . .

Wrenching at the key, French fired the cruiser and stepped on the gas, spraying dirt and gravel. Watching his partner in the rearview, he felt a twinge, but the river took that, too.

Sooner or later they'd find her name.

Jason's would be next.

The heavy cruiser blew down the dirt road, but traffic at the four-lane held him up. A city bus. A tractor trailer. When a gap opened, he turned for the quarry, and stepped on it. Jason mattered, but Gibby came first.

It was Friday.

Senior Skip.

French found him in a field above the stony beach, sitting with Chance on the hood of a car. They were laughing and drinking, and terribly young.

Chance saw him first. "Oh shit." He hid the beer behind his back.

"Chance, I need a moment with my son." He took Gibby by the arm, and guided him into the field. "Have you seen your brother?"

Gibby's eyebrows went up. "Why?"

"Yes or no?"

"Then no."

"I want you to stay away from him."

"We've had this discussion—"

"No, we've not, not like this. Stay away from your brother. I don't have time to explain. Just do it. Spend the night with Chance, if you want. Go home or go to the movies. Go to a party, I don't care. Anywhere your brother is not."

"You're starting to freak me out."

"Good. Great. That's what I want. But I have a question, too, and it's important. Last Saturday, you went driving. Out in the country, you said, you and Jason and two girls." French took a deep breath, and said a silent prayer. "What were their names?"

"The girls?"

"Yes. Please."

"Tyra and Sara."

"Tyra's a brunette? Five-two, five-three?"

"And Sara's blond and tall. What does this have to do with anything? Why should I stay away from Jason? Dad, where are you going? Dad . . ."

The boy continued to speak, but French was underwater now, deep in the current, half-deaf and drowning.

Sweet Lord, help us, he thought.

Gibby knows her, too.

11

I watched my father walk away, then returned to Chance, who handed me a fresh beer. "What the heck was that about?"

I leaned beside him, metal hot where the sun had baked it. "He's looking for Jason."

"You didn't tell him?"

I shook my head. "He was being kind of a dick."

But that was only part of it. He was still treating me like a kid. I didn't like it. Sipping beer, I stared out at the water. Twenty kids were rafted up a hundred yards offshore. Beyond them, a lone figure floated on an inner tube, his legs bent at the knees, his head tipped back. "You good for a minute?"

"Yeah, sure."

"Sit tight."

I walked to the water's edge, skinned off my shirt, and made a shallow dive. At the raft of kids, people called my name.

Yo, Gibby. Yo . . .

Jason saw me when I was twenty yards out, but he barely moved. His head turned. His hands made lazy circles in the water. "Gibby in the house."

Hanging on the edge of his tube, I saw the lazy smile, the sunburn on his prison skin. Half a six-pack hung from plastic rings. "Dad is looking for you."

Jason's head rose a few inches. He cracked one eye to stare off at the shore, then shrugged without actually shrugging. It was a vibe, the way he settled his head back against the tube. "He was asking about the girls."

"What girls?" Jason closed his eyes, a beer can cradled on his chest.

"Tyra, mostly, but Sara, too. I think it was a cop thing."

"She probably wrecked another car."

"He told me to stay away from you."

"How's that working out for you, little brother?" Jason smiled but kept his eyes closed, as if his joke was the end of it.

"It was weird. He looked scared."

"That is also not my problem."

But I played the conversation again: my father's hands on my shoulders, and how they'd squeezed hard and then fluttered like feathers. "Do you ever get scared?"

"Of what?"

"Anything."

"Nope."

"Not ever?"

"Well, that's the thing about war, isn't it? Once enough people try to kill you, the little things don't matter. Cops. The past. Not even dying."

"What about prison?"

I knew the question was unfair, but so was his talk of fearlessness and little things. My life was *made* of little things. Jason understood, I thought, but I'd made him angry, too.

"Prison is different."

He tried to end the discussion, but I was tired of being the youngest, the sheltered, the only one unproven by combat or adulthood or a long dive from a tall cliff. "But you're scared of it," I said. "You have to be scared of something."

"Why? Because you are?"

"It's not like that."

"But you throw prison in my face when you know fuck-all about it."

"Only because I saw you on the road that day."

"You have no idea what you saw."

"I saw your face, man, your face."

My voice was too loud, and if someone asked, I'd be hard-pressed to say why any of it mattered so much now, on this day. Maybe it was because my father was afraid and my brother calm, or because the cliff rose above us. Perhaps it was due to thoughts of war and graduation, or the fact that Chance was dodging the draft, and made no bones about it. Whatever the reasons, I needed to see something of myself behind the armor my brother wore as easily as a T-shirt. If Jason understood that need, he didn't care. His eyes were equally hard, his mouth the same tight line. "Just swim away," he said. "Swim away, little fish."

When French left his son at the quarry, he understood the hurt feelings he'd left behind. But what else could he do? Even if Jason was not involved in Tyra's death—*Please, God, don't let him be involved*—he'd still be swept into the investigation and tarred with the doubts born of his own poor choices. He was the killer, the user, the convict. How many people would resist the certainties of guilt by implication? French had few illusions.

Oh, you don't know about Jason French?

The war?

The drugs?

They say he killed a hundred people . . .

Charlotte was a big city, but not that big. People knew your business, or thought they did, or thought they had the right. Gibby would be tarred with the same brush. So would Gabrielle.

But that wasn't the worst, not even close.

"Jesus Christ, Gibby knew her, too."

His good boy . . .

His youngest . . .

Murder cases swept up innocent people all the time. He'd seen it before: prison, shattered lives. Suspicion alone could tip the world on its side. "Damn it, Jason. Can't you think, just for once? Can't you make a decent, goddamn choice?"

It sounded unfair, but French had no idea what his oldest son did with his days and nights. Was he still abusing drugs? If so, where did he get them and from whom? Was he violent? Committing crimes? Where did he get money? How did he live? Whispers from other cops said Jason might be involved in something big. Guns, maybe. Or maybe gangs. The only certainty was that minutes led to hours, hours to days, and days to patterns of life. That was the math behind every bad case he'd ever worked. Small decisions. The wrong step. After that, it was all about the road.

French gave himself those seconds—those hard, dark moments of frustration and doubt—then locked the emotion down. He'd bought a few hours.

Not enough . . .

Going first to the house at Water and Tenth, he found two men on the sofa, hip-deep in chicken wings and beer. Neither had seen Jason for days. "He's still paying rent?"

"Two months, cash in advance."

"But he's not sleeping here?"

"Money is money. I don't care where he sleeps."

"Any idea where I can find him?"

"The man has ladies."

"Who and how many and where?"

"More than us, is all I know."

Feet went up on the coffee table, and French let his eyes move over the room. The air smelled of grease and smoke and spilled beer. On television, Muhammad Ali was trash-talking some other fighter. "What about a woman named Tyra?"

"Tyra Norris . . ." One man shook his head. "He won't be anywhere near that girl . . ."

"Not after what went down."

French gauged the interruption, looking from one to the other. "What do you mean?"

"I mean it was a scene, man."

They shook their heads, and drank beer and watched Ali. It took a minute to get the details, but once they started talking, both men reveled in descriptions of the ruined Mercedes and Tyra in the dirt, of how she'd screamed and pulled a gun, and how her skirt tended to ride up on one side. French raised a hand to slow them down. "Say that last part again."

"She said your boy fucks women and kills dreams . . ."

"A direct quote . . ."

"She was yelling it up and down the street . . ."

"But she still tried to make out with him . . ."

"Truth, brother. Like . . . aggressively."

"She's crazy, but crazy hot, you know?"

"Lively, I'd say . . ."

"Like a wall socket is lively . . ."

They high-fived. They laughed.

"How did Jason handle it?"

"Oh, hey, man, Jason was cool. He rolled, but he's like that. I told him to his face he was one badass dude. I said he was an iceman . . ."

"Like falling snow."

"Yeah, yeah, cold but quiet. Just like that."

"Anything else I should know? Did she say anything else? Do anything else?"

Both men shook their heads. "Nah, man. She tagged a few more cars, and split. Haven't seen her since."

French looked for signs of deceit; saw none. "If anyone else asks, you tell them what you told me, that Jason was in total control at all times."

"Truth is truth."

"I need to check his room."

They went back to their beer and television, and French took the staircase up. In Jason's room he found clothing, condoms, and in the back of a drawer, a .38 Special that he pocketed. Nothing else seemed remotely personal: a rumpled bed, a novel by Leon Uris called *Battle Cry.* Back outside, French knelt by the tree where Tyra had supposedly wrecked her Mercedes. He had no reason to doubt the men inside, but no reason to trust them, either. Gouged bark made him feel better. So did the shredded lawn, the bits of glass and broken plastic. Tyra had been here. She'd argued with his son; threatened him with a gun.

A shard of red plastic glinted in the sun.

Even if he was on drugs . . .

Even if the war had messed him up . . .

But French no longer knew his son. Drugs, prison, life in the dark parts of the city . . .

He needed more, so he worked the back alleys and informants, the off-license bars and drug dens and flophouses. He shook the trees, hoping his boy would fall out.

It didn't happen.

By dusk, he could no longer ignore the radio. It squawked the moment he got back in the car. "David 218, Dispatch."

He keyed the mic. "David 218, go ahead, Dispatch."

"Detective Burklow has called four times now."

"Stand by, Dispatch." French lowered the mic and took a final moment for his sons.

What else could he do?

Gibby was safe—he'd made sure.

But Jason . . .

French stared out at a broken street lined with warehouses and bikers and women in short skirts. It was his seventh stop, and the story was the same as everywhere else. People knew Jason, but none had seen him, none would talk.

"Dispatch, David 218. Please tell Detective Burklow I'm 10-49, ETA twelve minutes."

12

From a window above, Jason watched his father drive away. He saw the top of the car, the rear windshield and taillights. When his father was gone, Jason lit a cigarette and turned. "What did he want?"

A big biker stood at the top of the stairs, a mountain of muscle and denim and faded ink. "He wanted you."

"Did he say why?"

"Didn't say, and I didn't ask."

Jason left the window, and sat at a scarred, wooden table. The floor beneath his feet was old, the windows behind him dirty glass in metal frames with peeling paint. The room had been an office once, with views down on to a factory floor where they'd made phone books back in the forties and fifties. Some hard-ass bikers owned it now, a club moving south from Jersey, Maryland, and Pennsylvania. *Pagans*. They'd turned the factory into a private club with garages in back and rooms upstairs to crash. They had members, cash, credibility.

"Is your old man going to be a problem?"

The biker's name was Darius Simms, a chapter president with ties running all the way back to the club's early days in Prince George's County, Maryland. He crossed his arms, and blue ink bulged on his biceps, the *Argo* tattoo as ubiquitous to Pagans as the patches on their denim cuts.

Jason said, "No. No problem."

"As long as that's true, our deal stands. The room. The privileges. But no one here likes cops with a reason to show up, unexpected."

"It won't happen again."

"Make sure it doesn't."

The biker clumped back down the stairs, and Jason moved to the big, interior window with views on to the old factory floor. The machines had been removed years ago. Now a bar ran along two sides, with booths and tables in the center. The crowd was not too big, maybe twenty bikers and twice as many women. A 1946 Flathead hung from the ceiling on chains. The lighting was poor. Gray smoke made a haze.

"Hey, baby. Are we doing this or not?"

Jason had almost forgotten about the woman, half-reclined on the low, long sofa. "What was your name again?"

"Angel."

"How old are you, Angel?"

"Twenty-five."

"I'm thinking nineteen."

"Twenty-five. Nineteen. Does it matter?"

Jason studied her from across the room, the short skirt and tall boots. The red hair was nice. "I'm sorry, sweetheart. I don't do that anymore."

"Don't do what? Pretty girls? I have friends who say different. They say Jason French always has the dope, and that he screws like a rock star, too."

Jason looked away from the smile she'd conjured like a two-bit magic trick.

"Come on, baby doll." She swung her feet to the floor, revealing more of her long, pale thighs. "Can't you help a girl out?"

"Here." Jason put a bottle on the table. "Go crazy."

"Johnnie Walker?"

"That's Johnnie Walker *Blue*."

"This wasn't the deal."

"What deal? You knocked on my door. You came inside."

"If you're not dealing, why does the club let you stay here?"

Jason shrugged. "That's between me and the club."

She tried again, soot-eyed and willing and far too young. "You don't think I'm pretty enough?"

"I think you're beautiful."

She stood, half-pouting and half-angry. "You could have stopped me at the door, you know."

"I should have done that. You're right."

"You're being a real jerk face."

Jason could barely hide the smile. "No one has ever called me that, but yes. I suppose I can be a real jerk face."

"What do I tell my friends?"

Jason glanced down into the club, and saw her friends at the bar, four or five pretty girls, jaded, no doubt, but not one over nineteen. "I think you and your friends can find a better place to party."

Dinner that night was no better than the last. Dad didn't show up. Mom asked enough questions to make sure I'd not been with Jason. Afterward, in my room, I read of war and communism and riots in a northern prison. It was a bad night, a lonesome one. That changed when the doorbell rang.

"Gibby." My mother called up the stairs. "You have a visitor."

I went down barefoot, in jeans. My mother, at the open door, said, "Not too long," then ghosted away with a frown on her face.

"Sara." I stepped outside, closing the door. "What are you doing here?"

"Hey, I'm sorry to show up like this. I tried to call all afternoon."

"My mother." I waved off the apology. "Sometimes she answers. Sometimes she doesn't. Do you want to come inside?"

"Maybe we could talk out here."

"Sure." I followed her off the porch and into the night air. She wore cutoff jeans, sandals, and a white top that tied behind her neck and left her shoulder blades exposed. "How'd you find me?"

"There are only three listings for *French* in the book. I thought I'd take a chance."

"I'm glad you did." We stood on the walk as moths flickered in the lights behind us. Sara looked lovely but vulnerable, her arms squeezed so tightly beneath her breasts I wondered if she was cold. "Would you like a jacket?" I asked.

"No, no. It's nothing. Listen, um . . . Do you mind if we take a drive or something?"

She nodded toward a window, and I saw my mother inside, watching us through the glass. The frown had deepened. She tapped her watch. I said, "Yeah, sure. Understandable."

We walked to the driveway, and I recognized Tyra's Mercedes, still battered and scraped. I hesitated, but Sara understood. "It's part of the reason I came."

"The car?"

"The car. Tyra."

I glanced at the house. My mother stood in the open door. "We should go," I said. Sara slid behind the wheel, and I got in the other side. My mother moved onto the porch, then the walk. "We should go quickly."

Sara reversed down the drive, and I half-expected to see my mother running after us. She didn't. The car shuddered as we rocked onto the road, but steadied once we started moving. The top was down. Wind took Sara's hair, and she looked sideways with an amused smile. "Is your mother always like that?"

"Pretty much."

"It could be worse." She raised a narrow shoulder. "I don't talk to my mother."

"Not ever?"

"Not for eight years."

I didn't know what to say to that, so we drove in silence as buildings rose, and city lights climbed higher. Sara fiddled with her hair, chewed her bottom lip. When she spoke at last, we were at a stoplight with cars lined up across the road, their headlights on her face. "Have you seen Jason?" she asked.

"I thought this was about Tyra."

"I was hoping they might be together."

"I saw him today. He was alone."

"Did he mention her?"

"Not really."

She smoothed hair away from her eyes, and when the light turned, she drove faster, the little car tilting on the curves. A mile later, I recognized the street. "This is where you live." She nodded, and I thought maybe she was crying. I didn't know what to say or do, or how to help. She was a grown woman; I wasn't even wearing shoes. In the driveway, I asked her, "Sara, what's going on?"

"I can't find Tyra."

She turned off the engine, and I looked at the condo, at all the light spilling out. "Since when?"

"Last night."

"Some other guy, maybe. Some other party."

"Not this time."

"You can't know that."

That made sense, I thought, but Sara told me about their argument and her missing car and a box of doughnuts, abandoned in the driveway. "She wouldn't have left them. Not like that, not crushed in the drive."

"You called the police?"

"They said twenty-four hours. Maybe your dad . . . ?"

"He's working. I don't know where he is. We can call the station." She looked hopeful, but I wasn't. When Dad worked late, he was impossible to reach. "How long until the twenty-four hours are up?" I asked.

"A few hours, maybe."

"There you go. Not bad."

"Will you come inside with me?"

"Um . . ."

"To be honest, I'm a little afraid."

When French arrived at the hospital, Burklow was waiting outside the emergency room entrance. "I'm sorry, Ken. I know you had to wait."

"It's not like you to run silent."

"Radio problems, some other stuff. Is he ready for us?"

"He said to bring you down."

They passed through the emergency room doors, and into a waiting room. Bypassing the elevator bank, French took the stairs down, Burklow at his heels. At the bottom, a keypad allowed entrance to a hallway that served the medical examiner's office. "Radio problems, huh?"

"I don't want to talk about it, Ken."

"But later, you will."

"Later. Absolutely."

They moved past offices, labs, refrigerator banks. The autopsy suites were last in line, a group of rooms built around a central hub of scrub sinks, and observation windows. It could be a busy place, but was quiet now.

"There's our vic."

She looked worse under bright lights: the wounds that killed her, the Y cut, the open cavity. Most of her organs were out, but the medical examiner was still wrist-deep. "Gentlemen, come in." He lifted his hands, and held them awkwardly. "Let me walk you through what I've found so far." He did it methodically and precisely. It took time. "It appears that different blades were used at different times."

"Multiple blades," French said. "Does that mean multiple assailants?"

"Uncertain, but possible. Some cuts imply a certain amount of strength and viciousness. Others were of a more delicate nature."

"Any kind of pattern?"

"The more precise incisions hurt the most."

"Meaning?"

"Whoever made those cuts knew the big nerves, the sensitive areas. Something tells me he took his time. See the precision. Here and here."

"And the breast tissue?"

"I'd argue that those excisions were made with the smaller blade and with exceptional care."

Burklow said, "Jesus Christ."

"Keep going," French said.

The ME continued with the same dispassion. "No tattoos or birthmarks. She's had a recent manicure, a pedicure." He pointed at her hands and feet. "Expensive dental work. Little sign she's ever done manual labor. I'd speculate that she had resources. We'll know more when the roommate arrives."

French nodded before the weight of that comment sank in. "Wait a minute. What did you say?"

"I said, when the roommate arrives. Tyra's roommate."

Tyra . . .

They had her name.

"I tried to reach you about this," Burklow said. "We found clothing and personal items in a dumpster six blocks west of the crime scene. The victim's name is Tyra Norris. Twenty-seven, local . . ."

"Local? Wait. You have an address?"

"Martinez and Smith are en route now."

"We need to go."

"There's more here to discuss."

"Later, Doc." French moved for the door, pulling his partner behind. "We need to go now."

The doctor said something else, but French missed most of it. He moved fast, and they hit the stairwell, the lobby, the warm air beyond the double doors. "Ride with me," he said.

"Why?"

"Because we need to talk."

"Yes, I believe we do."

"Address?"

Burklow gave him Tyra's address. "The other side of Myers Park."

"I know the street."

French got behind the wheel, and pushed it—the parking lot, the two-lane, the big artery that was the shortest route to the other side of Myers Park. Burklow watched the city pass, but fooled no one. As a cop, patience was his great strength, as was his fundamentally unforgiving nature. He would tolerate self-indulgence in a friend, but rarely in another cop. Victims came first. Resolution for the wounded. Justice for the dead. French checked the speedometer, but didn't back it down. He worked the road at twice the posted limit: inside lane, outside. Seventy miles an hour, he threaded the needle with one hand tight on the wheel, the big cherry flashing on top.

When Burklow finally spoke, he kept his voice level. "I'm thinking now is probably a good time."

"It'll sound worse than it is."

"Nevertheless . . ."

Burklow was watching intently, pricks of light in his eyes as the car threaded traffic and blew through lights. There was no easy way to explain. How could there be? "I've met the victim," French said. "Before today, I knew her. I met her. Last week, I walked in on her with Jason. They were, uh . . . you know."

"Sexually engaged?"

"I said it would look bad."

Burklow stared through the side window as he'd done a million times, the tension apparent in his shoulders and jaw. Even the skin beneath his eyes was tight. "You recognized her at the scene?"

"It took a few minutes."

"That's why you left in such a hurry."

"To look for Jason. To get ahead of it." French took his eyes off the road to risk a glance at his friend. "It gets worse."

"Not possible."

"Gibby knows her, too."

Burklow's head snapped around as if he'd taken a punch. He loved Gibby like a son. They fished together, and watched football on Sundays. If Gibby needed advice, Burklow gave it. He was there when Gibby was born and the day he'd learned to drive. "Start at the beginning," he said. "You leave something out this time, and I will fucking pound you."

French dipped his chin, and did as Burklow asked. "There's a rental house at Water and Tenth. There's a bedroom upstairs . . ."

Inside Sara's condominium, I poured wine, and her hands trembled as she took the glass. She sat on a white sofa in a room that was elegant and very adult. "I like your place."

"It's Tyra's. She comes from money."

It showed, I thought. Rich leathers. Real art.

Sara lit a candle, and sipped her wine. "Will you kiss me?" she asked.

"Are you sure?"

"Just for a little while. Just until."

It felt strange, the way she asked, but I knew nothing of grown

women, and that made everything strange: the tasteful furniture, her
readiness when I sat beside her. She took the glass from my hand, then
pressed me down and spread across me like a blanket. At first, she clung
tightly, but then she kissed me, and the touch of her lips was as gentle as
rain. Her fingers, too, were light on my skin. They brushed my face, my
chest. In time, she rose, and our shirts came off, and still the moment was
hers. The eagerness remained, but she'd coiled it someplace deep: a vibration at the small of her back, a catch in her breathing. We kissed until the
coil loosened, and when it did, I felt it in her breath. It came faster and
hotter, and the heat was in her skin, too: her hands on my face, the press
of her legs. Under shadowed eyes she pushed me down, and I knew she
wanted an excuse, a reason to move and do and forget. I was a tool for
her, but didn't care. The heat was mine, too, the same catch in my breath.
I closed my eyes and saw a wash of red as if the heat we shared had rolled
into the room itself. Bloodred, it brightened and pulsed, and Sara's skin
was slick beneath my hands. She said, "Oh . . ." And I thought, *Yes.*

But that's not what she meant.

"Oh shit, oh shit, oh shit . . ."

My eyes opened as she rolled away.

The red light was real.

Cops were in the drive.

Sara ran to the window, and for those seconds looked like something from a world I'd never really known: the giant shadows, the red
light on her skin. It felt like a scene from a movie, set in a great city and
starring someone larger than myself. I felt nothing but awkward. Pulling
on my shirt. Looking for hers. I found it beneath a pillow, and carried
it to her.

"Here, put this on."

The curtains were diaphanous. She held a bit between two fingers.
"Why are they here?"

"Come on. Get dressed."

Outside, men crossed in front of the car lights. I got the shirt over
Sara's head; helped her with the straps that passed for sleeves.

"It's Tyra. It has to be."

"We don't know anything yet." But I actually did. The cops were named Martinez and Smith. They were murder cops. They worked with my dad.

"Don't leave me, okay?"

My arm went around her shoulders. She was scared. We both were. "Come on," I said. "Let's see what they want."

At the door, Martinez and Smith were already on the top step. Their shock at seeing me would have been comical in other circumstances.

"Gibby? Jesus." Smith spoke first, his gaze moving to Sara's face and mine, then to my arm on her shoulder. He was a small cop with soft eyes and narrow hands.

Martinez, beside him, looked harder and crueler and cynical. "What are you doing here?"

"Nothing."

It was a kid's response, but Martinez was like my father at his worst: the cop eyes and distrust. He glanced at Smith, and cleared his throat. "Why don't we speak separately? Gibby, will you come with me?"

"Is this about Tyra?" I asked.

"What do you know about Tyra?"

"Only that she's missing."

"You know her, then? Personally?"

"Yeah. Course."

"*How* do you know her?"

Smith said, "Martinez . . ."

But Martinez ignored the note of warning in his partner's voice. "I said, how do you know her?"

"Come on, man. It's Bill's son."

"Don't tell me to come on! You saw her, same as me."

I didn't know what he meant, but thought, *Tyra*, first, and then that it was bad. Martinez was so hot and bothered I looked for smoke in his ears. "We have questions," he said. "Cop questions, important ones. And I expect you to answer them right here and right now, same as your little friend."

He stabbed a finger at Sara's face, and I saw blood on the cuff of his shirt. He followed my gaze, and saw the same thing. "Son of a bitch . . ."

He tried to wipe it off, and Smith took the lead, his voice softer.

"You're confused. I understand. Worried, too, I'm sure. But we need to ask the questions first. You know how this works."

I did. I didn't care. "Tell me about Tyra."

"I can't do that . . ."

"Gibby, what's happening?"

I pulled Sara closer, squeezing her shoulders. "We'll wait for my father," I said.

"Your daddy's not coming," Martinez said. "Even if he did, it wouldn't make a difference. This is happening like I said. Right here. Right now."

Smith showed his palms. "It would be helpful . . ."

"You're damn right," Martinez said.

"Not until I know what happened to Tyra."

"Goddamn it, kid. You don't ask questions, and you don't get to see your daddy."

But a car was racing down the street, red light on the roof, the engine running hot. It was my father's car; I knew it. So did Martinez. He stepped back, and I heard the words under his breath: *Motherfucker, son of a goddamn bitch . . .*

The car braked hard, and the doors flew wide. "Not a word, son, not a single word."

"What are you doing here, Bill?"

"Not now, Martinez. I need to speak with my son."

"So do we."

"And I'm saying, *not now!*"

"He knows our victim." Martinez stepped into my father's personal space, crowding him. "Personally." Martinez stressed the word. "He knows her *personally.*"

"We can talk about that later. Gibby, get in the car."

"But Sara . . ."

"I said *get in the car.*"

"What happened to Tyra?" I made it a demand. No one cared.

"Not now," my father said.

"Then when?"

"Son, get in the *fucking* car."

His eyes blazed, but the profanity frightened me more than anything else. Burklow was gentler. "Go ahead, son. You can see your friend tomorrow. She's not in any trouble."

Keeping his eyes on Martinez, my father said, "Ken, if you would."

Burklow took my arm, and pulled me down the steps.

Martinez said, "We still want to talk to your son."

"I know you do, but it's not happening tonight. Ken, please."

The big cop dragged me all the way to the car, and stuffed me in the back seat, locking me inside. I looked for Sara, on the stoop.

Her face was in her hands.

She was crying.

13

At Lanesworth, X was frustrated and restless. He stretched out on the bed, got up, stretched out again. When Reece appeared, at last, a glance at his face told X it was done. "It went well, then?"

"So well I am disinclined to charge you. The young woman was . . . delightful."

X mirrored the man's thin smile. "It's no crime for a man to enjoy his work. Expect the usual fee in the usual manner."

"Thank you, sir."

"I assume you have something for me?"

Reece withdrew an envelope full of Polaroid photographs, and handed it over. "We did it like you said."

X opened the envelope, removing the photographs. "Chronological order?"

"Beginning in the driveway outside of her condominium."

X took his time with the pictures: the girl in the car, then chained, then dead. "How long?" he asked.

"Five hours, once we got her up."

"She was conscious throughout?"

"I took the usual pains."

X had no doubt. Reece was immaculate in the execution of his passions. Going through the stack a second time, X culled out a few photos and handed them to Reece. "You know what to do with those?"

"No fingerprints. Untraceable."

"As soon as possible, please."

"I have the address."

X returned the remaining photos to the envelope, and passed them to Reece. "There's an inmate on cellblock C, Francis Willamette. These are for him. Use appropriate discretion."

Reece would, of course. He knew the guards, the protocols. "Is there anything else I can do for you?"

"You saw Jason, of course."

"I did."

"Good." X sat, and offered Reece a second chair. "Tell me what you saw. Leave nothing out."

14

Burklow took me home, and stayed late at the kitchen table, nursing a beer, and deflecting questions. "You'll need to ask your father that."

"Where is he?"

"Dealing with stuff."

"When will he come home?"

"He'll be here when he gets here."

"Tell me about Tyra."

"Forget it, kid. I mean it."

When lights finally appeared in the driveway, he told me to sit and wait, then went outside to meet my father. I didn't sit. And no way in hell was I waiting. I crept to the front door, and watched Burklow argue with my father, poking him in the chest not once, but twice. I'd never seen him show such disrespect, but my father took it, responding in a fierce, quiet whisper that looked like pleading. When Burklow turned away, red-faced and still angry, my father followed like a whipped dog.

"Ken. Buddy . . ."

I missed the rest, but they looked nothing like buddies. For five full minutes they argued, and when it ended, it did so badly, Burklow's voice rising as he towered over my father. "I don't care about that. You should have told me at the scene. And don't tell me I'd do the same thing, because I wouldn't, not on a case like this."

"You say that now—"

"Don't. No."

"You don't have kids. You can't understand."

Burklow turned away, and I lost what came next. I stepped off the porch to hear better, and my father noticed without actually looking my way. He raised a finger, stopping me where I stood. He said something else to Burklow, who said, "No. Hell no."

"Another day, twelve hours . . ."

But Burklow was done talking. He got in the car, slammed the door, and left rubber on the driveway. My father stared after him for a long time, then came to me, looking utterly worn. "Did you hear that?"

"Some of it. Not much."

"Whatever you heard, forget it."

"Was that about me? I heard him talk about *your son*. I saw how Martinez was acting."

"It's not about you. Don't worry about Martinez."

"It's hard not to."

He nodded once, but bleakly. "I need to speak with Jason."

"That's what this is about?"

"He may have information I need."

"About Tyra?"

"I can't talk about that."

"Martinez and Smith are homicide cops."

"Son . . ."

"Is she dead?"

"I told you, son. I can't *talk* about that!"

The explosion pushed me back. The look in his eyes. The lines in his face. It was easy to forget that he hunted men for a living, but I saw it now, like he could chew me up, spit me out, and not taste a thing. I stepped back on instinct, and it was a bad moment between us, his hands rising once before dropping like leaves. I had nothing else to say, and neither did he; and when he turned for his car, there was a drag in his step. I watched his taillights fade, then took my hand from my pocket, considering the scrap of paper I'd carried there since the quarry.

On it was a phone number.

It was local.

Inside, the house was eerily quiet, so I went alone to the kitchen, and lifted the phone from its cradle on the wall. The cord was long enough to reach the pantry, so I shut myself inside, and dialed. On the other end, the phone rang nine times before someone answered. I heard laughter, loud music.

I asked for my brother.

Eventually, he came.

It took forty minutes to find the area Jason described, and again it felt like a scene from a movie, a grim night in some larger city. I cruised one side street and then another. When I found the right building, I knew it by the motorcycles and the women and the noise.

Lots of chrome and plenty of skin . . .

Just like Jason said.

I found a place to park, and backtracked two blocks to where a row of motorcycles angled in at the curb. I was out of place there, and everyone knew it. Bikers gave me the dead-eye or blocked my path or streamed smoke in my face. A crowd milled near the door, and as I squeezed into it, women crowded me back, and touched me and laughed.

Hey, sugar . . .

Hey, baby boy . . .

One hung on my shoulder and cupped me between the legs.

"Excuse me," I said, and she laughed again.

At the door, a biker stopped me. Muttonchops. Long hair streaked with white. "Members and ladies," he said.

"I'm looking for Jason French." Nothing moved on his face. A beer bottle went up and down. "He's waiting for me, I promise."

"Well, if you promise . . ."

His voice rose on the last word, lips twisting. Problem was, I wanted inside, and he wanted me to try. It was a tense moment until Jason appeared behind him, and dropped a hand on his shoulder. "Take it easy, Darius. He's with me. Come on, little brother."

I followed Jason into a dark room, then through another crowd to a metal staircase at the back wall. Upstairs, Jason led me into a square room with brick walls, sparse furnishings, and a massive safe that looked as if it had been there forever. Jason saw my reaction to it. "Diebold cash safe—1905, I think."

I smoothed a hand across the steel door, the enormous hinges. "It must weigh tons."

"Three or four, at least. This place was built with steel beams in the floor to carry the weight. You can see them from a storage room downstairs."

"What's it for?"

"Originally? Payroll, I'd guess. Records, maybe."

I sat at the table, and he leaned against the wall with his arms crossed. "What's in it now?" I asked.

"What makes you think I know?"

"There are a million rooms in this city, but you're in this one. Plus, you said *originally*. That implies that the safe, now, has some other purpose." I rolled my shoulders. "Words matter."

Jason looked at me strangely after that. He didn't answer my question, but poured whiskey into shot glasses. "You're a sharp kid, Gibby. Let's drink to that."

He handed me a whiskey. It burned going down.

"So why are you here?" he asked.

"I think maybe Tyra's dead."

"Bullshit."

"Seriously."

He was unconvinced, so I told him how Tyra had gone missing, and how Martinez and Smith had rolled up to the condo, hot, distrustful, and angry as hell. That led to a description of Dad and Burklow, of how they'd rolled up the same way, bundled me into a car, and argued, later, about things they did not want me to hear. "Murder cops," I said. "All four of them. It has to mean something. I think it means that Tyra's dead."

I'd hoped to see his face in an unguarded moment. Instead, I got a raised eyebrow as he poured another whiskey. "None of that means Tyra is dead. It could mean anything."

"I don't know, man. They were arguing hard, and Dad looked pretty scared. He's looking for you, too. I thought you should know as soon as possible."

"That's why you're here?" Jason frowned, and lowered the whiskey, untouched. "Why, exactly, do you think I should know something like that as soon as possible?"

"You know, in case they show up here."

"You could have told me on the phone."

"You're my brother. I wanted to come."

Jason's eyes narrowed, and the frown deepened. Standing abruptly, he checked the street, left and right. "You should have stayed home, Gibby." He closed the blinds; checked the stairwell. "These people. This place . . ."

"Are you angry?"

"Only with myself." He snatched a duffel bag from the closet, stuffing in clothes. "This is a dangerous place. You shouldn't be here."

"I can handle myself."

"No, you really can't."

"Don't say that."

"Listen, kid. You think you know me, but you don't. You want to be in my life, and I think that's cool. I wanted to be in your life, too, but I'll drag you down, you give me half a chance. I see that, now. Hell, I've already done it. Tyra. The cops. I mean, damn. If they raided this place right now, with you here . . ." He pinned me with those cold, bright eyes. "You should be hanging out with Chance or some other kid or that pretty girl from the quarry. That's your life, and I should have left you in it." He tossed the bag on the bed. "I shouldn't have come home at all."

"I can help you. Whatever this is . . ."

"Jesus, kid. You won't listen!"

He stormed across the room, and I followed him. "What are you doing?"

"Making my point the best way I can." He braced one hand on the safe; spun the dial with the other. "You tell me words matter, and that's true, they do. But actions matter even more." The door swung wide, and I saw dark metal as Jason stepped aside. "Now, do you understand?"

I did. I didn't want to.

He pulled out a rifle, cleared the action, and tossed it to me. "That's an M16A1 rifle, fully automatic and highly illegal. I have thirty of them."

He pointed at other weapons. "Those are CAR-15s." He pointed again. "Thompson submachine guns, very hard to come by. Those are AK-47s, Russian-made, the good stuff, Colt 1911s, of course . . ."

"Slow down, man. I don't understand."

He dragged a satchel from the safe, rolled back the zipper, and showed me all the cash inside. Thousands of dollars. Tens of thousands. "This is what I do," he said. "It's who I am." He took the rifle from my hands, and racked it with the others. "I'm not a good person. You shouldn't be here."

In bed that night, I dreamed of brother Robert. He stepped from the deep jungle, and I saw the hole in his chest, the shattered bone and the ruby-dark stain. When I whispered his name, he looked up, and blackness filled the place his eyes should be. He tried to speak, but his tongue was gone, too; and when he fell at my feet, I knew in the way of dreams that I should lean close, so that's what I did. I ignored the smell of him and the empty sockets, the night sounds and the grass and the speckled sky. I poured my soul into knowing my brother, but none of that mattered. His last breath was gone, and the knowing of him with it.

I woke from that dream with tears in my eyes, then dressed in the quiet, and slipped outside to cool air and light that was watery and gray. In the car, I thought how strange it was to be born with two brothers, yet be so ignorant of both. I was a child when Robert died, and missed the chance to know him man-to-man. Jason was a mystery, too, and de-termined to stay that way. That left a distant father and an unknowable mother, the whole situation so fucked up and faceless that when I drove, it was to the quarry, where I hiked to the cliff's edge, and stood alone to watch the day break as a red sun rose.

I thought this was the time to do it. Robert had died hard, no matter what the government said, and standing there, I felt the same emotions that had driven Jason to enlist and take action. My father said once it was a stupid war for stupid reasons, but he'd been drunk at the time and had never said anything like it since, so I thought maybe Jason was right to fight and kill and get even.

I stared into the quarry, a hole in the world still filled with the dark-ness of night. At my feet, the stone was sunrise red, but only as far down as a tall man could reach. Beyond that was the blackness, like there was no water at all, and maybe I would fall forever. Stripping off my shirt and shoes, I pictured Robert's perfect dive, the way he'd hung and fallen and risen beside me, laughing. *Let the Vietcong touch that,* he'd said; but they'd killed him, anyway. I thought of Jason, who'd made the dive, too, but wanted nothing to do with me. For a long time I stared into the pit.

"Just dive," I said, but did not.

I wasn't like my brothers.

I was afraid.

Later that day, I was in my room when Chance walked in. "Dude, what the hell?"

I looked up from the book I'd been reading. "Is there a problem?"

"Batting cage. Duh."

"Oh, man." I closed the book, and got up off the bed. "I'm sorry, Chance. I totally forgot."

"Ahh . . ." He waved a hand, and his features softened. "Don't sweat it."

But I did. Chance loved baseball with a passion. He wasn't very good at it, but Saturday at the cages was ritual.

"You sick or something? Hungover?" He said it with a glint. I shook my head. "So let's take a walk. Maybe the twins are out."

He meant the Harrison girls down the street. Seventeen. Seriously cute. "I'm kind of waiting for my dad. How about some TV instead?"

"Yeah, sure. Whatever."

We stretched on the floor and watched *Star Trek* reruns. Once, I went downstairs to see if my father had returned. "Bring beer," Chance said, but was joking, sort of. In late afternoon, we did go outside, but the Harrison girls were nowhere to be seen.

"You have plenty of time," Chance said.

"What?"

"You keep looking at your watch."

Guiltily, I looked down at my wrist. I didn't remember checking the time, but I didn't remember leaving the yard, either. "I just want to see my dad."

"I know better than that." The same grin twisted Chance's face, so I stopped beside a telephone pole that smelled like creosote and hot wood. "Becky Collins," he said.

"What about her?"

"Yeah, right."

"No. Seriously. What?"

Chance squared up on me, disbelieving. "You forgot your date with Becky Collins?"

"That's today?"

"Seven o'clock at Dana White's house." He looked up as if the sky had caught fire. "You mean you forgot? Like . . . for real forgot?"

"I guess I did."

"But it's Becky Collins." Chance closed his eyes, repeating himself. *Becky . . . freakin' . . . Collins . . .*

He could go for a while like that, so I sat on the curb to wait him out. Of course, his confusion was legitimate. I'd had a crush on Becky since forever. *Everyone* crushed on Becky. She was smart and pretty and different from other girls. The confidence. That steadiness.

"You want to tell me what's going on?" Chance settled at last, standing above me, looking down. "You're inside all day. You forget batting practice, then a date with the hottest girl in school. What's wrong with you?"

"I don't know. Family stuff. I don't really want to talk about it."

"Do you want to kiss the girl?" I met his eyes, and they showed his amusement. "Come on, Cinderella." He pulled me up. "Let's get you ready for the ball."

In the shower, I tried not to dwell on Jason or his guns or the chance he might go back to prison. Instead, I thought of Tyra, thinking she might really be dead. I imagined blue skin and a metal table, all the cops on the city beat, frustrated and smoking cigarettes and driving around town.

In the bedroom, Chance had clothes laid out on the bed. "Seriously?" I asked.

"What? I can't help you get laid?"

"It's not like that with Becky."

"Not yet."

"Chance . . ."

"I'm kidding. Come on. Take this." He handed me a shirt, and tried to coach me as I dressed. "Remember. Becky's poor, but sophisticated. That means smart and ambitious and not into your typical bullshit."

"I know Becky Collins as well as you."

"No, you don't. So listen." He riffled through my shoes, speaking over his shoulder. "She's a cheerleader but doesn't care about sports, same with the Latin Club and Young Entrepreneurs and student government. She does those things, but don't depend on them for conversation. She's been counting on a scholarship, so some of it will be window dressing. You'll need to figure out what really matters to her. Don't make assumptions." I looked at him sideways, and he shrugged. "What can I say, man? I've been mind-stalking that girl since fifth grade. Here, put these on."

I put on the shoes, and checked the mirror. "Disco, baby."

"Don't use that word, not ever." Chance looked at his watch. "Almost time. You have condoms?" My jaw dropped, and he laughed. "God, you're easy. Relax. Shake it out." I tried, but was nervous. "She's only a girl. Say it out loud."

"She's only a girl."

"She's lucky to have you. Say that, too."

It went like that for most of the drive. I put Chance's bike in the back seat, and took him home the long way, his request. Eventually, he was making jokes, telling stories. By the time we reached his street, I wasn't thinking of Tyra or my brother or all the years I'd had a crush on Becky Collins. The top was down. We were laughing.

"You all good, brother?" Chance dropped his bike in the dirt, then leaned on the car. "You have money? You know where you're taking her?"

"Yeah, man. I'm good."

"Be adult, all right? Talk about the war or Nixon or Brezhnev."

I laughed. "No."

"Inflation, then. The recession."

"Are you finished?"

"Just knock her panties off." He winked and grinned, and went inside.

Chance, I thought.

He was in my head.

Pulling from the curb, I watched the time as I drove. I didn't want to be early. I didn't want to be late. On the sidewalk at Dana White's house, I checked my watch a final time, then smoothed my hair, practicing silently.

Hello, Becky. You look beautiful this evening . . .

I walked toward the door, feeling I should have brought flowers. I'd never been on a real date . . .

Flowers. Damn it.

I hesitated at the bottom step.

Hello, Becky . . .

I was still there when the door opened, and Becky appeared, her face in the crack of the door, a glimpse of T-shirt and jeans.

"Gibby, come on." Her voice was low, almost a hiss. "You can't be here. You know that."

"What? I don't . . ." I shook my head, confused. She glanced away, showing the curve of her jaw, a tumble of hair. Turning back, she gestured with a hand. "Around the side. That way."

The door closed before I could ask what she was talking about. Instead, I followed a line of bushes to a gate and the backyard and an open window. Becky was there, Dana White behind her. I squeezed through the landscaping, my face at the sill. "What do you mean I can't be here?"

"Hush, all right?"

She made a shushing noise with her hands, and Dana pushed closer. "Becky, this is dangerous."

"Not if you be cool."

"My father will kill us—"

"What's going on?" I interrupted.

Becky looked from Dana's face to mine, and the conflict was obvious. "Screw it," she said. "Get in here."

"Becky, no."

"Quiet, Dana. It's not up to you. Gibby, come on before somebody sees."

I didn't know what was happening, but scrambled though the window, where I found Becky flushed, and Dana, beside her, pinch-faced and angry and pale. "If my parents find out, I'll tell them you made me."

"Button it, Dana. I mean it." Becky studied my face, then put her hands on my shoulders, and stared into my eyes. It was like standing on a mountaintop. "You don't know, do you?"

"Know what?"

"Jesus. Okay. All right. Dana, check the hall."

"No."

"You know you'll do it eventually, so stop wasting time."

Dana crossed the room, saying, "This is bullshit, it's bullshit . . ." Nevertheless, she cracked the door to check the hall. I heard a television, the sound of adults in muted conversation. She closed the door.

Becky said, "Lock it," then took my hand, and led me to the edge of Dana's bed. "There's no easy way to say this, so I won't. Just sit, okay? Just . . ."

She showed both palms, as if to keep me on the bed, then turned on a small television, and fiddled with the antenna. When the picture firmed, I saw a reporter, and then my brother's face. Becky sat beside me, but it was Dana White who found the words. "Murder," she said. "Your brother's wanted for murder."

15

By the time I reached home, I remembered nothing of the drive but darkness and speed. "Mom. Dad." I spoke from the entry hall, but neither noticed me. My mother was yelling. Broken glass was everywhere.

"Of course he did it! Of course he did!"

"Gabrielle, please . . ."

"Why didn't you warn me? Tell me?"

"Because I didn't know . . ."

"I saw it on the news, William! My own son! I saw it on the news!"

"Gabrielle, please . . ."

"Now he's back, and with Gibby! Now Gibby's at risk!"

"He's not with Gibby. Gibby's fine."

"Where is he, then? My good boy . . ."

She folded at the knees, and my father knelt beside her. He saw me then, and gestured me back; so I went outside to wait by the cars. Through the window, I saw him get my mother to her feet, and guide her toward the bedroom. She stumbled twice. He never let her fall. When he came outside, we met where the driveway ended. He seemed unwilling to speak, so I started the conversation. "Is it true about Jason?"

"It's true there's a warrant for his arrest."

"So, Tyra *is* dead?"

"She was murdered, son. That's all I can tell you. You *will* have to talk to Martinez, though. You knew her. You may have insights."

"Martinez? Why not you?"

"I'm too close. They won't let me near it."

"Dad, come on . . ."

He shook his head, waved me off. "Is there anything you want to tell me first? Anything I need to know? You knew Tyra. You knew her with Jason."

"I didn't really know her at all. We spent a day at the lake. That's it."

"I need to find Jason." He palmed his face, so distracted he was barely there. "I need to bring him in."

"*Bring him in* . . ." I couldn't believe it. "Listen to yourself!"

"Safely, Gibby. Bring him in safely. Tyra's death was . . . hard. Cops aren't taking it well. Emotions are running high."

"Jason didn't kill her."

"But they *were* sexually involved. They fought in public, and it got violent. She pulled a gun . . ."

"I know. I was there."

My father froze. Three full seconds. "Please tell me that's not true."

"Yeah, I was there. She was out-of-her-mind drunk."

"Did she threaten you?"

"Why would you ask that?"

"Motive. It's the first thing cops look for."

"You keep talking like you're not the cops."

"Do you know where Jason is or not?"

"I don't."

"I think you're lying."

"I'm not," I said, but was. Jason had a safe full of guns and cash. What would happen if the cops found it?

Prison, I thought.

No question.

My father threatened and begged, but I had nothing else to say; and when he left, he was furious about that silence. I gave him a thirty count, then rolled my car to the bottom of the driveway.

Ten minutes to the city line.

Another twenty to my brother.

I drove fast, and thought of Tyra, not dead on a slab, but as I'd seen her at the lake, naked and unashamed and laughing.

I didn't see the headlights behind me.

I didn't even care.

When I reached the Pagans' private club, I parked at the curb, and jogged for the door. No guard. No people or music. Inside, it was quiet enough to hear the argument upstairs, the raised voices and the clank of metal on metal. Halfway up the stairwell, I recognized Jason's voice. "I hear what you're saying, Darius. But it is what it is. I'm out of here, and all of this goes with me."

A mumbled response.

I climbed higher.

"No." Jason again. "That was not our deal."

"You're not taking the guns or the cash . . ."

At the landing, I risked a glance through the door. Guns were stacked on the bed, others still in the safe. Jason was there, too, raking out cash as three bikers crowded around him, two with pistols wedged in their jeans. The oldest one spoke—Darius, I thought. He looked familiar. The muttonchops. The white in his hair. "I'm not messing around, Jason. The cops want you. That's tough, but it happens. You can leave right now, and none of us will say a word. But the guns stay. Same with that money."

"You've had your cut." Jason dropped bricks of cash on the bed, and went back for the duffel that held the rest. "The guns are mine. Cash, too."

"You think that matters now? How long 'til the cops raid the club? Call it *hush money* or *compensation*—call it whatever you want—but that stuff stays." He gestured to one of the bikers. "Do it, Sean." The biker reached for the cash, and Jason hit him so hard and fast he went down like a dropped rock. Darius reached for the weapon in his belt, but Jason moved in a blur. He caught the wrist, twisting it up and back before taking the pistol himself, and putting a bullet in Darius's foot and a second in his knee. Darius fell screaming, and Jason pushed the barrel at the last biker's face. "Gibby, anyone else downstairs?"

I pointed dumbly at my chest. I didn't know he'd seen me.

"Gibby? Anyone else."

"No. Uh. No one."

"Go downstairs. Lock the door."

"Um . . ."

"Go ahead. I won't let you miss the good stuff."

It was something Robert used to say. *Do your homework, little brother. I won't let you miss the good stuff.* Stumbling from the room, I locked the door and ran back upstairs.

"We're good?" Jason asked.

"It's locked."

Jason gestured with the gun. "On your knees."

The third biker knelt, but did it slowly. "Look, man . . ."

Jason took the pistol from the biker's belt, and tossed it on the bed. Then we heard the banging downstairs, someone pounding on the door. "Gibby, if you would." He tipped his head at the window, so I peered out and down.

"Oh, man, I think it's Dad."

Jason pointed at the biker. "You. Keys."

"What keys?"

"The van out back. Front pocket. Toss them to the kid."

I caught the keys. On the floor and bleeding, Darius said, "I'll kill you for this, French . . ."

"Shut up, Darius, before I put a third one in your head."

"You'd best do it now. Pagans don't forget or forgive. We'll find you and we'll fucking kill you."

"Yeah, maybe." Jason pistol-whipped the kneeling biker; knocked him cold. "And then again, maybe not."

Darius said, "Damn it, goddamn it . . ."

Jason ignored him. "Gibby, get the rest of the guns. Put them on the bed." I did what he said. "Good. Grab those corners." I pointed at the blanket, still numb. "It's a lot to ask, I know. Gibby, look at me." Jason raised his eyebrows, nodding once. "If Dad's here, then other cops are coming. Understand? Gunshots. Men down. He'll call it in." As if to confirm, the pounding below us grew louder. "This is all I have in the world, little brother, what you see on that bed."

"Shit, man . . ."

"Pick 'em up. Let's go."

He shoved the pistol into his belt, and I helped him drag guns and cash off the bed. A couple of dead men would have weighed less.

"Down the stairs. Out the back."

We dragged guns and cash down the stairs, then through a narrow hall to concrete steps that took us into the alley. I stumbled on the last step, and a rifle clattered on the ground.

Jason said, "Leave it. Just get us to the van."

We made it to the van, and none of it was real: the alleyway damp, the stink of gun oil and grease as we shoveled guns and cash. A brick of fifties split open, and Jason raked the bills like leaves. "Do you hear that?" A far-off siren, and then others. Jason rolled the door shut, then put his hands on my shoulders, and tried to steady me as Robert often had. "Decision time, little brother."

"What decision?"

"Come with me."

I looked the length of the alley, then back. "You told me to stay away."

"That was then, and things have changed. I can't come back here, not ever."

"Where are you going?"

"There's a place up north. It's what the money's for. A dozen acres of rocky coast, a fishing boat and room to breathe. It's beautiful. Trust me."

"Where up north?"

"Only if you're in. Only if I *know*."

"But the guns . . ."

"Escape money, pure and simple. Pay for the land. Pay for the boat." His hands were like steel, the sirens closer. "Ticktock, little brother."

I hesitated because he looked like Robert, but that was mostly bone and skin and the color of his eyes. He saw the decision before I could get the words out. "Hey, kid, I get it. We don't know each other anymore, not really." His hands fell away. He stepped back. "You have a life. I shouldn't have asked."

"It's not like that," I said.

"Sure it is, and it's cool. Take care of yourself. Tell Dad I didn't kill her."

"Jason, wait . . ."

But he didn't. He sprang into the van, keyed the engine, and rolled down the alley without once looking back.

Jason took a right and gunned it from the alley, then hung a left and felt the back end slide. After that, he was hammer down, buildings flicking past as he checked for cops, and hung a second right. He drove faster, and saw light bars flash at an intersection two blocks west. More lights split the night ahead, so Jason cut down an alley, left paint on a parked car. At the next street, he clipped a phone pole, and overcorrected, tires screeching. The street was a three-lane, so he took it down the middle, the needle passing sixty-five, then eighty. Two cruisers drifted onto the street four blocks back, so Jason braked hard, cut right, and killed the headlights. He gave it a block, took another right and thought he was out clear; then a third cruiser locked up the brakes as it flashed under a red light one street over. Jason didn't need a radio to know the cops were talking.

Three cars close.

More coming.

Lights still off, he accelerated until dotted lines blurred on the street. At ninety-five, the engine maxed out. Another mile, and he thought he was out clean—nothing behind or in front. He gave it two more blocks, then dropped to forty, turned on the lights and tried to look normal as the road dipped, then rose. He crested the hill, then light speared down as a helicopter thundered overhead, spinning to put the light in his eyes. It matched his speed; banked when Jason cut right. For an instant, the van was in front, but Jason was screwed and knew it. Four turns, another hill, and cars came in from every side, six of them and then a dozen. Jason's run ended where two roads met and streetlights burned, high and white. His foot an inch off the pedal, he watched the cops spill out, weapons up.

He couldn't go back to prison . . .

Better to die here and now . . .

After years of war, the thought was an old friend, and all else, white noise: yesterday, tomorrow, the whole of it, white noise. But then he saw his father. Cops were holding him back, but he was fighting, too. "Don't do it! Jason! Don't!"

Jason looked down at the gun in his hand.

MAC-10.

Fully loaded.

"You don't have to die, son! No one has to die!"

Did Jason even care? He'd killed so many men . . .

"Think about your brother! Think about Gibby!"

Jason didn't want to, but did, picturing him as he'd hung on the side of an inner tube, far out in the quarry. He'd needed something then, but Jason had been distant and angry and ungiving.

Swim away, little fish . . .

That's the face Jason saw, all hurt and need and little boy.

"Well, shit . . ."

Jason lowered the weapon, and showed his hands.

It seemed his father knew him after all.

16

I learned about the arrest at three that morning. "Dad?" The word escaped before I even registered the noise that stirred me from the sofa: a hum and a rattle, the garage door going up and then back down. Rising, I reached the back hall as he entered the house.

"Not now, Gibby."

He showed me his palm, but I trailed him to the kitchen. "Where's Jason?"

"It's late, son."

"You followed me. You used me."

He stopped, at last. "Because you lied to me. You left me no choice."

"That is bullshit." He sighed; I hated that. "Did you arrest him?"

"I need to speak with your mother." I blocked his way, and thought, at first, he would argue. Instead, he said, "I'm sorry, son. I truly am."

That's when I knew for sure.

As the sun rose hours later, I heard my father leave the house. For some time after that, I lay in bed thinking of Sunday mornings and church and how it used to be. For all my childhood, we'd attended as a family, but that ended when Robert was killed, and we sank into this strange half life without smiles, vacations, or Sunday service. Today, that bothered me, so I showered and gave myself a rare shave. I dressed with exceptional care, and went to church on my own, arriving a few minutes after the start of the early service, and slipping into a pew at the back, all of it so familiar: the dark wood and the people, the organ and the colored glass. I opened a hymnal, but didn't sing along. Afterward, there were readings that made sense to me, but then the minister took the podium to speak of war and sacrifice and salvation for all people. With one brother dead and the other arrested, I found his words so hollow that I almost left. I actually rose to my feet, but then I spotted Becky Collins four rows down, seated across the aisle with Dana White's family. Her hair was up—which I'd never seen before—and the curve of her neck struck me as the most vulnerable thing, pale as it was, and fringed by a spill of small, soft hairs. She must have felt me staring, for she turned and saw me and blushed. Dana's father turned as well. He stared at me for long seconds, then stood and squeezed past his family, working his way into the aisle. A large man with wide, rough hands, he was a foreman at the Freight-liner factory, a man used to telling others what to do and how to do it.

"Gibby." He slid into the pew beside me.

"Mr. White."

"How are you, son?"

He spoke with gentle concern, and I smelled hair tonic and after-shave. I'd met him only once, on a Friday evening last year, a football game at home, halftime at the concession stand with Dana tucked against his side. He'd been pleasant then, and even now his eyes were kind. I nod-ded to his question, but didn't really answer. People were watching. Not all of them, but enough.

"Listen," he said. "I know about your brother." He raised a hand, as if I might interrupt. "No need to speak of innocence or guilt—I'm sure you would say all the right things—but, at this moment, I'm responsible for Becky's well-being. She's a guest of my family. That means I must act in her interests, almost as a father. Do you understand that, son?"

"Listen, sir—"

"Please don't *sir* me. I know you snuck into my daughter's room last night. I won't pass judgment on that alone—perhaps you felt justified, somehow—but it does speak to your character." I felt heat in my neck, a sudden dryness in my throat. "What matters most is this: I can't have you speaking to Becky today, not in church and not afterward, not until I return her to her own father. Do you understand?" He leaned closer, his arm along the back of the pew. "I'm not judging you, son, not on this murder business, and not on the actions of your brother, but this is a difficult thing whose full meanings are not yet known. Work with me, okay? Do the right thing, today of all days and here of all places."

He gave my shoulders a squeeze, then slid out of the pew to rejoin his family. Becky looked my way, but I was burning too hotly to meet her eyes. Instead, I stared at the woman in front of me, at the lacquered hair and the floral dress. I thought everyone in church had heard what Dana's father had said, and could see the shame he'd put inside me, this thing that was a flame. Pride alone kept me from leaving before the service ended, and even then, I kept my seat, watching to see who nodded or spoke or simply stared. Becky was the only one I cared about, so I rose as she entered the stream of people and found a place on my side of the aisle. Dana's father was watching from behind, so she kept her eyes straight ahead, and said nothing at all to me, choosing instead to press her church bulletin into my hand as she passed. I waited until the church was empty, then looked down to see four fine words in Becky's lovely hand.

Five o'clock.

The quarry.

The rest of the day was a lifetime. I met Chance, and we played pinball at the 7-Eleven, then sat on the curb and ate sandwiches sold cold for twenty-five cents.

"What'd you get?"

"Pimento cheese. You?"

"Egg salad."

That's how the conversation had been all day. It's not that we couldn't run deep, but that Chance understood the way our friendship worked. If he was down, my job was to be there and be cool. Same thing in reverse.

"I'm thinking something cold and wet." Chance dunked his trash in the can, went back inside, and came out with a six-pack under his arm. I looked up with sun in my eyes, and he passed me a can. "This will help."

"I guess you heard, huh?"

"That Jason killed a girl? Yeah, pretty much everybody's talking about it."

"That's not all." I told Chance about the guns and cash, and the biker

Jason shot in the foot and leg. "Darius something or other. I was there. I saw it."

"An actual shoot-out?"

"I guess. They arrested him right after. I was basically with him."

"Okay, time-out. Back up."

Chance wanted specifics, so I gave him the story in detail. "He was going to run, start a new life. He asked me to go with him."

"You said no, of course. Please, God, tell me you did."

I didn't answer right away. Cars passed on the street. "I saw Becky in church today."

It was a hard right turn, but Chance gave it to me. "Was she hot?"

"Sundress. Pretty hot."

"Becky freaking Collins . . ."

"She wants to meet me this afternoon."

"Be still my heart."

He was trying to lighten the mood, but I felt cheap, like I shouldn't have mentioned Becky at all. "Listen, I'm going to get out of here."

"Something I said?"

I stood, shaking my head. "No, brother. We're good."

"Well, damn . . ." Chance stood, too, looking unhappy. "I know you're upset about this—your brother and all—but we could go to the movies or the mall, take your mind off things."

"I need to think this through."

"One for the road?" He offered another beer. In response, I handed back the one I'd not yet opened. "Okay, all right. But call me later, yeah. Tell me what happens with Becky."

I said I'd try, but doubted it would happen. Something had changed in the church. Maybe it was the way blood had risen in her cheeks at the moment she'd first seen me, or the curve of her neck, the vulnerability of that pale, smooth skin and the small hairs that brushed it like lashes. I knew only that something was different between us, like I was on the mountain once again, and too high above the world to breathe.

I took a drive to clear my head, but found no clarity at all. My thoughts wandered, and so did I, driving past the house, the police station, even the school. When I reached the quarry, I found a dull sky that pressed down on whitecaps and dark water. A single car was in the field, so I parked beside it, and walked down to the stony beach. Becky was there in blue jeans and a buttoned shirt. The wind took her hair, and streamed it like a flag. She wore no makeup, no shoes. If anything, she was prettier than she'd been in church. When she saw me, she pushed her hands into her pockets, so the jeans rode low on her hips. "It's strange," she said. "This place without our friends."

Stupidly, I said, "I got your note."

Tucking a strand of hair behind her ear, she smiled shyly. "I'm sorry about Dana's dad."

"Ah, Mr. White's okay."

"He thought people would talk. He just wanted to help."

"You looked beautiful," I said.

"It was Dana's dress."

"I'm not talking about the dress."

The smile came again, and she led me along the shore, and it was quiet for a while. Barefoot, she picked her way along the quarry's broken edge until we reached a stand of pine, where we sat on a bed of needles, and spoke of things like school and Chance and the future. She asked for my thoughts on Vietnam, and I struggled to find the right answer. The war was a mess, but others my age were fighting and dying.

"Do you think you'll be drafted?"

"Odds are against it."

She drew her knees to her chest, and watched me with those cornflower blues. "Are you thinking of enlisting?"

No one had ever asked me that straight on. Maybe no one saw me so clearly. "Why do you ask?"

"I know your brother died in Vietnam. I know you were close."

I had no easy response, so we stared across the water, her shoulder against mine. "You haven't asked about Jason."

"Do you want to talk about him?"

"Not really."

"Then let's not."

She touched my hand, and we found other things to discuss. It turned out that Chance was right about one thing. Becky had been accepted to Princeton, but wasn't going. "Too expensive," she said; but I saw no bitterness. "Come on, there's more to see." She led me farther along the water's edge, and when we reached a finger of rock, she clambered down to a place where water almost covered the stone. Once down, she crossed her arms as cool wind raced across the water. "My parents told me about Princeton two months ago, that it was impossible, even with financial aid."

"That blows. I'm sorry."

"It's life. Besides, it taught me the difference between things I can control and those I can't. It's why I brought you here."

"I don't understand."

"Don't you?" The same cool wind streamed hair across her face, and she smiled at my confusion. "Kiss me, Gibby."

"Really?"

"I've wanted to kiss you since sophomore year."

"But you never said . . . I had no idea."

"Well, now you do." She stepped closer, so I kissed her, lightly at first, and then not so lightly. Her hands found my shoulders, and mine, the small of her back. She drew away, in time, but her eyes were bluer and deeper and smiling. "That was my first kiss," she said. "My first kiss ever."

17

At the police station, Jason was moved from holding cell to interview room, then back and forth again. It lasted all day, and most of the questions were about Tyra. He knew better than to talk about that, so he didn't. Besides, the cops were assholes.

Smith.

Martinez.

Late in the day, they left him alone, so he stared at the mirrored glass, thinking of Tyra. She was dead, he felt certain, though the cops had been careful to share nothing but their questions. *How did you meet? When did you see her last? Why the fight? What happened to Tyra's gun?* They had other questions, too, but Jason learned early how to tune them out.

Eventually, a man entered that Jason didn't know. He wore a suit and a wedding ring. "My name is David Martin. I'm captain of the homicide division." He sat, lacing his fingers on the table. "The recording devices are off. It's just us."

Jason gave the man a dead-eyed stare.

"You've not asked for a lawyer. As a gesture of respect to your father, I'm here to suggest, most strongly, that you do." The captain leaned forward, his features plain but intent. "Silence is not a valid defense. You should have an attorney."

"I hate attorneys."

"Everyone does until they need one."

Jason shifted in the seat, chains rattling where his hands were secured to an eyebolt in the table. "The last lawyer I had talked me into a plea I should have never taken."

"Twenty-seven months for felony heroin, a good deal by any standard."

"Only if I was distributing. I wasn't."

"Still . . ."

"Have you ever been to Lanesworth?" Jason asked. "You would not be so glib if you had."

"Very well." The captain rapped on the mirrored glass. "We're recording now."

"I have nothing to say about Tyra Norris."

"So let's talk about this." The captain withdrew photographs of the van and its contents. "Ninety thousand in cash, and enough weapons to fight a small war."

"I've had enough of war."

"So has the city."

Jason studied the cop's face. He seemed decent enough, smart enough. "Is my father behind the glass?"

"He can't help you, son."

"What happened to Tyra?"

The captain leaned back, considering. "What would you like to know?"

"How she died and why you think I'm the one who killed her."

The captain drummed his fingers, then shrugged. "Some days ago, you rented a room from Charles Spellman."

"Yeah, 1019 Water Street. It's no secret."

"Your room is on the second floor on the northwest side."

"It is."

"And you're still the registered tenant."

"What's your point?"

Captain Martin didn't respond. Instead, he placed three evidence bags on the table, each holding a Polaroid photograph. He fanned them out, and Jason paled. He'd known more blood and death than most, but that was another life in a different world. "That's Tyra?"

"It is."

Jason struggled to imagine it, but the shape of her was right. The hair. The cloudy eye. "I would never hurt Tyra. Not like that."

"And yet . . ." The captain laced his fingers on the table, leaning close. "When we searched the Water Street house this morning, we found those photographs in your room, beneath your pillow, in fact."

"I did *not* kill Tyra Norris."

"We found this as well." The captain produced a fourth evidence bag. In it was a scalpel, mirror-sharp and stained blackish red. "That's Tyra's blood on the blade. So you see . . . Murder weapon. Photographs." The cop leaned back this time, sad but certain. "If there are mitigating circumstances, something from the war, something you think I should know about . . ."

Jason reached for the photos, but the chain was too short.

"Nothing?" the cop asked.

"No." Jason could barely speak. "Nothing."

"I'm sorry, son." The cop gathered up the evidence, and stood. "I'm sorry for Tyra Norris, for her family, and for yours. It's a bad case, truly horrible. That being said, you're still your father's son. If you think of something you'd like to say, either to him or in mitigation, I will always be willing to listen."

Saying goodbye to Becky was not an easy thing to do. We were at the cars. She was standing close. "Why sophomore year?" I asked. "Why then? Why me?"

"You really don't know?"

I shook my head.

"Math class, first day." Her eyes twinkled as she spoke. "Mrs. Ziegler called me to the board to work a problem. You remember?"

"What I remember is how much you'd changed over the summer."

"Yeah, you and every boy in school. The legs. The boobs. But that first day in math class, you were the only one who looked at my face. You watched my face and you nodded and you smiled."

"I promise, I was no saint." Becky blushed, and dug a toe into the grass. "You seemed confident, though. Very self-assured."

"But I wasn't at all. No boy had ever looked at me the way those other boys did. Standing at the board, I could barely think straight. I still don't know how I finished the problem. I kept asking myself, *Why did I wear a skirt this short, a shirt this tight?*"

"And that's the reason you wanted to kiss me?"

"Not the only reason. Your life seemed so tragic from the outside: your brothers and the war, what people said about your mother. I liked the way you carried that weight." She lifted narrow shoulders, smiling. "Plus the way you look in those jeans."

"These?" I asked.

"Those jeans." She pressed into me. "Any jeans."

On the drive home, I thought of the things Becky had said, of her toes in the grass, and the small, possessive smiles. I'd have to break it off, with Sara, no question. It would be hard, I knew. She'd just lost Tyra. I didn't want to pile on the hurt.

But maybe she wouldn't care.

Maybe I was the smallest of distractions.

At home, I found the kitchen cold and empty, my mother on the sofa, drinking vodka. I'd not seen that in a while. "Hey, Mom. I'm sorry I didn't call."

"This time it's okay."

"Did you eat something?"

She held up the glass, then put it down. "Come sit." She patted the cushion beside her. "How was your day?"

"It was fine. You know. Considering. Where's Dad?"

"In his office, looking for lawyers, though what luck he expects on a Sunday night is for him alone to know."

I studied my mother's eyes. They were glazed. The vodka bottle was four inches down.

"How was your day?" she asked again.

"Mom, look at me." She did it, but slowly. I thought, *Pills, maybe, or maybe an earlier bottle.* "What are you doing?" I asked.

She shook her head, but I knew the answer.

Hiding, I thought.

Like me.

At my father's study, the door was closed, but I could hear him on the phone. "I don't care what the fee is. His first appearance is tomorrow morning. I need you there."

I felt guilty, but eavesdropping seemed a small sin, considering. When the call was over, I knocked on the door.

"Come."

My father was unshaven and exhausted, with enough color in his face to hint at the frustration I'd heard in his voice. "Lawyers," he said.

"Did you find one?"

"I believe so."

"A good one?"

"An expensive one. Where have you been?"

"With a girl, actually." I sat across the desk, which I'd only done once before in my life. *Too much murder,* he'd told me once, meaning files and photos and autopsy reports. "Will the lawyer help?"

"Who knows with lawyers?"

"He didn't do it," I said.

Across the desk, my father slumped more deeply into his chair. "Are you sure about that?"

"Yes."

"Sure enough to promise me? To bet your life on it? To bet your mother's life?"

"Why would you phrase the question like that?"

"Because it looks bad, son. It looks really, truly bad."

I went to my bedroom, but that image of my father stayed with me.

The helplessness.

The heartbreak in his eyes.

I needed to know what he knew, and could think of only one way to get the information. It was late, but that didn't stop me. Dad was in his office, Mom in the bottle.

I walked through the front door, keys in hand.

No one noticed or cared.

It took time to reach Ken Burklow's house. He lived across the city line in a small house on a neat street.

"Gibby. What are you doing here?"

He filled the door, surprised to see me.

"May I come in?"

He stepped aside to let me pass, then studied the street with cop eyes like my father's. "It's late. Are you okay?"

I'd thought I was. Now I wasn't sure.

"Sit down, son. Before you fall down." He put me on the sofa, and came back with a glass. "Drink that."

"What is it?"

"Very expensive whiskey." He sat across from me, a big man in jeans and loafers. "So . . ."

He let the word hang, and I found myself strangely uncertain. I'd come for answers about my brother, to guilt Ken if I had to. Instead, I was swept up in visions of my family as it had once been. Against the backdrop of *now,* it was too much, so I went elsewhere. "I think I have a girlfriend."

"Is that really what you came to talk about?"

I shook my head, staring into the whiskey. "Dad thinks he did it."

"Maybe he did."

I looked up. He was serious. "What is it with you cops?"

"What is with you *kids*? Your brother put two bullets in a biker's leg. You saw him do it. He's trafficking illegal weapons. Is murder such a stretch?"

"The murder of an innocent woman."

"This is a discussion for your father."

"He won't talk about it."

"Then be patient."

"How, exactly? Jason's my brother."

Ken frowned more deeply, then stood and crossed to a collection of framed photographs. I was in some of them. So was my father. He stood for a long, reflective moment, and then lifted a frame from the shelf. "Did you know that I fought in Korea?"

"I did. I do." So had my father.

"Eighth Army, Second Infantry Division, Ninth Infantry Regiment. That's me on the end." He handed me the frame. In the picture, a double row of young men faced the camera. Ken was grinning. They all were. "That was taken the day before we deployed. I was twenty-four years old, a newlywed, a recon sergeant. Most of the others were about your age."

In the photo, Ken was wide and rawboned and lean, his face clean-shaven, the grin brash and self-assured.

He spoke as if reading my mind. "I wasn't afraid of much."

He took the picture back, and studied it with a distant expression. "By July of that year, we were on the Naktong River, not far from the city of Pusan. Ever heard of it?" I shook my head, and he shrugged. "Different war, different time. For us, though, it was about as real as real gets. North Koreans had crossed the thirty-eighth parallel and pushed us into a de-fensive line along the river. Fighting was constant, weeks of it, day and night, as bad as you can imagine. By August, we'd taken heavy casualties, and were short on everything: troops, supplies, even ammunition. I was a forward observer, tasked to monitor NKA movements. That put me way out front, usually on a hilltop, usually exposed. The terrain was rough on our side of the river, our lines too thin to deal with the incursions, the coordinated attacks. Some days, every foxhole had someone in it that was dead or dying. Rifle fire. Mortar rounds. Even hand to hand, at times. I got cut off more times than I can remember, me and my crew alone on one hilltop or another. Sometimes I'd see North Koreans coming over the river, thousands of them, this wave of humanity determined to kill every last one of us.

"You wonder if there's a point. Here it is. Our battalion had nine forward observers, people like me. By the time October rolled around, I was the only one left alive. We learned later that those were the bloodiest weeks of the entire war, that nothing else even came close. Five thousand Americans killed, twelve hundred wounded, another thousand MIA. Hell, the South Koreans lost forty thousand.

"I saw more heroism in those days than most men see in a lifetime, and I saw the bad stuff, too, the way men turned coward or turned cruel. Of the thirty-six in that initial platoon, only four of us came back alive. One killed himself a year later, Charlie Green, a corporal, a Kentucky boy. James Rapp robbed a bank, pulled eight years of hard time, then got out, stole a car the same day, and drove into a phone pole. Some said it was intentional, another suicide. No one really knows. The third survivor was from California, Alex Chopin, a good kid, a little flaky but solid in a fight. After the war, he lived rough for a while in LA, then disappeared into some kind of commune up the ass end of Humboldt County. As for me, number four . . ." Ken sat, his eyes dark and distant. "I lost my wife. I struggled."

"You said there was a point."

"People change. That's the point. They change in wartime most of all."

"Do you really think he killed her?"

"I think it's possible."

I put down the glass, and rose to my feet, dry-mouthed.

"Sit down, Gibby."

"I think you've said enough."

"You don't have the facts, son, not about this case or your brother or what war can do to a man."

"So give them to me."

"I told you, kid. It's not my place."

"He couldn't have changed that much."

"War and prison and drugs." Ken reached for my untouched glass, poured the whiskey into his, and leaned back. "*You* do the math."

At home much later, I stayed awake for hours, afraid that if I slept, I would dream of a river and mud, and small men come for killing. I pictured Ken on a windswept hill—this friend of my father who'd fought young, and lost some piece of himself. He'd known war, as had my brothers; and without meaning to, he'd put some of that war inside me.

The Jason I'd known.

Jason as he might now be.

I didn't know what to believe, so I twisted and turned, and each time

I drifted, I started awake. Eventually, though, I slept, and the dreams that came were not of war or pain or prison but of Becky Collins, who smiled in the sun, her eyes like blue flowers.

Have faith, she said. *Life is beautiful.*

I woke in a sweat, hoping she was right.

18

Detective French rose early and left the house before the sun had cleared the trees. He'd spent most of the night wrestling with thoughts of his son and murder and a dead girl's cloudy eye. It looked bad for Jason: the photos of Tyra's torture and death, the bloody scalpel taped to the back of his son's dresser.

But still the doubts lingered.

Still, these images of the boy he'd raised.

Captain Martin had locked him out of the case, and word had gone down the line. Only Burklow had the balls to break ranks, and what he'd shared was not enough. French had not seen the knife or the photographs. He knew nothing about witnesses, forensics, the specifics of the autopsy results. Patience had been urged, and French, half-broken, had agreed.

But that was last night.

Like most in law enforcement, the medical examiner was an early riser, and was still at home when French parked the car and killed the engine. He hesitated because there were boundaries in the murder business—there had to be. Putting his uneasiness aside, he climbed out into the morning sunlight as a young man jogged past, and a kid on a bike flung papers. French waited until one landed in the ME's yard, then picked it up: *The New York Times,* which was good.

Nothing local.

No mention of his son.

On the porch, he raised his hand to knock, but the door opened before he could. "Detective French. What are you doing here?"

"I brought your paper." He tried to keep it light, but Malcolm Frye declined to return the smile. "I'm sorry, Mal. I know it's early."

"I can't discuss the case with you."

His reticence was understandable. Going against the captain's orders would get any medical examiner in trouble, especially in a case as politically loaded as Jason's. And Malcolm Frye wasn't just any ME. He was the only black one in the city, no small accomplishment in a county that had only recently integrated its public schools. That made Malcolm an important part of the civil rights movement. He was visible. He had a lot to lose.

"He's my son, Malcolm. I don't know where else to turn."

The moment stretched uncomfortably. Neither man would call the other a friend, but the respect had always been there: all the years, dozens of cases. The ME frowned, then softened. "You still drink coffee, don't you?"

"Only in the mornings."

"Coffee, then. Come on." He led the way into a neat kitchen. "Two things first." Malcolm poured the coffees. "If anyone asks, you were never here. Second, the autopsy file is at the office. Even were it here, I wouldn't share it with you. That's a line I can't cross."

"Hey, we're just two guys talking."

"All right, then."

French had a thousand questions, but one rose first in his mind. "You've seen the scalpel recovered from Jason's bedroom. Is it consistent with Tyra's injuries?"

"With the more precise cuts, yes."

"Would most scalpels be consistent?"

"Bear in mind that two blades were used on Tyra Norris, one very thin and incredibly sharp. It takes high-grade steel to hold that kind of edge. A scalpel is specifically engineered to that purpose. Telling one from another . . ." He made a face that meant *probably not*.

"And the blood on this particular scalpel?"

"It matches Tyra's."

"Do two blades mean a second cutter?"

"It means a second blade, something like a kitchen knife, nothing special, sharp enough but not surgical. Beyond that, we move into speculation."

"At the scene, you said some cuts indicated a higher level of skill or knowledge. A corpsman, you thought. Maybe a med school dropout."

"Yes, but again, that was off-the-cuff speculation."

"Not enough to rule out my son?"

"I'm sorry, but no. Everything that led me to that initial impression could be learned in a book or on a battlefield or working on stolen cadavers. I can't testify to a specific level of skill or training. Whoever did this had patience, a steady hand, and a general knowledge of anatomy."

French stared through the window. Outside, the day was brighter: a high blue sky, the shadows rolling back. "Walk me through it. Front to back."

The ME kept it clinical. The specifics. "In the end, she died from blood loss and mass, diffuse trauma. The murder took time."

"How much time?"

"Hours. She suffered."

French walked to the window, and peered out. "You have a background in psychology, don't you?"

"Before medical school, I was a clinical psychologist."

"Forensic, as I recall."

"I worked with police departments, yes. Miami-Dade. Los Angeles."

French pinched the bridge of his nose. He was about to leave the *cop* behind, and it was hard, losing that shell. "How does it happen, Malcolm? What makes someone capable?"

"Of torture like this?"

"The psychopathy."

"Come, Detective, you know the answer as well as I." The ME showed his pale, pink palms. "There are some killers we'll never understand, even after trial and conviction and years of study. You won't hear this term in clinical circles, but people like that are born *wrong*. We both know the names. We've read the cases. Perhaps one day we'll understand that level of innate psychopathy, but right now, we don't."

"What about those who aren't . . . *born wrong*?"

The ME rolled his shoulders. "Something in life makes them that way. Childhood trauma, abuse."

"And if it's not related to childhood?"

"Something violent, then. Something big."

"Like war?"

"That depends on the person and the war."

"A bad war. My son."

"Ah, now I see." The ME sipped his coffee, very intent. "How long did Jason serve?"

"A bit less than three full tours."

"Was he physically injured?"

"Burned, shot, and stabbed."

"Did he kill men in return?"

"Twenty-nine, at least. Would that be enough to change him, to make him capable?"

"Of murder like this?" The ME leaned back, and showed the same pink palms.

Maybe he had no answer to give.

Maybe none was needed.

Court opened at nine, and I was there early, watching from across the street. My father would use the secure entrance in the rear, but I wasn't taking chances.

If he saw me, he'd stop me.

Leaning against a light pole, I tried to sort the people into groups. The lawyers were easy. They carried briefcases and files, and huddled with people that looked like clients. I knew enough about court to know they weren't the killers or the rapists—they'd come later, shackled and under guard. What troubled me were the reporters. They stood by a line of news trucks, and I knew they were here for my brother. Details of Tyra's death remained thin, but the rest of it made a hell of a story. *Bikers. Guns. A cop's kid.*

"Jeez, look at these people."

I turned at the voice, and found Chance at my right shoulder. "Why do you always sneak up on me like that?"

"Because you make it so easy." He leaned against the other side of the pole, dipping his head at the crowd. "Those are people you never want to see late at night or moving in next door. Jesus. Look at them." He pointed toward the crowd. "Hey, we know those guys."

He meant the last group, and one I'd tried hardest to ignore: mothers, fathers, people who knew my family. "Moral support, I guess."

"Don't believe it for a second. They're here for the show. Look at that one. He's laughing. Fat bastard just told a joke."

I watched the big man shake. He'd been my football coach in sixth grade.

"They're opening the doors. Let's go."

Chance pulled me across the street, and we followed the crowd through double doors and into a long hall. I counted eight courtrooms. Almost everyone made their way to number six. I looked for my father, but didn't see him.

"There, that's a good spot." Chance pointed at a crowded bench near the front. We took seats on the aisle, and I wondered if this was the same courtroom where Jason had made his plea and been sent away. I thought it was. It felt the same.

After a few minutes, an armed bailiff led the judge into the room, waiting for him to ascend the bench, then calling court to order. "All rise." People stood, and then sat, and I thought how like church it was, the same rustle and sigh, the roomful of sinners staring up.

"Good morning." The judge settled like a king on his throne. "We have a lot of cases on the docket, so I'll try to move things along as quickly as possible. Bailiff." He gestured, and a second bailiff unlocked a door so other armed men could bring out the prisoners slated to face the most serious charges of the day. A line of them emerged, all in orange jumpsuits, all cuffed. Jason was the last out and the only one in full chains.

"There's your old man."

Chance nudged me, and I saw my father beyond the bar in the left corner, talking with an older man. The lawyer, I thought.

"Madam Clerk, call the first case."

A woman to the judge's left read from the docket. "Case number 72 CR 1402, *State v. Jason French*."

A bailiff led my brother to the defense table, and the attorney left my father's side to meet him there. "Good morning, Your Honor. Alexander Fitch, for the defense."

"Mr. Fitch, nice to see you in my court." The judge glanced at the prosecutor's table. "Is the State ready to proceed?"

A young woman stood, but before she could reply, a small man rose from a nearby bench. "Brian Gladwell for the State, Your Honor."

He moved behind the prosecutor's table, and the judge frowned, perplexed. "Not that you are unwelcome in this court, but we rarely have the pleasure of the district attorney himself on matters as perfunctory as a first appearance."

"I have my reasons, Your Honor."

"The privilege is yours. Madam Clerk."

The clerk read the charges. I missed a few, but the big ones stood out. *Attempted murder in the second degree, felony weapons trafficking, felony fleeing to elude arrest, felonious assault, assault with intent . . .*

She kept going, but I kept my eyes on the DA. Fine lines creased the side of his neck, but that's not what I noticed first.

He was sweating.

He was pale.

When the clerk finished, the judge addressed Jason's attorney. "Mr. Fitch, how does your client plead?"

"Not guilty, Your Honor."

"Preferences for probable cause?"

"Only that you schedule the hearing as soon as convenient for the court. We intend to refute these charges and would like to do so at the earliest possible time."

"Mr. DA?"

"We anticipate further charges, Your Honor. As much time as you can give us would be welcome."

The judge drummed his fingers. He knew about Tyra Norris. Everyone did. "What kind of charges might you bring in the future?"

"Felony kidnapping. Murder in the first degree. The investigation is ongoing."

The crowd around us stirred, the sound like a rustle of feathers. The judge consulted his calendar, and offered a date fourteen days in the future. "I assume that's acceptable to all parties."

"There's one last thing, Your Honor."

"Mr. DA?"

The district attorney cleared his throat and, for an instant, glanced at someone in the courtroom. "Ah, Your Honor . . ." He cleared his throat again; shuffled some papers on the table. "The State requests that the defendant be remanded to the authorities at Lanesworth Prison."

The judge was clearly puzzled. "On what grounds?"

"Ah, safekeeping, Your Honor. After consultation with authorities at the local jail."

"In my experience, Mr. DA, safekeeping orders are for defendants too sickly or frail to manage outside the types of medical facilities available at fully staffed and funded state institutions. Are you suggesting that Mr. French is too unwell to survive two weeks at the local jail?"

"Actually, Your Honor, I'm suggesting he's too dangerous."

Another murmur stirred the courtroom. The judge waited for it to settle. "Perhaps you could explain."

"Your Honor, the defendant served three combat tours in Vietnam, a time in which he learned to kill and do it well. Many here have heard the stories—"

"Rumors, Your Honor." Jason's lawyer interrupted. "Unadulterated and irrelevant."

"Be that as it may"—the DA raised his voice—"the defendant was dishonorably discharged after attacking a highly decorated superior officer. It took four men to subdue the defendant, and three were severely injured in the process, two to the point of hospitalization in intensive care. It takes a dangerous man to do that kind of damage, and local authorities don't relish the responsibility of keeping someone like that in custody. Our jail is overcrowded. Its officers lack the training necessary to deal with someone as demonstrably violent and capable as this defendant."

"Your Honor—"

"I have a letter, Your Honor, from the warden at Lanesworth Prison attesting to the dangers of holding Mr. French in custody. Even at a state prison farm—with all its facilities and experienced officers—this defendant was suspected in two unsolved killings and multiple beatings—"

"*Suspected,* Your Honor. Neither tried nor convicted."

"Your Honor, if I may approach with the letter."

"Hardly necessary, Mr. DA. Your request is unusual but well within the prerogative of your office. If you want the defendant in state prison, that's where I'll send him. Madam Clerk, enter the order and call the next case."

An hour passed before they came for Jason. He spent that time alone in a cell.

"Open five."

When the door opened, Jason blinked but stayed where he was.

"Come on, let's go. Your ride is here." Jason waited five beats, then rose as if from a Sunday nap. The guard stepped back, and four others entered to bind Jason in full restraints. "All right. Nice and easy." They formed up around him, and Jason began the shuffle step that kept him on his feet and moving. They traveled one hallway, and then a second. A bus waited in the parking bay. LANESWORTH PRISON. INMATE TRANSFER. "Stop here."

Beyond the bus, a concrete ramp sloped to the open street. Jason heard distant traffic; tasted the fumes. When the bus door opened, a uniformed corrections officer stepped down. The name tag said RIPLEY. Jason knew him. "Paperwork?" He held out a hand, and one of the local officers gave him a clipboard. Ripley dashed off a signature, and handed the clipboard back. "Any problems I should know about?"

"Meek as a kitten."

"We'll take it from here."

Ripley summoned two officers from the bus, Jordan and Kudravetz. Jason knew them, too. They got him up the steps and onto a bench. When Ripley mounted the bus, he threaded between the seats until he reached the place Jason sat. He was midfifties, broad, strong, and prison-pale.

Jason met his eyes, and said, "Captain Ripley."

"Prisoner French. Do you understand what's happening and why?"

Jason nodded once. He knew.

"Would you believe me if I said I'm sorry for you?"

Jason met the guard's steady gaze. Captain Ripley wasn't a bad guy, just trapped, like the warden was trapped. "I would," Jason replied.

"It's a long drive," Ripley said. "At least you have that."

He returned to the front of the bus, locked the steel mesh door, and sat on the other side with Jordan and Kudravetz. The driver cranked the engine, and rolled them into traffic. Jason watched the city slide past, the businessmen and tall buildings, the construction crews and pretty women. A clutch of hippies filled a street corner, protesting the war; and Jason watched them slide past, too: the men who'd never fought, the women with angry faces and flowers in their hair. A moment's resentment flickered, but Jason was too much a prisoner to really care.

He thought of Tyra, instead.

He thought of X.

When the city fell away, it took little time for the fields to spread out and the forests to rise. The bus made multiple turns, moving ever eastward until the roads narrowed and buckled. The driver downshifted when it got bad, but the old bus still rattled and clanked.

The prison was close.

Jason saw it in the tangled woods and narrow cuts, and in the ditch lines filled with stagnant water.

Not just close, he thought.

Here.

The bus slowed on cue, turning at an enormous block of stone where words, carved long ago, told the sad, grim truth of things:

LANESWORTH STATE PRISON FARM, 1863

ABANDON ALL HOPE, YE WHO ENTER HERE

Before his time at this place, Jason had never read Dante, but could now quote entire passages. "Through me the way to the suffering city; through me the everlasting pain."

Ripley turned his head, his fingers hooked in the mesh. "What's that, prisoner?"

"Dante's *Inferno,*" Jason replied. "*Divine Comedy.* The gates of hell."

"I don't get it."

"I just hate that sign."

Ripley didn't understand or care enough to ask again. "Four miles," he said; but Jason knew that, too.

Four miles of private road.

Eighteen thousand acres.

The prison crowned a rise in the center of all that emptiness, and Jason felt a familiar chill when he saw the blackened stone. Ripley said, "Welcome home," but Jason heard a softer voice, instead, a knowing whisper and the long-ago words of Dante Alighieri.

Nothing was made before me but eternal things,

And I endure eternally.

The voice belonged to X.

Jason was home, indeed.

19

After Jason's court appearance, we sat in my car, waiting for a bus to slide out from the belly of the courthouse. Chance was not happy about it. "Tell me again why we're doing this."

He'd said it before, but few things were real to me now: Becky, my brother, this question of manhood and war.

"Can't we go to the quarry or something?"

"Chill," I said. "That's the bus."

A bus emerged and rolled past us—same white paint and black letters—and I saw my brother inside. I knew where they were taking him, so I couldn't explain this need, but I wanted to see the prison and make it real. I stayed far back, but kept the bus in sight as it moved through the city and into the countryside. It took an hour to reach the far, empty place where Lanesworth waited for my brother, and when we got there, I stopped on the verge of the state road, and watched dust rise as the bus split a brown-green field and disappeared under a canopy of trees.

"We're not going in?" Chance asked.

"This is far enough."

"Finally, some sense."

He spit through the open window and I felt a wave of anger. "How many times have I been there for *you*, Chance? When your dad left. When your mom got sick. I could name a hundred others, and I didn't bitch about any of them, did I? I went to the hospital. You lived in my room for a month."

"Dude . . ."

"Two damn minutes, all right?"

He didn't apologize, but Chance played tough about the things that really mattered. His mom was one. I was another. When dust settled in the field, I turned across the road, and drove us out.

"Did you get what you needed?" Chance asked.

"I'm not sure what I needed."

"Look, man. If he didn't do it, he'll get out. Not for the guns, maybe, but you know . . ."

I had no response, and the rest of the drive was like that. In the city, I dropped Chance at the mall. His reasons were simple. "If I'm going to cut school, I may as well have some fun. Sure I can't talk you into it?"

"Not today."

"I can come with you if you want."

"Nah, go on. I'll see you later."

I left him on the sidewalk, and drove to Sara's condominium. There was no answer when I knocked on the door, but I saw an upstairs curtain twitch. "Sara, come on." I knocked again. "Sara!"

When the door opened, she looked puffy and pale. "What are you doing here?"

"I don't know. I wanted to check on you."

"Well, now you have."

She leaned on the door, but I caught it before it closed. "Sara, wait."

"We should have never gone out with you." She showed her face again, pinch-lipped this time. "You. Your brother. She'd be alive if we hadn't."

"You can't believe that."

"Do you know how she died?"

"How could I possibly know that?"

"Her parents know. The cops told them and they told me."

"Sara, listen—"

"She was cut to pieces, chained up and tortured and cut to pieces. They say it took hours."

"I don't know what to say." I truly did not.

"Your brother's an animal. Don't come here again."

She slammed the door, and I tried to *not* see Tyra as she'd described her.

What if it's me? I wondered.

What if I'm the one who's wrong?

When I turned away from Sara's door, I noticed the man in a car across the street. I didn't think about him one way or another until I stepped into the road, and saw that he was not so much old as old-looking. That seemed familiar, somehow: the loose skin, and how he watched me walk. Even in my car, I thought he was watching. I told myself it didn't matter. He was just a creepy old dude in a creepy black car.

It took four blocks to remember.

I'd seen him in the courtroom crowd, three rows back and staring at the DA. I took my foot off the gas, and replayed the scene: the judge on his bench, the DA, sweating bullets as he stammered at the judge, and looked fearfully into the crowd. The old man from the car had been right there.

Lanesworth . . .

The DA had been talking about Lanesworth.

The same man on Sara's street could not be a coincidence.

I turned across traffic, and everything was fast: my heart, the drive. On Sara's street, I drove faster.

Be there! I prayed.

But he was gone.

I pounded on Sara's door, thinking she should know about the man on her street, or that maybe she already did. "Sara! Open up!" I beat on the door for two full minutes. I wanted answers. I wanted to talk.

Sara, apparently, did not.

I thought about it as I drove from the city: Sara's anger, the man on her street.

At home, I found my mother in the kitchen, beautifully dressed and made up to perfection, humming as she swept about the room, stirring pots on the stove, bending to remove a tray of cookies from the oven.

"Mom?"

She saw me, and beamed. "Gibson, hello! Such a lovely day!"

There was no mention of Jason or court or the fact I should be in school. She kissed my cheek, and I smelled her perfume. "What *is* all this?"

"Can't a mother cook for her family?" She turned on the same smile, the same glittering gaze. "Are you home for lunch? This is for dinner tonight, but I can whip something up in a jiffy."

I had no easy response. The whole scene had a patina of make-believe: the sunlight and the apron, another burst of day-bright smile.

"They say the temperature will break by dusk. Perhaps we should dine on the patio. Your father always liked that." She dipped a spoon in sauce and tasted it. "Paprika," she said; and I realized then that she was strangely, deliriously happy. Worse yet, I realized why.

The bad son was in prison.

She thought the good one was safe.

Too troubled to stay in the house, I drove back to the city, ending up in a parking lot I knew better than most. The building was redbrick and small, its windows as spotless and crisp as the poster taped inside:

THE MARINE CORPS BUILDS MEN

A recruitment officer was watching through the window, and waved at me to come inside. He'd done the same thing a dozen times on different days, but today, I got out of the car and actually went inside. The officer was medium-sized and medium-aged, but his feet rode the linoleum at shoulder width. An empty sleeve was pinned on his chest beside a name tag that said MCCORMICK, J.

"I've seen you before," he said. "Ten times, at least." He gestured to the desk, and we sat, one on either side. His eyes were dark, the gaze measured. Medals hung beside the empty sleeve. "You're wondering about the arm. Most do. Enemy bayonet. A severed artery."

"Vietnam?" I asked.

"Khe Sanh in '68."

"Is that why . . . ?" I trailed off, pointing at the Purple Heart on his chest.

"Is that the reason you're here? You like the idea of medals?"

"I never think about them."

"Every boy does."

"I'm not a boy."

"You sit in the car like a boy."

It was flatly said. Heat rose in my neck and face, and I hated that. "Aren't you supposed to recruit me?"

"This is the Marine Corps, not the army."

I started to stand, the air between us like the edge of a storm.

"First, tell me why you came inside. Why today? What changed?"

It was a good question. I had no ready answer. "My brothers fought," I finally said. "I graduate soon."

"Were your brothers marines?"

"My father, too. He fought in Korea, my brothers in Vietnam. The oldest died at Cam Lộ in '67."

"What unit?"

"First Battalion, Third Marines."

"I'm sorry for your loss, son. I'm sure he was a fine marine."

"PFC Robert French. He was."

The officer blinked at last. "You said *French*?"

"Robert, yes. Drafted out of high school. When he died, my other brother enlisted."

The officer leaned forward, the same fixed look in his eyes. "Your other brother is Jason French? Gunnery Sergeant Jason French, from here in Mecklenburg County?" He slid a newspaper across the desk, and pressed his finger on the headline. "This Jason French?"

I saw a picture of my brother beneath a headline that spoke of murder and court and custody. "He didn't kill that girl," I said.

"I believe you."

"No one else does."

"Those people don't matter, civilians. They don't understand the man your brother is, they can't."

"Understand what, exactly?"

The officer leaned even closer, his mouth a firm, straight line. "I want you to give your brother a message. Tell him it's from First Lieutenant John McCormick, Second Battalion, Twenty-Sixth Marines. He doesn't know me, but that won't matter. Tell him it's from every combat marine who knows what he did in Vietnam."

"I still don't understand."

"Kid, you're not supposed to."

Something in the air had changed, not the edge of a storm, but the stillness, behind. "What message?" I asked.

"Simply this."

The officer gathered himself, dark eyes glinting as his chair scraped in the empty room. He blinked away what looked like tears, and I watched in quiet dismay as he stood tall behind the desk and, with his last good arm, saluted the marine who was my brother.

20

The intake officers processed Jason as they would any prisoner. They pho-tographed and fingerprinted him, then took off the chains, the county-issued clothing. The strip search was perfunctory, and Jason endured it without comment. The smells were the same, same colors and sounds. He didn't know where in the prison they'd house him, but knew how the walk in would play. The first time, there'd been jeers and threats; no one had known him.

This time, there'd be silence.

Just like when they'd walked him out.

Jason looked at the observation window on the second floor above the intake center. A man stood behind the glass, lights dimmed, but Jason knew it was the warden. He had the same narrow shoulders, the same defeated slump. Seeing him there, some part of Jason was angry—he wouldn't be at Lanesworth without the warden's approval and participation—but it was hard to hold on to the emotion. The man was his own kind of prisoner.

"Are you ready?" Captain Ripley put his hand on Jason's shoulder, but Jason didn't move.

"Where are we going?"

"Not to X, not yet."

Jason studied the man's features. He had a square face, wide-set eyes, and a nose like a fist. "You're still running his detail?"

"I am."

"Still six of you?"

"Other than his fast-approaching execution, not much has changed."

"How soon?" Jason asked.

"Not soon enough."

Ripley nodded at another officer, and a steel door slid on metal tracks, a hallway stretching away beyond it. Jason took the first step, and Ripley fell in beside him. They walked in silence, down one hall, then another. "The warden wants to make you comfortable. Isolation wing. Private cell." He stopped at the main door of the isolation wing. A second guard let them in. The first cell was empty. "This is yours." Jason stepped inside, but Ripley seemed loath to leave. "You didn't kill her, did you?"

"What do you think?"

"I think X has long arms and some reason to want you back inside. Any thoughts on *reason*?"

"None."

"Either way . . ." Ripley shrugged with sad eyes, and Jason felt a moment's pity. No guards on X's detail had a wife or kids. Too dangerous. The warden's call. But there were means of hurt beyond torn skin or broken bones.

Ripley gathered himself as if remembering that one of them was an inmate. "Anyway. He wants to see you at five o'clock. Those are for you." He meant clothing, stacked on the bed: jeans, a linen shirt, and loafers. The guard offered Jason a pack of cigarettes. "Here, you'll need these more than me."

He left and locked the door, and Jason contemplated the scars on his hands. Some were from the war and other fights, but most had come from fights with X. Same with the headaches, the nightmares, the poorly healed ribs. Lighting a cigarette, Jason stared at the cold, blank walls. The men he'd fought with in Vietnam were dead or scattered. His father could barely meet his eyes, and he'd not seen his mother in years. Only Gibby seemed to care if he was in prison or not.

Only Gibby and X.

I left the recruiting office overcome by something close to religious awe. I'd never seen such respect and conviction, and tried to imagine what kind of act or action would make a stranger rise and salute with tears in his eyes. What had I done in life that even came close?

With that thought in my head, and nowhere I had to be, I decided to find Becky Collins. On her street, I passed a shattered tree and a hollow-eyed woman who watched me roll by. When I reached the right house, Becky was in the yard as if she'd known I was coming. I was afraid the unannounced visit might make her angry, but that's not how it played. She waved broadly, and smiled as I parked.

"This is a nice surprise."

"Chance thought you'd be upset with me if I showed up uninvited."

"Chance is an idiot. Can you stay?" I said I could, and she took my hand to pull me from the car. "Come with me, then."

She led me into the backyard, then into a stand of trees, and down a red-clay bank rutted out by heavy rains. At the bottom, we picked our way into deeper forest and along a footpath to a creek that gurgled among the stones.

"I found this place when I was six."

Becky spoke over her shoulder as she led me deeper, parting a tangle of vines so I could follow her into a clearing where the creek spilled into a basin dappled with light, its loveliness so unexpected and complete it startled me.

"Isn't it something? Sit here." She gestured at a mossy spot near the water's edge. "Give me a second, okay?"

I watched her gather bits of trash washed in by the creek, making a neat pile of it beside the trail.

"I have to stay on top of this, especially after it rains." She dropped a final bit of plastic, then sat beside me with her knees up and her arms crossed to make a place for her chin. "So," she said. "Gibby French."

"Becky Collins."

"You want to talk about it?"

"What?"

"Whatever it is I see down in the bottom of those pretty green eyes."

I didn't want to talk about Jason or Tyra, so I changed the subject. "This place is pretty amazing. How'd you find it?"

"Any kid would have."

"Have others?" I asked. "Found it, I mean."

"Not for a while, I guess. I don't see people here. There are houses that way—a whole other street—but there are brambles and kudzu. The drop is steeper."

"Do you ever swim?"

She raised one eyebrow into a perfect arch. "Do you want to?"

I did want to. It was the coolness and the depth, the vines that made a curtain, and the stillness of the deep, green shade.

"I'm not taking off my clothes," she said.

"Me, either."

"Underwear, then?" I looked for the joke, but there was no such thing in her eyes. "You first," she said, and then watched as I took off my shoes, stood awkwardly, and fumbled at my belt. "Do you want me to turn around?" I nodded stupidly, surprised when she closed her eyes and covered them with her hands. "How about this instead?"

I took off my shirt and pants, realizing then that her fingers were spread and she was grinning as she watched. I said, "Cheater," then stepped into the pool, which was deeper than I'd thought. I moved to the middle and sank to my chin.

Becky stripped as if the act were devoid of sexuality. Tossed shoes. A quick roll onto her back to pull off the jeans. She stood to remove her shirt, and I looked away because her sexuality was obvious, whether she meant it to be or not. In the water, she said, "This is nice," then went under and rose, dripping. The pool made her eyes look something other than blue, and the water made the bra translucent. "Do you want to talk about it, now?" she asked.

I wasn't sure if she was teasing or not, but words had never been hard for me. I spoke of my father, who thought Jason might be guilty, and of my mother, manic in the kitchen. That led to Chance and prison and the question of college versus war. When I reached the place that hurt the most, I looked away and shared my thoughts on brothers and death and the guilt I harbored for my easy life. When the words ran out, I found Becky close in the water, not touching me, but nearly so.

"What do you think?" I asked.

She stared for a handful of seconds, still silvery-eyed and lovely. "I think you have troubles, and that none of them are bigger than you."

"What do you think I should do?"

"With your life? I can't answer that question."

"What about now? Today?"

"Be there for your brother. Let him know he's not alone."

"That's it?"

"It's enough," she said; but the words, in my ears, were strange.

Be a man, I heard.

For once in your sheltered life.

Ripley returned at ten minutes before five, and Jason considered how strange it was to walk the prison halls in loafers and jeans. He'd served twenty-seven months behind these walls, a full twelve of them before he'd met X.

But those last months . . .

He'd fought and bled, and been brought back to fight again. Fifteen months. A blur of pain, blood, and bandages. No one had fought X so many times or come so close to beating him. For a time, the guards had wagered in secret on the conflicts, but X didn't fight for sport—not that kind—and two days after he'd learned of the wagers, one guard lost an ear in an unprovoked bar fight, and another, his home to fire.

After that, there were no wagers.

"This way."

Ripley led Jason down a series of halls, then outside and through the main yard. Jason watched the prisoners, and the prisoners watched him back. Blacks. Hispanics. The white prisoners paid the most attention. Nazis. Bikers. Loners with the right ink. They had a corner of the yard, and it seemed every eye was on Jason as he passed.

"Because of the Pagans," Ripley said. "Word is out about what you did to Darius Simms."

"Is that why I'm in solitary?"

"Let me put it this way. If guards come for you that aren't on X's detail, tread with serious care. X is not the only one with deep pockets and corrections officers on the payroll."

They kept moving. So did every eyeball in every white face. After that, it was all about death row. The building was the oldest at Lanesworth, a onetime weapons depot modified in 1863 to hold Union army prisoners of war. Security inside was unpleasant, but Jason knew the guards, the protocols.

"Open one."

A buzzer sounded, and the old hinges groaned. A second guard appeared, not one of X's. He was midforties and florid, same buzz cut as every other guard.

Ripley said, "You got him?"

"I do."

Ripley met Jason's eyes for half a blink, then turned on a heel, and left without a word. A red hand settled on Jason's arm, and put damp marks on his skin. "I'm sure you remember the rules. Stay in the center of the hall, clear of the cell doors. Don't talk to anyone. No eye contact. Make it easy for me, I make it easy for you."

They turned to face the *row,* and it was like every nightmare Jason had had since getting out: the small, hot cells, and pale faces against the metal, the long walk to the end, and then down the stairs to X.

"Walk on, prisoner."

Jason squared up, and took that first step. If X wanted him dead, he wanted him dead. If it was something else . . .

He kept his eyes down as cells slid past, and one inmate hissed, *Hey, slickness . . . hey, slick . . .* At the end of the row, another guard stood at the top of the stairwell. He was part of X's detail, and had been for years. Jason could not remember the name, but the face was familiar. He waved off the red-faced guard, and put a hand on Jason's arm. "I'm sorry to see you back. You okay? You good?"

"Well enough."

"We'll do it like every other time." The guard turned a key. "He's in a good place today. You should be fine."

Jason stepped through the door, and faced the stairs with the usual anxiety. X could speak of history and philosophy, of literature and art, the great works of mankind. In a single hour, he could show the world through fresh eyes, then just as quickly recall some far-off murder in detail so exquisite it turned your stomach. X was brilliant; he was insane.

Then there was the rest of it . . .

Jason flexed his oft-broken hands, and twisted once to take pressure off the poorly healed ribs. When he reached the bottom of the stairs, he looked up as the guard nodded, and locked the steel door to leave Jason alone in the shadows beneath death row. There was a stone archway at the bottom of the stairs. Beyond that was the corridor and X's cells and X.

"Hello, Jason."

The voice was the same. So was everything else. Jason had wondered at this moment: his physical reaction, his first words. He wanted to vomit. He wished for a .45 in his hand. "You told me I was free of this place and of you. You said I was out clean."

"I meant it at the time." X stood center corridor, a lean man of average height, casually dressed. "Things change."

Jason moved beneath the arch, and into the corridor. "Things like what?"

X shrugged, but seemed happy. "Let's say that a date certain for one's execution tends to sharpen the mind until some things become painfully acute."

"Such as?"

"Old regrets. Final aspirations."

"You had Tyra killed to bring me back." It wasn't a question. For Jason, it had never been a question.

"Sadly for the young woman, I didn't know that you would be arrested on gun and assault charges, that I might have simply waited."

"She was an innocent woman."

"But was she really?" X took a few steps, eyes glinting. "She taunted the men on that bus, forgotten men with little dignity and few reasons to live. She teased and tormented them, and did it for what, exactly? A moment's distraction? Her own venereal pride?"

"Please spare me the false indignation. You don't care about the men on that bus. And any sins of Tyra's pale beside your own."

X raised his shoulders, both hands behind his back. "I'm merely deconstructing whatever narrative you've built in that otherwise fine mind of yours. The men on the bus are irrelevant, yes, but any positive qualities your young friend may have had, she was, at the core, selfish and unworthy."

"Of her life?"

"Of you, Jason. For God's sake, did you learn nothing from me in our time together?"

Jason took a deep breath, trying to steady himself. It had always been like this with X. "Why am I here?"

"Can't two friends simply visit?"

"We are most certainly not friends."

"Kindred spirits, then."

Jason shook his head. It was all so familiar. "I've never understood these delusions of yours."

"Delusions!" X raised his voice for the first time. "How many men have you killed, my friend? And how many of those deaths do you actually regret?"

"That was war. It's different."

"But is it different there?" X pointed at Jason's heart. "Does a song not play each time? You alive, another dead . . ."

"I'm not doing this with you. Not again." Jason backed away, knowing X could kill him if he wished. There'd be a blade nearby, a shard of glass, a twist of wire . . .

X trailed languidly behind. "I did take pains to bring you here."

"Tyra's pain. My pain."

"You're upset. I understand. We can try again tomorrow."

"Tomorrow will be no different."

"Yet time is not our friend."

"The electric chair. Yeah, I heard." Jason kept moving: the second step, the third.

"If you knew my heart, you would feel differently."

Jason climbed higher, and X watched him go, a smile on his face. "The heart, my young friend, and all the songs that play."

21

An hour after we climbed from the creek, I was back in the car, and Becky, again, was leaning above me. The sun hung below the trees. The light was soft on her face. "This was good," I said.

"Come anytime, Gibson French."

Without intending it, my gaze slid to the house behind her. The porch had collapsed on one side. The screens were rusted and torn.

"Hey, handsome. Eyes front." Becky touched my cheek, and turned my head. "It's just a house. It's not who I am."

"Chance told me not to come."

"And I told you, Chance is an idiot. Will you stay a little longer?"

"I need to go."

"Important business?"

"Kind of. Yeah."

A hint of doubt showed in her eyes. She sensed my unease, but misunderstood the reasons. "I'm a cool girl, you know. We can talk about other things. It doesn't have to be so heavy."

"I think you're the coolest."

"So let's go somewhere. Sunset. Dinner. The place doesn't matter."

Her words made sense, but others did, too.

Be a man . . .

For once in your sheltered life . . .

"I'm being pushy," she said. "And that's not normally my thing. Just tell me you're not blowing me off."

"I'm not."

"Is that a promise?"

"It is."

She bent low, her elbows crossed on the window frame. "Tell me I'm beautiful."

"You're gorgeous."

"Why should I believe you?"

"Because you're a gorgeous, beautiful girl, especially in your under-wear."

She blushed and looked away, but was not unhappy. When she turned back, we kissed, her lips softly parted, her breath warm and sweet. When she drew back at last, the grin was in her eyes, and she held up two fingers.

My second kiss . . .

That's what she meant.

I held up the same two fingers, then put the car in gear, and watched her dwindle in the dusty light. She shielded her eyes to watch me, too; and I considered how fast the world was changing. A week ago, life was the quarry, the dive, a few cold beers with Chance. Now there was Becky and Jason, my father and mother, a house full of lies.

Maybe this is how it feels, I thought.

Adulthood.

I preferred the clarity of single-mindedness, so I thought about the best way to help my brother. Before, the answer would have been simple. My father was a cop, with his own kind of clarity. But I couldn't ask for his help—he'd worry more for me than Jason, and act accordingly. *Should I visit Jason in prison?* I debated as I drove, then stopped at a pay phone and lied to my mother.

"How late?" she asked.

"I'm not sure. A few hours."

"What are you doing?"

"Something with Chance. Nothing big. Hanging out."

"But your father—"

"Just tell him for me, okay?"

I hung up because I knew how the rest of it would play. On Chance's street, I parked a half block down, and watched my back as I walked to his house. It was that kind of street. His mother came to the door when I knocked, her hair streaked with gray and pulled back in a kerchief. She'd worked two shifts already, but none of that tiredness touched her eyes when she saw me. "Gibby, sweetheart. Come inside. You're in time for dinner." She gave me a hug, then called out to Chance. "Chance, come say hi to Gibby."

Chance emerged from the back hall, surprised to see me.

"Can we talk?" I asked.

"Yeah, sure. Mom?"

"Dinner in ten minutes. Gibby, do you like creamed chipped beef on toast?"

"Sure. Thanks."

Chance led me to his room, a small space with a single window. "Have you ever had creamed chipped beef on toast?" He closed the door. "Dried beef, milk sauce, and Wonder Bread. Your basic staples."

"I'm sure it's awesome."

"I guess you're here for a reason."

I said that I was, and told him what I wanted to do.

"Are you nuts?" he demanded. "Are you fucking high?"

"I don't know. You tell me."

"You want to figure out who killed Tyra Norris? You? Not the cops?"

I nodded.

"Then yeah, I'd say you're nuts, like off-your-rocker, nuthouse nuts. Leave it for the cops, man."

"The cops think Jason did it."

"Not your dad, though."

"I don't know. I think maybe he does. He won't talk about it, but he's got this grimness, like he's braced for it. And the other cops are watching him. I can tell you that. They're looking at him strange."

"Dude, you're just a kid . . ."

"Am I, though? I can vote, drink, go to war."

"Forget that bullshit. Let's break the rest of it down. We have a murdered woman—"

"Tyra."

"Tyra, fine. I know her name. This Tyra's been seriously, hard-core murdered, and you want to prove your brother didn't do it." He leaned into the next word, pausing with one hand up, as if to throw a dart. "How?"

"That's why I need your help. It's why I'm here."

"Who am I? Kojak? Columbo?"

"Screw those TV guys. You're the smartest person I know."

"All right, that part's true. So what? You want to brainstorm this thing?"

"I do, yeah."

"Dude, we don't need to brainstorm anything. There's nothing to talk about. You can't do it."

"Why not?"

"Because you haven't thought this through. You want to save your brother. Fine. Fair enough. But what's on the other side of that coin? You need to prove he's innocent. Straightforward, right? So you find the guy who killed her. You go out in this big, bad world, in the black of night, and you find whatever sadistic, soulless, murderous son of a bitch decided, at some point in life, that torturing women to death is what he really wants to do with his time. To find *that* guy, you'll have to ask questions and get up in his business, up in the place he lives, where he eats and hunts and sleeps, and that, my friend"—Chance used a finger to jab me in the chest—"that is some serious, scary, crazy-dangerous business."

"I don't care about that."

"You should."

"After dinner," I said. "After dinner, we figure this thing out."

In the subbasement beneath death row, X ate and drank, but tasted little beyond the salt of disappointment and the sweetness of his pride. He saw so much of himself in Jason. Did that make his feelings venal in some way? It felt profounder than that. There was compassion in Jason's fierceness, and pity, even when he loathed. Such contradictions were rare in fighters so attuned, and X struggled to understand how Jason could be so vicious and tactically brilliant, yet remain a man of such deep feeling. Pushing away his plate, X replayed the first time he'd forced Jason to fight. He'd not expected much. Jason had appeared more or less as they all had. He'd been leaner perhaps, and sad somehow, though X admitted the impression of sadness might be revisionist.

Why? he'd asked.

Why are we doing this?

Why me?

Had X cared enough to explain, he might have used words like *dominion, distraction, mechanical release.* But there'd been so many fights and fighters, so many conflicts that left him empty.

Jason's skill had been obvious in the first seconds, and X remembered feeling mild interest. There was some talent. He saw no fear. True understanding came later, as X stood bloodied and awed and nearly beaten. Even now, he could feel that sense of near-religious awakening. Fighting Jason made X want to be *more,* and X had not wished to be more for a very long time.

"Guard!" he called out, impatient. "Take this away." X meant the remnants of his dinner. Normally, it was a quick and silent affair. This time the guard lingered. "What?" X could not hide the impatience.

"I'm sorry to bother you . . ."

"Speak."

"Your lawyer is here. He's been waiting."

X frowned. He'd not summoned Reece, and Reece would not come without reason. "Very well. Send him down." The guard scurried away, then returned with Reece, and left. "Sit." Reece looked nervous. That was rare. "Speak, for God's sake."

Reece gathered himself, then spoke softly, as if to do otherwise might trap the words in his throat. "I've been watching the girl. I know I shouldn't be. I know that, I do, not without talking to you first. It's just that I saw her, and she has this look, and she's stuck in my head, stuck there, and spinning . . ."

"Just a moment." X raised a hand, stopping him. "What girl?"

"Um, you know, from the car, the blonde, the other one."

"The one you didn't kill? The one I specifically instructed you to leave alone?"

"The blonde, yes, sir. Her name is Sara . . ."

X stopped him again. Reece was his right hand, one of his many extensions into the outside world. In exchange for his service, X provided money and lawyers and quiet places for Reece to do unspeakable things. Such were the rewards, but there were expectations, too, and penalties should Reece fail. "I find this development troubling," X said.

"I knew you would. I'm sorry."

"And you've come to me because . . . ?"

"I want your permission."

That meant permission to take her, to take his time with her. There was *need* in Reece's eyes, but a real fear, too. He was not the only fixer, and knew it. X could kill Reece with a phone call, and it would not be an easy death. "This must be important to you."

"I can't explain it."

He didn't need to explain. X remembered how it felt to be triggered. A glance on the street. The way a woman walked or smelled or how she twisted her hair. X had once tracked and killed a man for whistling a tune reminiscent of a ferry ride X had taken with his grandfather, as a child. He couldn't say why that had triggered him. It simply had. "What's your timeline?"

"Now," Reece said. "Yesterday, if I could."

X saw all the ways it could play out: the levers and the pieces, strategic moves that went beyond the purely tactical. "I would need something first, and there's a condition attached."

"Anything. Name it."

"Jason has a brother. He was in the car with your blonde."

Reece nodded, his eyes predatory. "Gibson French. Eighteen years of age. The Mustang is his. I saw him at Sara's condo, too. It's possible they're together."

"Bring me pictures," X said.

"Of the brother? Doing what?"

"It doesn't matter." X shrugged to make the point. "Reading a book. Walking the dog. What I require is a current photograph of good quality."

"That's it?"

"Bring me that, and the blonde is yours."

Reece licked dry lips, nodding in ill-concealed eagerness. "You said there was a condition."

"There is, and it's important." X leaned closer, so there would be no mistake. "You'll take the girl after I'm dead, and not before."

Sudden emotion flared in Reece's eyes, panic first, then disappointment and anger, his need for the girl as great as any junkie's need for a fix. "I'm sorry, sir. I don't understand."

"If you think about it, you will. Take a moment." X studied Reece's face as the wheels turned. The man's need was a living thing, and it warred with his very legitimate fear of retribution. He'd seen what happened to men who crossed X—Reece had killed a few himself—and none of those deaths had been slow or easy. X repeated his condition. "After I'm gone, and only then."

"Yes, sir. It makes sense."

"Explain it to me so I know you understand."

"Umm, you want Jason French to remain here at Lanesworth. That means there can be no doubts about who killed the brunette."

"And if the blonde turns up dead?"

"People might wonder if Jason really is the killer."

"Police." X stressed the word. "Prosecutors."

"Yes, sir."

"And you understand how unhappy I would be if something like that happened?"

"I do."

"So tell me the terms of our agreement."

"Bring pictures of the brother. Wait for the girl until after you're dead."

"It's very simple."

Reece nodded a final time, and stood. "Is there anything else I can do for you?"

"Just the pictures, please."

Reece said he would handle it, and X knew he would do it quickly. Calling the guard, X waited as he led Reece to the world outside. When the guard returned, X was pacing restlessly. He felt better with Jason inside, not *alive* but close enough to remember how it felt; and right now, it felt good.

"I want a fighter," he said. "Now. Tonight."

The guard asked for a preference, and X thought for a moment. He knew everything about Jason French, and much about the doings of the prison.

"A Pagan," he said at last. "The biggest one you can find."

22

Dinner at Chance's house was simple and pleasant. His mother told jokes, and asked about his day. When the meal was finished, they argued over who would do the dishes. "Don't be silly." His mother stood, gathering plates. "Be with your friend."

In Chance's room, he hooked a thumb at the kitchen. "Sorry about that."

I wasn't sure what he meant, but thought he was embarrassed by the small portions and his mother's talk of overtime. "Dude, it was great. Your mom's as cool as they come."

"So. Your brother." Chance turned a chair backward, and sat. "We're only talking, right? If I come up with the perfect plan, you won't go off and do something stupid?"

"We're just spitballing."

"Purely hypothetical."

I put a hand on my heart, another lie. I felt bad about the deception, but Chance was the smartest person I knew, and likely to see things I'd missed. That said, he was his mother's entire world, and I didn't know how far this thing would go. What I knew was that Jason needed help, and there was no middle ground. He didn't kill Tyra, end of story. I just needed to prove it.

So we brainstormed like we did on Saturday mornings with nothing to do, only the questions were more life-and-death than what movie to see or whether hoops in the driveway made more sense than sandlot ball with the Miller kids down the street. I told Chance everything I knew about Tyra and Jason, beginning with our day at the lake, and ending with a prison bus on a stretch of empty road, and Tyra falling drunk from the car at her condo on the rich side of downtown. He listened without interruption, then asked me to repeat the story.

"To be clear," he said. "You're saying she was naked in the Mustang?"

"Topless," I replied. "She was naked at the lake. Can we focus now?"

"A grown woman, though. Come on . . ."

In other circumstances, I might agree. This was not the time.

"Did she have a job?" he asked.

"I don't know."

"Family in town? Other friends?"

"I don't know that, either."

"We should ask Sara."

"Definitely."

"She really screwed your brother right in front of you?"

"In the flowers, dude. Deep in the flowers."

"What about enemies?" Chance asked, serious again.

"Probably a few. The lady had a streak."

"What do you mean? How so?"

"A streak, man, this unpredictable wildness, like she could be playful one minute, and nasty the next. We know she dragged Jason into a bar fight, and I told you about the prison bus. She was shameless. Maybe she flirted with the wrong guy at the wrong place, or said the wrong thing at the wrong time. She was capable of anything. She crashed a car. She pulled a gun . . ."

"So she's crazy."

"Also selfish, provocative, and stupid drunk."

Chance shook his head, unhappy. "I don't see how any of this helps. It's vague. There's barely a place to start."

"Somewhere, she met the wrong person." I said it with a little heat. "At the Carriage Room, or at work. Maybe somewhere with Sara . . ."

"Maybe Jason didn't like a gun shoved in his face."

"Don't joke like that."

"Maybe I'm not joking."

"Come on, Chance. Now you're pissing me off."

"Truth, then, the deepest kind. Your brother scares me, all right? He's a dead-eyed, hard-core, scary motherfucker, and you need to think about that. Three years in Vietnam, two and a half in prison. You don't even know him."

"I know enough."

"Do you, really?"

"This is what happened." I raised my voice, but otherwise ignored the bait. "Sometime, somewhere, Tyra Norris met the wrong person or did the wrong thing. She made someone angry or stole something or screwed the wrong guy. We need to find out who and what and when. It's that simple."

"Simple? Really?" Chance frowned, looking washed-out, jaded, and afraid. "It's a big world, man."

"A big world," I agreed.

But a fairly small city . . .

When we ran out of things to talk about, Chance walked me to the car, and tried to sum up the ideas we'd scraped together, the places we could theoretically start. "Bikers. Carriage Room. Sara."

"Jason's housemates." I opened the driver's-side door. "A job, if she had one. Old boyfriends. Any other places Jason might have taken her."

"It's not enough," Chance said.

"It's a start."

We'd argued this point for a while. Swinging blind was dangerous.

"This whole thing," Chance said. "It's not hypothetical, is it?"

He leaned on the car, and I cranked the engine, gunning it hard to pretend I hadn't heard.

"Look at me, dude." He waited for my foot to come off the gas. "I'm not stupid, you know. I know you're lying to me. Do you think I'm afraid to go with you?"

"Why would you ask that?"

"Because things have been different between us," Chance said. "Since the other day, I mean. We were in the car, coming back from Becky's street, and we saw that billboard about the draft and all. You asked if I'd

registered, and I said no, and I saw the way you looked at me." Chance
held my eyes, but swallowed hard. "Your brothers fought, and your father
fought. I know you think about enlisting."

"That doesn't mean I think you're afraid."

"Do you remember the letter?" Chance asked. "The one requiring
you to register for the Selective Service? I burned mine in the backyard.
I've had two more since then, and I burned them, too. When I check the
mail now, I want to vomit." He looked away, shaking his head. "I don't
want to be afraid, but I don't want to die, either."

What I was hearing made a sudden kind of sense. Chance and I used
to follow the war together. We tracked the battles, the politics. We knew
what carrier groups were deployed, and where. Lately, that had changed,
and the more time passed, the starker those changes seemed to be. If I
brought up the war, Chance got quiet. My talk of enlisting made him
increasingly nervous.

"It's Vietnam," I said. "Everyone feels that way."

Chance nodded once, but this was a hard thing between us. "So
you're going home?"

"It's getting late."

It wasn't an answer, and Chance knew it. "Call me later?"

"Sure. Course."

When his friend was gone, Chance stood long in the twilight, thinking
about the parts of his soul he'd just laid bare. It didn't matter what Gibby
had said or how calm he'd kept his features. A new doubt was in his
friend. And it *should be,* Chance thought. The war was real. People like
them were dying.

Inside the house, Chance knelt at the bed, and dragged out a box
of magazines he'd collected about the war in Vietnam. The photographs
were graphic. On one page, thirteen bodies were trampled into the mud,
a soldier in the ditch with his jaw shot off. Another page showed a blinded
marine no older than Chance and a North Vietnamese soldier trapped
in a burning tank, bubble-skinned and screaming as his face melted and
flames danced from the crown of his head. There were a thousand images
just as bad, and Chance could spend all night with them.

He spent an hour this time, then tucked it all beneath the bed: the magazines he hid like pornography, the secret of his schoolboy shame.

I thought of Chance as I worked the car south. I didn't know what he needed or what to tell him, but it was true I didn't want him involved. As the Carriage Room drew closer, I thought less of my friend and more about what might happen next. When people got murdered in Charlotte, odds were pretty good they'd die within a two-mile radius of the Carriage Room. Drugs. Gangs. Pick your poison.

The bar was redbrick and narrow, a single story surrounded by cracked tarmac. Motorcycles and pickups filled the lot. The women going in and out showed mostly skin, and the men, mostly leather. I stood in the lot, and came very close to changing my mind. The sun was falling, darkness rolling out. I took a deep breath, and started walking, three men staring hard when they saw me. Patches on their vests said HELLS ANGELS instead of PAGANS, but no one stopped me, so I wedged myself at the bar, and waited for the bartender to notice me. A tall man with a towel on his shoulder, he said, "I think you're in the wrong place, kid."

I flashed a fifty. "It's yours if you help me."

"All right." He made the money disappear. "Tell me what you need."

I opened my mouth, ready to save my brother's life.

I had no idea what to say.

At first, the bartender seemed amused. It didn't last. "Fifty bucks is a lot of money, but it's not *that* much. I'll give you ten more seconds."

"My brother is Jason French."

"Yeah. So?"

"Um, do you know him?"

"Maybe."

"He was here a while back. He got into a fight with some bikers."

"Look around. We have lots of fights and lots of bikers."

"He was with Tyra Norris."

"Oh, that one."

He rolled his eyes, shaking his head. It could mean anything, so I tried again. "She may have started the fight. Does that help?"

"Tyra Norris and a fight with some bikers." The bartender's face shut down, a cold, blank slate. "We're done now."

"If it's about more money . . ." I emptied my wallet, and spread bills on the bar. "Sixty-three dollars. It's all I have."

He looked at the money, but didn't touch it. "You don't want to go this way, kid. Trust me."

"Take the money. Please."

The bartender took another look around the room, then pocketed the bills with a world-weary shrug. "I know your brother, and I know Tyra, too, tart little sex pistol that she was. And yeah, I was here when the fight went down, five on one against your brother. It cost me two busted tables and about thirty broken glasses. It started here, and spilled outside when they tossed your brother through that window."

"What was the fight about?"

"What I told you is all I know."

"It's not enough."

"Jesus, kid . . ."

"Tyra's dead and my brother's in prison. What would you do if you were me?"

"Look, I'm trying to save your ass."

"So give me back the money."

I held out my hand, but he didn't reach for any bills. With another I-don't-care-about-this-anyway kind of shrug, he said, "All right, tough guy. It's your funeral. Wait here."

He slid a bottle of beer into my hand, then ambled to the end of the bar where an older man hunched above a glass of brown liquor, four other bikers sharing the same corner. The bartender whispered a few words and then returned. "I told him you want to talk, and what about."

"So I wait?"

"If you know what's good for you, you'll go home and go to bed. Other than that, yeah, you need to wait."

But I had no desire to do that. Pushing through the crowd, I saw that the old man was younger than I'd thought, sixty maybe, or maybe a hard-won fifty. He was bigger than I'd thought, too, with hands like a mechanic's. When I was five feet out, he said, "You don't want to be here, kid."

"I just want to ask a few questions."

"Last chance, son."

After that, three things happened simultaneously. I opened my mouth, took a step, and someone hit me in the stomach so hard and fast it bent me in half. The old man said, "Outside," and that's where they took me, through a metal door and into the dark behind the building. They threw me down. I tried to breathe.

"Do we know him?" An unfamiliar voice.

Someone else said, "He looks like his older brother."

"What brother?"

"Jason French."

"No shit?" The old man gripped my hair and twisted my head for a better look. "What's your name?"

"Gibby . . ." I choked on the name, tried again. "Gibby French."

He twisted harder, got some light on my face. "Here's the thing, Gibby French. Angels' business is my business. Why are you asking about my business?"

"All I want to do is help my brother."

A voice said, "Tyra Norris. Somebody cut her up."

"Yeah, well. Tyra. I can't worry much about her." He let me go, and my head hit pavement. "I don't mind the idea of your brother in prison, either. Good for the club, good for me."

I rolled onto my back, gravel and grit grinding into my skin. "He didn't kill her."

"Nobody here cares."

"I want to talk about the fight."

"Talk? That's it?"

"That's it and that's all."

"Well, I've got news for you, kid." He dragged me up, crazy strong. "This has never been a *talking* kind of place."

He hit me hard; bent me in half a second time. He swung again, high to low, right in the face. I hit the ground, blood streaming.

"Get up," he said.

I tried to do it, but took a boot in the ribs because I didn't do it fast enough. I heard a door open, and saw the bartender looking down, skinny and pale as he said, "Hey, uh, can you maybe, uh, not do it here? This job is all I have, and the manager is already looking to fire me. I'm thinking . . . you kill this kid, then cops and such . . ."

"Oh, is that what you're thinking?" A disgusted look crossed the old biker's face. "Go on, then. Bring your truck around. We'll take this party down the street."

The old biker turned away, and I didn't even think about it, just drove with my legs, put a shoulder on his belt, and slammed him into the wall. With blood in my eyes, I couldn't see much, but I could feel him, the old fucker. I got two good ones on the ribs and a couple on his face before someone pulled me off. I swung wild, and felt a lip burst. Then I was on the ground, and a dozen boots were working hard to keep me there. They swung in and out, and the world became a simple thing.

At first, it was pain.

Then it was the truck.

Then it was the ditch.

23

Across town, Gibby's parents ate a late dinner alone. French was angry at his son's absence, but so pleased with his wife the anger didn't matter. She laughed, and touched his hand, her lips bright with five years of forgotten smile. Pouring wine, he asked, "Why are you so happy tonight?"

Strangely timid, she shook her head. "I feel guilty talking about it."

"You're allowed to be happy."

"But Jason is still . . . He's still . . ."

"Sweetheart, Jason is beyond us now. Whatever we believe or wish to believe, it's up to the system."

"What *do* you believe?"

She posed the question in such a quiet, small manner that she seemed childlike to French. He placed his hand on hers. "Tonight, all I want to talk about is you." She looked away, but it was clear the comment pleased her. "This feels fresh—this moment. I don't want to lose it. Look at me, okay? Tell me your thoughts."

"You'll hate me for them."

"I won't."

"But you will. I know you will." She lowered her eyes, and a single tear hung on her lashes. "It's been so hard . . ."

"But you're happy now. Won't you tell me why?"

"You won't be angry?"

"Never."

She looked up, and her damp eyes filled with trust. Leaning so their faces were inches apart, she said in a soft and smiling whisper, "I don't feel him anymore."

"What do you mean?"

"In my heart, I don't feel him. Jason," she said, and the childlike smile was back.

That image stayed with French long after he'd taken his wife to bed. Lying in the darkness beside her, he studied the workings of his own troubled conscience.

What do I believe about my son?

Since Jason's arrest, French had walled himself away from as much emotion as possible, and, perhaps, he admitted now, from critical thought as well. That detachment had offered shelter and security, but he felt cracks in the foundations of those walls; and it was his wife who'd unsettled his defenses.

In my heart, I don't feel him . . .

French understood the need for self-protection, but could no longer hide from the more difficult truths. Too much of his son remained: the memory of his birth, the smallness of his hand. Rising in silence, he carried his guilt to the study, where he kept things dark, and dialed his partner's number from feel. "Are you still up?" he asked.

"Definitely."

"I'm coming over."

On the crosstown drive, French was as much cop as father.

Could he have done it?

Not possible.

But maybe . . .

It came down to a single thing.

"Hi, Ken. Sorry. I know it's late."

"Don't worry about it." Burklow stepped back to let him inside, then made drinks without asking. "Here. You look ragged. You okay?"

"It just hit me, is all."

"Jason, you mean?"

"Everything."

French kept his wife out of it. Her regression to near-infantile contentment was too personal to share.

"So." Burklow sat across a low table, his long, heavy frame cradled in a worn leather chair. "What can I do for you?"

"A favor."

"Ask it."

The response was automatic and honest. If French killed a man, Burklow would scream and fret, but, in the end, he'd help bury the body. It was that kind of friendship. "You spoke to me once of a friend at the Defense Department. He told you there's *war* and then *WAR,* and that Jason fought the second kind."

"Chris Ellis. He's high up."

"A good friend?"

"Good like you're good. Is he the favor?"

"It's time I knew more about Jason."

Burklow immediately stood, tall and unsmiling. "Wait here." He went to the back bedroom, and came back with a manila envelope tucked beneath his arm. He dropped it on the table between them.

DEPARTMENT OF DEFENSE

INTERNAL USE ONLY

Beneath those words were Jason's name and rank and serial number. "Jason's military records." Burklow sat again and picked up the whiskey. "I knew you'd want them."

"But . . . when?"

"I made the call yesterday. Drove up last night to collect them." French leaned away, as if afraid of so much unadulterated insight into the life of his oldest living son. "Most of it is classified. If you get caught with it, we're both screwed, and I mean *federally.*" He sipped again. "Are you sure you're ready for what's inside?"

French had been sure, but now was not. People said twenty-nine kills, but it could be fifty or a hundred; and both men understood enough of war to know it could be even worse than that. Friendly fire. Civilians. Black ops.

Not all kills were clean.

"After we found her," French said. "Tyra, I mean. I asked the medical examiner what could make a good man do bad things. What could break a man so horribly and irretrievably? He said it would be something big."

"And you're thinking, *War.*"

"Do you know anything that's bigger?"

A silence followed, both men lost in their own memories of war, and in the stillness, a phone rang, shrill enough to make them flinch. Burklow answered the phone and listened. "Yeah, he's here. Hang on."

He held out the receiver.

"This is Detective French."

"Detective, hi. This is Lauren at dispatch. I'm sorry to bother you so late. I tried your home first, but no one answered."

"It's all right, Lauren. What's the problem?"

"I hate to give you more bad news."

"Best just say it, then."

"Yes, sir. Four minutes ago, I took a radio call from a patrol unit working the industrial corridor on the south side. They found your son beaten senseless, facedown in a ditch two hundred yards from the Carriage Room. He's alert now, and declining medical attention. Patrol is still on-site, but they say he's hurt pretty badly. I can send paramedics, but thought you might want to keep this one quiet, given the past few days and the news and all."

French felt disconnected from the voice, the room. Maybe it was sleeplessness or the scotch, but what he'd heard made little sense. "I think you have a bad ID, Dispatch. Jason's in lockdown at Lanesworth."

"I'm sorry, Detective, but I'm not talking about Jason."

French drove fast, Burklow on shotgun. Beneath the hood, the engine screamed. On the roof, the cherry flashed. "You can't help him if you kill us getting there." They crested a hill, and the car rose on its shocks. "He's safe. He's with our people."

But the hammer stayed down. Words. None of them mattered.

"Bill, slow down. I mean it." They blistered an intersection, the stoplight steady red. "Jesus Christ."

French understood the concern, but something wild had filled his heart. "He's different, Ken. He's changing."

"Your son is changing. Fine. Slow down and we can talk about it."

French drifted a hard right, and left rubber on the road. "I think it's Jason," he said. "He's opened up something rebellious and dark. Watch Gibby's eyes, the way he looks at his mother and me, his whole life. He's trying to prove something."

"How about you get us there alive, and then we see what's what?"

It was hard to do, but French slowed enough to get them across town in one piece. It was a dismal part of the city, a place people lived because they had no choice, or because they wanted the drugs, the bought sex, the loss of self. Cops patrolled, but rarely.

Gibby shouldn't be here . . .

And yet he was. French saw the lights from four blocks out. They split the darkness; painted the ground. His youngest son sat on the curb, and looked painted, too: wet and red, and in places, black.

"Head wounds. You know how they bleed."

French did not respond. He cut across four lanes and smoked the tires when he stopped. One cop stood at the edge of an empty lot, the Carriage Room beyond him, down the street. The other cop was on the curb, talking to Gibby. When French got out of the car, he said, "Here's your father."

"What happened?"

"Somebody beat him badly, and dumped him in the ditch. He was crawling out when we saw him. I couldn't tell if he was white or black, male or female. Nothing but blood and mud and ditchwater."

"Son, are you okay?" He knelt, but Gibby looked away. "How bad is he?" French looked back at the uniformed officer.

"Cuts and bruises, maybe some damaged ribs. Most of the blood is from gashes in the scalp. I'd say somebody got him on the ground and kicked him pretty good. I don't think the blood is all his, though. Looks like he gave a little back."

"Has he said anything?"

"He didn't want me to call you."

"But he's lucid?"

"If not, I'd have transported him myself."

"Okay, thanks. Both of you."

The cop squatted beside Gibby, one hand on his shoulder. "Your father knows what's right for you. Hospital. Doctors. You listen to him. Talk to him."

"Yes, sir."

No slurring or confusion. That was something. Hell, it was everything. When the patrol car left, French sat beside his son, their shoulders almost touching. "Do you remember what happened?"

"I don't want to talk about it."

"I need something better than that."

Gibby shrugged, and French caught his partner's eye.

Rebellious.

Dangerous.

"Were you at the Carriage Room? Are the people who did this to you there? Would you know them if you saw them?" Still nothing. Not even movement. "Is this about Jason?"

"Can we go home now?"

"No, son. Hospital. Come on."

French got his son in the back of the car, then turned across traffic, watching the Carriage Room as he did. It was the only place open for three full blocks. He wanted answers, and thought he'd find them there. He wanted to kick in doors, tear the place down.

"Just be cool, Bill." Burklow kept it soft. "We can come back later."

At the emergency room, Gibby walked on his own, but it wasn't pretty. French spoke to the doctor, and dashed off a final signature. "If he tells you what happened, I want to know."

"You're aware of patient confidentiality, Detective."

"He's my son."

"Your son is eighteen."

"Just do what you can, Doc. Patch him up. Cover the worst of it. His mother will have a fit as it is. Bandages can't make it any worse."

An orderly got Gibby into a wheelchair, and pushed him toward the double doors. "I'll be right here, son."

Gibby did not respond or look back. When he was gone, Burklow said, "He's in shock. Give him time."

"I think I'm out of time."

"That's the worry talking."

"Why would he go to the Carriage Room? Or be on that side of town at all? It has to be about Jason." French moved, unable to stand still. "We should canvass while it's fresh. We need witnesses, the location of Gibby's car. I want the bastards who did this."

"Let's go, then. Let's do it."

"I told Gibby I'd wait. I can't leave him."

"I'll stay. I'll get him home."

"Yeah?"

"You're coming out of your skin as it is. You do what you need to do, but call in backup for the Carriage Room. I don't want you in there alone."

The idea moved through French like a drug. He wanted to move and do, to cop the shit out of that bar.

"One last thing." Burklow put a hand on his partner's shoulder. "Young men push back. They test the world, the father. It's part of growing up."

"I know that, Ken. I *have* raised two others."

"What I'm saying is that any kid but this one would have pushed back years ago. Right or wrong, you and Gabrielle have kept him in a bubble, and the bubble has kept him quiet."

"Maybe you're right. Maybe this is my fault."

"Listen, brother. Rebellion is natural in any red-blooded kid. Whether Jason stirred something up or not isn't the point. Same with the way you've raised him. The cause could be as simple as a girl or graduation, or it might simply be Gibby's time to crack the shell. All I'm saying is this: That silence you hate . . . the pushback. Don't make it personal."

French understood the logic, but the understanding didn't help. He needed the *why* and the *who*.

Why had his son been on that side of town?

Who stomped him bloody and left him in the ditch?

In the car, French radioed dispatch, requesting backup at the Carriage Room and an all-points on Gibby's Mustang. He'd parked it somewhere, or someone had ditched it. The location would tell him a lot. After the call, it was another fast drive back to the dangerous side of town. By the time he arrived, it was after midnight, and felt like it. Even the Carriage Room seemed quiet, with only a few cars in the lot and not a soul outside. French studied the scene from fifty yards out, then rolled in soft and slow, flashing his lights once when he saw a patrol car, dark in the shadows. He parked beside it, and found the same officers who'd discovered Gibby in the ditch. The driver said, "How's the kid?"

"Still with the doctor."

"Is he talking about what happened?"

"Not yet. How long have you been here?"

"Eight minutes. Maybe ten."

"Any movement?"

"The bartender's there, and a skinny girl, sweeping. Two old drunks are pretty much facedown on the bar. Everything else looks quiet."

French studied the building and the darkness around it. Quiet could be dangerous at times, but this did not feel like one of those moments. "It wasn't like this before."

"It's been two hours since we found your son. Blue lights. The cherry. Some people spook easy."

"Yeah. Maybe."

"Listen." The uniformed cop hooked an elbow through the open window. "We'll play this any way you want, but I'm not sure you need us. The bartender. A couple of old drunks."

French didn't blame them. End of shift. A long night. "It's fine. You boys go on home." He watched them go, then locked the car, and walked to the bar. The lights inside were up, a record spinning on the jukebox.

Allman Brothers.

"Ain't Wastin' Time No More"

The uniforms had been right about the men at the bar. One slept. The other slumped, peeling the label off a bottle of Budweiser. The skinny girl with the broom was sweeping up dust in the far right corner. As French watched, she did a little dance move with the broom, startled to complete the turn and see a strange man standing where none had been a moment before.

"I'm looking for the bartender." He flashed the tin, and she pointed at an open door as a man stepped through from a back room. Tall and narrow-shouldered, he seemed familiar to French, a round-faced man with a twelve-pack under one arm, and two vodkas bottlenecked in the other hand.

"We're closed," he said.

"Sign says *Open*."

"We're closed to cops." The bartender put the bottles on the bar, then barked at the girl with the broom. "Eyes on the floor, Janelle. It won't sweep itself."

Janelle twitched into motion, no dance left. French assumed there was a gun behind the bar, so he drew back enough coat to show the revolver on his hip.

Just to be clear.

To be sure.

Crossing the room, he kept his eyes on everyone, but mostly the bartender. He'd seen him somewhere before, ten or twelve years ago. Snapping his fingers, he said, "Hey. Lawnmower man."

The bartender scowled, shaking his head.

But French was right. He couldn't remember the name, but in the spring of '61, this guy and some idiot friend robbed a late-night market, and tried to escape on a riding mower. He'd caught them a mile down the road, still holding cash and stolen beer, still drunk, and entirely, hilariously out of gas.

The booking officers had had a field day at their expense.

So had the local paper.

French said, "Ah, good times," but that's not what showed on his face. He wanted the man afraid, so he put that in his eyes, instead, the kind of cop who could beat an innocent man into confession, then take a child for ice cream with the blood still wet on his knuckles. "This kid." French placed a photograph on the bar. "Was he in here tonight?"

"Never seen him."

"Someone beat him half to death, then dropped him in a ditch two hundred yards from your front door."

"What happens beyond that door is not my problem."

"Thing is, lawnmower man, the kid is my son. I mention that simple fact so you might imagine the kind of fire I'll rain down on anyone who lies to me about this. It's a pot you don't want to stir. Not tonight. Not with me at the bottom of it. Look at the picture again."

"I don't need to."

"You really do."

"It's like I said. We're closed to cops."

The bartender began to turn away, but French caught his wrist, and jerked him halfway across the bar. He fought back, but fear had always made French strong, and he was afraid for his son. "I have three questions," he said. "So I suggest you look closely at this photograph." He held the photo in one hand, and used his other to squeeze so hard that bones ground together in the bartender's wrist. "Was my son here? What was he doing here? Who was he with?" The questions came fast, but need was the other side of fear. "We'll start at the beginning. Was this young man here tonight?"

"No, man. No. Jesus." The bones ground audibly. "No kid, not tonight. Dude, I swear. Come on, that hurts!"

"I don't believe you."

"Why would I lie?" French twisted harder, and felt bones flex. "Oh God! Oh Jesus!"

The pressure stayed on until tears sprang up in the bartender's eyes. "What about you?" French swung on the drunks at the bar. One shook his head, terrified. The other fell off the back of his stool, then ran for the exit, stumbling twice before French tripped him from behind, and pinned him with a knee. "Why are you running? What are you so afraid of?"

The old drunk was thin and frail, but a creature had torn loose in French's chest. "Look at the picture." He shoved it at the old man's face; caught the jaw, twisting it back. "I said, look at it! He was here, yes?" Fingers pressed on whiskers and brittle bone. The old man moaned in pain, but there were answers here, and French would tear them out if he had to. *The bartender. The old men.* In some dark place, he knew not even the girl was safe. "Was he here? Who was he with?" The old man began to cry. "I'll ask you one more time . . ."

"Stop it, please! You're hurting him!"

It was the girl, ashen and afraid. She had both hands on her heart, a slip of a girl.

"He can't even speak. Don't you see? He never has."

She touched her mouth, and French looked down at the old man, seeing him for the first time, a frail old drunk, wild-eyed and afraid, moaning wetly as he worked a mouth with no tongue.

French stumbled back, horrified by the extent of his fear and rage, and by the creature that followed behind. He wanted to apologize, but knew there were no sufficient words. So he showed his palms instead, backing away until he found night air and the quiet and his car. From behind the wheel, he watched people flee the bar, the old men stumbling off together, the bartender leaving next, and then the young woman, who locked the building's door before shaking out a cigarette and placing it between her lips. She didn't notice the police car until half the cigarette was gone, then she started his way, and he watched her come. The narrow waist. The shadows for eyes. If she was afraid, it didn't show. She put a hand on the roof, and looked inside. French was unsure what to say, so he spoke in cop. "You shouldn't lock up alone in a place like this. It's dangerous."

"Normally, I don't, but you scared the bartender pretty bad."

Up close, the girl was pretty and younger than she'd first seemed, maybe only eighteen. "About what happened in there . . ."

"You kind of lost your shit. Yeah, I saw it."

"Is he okay?"

"Old Tom? He's tougher than he looks."

"He's a regular?"

"Like the rain."

She smoked more, and studied him with a contemplative air. French thought something was happening, but couldn't think clearly. The way he'd behaved, that blind rage. The girl was still watching him, her eyes either gray or dark blue. "How old are you?" he asked.

"Eighteen."

"And your parents know you work in a place like this?"

"So what?" She frowned around the cigarette. "Now you're the good cop?"

"I've pulled bodies from this place. Before your time, but more than once."

She shrugged, quietly amused. "I think I'm safe enough."

"You can't know that."

"My father is pulling a dime for the club. Central Prison."

"So this place?"

"It's easy money, and it's like I said, no one touches me unless they want every Hells Angel in the state gunning for them."

"This is a club bar?"

"Yes and no. A couple nights a week."

"And the bartender?"

"A wannabe."

French was feeling better now: slower thoughts, some kind of order. "It's Janelle, right?"

"It is."

"What can I do for you, Janelle?"

She looked away, and small teeth appeared as she caught her bottom lip. "That boy is really your son?"

"He was here, then. Did you see what happened?"

"I'm no rat. I noticed him, is all."

"And . . . ?"

"And he was my age and cute and kind of sweet-looking."

"He almost died, right up there in the ditch, dumped like trash with his head kicked in." She shook her head, then showed the same twilight eyes. "It's just us, Janelle. All alone, no one around." She hesitated, but French was close. "What would your father do if it were you, half-dead in a ditch? What would you want him to do? My son is only eighteen. He's your age . . ."

"Okay, all right. Enough. Jesus." She lit another cigarette. "Look, it's like I said. I was working, and I saw him, and I paid attention. Good-looking. Kind of earnest. I couldn't hear everything he said, but I know he was asking about Tyra Norris . . ."

"*Tyra Norris.* You're certain about that name?"

"Hey, I'm no rat, but I'm not stupid, either. He was asking about Tyra Norris—I heard it plain as day—and before someone killed that bitch dead, she was the original slut-whore from hell. Bikers. Truckers. Even a few cops." She pointed with the cigarette, one eye half-closed. "Maybe that's what got your boy beat."

In the driveway an hour later, French saw a light in Gibby's room. He wanted desperately to see his son, to know he was okay, but also to push hard about Tyra Norris and the Carriage Room. But time, he decided, was a friend. Let the resentments settle, the angers fade. Going to his office instead, French poured a drink, and squared Jason's military records on the desk, staring at the envelope until the drink was gone.

Three in the morning.

Lots of dark left.

Taking a breath to steady his resolve, he broke the seal and started reading. It was all there in photographs and plain print: the lost years and the war, the life of his middle son. It took an hour to skim the file, and two more to read it again more slowly. Turning off the light, French tried to understand the things he'd learned of his son and the darkness of this particular war. It was not easy. There was no clear path. He was exhausted and hurting, but when the sun rose, he was still at the desk, still dumbfounded, thunderstruck, blown the absolute fuck away.

24

Jason woke on a hard bunk, and knew, even without windows, that it was not yet sunrise. That was the rhythm of war and prison. Too many bloody dawns and dead friends. In the dark, he did push-ups and stretched, then trained for forty minutes, not just the close-quarter combat techniques taught to every marine in Force Recon—the combination of Okinawan karate, judo, tae kwon do, and jujitsu perfected by Bill Miller in 1956—but also a devastating blend of Van An Phai and Vovinam, learned across two years from a colonel in the South Vietnamese army. The movements were fluid, fast, precise. He worked until the sweat poured and the guards came to take him back to death row. One, he knew. Kudravetz. The other was new to X's detail. They shackled him in silence, and no one spoke on the long walk. No one needed to. At death row, they removed the restraints and sent him down to X.

"Good morning, Jason."

Jason took the final step down, and met X where he stood beneath the stone arch. "It's a little early."

"And yet you're not my first visitor."

Jason frowned because X did nothing without reason; *said* nothing without reason. He wanted Jason to ask about the visitor, so Jason did not.

Eventually, X shrugged. "You remember Reece, I'm sure. A blunt instrument, admittedly, but predictable when such things matter."

Jason was still trying to gauge the moment. A smile. A frown. In the subbasement, they rarely meant the normal things. "How about you tell me why I'm here."

"You're here because I found yesterday unsatisfactory. Because I went to bed unhappy, and woke thinking we should try again." X turned for the cells, and Jason followed with the same wariness. At the second cell, X gestured at a table set for breakfast. "Bacon and eggs, grapefruit and pastry. This is honey from the warden's wife. She's begun to keep bees, apparently."

He offered a chair, and Jason sat stiffly, watching X do the same. He was clean-shaven and finely dressed, but his face was bruised and taped, his knuckles scraped raw. X noticed the studied glance, and shrugged a second time. "One of the Pagans, late last night. I think his name was Patterson."

"*Was* Patterson?"

"Was. Is."

"Why a Pagan?"

"I may spend my days below ground, but I do hear things, rumbles of displeasure from some of the Pagans. They seem to believe you stole from the club and put a few bullets in one of their shot callers. I made it known that you are under my protection."

"Is that why I'm here? So I can thank you?"

"For now, it's about breakfast. For later . . ." X made an expansive gesture. "Discourse. Debate. A few well-fought contests in the days which remain."

"Discourse and debate."

"*Honest* discourse. *Vigorous* debate."

"You had Tyra killed for the sake of a conversation?"

"In part, yes." X frowned for the first time, shaking his head. "But also because she was cruel, selfish, and vain, an utter waste of life."

"And what of *my* life?"

"You'll lose a few days of it. A small price."

"No, X. Not a few days. I'll be here long after they kill you. The lights will flicker, and I'll be here to see it happen. Ten years later, I'll still be here. You've assured as much: the photographs, the murder weapon."

"Yes, well . . ." X poured coffee for them both. "You've known for some time that I am not a nice man."

He lifted a cup, his attitude so dismissive that Jason found it impossible to keep his anger in check.

Tyra's death.

His freedom.

X must have seen the conflict in Jason's face, yet acted oblivious. "Tell me again, Jason. How long since you left this place?"

"Two months and nine days."

"And, in that time, did you think of me? Beyond what I'd chosen to share, were you curious about my life before this place? Did you search out the articles, the documentaries? The public record is quite extensive."

"No." Jason clenched his jaw. "I left here knowing everything I needed to know about your life and the people you killed. If I forgot half of what you told me, I'd still know too much."

"Do you know how they caught me?"

Jason did, in fact, know a lot about X's life before prison. In spite of what he'd said, he'd watched both documentaries, read the articles and police interviews, the in-depth profiles in the glossy magazines. No journalist had all the facts, of course, and no cop alive knew how many people X had actually killed. But Jason could name them all. He knew what they'd looked like and how they'd died and what small flicker of life had drawn X like a moth from the dark. He knew their last words and how they'd begged and what they'd felt like and smelled like, and how X had placed his tongue, once, on a still-beating heart that *tasted of salt, and felt like warm vinyl.*

When the cops finally caught up with X, even the most arrogant admitted it was blind luck or providence.

But for this . . .

If not for that . . .

Now Jason had to wonder. X *had* raised the subject. That meant some part of him wanted to talk about it. Or it was part of some larger game.

Misdirection.

Distraction.

X's great advantage lay in the fact that his goals were his alone, and unknowable. He could spend six months plotting a single encounter, or envision, in an instant and with absolute clarity, the long weeks of torture that would lead at last to some poor soul's death. It was no different in the subbasement. Nothing could be taken for granted. Face value did not exist.

"How *did* they catch you?"

"I thought you disliked tales of my youth."

"I do. But you did raise the subject."

"The story is boring. I've already moved on." He waved his cigarette to underline the point. "To business, then. Reece came for a reason. So did you."

"Discourse and debate?"

X disliked the tone, but didn't make it an issue. "*Honest* discourse," he said. "*Vigorous* debate. And when we fight, I expect that same vigor and commitment. Yesterday, you gave me reason to doubt." X slipped one hand into a pocket. "This is to assure your commitment, to know that in these final days, I have the Jason I've so long admired." He placed a photograph facedown on the table. "Reece brought it just for you. We'll call it a *token*."

Jason reached for the photograph, and X gave him long seconds to take it all in: the young man's face, the light on his cheek, and the way he stood. "Your parents' driveway, I believe. He favors you, don't you think? The intelligent eyes. The generous mouth." Jason tore his gaze from the photograph of his little brother, and X was waiting with a smile on his face. "So we're clear," he said. "So we understand each other."

25

After the hospital, I stared for a long time at the stranger in my bathroom mirror. He had one good eye, the other swollen shut. A bandage wrapped the crown of his head, and the skin of his face was a camouflage of purples, greens, and iodine browns. The same stains mottled his arms and ribs, and when the stranger took the bandage from his head, I saw cruel black lines where his scalp had been laid bare and stitched back together. I frowned, and the stranger did, too.

That was about our father.

There should have been twenty cops at that bar: bright lights and guns and hard men asking hard questions. Instead, there'd been only me.

I blinked, and the stranger disappeared. I couldn't remember all of the fight, but the ditch stayed with me: the taste of water, and of his boot, the smell of his skin when, at last, he'd let me breathe. *Listen to me, kid. Die or not, I don't give a shit. But if you talk to the cops or anyone else or come out of this ditch before we're good and gone, I'll stomp a mudhole in your face so dark and forever you'll never see daylight again . . .*

He'd told me to stay, and like a dog at his feet, I'd done it. I'd waited as footsteps faded, and engines fired, and silence came behind. Even then, I'd stayed in the water, deep down in the grass and mud. I'd stayed until the crying ceased, then crawled up and out, into the headlights and the anger and the shame.

• • •

When the new day came, my father did, too. I was on the bed, and down to one emotion, but anger could wear a lot of faces: hostility, bitterness, the cold, quiet fury I'd come to know best.

"Come in."

I kept my voice flat, and stood because him looking down was not going to be okay with me. He came in, closed the door, and we met in that eye-to-eye place.

"Can we talk about it?" he asked.

"*You* can."

His eyes moved across my face and scalp. He made a small gesture, pointing at my head. "You should have left the bandage on."

"I shouldn't have needed it in the first place."

"You're angry."

"Because it should have been the cops."

He nodded as if some suspicion had been confirmed. "You were there for Jason. You were asking about Tyra."

"Someone should believe him, evidence or not."

"You're right . . ."

"Prison or not, Vietnam or not, drugs or not—"

"Stop, just stop." He reached for my shoulders, and when I stepped back, he followed, both hands up as if to gentle a horse. "You're right, son. I'm trying to tell you that. It's why I'm here. Just listen to me, please."

But the anger was simple and clean. I understood it. "He's all alone."

"I understand that."

"It could have been me."

That stopped him cold, but truth could be like that.

"I knew Tyra, too. She was in my car. I've been to her house. I've seen her angry and drunk and bleeding. What if the evidence said *I'd* killed her? Would you treat me like Jason? Let them send me off to prison?" My father stepped closer, and I said, "Don't touch me."

He looked away, out of embarrassment or decency. "I should have been there for your brother. I see that now. From the first moment, I should have been there. But I was also in shock. Son, look at me." He waited until I did. "Tyra's murder was the worst I've ever seen, so horrible I'll never forget it, not a bit of it. And the evidence against Jason is overwhelming."

He looked lost, but gathered up the threads of his conviction. "When Robert died, it killed me. It killed us all, I know. But then I lost Jason, too, not in the same way, but the boy I'd raised was gone, just . . ." He opened an empty hand. "But I still had you. I had you and your mother and this chest full of fear, this mountain, Gibby, this *mountain* of fear that if I slipped or made a mistake, I might lose you, too. An accident. The war.

"A few hours ago, I learned some things about your brother's past that help me understand the man he's become, not just the anger and the quiet but that maddening inflexibility of his. He's not the son I remember— not even close—but parts of him are still there, buried maybe, but not gone and not imagined." He rolled his heavy shoulders, all but begging. "I needed answers, son, and decided to go looking. Maybe I should have done it sooner. Maybe it would have made a difference."

"What kind of answers?"

"Things he won't talk about. His training and the war, the things he did there." He held up a hand, forestalling my questions. "It's classified, son, stolen information. I could go to prison for knowing what I know."

"I have a right to know, same as you."

"I can't allow you to take that risk."

"I'm eighteen years old. That's not for you to decide."

"You live under my roof. So yes, it is."

My hands clenched. His were fisted, too. "Is that your final word?"

"It has to be."

"Then I would like to be alone."

He searched my eyes, but I kept them cold and unforgiving. Even so, he lingered as if the rift between us was a wound that time alone could heal.

There weren't enough hours in the day.

I made sure he saw that, too.

Chance was outside when his mother stepped onto the porch. She had coffee in one hand, but looked tired. The sun was barely up. "Have you fixed it yet?"

Chance considered the bicycle in the dirt where he knelt. He'd gone over the curb too hard, and blown a tube, damaged some spokes. "The tube is patched, but a couple of the spokes are broken through."

"Well, leave it for now. You have a phone call. It's Gibby's dad." She shrugged as if the world rarely made sense and she'd long ago stopped trying to understand it. "Take the call, then come eat your breakfast."

They had a single phone, so Chance crossed old, brown carpet and sat on the old, brown sofa. "Hello."

"Chance, good morning. It's Bill French. I'm sorry to call so early, but I need to talk about Gibby."

The call was brief but troubling. In the kitchen, Chance's mother spoke from the stove. "What was that all about?"

"It was strange."

"Here. You can eat while you talk." She put a plate on the table. "Go on. Before it gets cold."

Chance ate some corn muffin; picked at the eggs. "He wants me to come over. He said Gibby needs me."

"It's a school day."

"He's not going to school. I think something might be really wrong." Chance waited until she lit a cigarette, and crossed her arms. "Can you give me a ride?"

The drive was out of her way and would make her late to work, but Chance's mother didn't complain. And when she parked and looked at her son, the smile came as easily as always. "You tell that Gibby I love him."

"Yes, ma'am."

"And this one's for you." Chance leaned close to take the kiss on his cheek. "You be a good boy."

He climbed from the car, watched her go, then mounted the broad staircase. A note was on the door.

Hi, Chance. Go on in. I had to leave for work, but Gibby's in his room.
Thanks for this.

Opening the door, Chance stepped into a familiar space that seemed eerily quiet. He and Gibby went way back, so he remembered the Christmas parties and the lively kitchen, the thunder of steps as Jason and Robert chased each other up one stairwell and down another. His envies had been simpler then. Brothers. A father. Even now, it was not about the money or the house. Nor was it a dark kind of envy. Maybe it wasn't envy at all. But there was a steadiness to his friend.

And then there was the war . . .

Chance lived in such *fear* of it! It's why he flirted shamelessly and picked fights and never backed down, because none of those things would kill him, or blind him or take his face. He'd seen that at the airport, once: a soldier with his skin melted from the hairline down. Since then, Chance had lived in dread of his eighteenth birthday, dreaming of all the ways to die in Vietnam, not shot cleanly like Robert, but disemboweled or impaled or tortured to death in Hỏa Lò Prison. He hadn't registered for the draft, and if he ever did, he wouldn't go if they called him. He was afraid and Gibby was not, a simple truth too painful to look at straight on.

So *was* it envy Chance felt?

It felt more like resentment.

That was impossible, though, and way too dark, so Chance made his way to Gibby's door, ignoring an unusual desire to turn and leave. Opening the door, he said, "Dude, you okay?"

"Chance, hey. I'm glad it's you." Gibby stood at the window with his back turned. "I thought you were my dad."

"Yeah, he asked me to come, believe it or not."

"Did he tell you why?"

Chance opened his mouth to answer, but Gibby turned so the light caught his face. "Oh shit, you did it." Chance covered his mouth, shaking his head. "Where'd you go? The Carriage Room?"

"Yeah."

"Bikers?"

"A few of 'em, I guess."

Chance moved closer. His friend's face was a wreck. "I told you not to do it."

"I know you did."

"You should have taken me."

"It wouldn't have made a difference."

Gibby limped across the room, and Chance got a better look at his face. "Man, I am so sorry. I should have tried harder to talk you out of it. When I saw how serious you were, I should have gone with you. But damn, you really are an idiot."

Gibby rocked his palm side to side. *A little of this, a little of the other . . .*

"You're not going back there, are you?"

"They'd kill me if I did."

The certainty in his voice made Chance realize how close it must have been.

"Did you learn anything?"

"They knew Jason and Tyra. I'm pretty sure that they're the ones Jason fought last week." Gibby dragged a faded sweatshirt over his head, then eased a ball cap onto his head. "How do I look?"

"Depends on where we're going."

"To see a girl."

"You don't have a car."

"My mother does."

"She won't let you take it."

"It doesn't matter." Gibby slipped dark glasses over his eyes. "I'm not asking for permission."

For French, the morning was about compartmentalization.

Lock down the personal.

Do the job.

First thing he did was go to the station and check the call logs for his son's car. Uniforms had discovered it outside an abandoned warehouse at 4:47 in the morning. French pictured the address, and worked the math in his head. Nine or ten miles from the Carriage Room. Too far for Gibby to walk.

Ditched, then.

From there, it was a short drive to the municipal impound yard. The shield got him through the gate. Finding the car was not so easy.

"Sixty-six Mustang?" The mechanic was grease-stained and bored.

"That's right."

"Color?"

"Maroon. It came in early."

"Well, now." The mechanic sipped from a Dr Pepper can. "I didn't get here 'til seven, and it's not on the clipboard."

"Check again, please."

He took his time, pages turning with the same slow, licked-finger rhythm. "Wait, yep. Here it is." He pressed a damp finger onto a single page, twelve sheets down. "Problem is, you said *Mustang*. The paperwork says *Ford*. You also said *maroon,* and this says *dark red.*"

"Are you screwing with me?"

"Why would anyone *screw* with a cop?"

The smile showed in his eyes, but city employees with a bitter streak were hardly rare, so French gave him the win. Working through the bay, he opened a door on to an acre and a half of parked vehicles, and found the car where he'd been told to look.

Registration in the glove box.

Plenty of gas.

French pulled on rubber gloves, and searched it front to back. Nothing. Returning to the small office, he found the same mechanic sipping on the same can of soda. "I want that car moved to deep impound."

"Huh? It was just a tow."

"I'll have a forensics crew here in thirty minutes." French reached across the desk, snatched up the phone, and spoke as he dialed. "In the meantime, move the car. Do it now. I'll need your fingerprints, too."

"Huh?"

"You and whoever hooked up the tow."

When French returned to the station, he went to see the captain. David Martin was a fair man, but a stickler for the rules. French didn't care. He barged into the office.

"I want in on the Tyra Norris case."

"There's this new thing." Captain Martin leaned away from the desk. "It's called *knocking.*"

"Yes, I've heard of it."

The captain regarded him carefully, twisting a pen between his fingers. "So your son, at last."

"I should have done this sooner."

"Why didn't you?"

"Shock. Disbelief. I don't know. Too much cop and not enough father. I thought like the rest of you."

That was about recovered photographs and the murder weapon, a slab of evidence thick enough to bury Jason alive.

"Kathy," the captain called out, and his assistant appeared around the door. "Two coffees, please. Cream for the detective." She left, and he gestured at a chair. "Let's talk about Gibby first."

"You heard?"

"A cop's son found half-dead in a ditch? Yeah, I heard."

"This is not about Gibby. War or no war, I don't think Jason is a killer."

"I still can't let you near the case."

"Unofficially. Off the books . . ."

"Not even that."

"Then dark. Just the two of us."

For an instant, the captain's conviction seemed to waver, but the door opened, and Kathy appeared with coffees. "Cream for the detective, and black for you."

"Thank you, Kathy. You can close the door." She did as he'd asked. The captain left his coffee untouched. "One question, Bill, and I want an honest answer. Did you recognize Tyra Norris at the crime scene? Did you know then who she was, that she'd been sleeping with Jason?"

French opened his mouth, but had no words.

Surprisingly, the captain's eyes softened. He nodded gently; his voice was soft, too. "Go see your son, Bill. Go be a father."

The warden was in his office when the call came from the front gate. "You're sure of that ID?"

"Detective William French. I'm holding his credentials right now."

"Hold on a second."

Bruce Wilson lowered the phone as if a few extra seconds would make the problem go away. He was not a bad warden or a bad man. He'd done the best he could in difficult circumstances. Of course, there was always the risk a moment like this would come, the first domino that would bring the rest down.

"Are you there?" the guard asked.

"Tell him he has to wait."

Dropping the phone onto its cradle, the warden left the office at a fast walk. His secretary tried to stop him with a question, but he said, "Not now," and left her looking hurt. At death row, he cleared security and took the stairs down. X was painting, his back to the cell door. The painting looked like Jason French. "We have a problem."

X declined to turn. "I suspect what you mean is that *you* have a problem."

"Jason's father is at the gate."

"Not *much* of a problem."

"He's a city detective who wants to see his son. If I say no, he'll want to know why. That means questions I'm not prepared to answer. Jason would not be here without my involvement. His father knows that."

"So let the man see his son."

"What if he talks?"

"He won't."

"You can't know that!"

X turned, lifting an eyebrow.

"I'm very sorry." The warden showed his hands, and lowered his voice. "What if this cop pulls on the wrong thread? What happens then?"

"Jason knows what is expected of him. There will be no threads. I assure you."

"Okay, okay." A nervous nod. "What else can I do?"

"You can remember, Warden Wilson." X dabbed his brush into bloodred paint, and touched it to the canvas. "You can remember your hard-learned lessons, and act accordingly."

French didn't know what to expect from his son, but this cold and distant emptiness was not it. His eyes looked vacuumed out, his voice monotone, as a guard secured his cuffs to the table. "I don't want you here. You shouldn't have come."

French struggled to understand. He'd expected *something,* anger, at least. "I came to talk. To apologize."

"Apologize? Really?"

"If you'll hear me out—"

"Why now and not before?"

French had no idea what to say. A moment earlier his thoughts had been clear—*so clear.*

"Just go," Jason said. "Go home."

"Not this time, son. There are too many things to say, and too many years between us."

"Oh, you came to talk *years.*"

"Mistakes made. Things I wish I'd done differently."

"Family history," Jason said.

"That's part of it."

"Okay." Jason blinked once, and slowly. "Let's talk about why I went to war."

"You went because of Robert, because he died a hard death, and you were young and angry—"

"Is that what you tell yourself?"

"Isn't it the truth?"

"Do you really want to talk about mistakes?"

"It's why I'm here."

"I heard her that night." Jason studied his father with those empty eyes. "The night we learned that Robert died, I heard what she said. That's the reason I went to war."

French thought, *Gabrielle, dear God . . .*

"Son, she was distraught."

"Distraught or not, she wished it was me instead of Robert, me with a bullet in the heart. How could I stay in the house after that? Or look at her? Or even at myself? Vietnam was all I had left."

French looked for the right words, but there *were* no right words. How could there be? Gabrielle had always loved Robert the most. He was the first and the gentlest, the closest to her heart of all their sons. Jason, in contrast, had always been sharp, sardonic, and quick, a needle to handle with care. It was a difficult truth to admit, but there it was. Gabrielle had a favorite; she'd always had a favorite. "Do you hate us, then?"

Jason shook his head. "I have no feelings for you at all."

"I refuse to believe that."

"Believe it or not. I don't really care. Just stay away from this place, and keep Gibby away, too."

"Son, please. Let's talk about this."

"You may not remember, but I tried that once." Jason stood, moving in such silence not even the chains made a sound. "Guard," he said. "We're finished here."

26

Chance rode shotgun in the big Cadillac, and looked for signs of the best friend he'd known for most of his life. This one seemed quieter, edgy, and unforgiving. He squinted as he drove, lines at the corners of his eyes. It seemed wrong to be in a "borrowed" car, but Gibby didn't seem to care about that, either. He spun the wheel with ease, like it was not his mother's car. When he nodded, the lines on his face seemed to deepen. "Last time I saw Sara, she wouldn't talk to me. This time will be different. Watch and see."

Chance knew little of what Gibby intended, only that Tyra was the dead girl, and Sara the roommate. "What do you think she'll tell you? I mean, best-case scenario, what are you hoping for?"

"I need information about Tyra. Where she worked. Other friends. Other boyfriends. Anything that's not right. I need a place to start. If anyone can give that to me, it's Sara." He slowed the big car. "This is her street."

"Looks expensive."

"That's her place, the third one down."

Chance watched the condo as the car slid to a stop at the curb. The curtains were closed. A banged-up Mercedes was parked in the driveway.

"That's Tyra's car. The one she wrecked at Jason's."

"Does Sara have a car?"

"I don't see it." Gibby stepped out onto the street, and Chance followed him to the sidewalk, then up five steps to the stoop. "That doesn't look right." The front door stood ajar.

"Come on, man. Just ring the bell."

But Gibby was already inside, so Chance followed him to a living room littered with empty wine bottles and dirty glasses. "That's not right, either." Gibby pointed at an open window, curtains stirring in the breeze. "Air conditioner is running. I can hear it. Sara!"

Gibby took the stairs two at a time, and Chance followed at his heels. The first bedroom was a mess, clothing everywhere, the bed unmade. "Tyra's, I think."

The second bedroom was more neatly kept, with pale, pink walls and views on to the park across the street. The bed was slept-in but empty, a pile of tiny clothes beside it. Terry cloth short shorts. A tank top. Chance picked up a framed photograph: two girls in the Mercedes, top down, one of them flashing a peace sign at whoever held the camera. "That's her?"

"The blonde with the peace sign. The other one is Tyra."

The blankets on the bed were thrown back, the fitted sheet pulled free at three corners. A water glass had spilled on the bedside table. The lamp was knocked over and broken. On the far side of the bed, Gibby found a wad of wet cloth balled against the second pillow. He picked it up. "It's wet. It stinks."

"What is it?"

Gibby dropped it on the floor, wiping his fingers on his jeans. "Something bad, some kind of chemical. I think we need to call the cops."

"You mean your father?"

"Not my father. Not this time."

It took Burklow twenty minutes to get there, and he came inside with a wary glance. "Your call was pretty cryptic."

"I thought we should talk in person."

"Tell me first why you're here."

His eyes flicked from Chance's face to mine, and I answered with a shrug. "I wanted to talk to Sara."

"I mean, why are you inside her apartment?"

"The door was open."

"So you walked in?"

"Basically."

"All right. Walk me through it."

There wasn't much, but I told him what I knew. The rumpled bed and broken lamp, the wadded-up ball of sticky, sweet-smelling cloth.

Burklow cocked an eyebrow. "Sweet-smelling, but with a *burn*?"

"Back of my throat, yeah."

"What else?"

"A back window is open, too, air-conditioning running on high."

"What did you touch?"

"The door. The banister. The rag on the bed."

"That's it?"

"The glass on the bedside table. I stood it upright."

He pointed at Chance. "What about you?"

"I didn't touch a thing."

"Which room is Sara's?"

"Top left."

He glanced at the stairwell, then studied the living room for long seconds, taking in the bottles, the dirty dishes. "Why didn't you call your father about this?"

"We're not really talking."

Burklow made a sound in his throat, his eyes on everything but me. "Stay here. Don't touch anything."

He examined locks at the door and window, then took the stairs up. He was back in two minutes, very cop. "Come with me." We followed him to the front door. He checked the sidewalks and the street. "Did anyone see you come inside?"

"I don't think so."

"But people were around?"

"Yeah, sure. Cars. Bikes. Regular people."

"Anyone especially close or paying particular attention?"

"Ken, what's going on?"

"You boys need to leave."

"Why?"

"Listen, kid. You called me for help, and I came. Now, I'm saying *jump*, and that's what I need you to do."

I didn't move. I made a point of it.

"All right, damn it. Fine." Ken leaned in close, more cop now than ever. "The window's been forced, but the front door is undamaged. That means someone came in through the back, and left by the front. Could be a simple burglary. Smash and grab. Happens all the time. But the rag you found—that sweet smell—that's chloroform. It's an anesthetic."

"What are you saying?"

"Forced entry. Chloroform. Signs of a struggle. Worst-case scenario, someone took her."

I said, "Jesus, Sara . . ."

"That's worst case for *her*. We haven't talked about you." I touched my chest, and his features hardened. "Listen, son. Tyra's dead and Sara is missing. Martinez and Smith already have doubts about you, especially Martinez."

Chance said, "Wait. What doubts?"

Burklow scowled, but answered the question. "After Tyra turned up dead, they found Gibby here with Sara. Given the circumstances and timing, any cop would wonder—victim's roommate with the suspect's brother—but these guys are assholes, too, and no fans of Bill, either. They're being quiet about it, but deep down, they're asking themselves if Jason was working alone or not, and if not, who else was involved. Gibby knew Tyra. He knew where she lived and what she drove, maybe her patterns and movements. He's been romantic with Sara—that means inside access, familiarity. Now this thing with Sara . . . the timing is a problem."

I understood at once. "Because Jason is in prison."

"If something has happened to Sara, it is literally impossible that Jason had anything to do with it. Martinez and Smith will think, *Accomplice . . .*"

"And if people here saw us . . ."

"Easy, now. Let's not panic." Burklow put one hand on my shoulder and the other on Chance's. "You boys were never here. You get me? You know nothing of chloroform or a jimmied window or a broken lamp.

You didn't call any cops. Understand?" We nodded, and he gave us both a squeeze. "Go on, then. Get the fuck out of here."

For me, the next minutes passed in a haze. I made a left turn. I stopped at red lights. Burklow thought Sara had been taken. Chance had little doubt that he was right.

"We could have walked in on him. Do you hear me? A few minutes earlier, and he might have killed us, too. This close, man. This damn close."

He'd said something similar twice already, but I didn't care about the same things as Chance.

"Dude, I am *talking* to you. This close!" Chance showed a thumb and finger, half an inch apart. "Can you at least acknowledge that?"

I shook my head, thinking entirely different thoughts. "We need to do something."

"Do what?"

I thought, *Find Sara, save Jason.*

Chance must have understood because he said, "Pull over, Gibby. Park the car."

"Why?"

"Just park the car."

I turned into a Rexall parking lot and stopped beside a strip of dirt littered with pull tabs and cigarette butts.

"Turn off the engine."

I did that, too. It was hot in the shade. Traffic blew past on the four-lane.

"Now tell me what you're thinking."

"I'm thinking we should find the guy."

"We talked about this."

"*You* talked about it. *I* listened."

"*Find the guy.* Shit. Just *find him.* I mean, look at your face! *Find him!*" Chance got out of the car, and traffic blew past. "I'm going to buy some smokes." He went inside, and stayed for a long time. When he came back, he was calmer. He lit a cigarette, and hung his arm out the window. "How would you do it?"

"I have no idea."

"And if you did find him?"

"I don't know that, either."

"Damn, Gibby . . . just . . . shit." He tossed out the cigarette, barely smoked. "You're an impossible friend. You know that, right? A pain-in-the-ass, impossible friend." I kept my mouth shut. "Don't smirk like that."

"It's not a smirk."

But it kind of was, and Chance knew it.

He said, "Okay, *genius*. What next?"

"We need a new car," I said. "Before my mother finds out we stole this one."

"How do you propose to find a car?"

"Come with me."

I walked to a pay phone across the lot, and dropped in two dimes. "Becky, hey. It's me."

"Gibson French, I was hoping you might call."

"Was there ever a doubt?"

"Well, you *did* see me in my underwear."

"All the more reason."

She laughed.

I got to the point.

"Listen, Becky. I need a favor."

When I stepped from the phone booth, Chance was waiting. "She'll help," I said.

"She doesn't have a car."

"No, but Dana White does."

I started walking, and Chance trotted to catch up. "You know that Dana White is not exactly our friend."

"True." I slid behind the wheel of the Cadillac. "But Becky said she only *looks* like a brittle bitch."

"She actually said that?"

"Yeah." I laughed a bit. "She did."

Half a block from home, I saw Becky, as lovely as ever in a T-shirt, denim shorts, and the same white vinyl boots where I'd seen a safety pin in the zipper, standing at the curb by Dana White's car. I stopped before I got too close, told Chance to get out, and drove on before Becky could get a good look at my face.

That part was going to be tricky.

My mother's car slid into the garage as if it had never left, and I skulked out of the driveway in a half crouch. On the street, I tried to keep the limp out of my walk, but Becky already had one hand up to cover her mouth. Either Chance had told her what happened or she had better eyesight than I thought. Up close, I saw the shine in her eyes, though she hardened quickly.

"Let me see," she said. "I can handle it."

I removed the cap first.

"Glasses, too."

I took off the shades, and Becky studied the cuts and the cruel, black stitches. "Chance said it was bikers."

"That's right."

"Because you were asking questions about your brother."

"He didn't kill anybody."

Becky said nothing.

"Don't you believe me?"

"I believe you have a good heart." She placed soft hands on my face, and kissed the places that hurt. "I believe I like you more now than ever."

Her hands stayed on my face until Chance cleared his throat, making it awkward. "Come on," I said. "I'll take you home."

"What if I don't want to go home?"

"You can't come with us."

"Because it's dangerous?"

"Look at my face, Becky. Something like this could happen again, or something worse. I don't even have a plan."

"I don't care about that."

"You should," I said.

But she crossed her arms, unmoved and unmoving. "Do you want the car or not?"

27

Reece prowled the secret hallways, and could barely contain himself. The girl. The risk. All his life he'd been a careful man. *Pros. Cons. Possibility.* Reece did not believe in God, but if he had a religion, it would be this: don't get caught. He measured his days by the discipline born of that religion. Target selection. Target acquisition. He could spend months making a choice and a plan only to abandon both at the slightest sign of risk to the secret life he'd made.

But that was before the girl.

X had said to wait, but Reece had not—*he could not*—and no scale in the world was large enough to measure that risk, not with X involved.

Still dazed by his own audacity, Reece checked the security feeds, verifying that the front gate had locked behind him and that the motion sensors were armed and active. The system was state of the art, designed and installed by an ex–Secret Service agent for a hundred-thousand-dollar flat fee, in cash and nonnegotiable. There were eighteen cameras on the grounds, another dozen in the house.

Leaving the monitors, Reece poured a glass of I. W. Harper bourbon. He was not a big drinker, but adrenaline was making him twitchy, and this particular bourbon seemed to help.

"The only bourbon enjoyed in a hundred and ten countries."

It was a popular slogan, and his father had enjoyed repeating it. Reece could see the old man, now, the quick wink and the quick drink.

Hurry on now before your mother gets home . . .

A railroad engineer, he'd died when Reece was seven, crushed between two cars after an unfortunate fall. Reece's mother had been strong enough to hold the family together, but she'd left him, too, killed by esophageal cancer when Reece was only twelve.

Finishing the bourbon, Reece left the security monitors, and followed one of the secret corridors that crisscrossed the north wing of his house. He had other places, of course—safe spaces of his own and others that X made available—but the north wing was for someone special.

Sara was the first.

At the next corridor, Reece turned sideways to squeeze between the wall studs and plywood. A single bulb gave enough light to see, but Reece didn't need it. He knew every corner and turn, every room beyond the gypsum board, and every safe place to watch. It's why he'd built the north wing in the first place.

The secret places.

The watching.

He imagined the rooms as he passed them.

Bathroom, bedroom . . .

The girl would stir soon, and he'd be there to watch and listen. He wouldn't touch her, of course—not for days or even weeks—but the intimate moments mattered as much: the dressing and the self-care, the small rituals enshrined in the days and nights of women across the world.

At the next intersection, Reece turned left, squeezing down another corridor.

Kitchen, living room, closet . . .

He stopped behind the wall of the master bedroom, where he could watch through the two-way glass or any of the small holes, so perfectly concealed. But this was the *beginning,* so Reece took a ladder up, and crept along the ceiling joists until he was above the bed, and could see down through the light fixture. Sara had not moved since he'd arranged her with such care: the blond hair on one shoulder, the sheet that covered her just so. He could have dressed her differently, of course, or undressed her. But Reece was a watcher first, and patient; so he closed his eyes, and in the dimness smiled.

Her name was Sara.

She was his.

When Sara woke, it was like rising through a black cloud, everything soft and supported, a slow drift upward. For a moment, she was at peace. But there'd been that splinter of a dream: gray light from the street and noise in the room, a man's face as he'd pressed her into the bed and clamped his hand across her face. She'd tried to scream, but choked, instead, on something sickly sweet and wet, his voice horribly gentle, as he'd leaned even closer.

Breathe it in . . .

In her mouth and lungs, the taste, like a sickness.

That's my good girl . . .

That part had been the worst: the lifted jaw and eager eyes, the small teeth in an expectant mouth. She'd tried to fight, but had no strength. *A fading room. A fading self.* At the end, she'd tried to beg, but the lips had gone, and the eyes had gone.

Just a dream, she thought.

But the taste was in her mouth.

Sara bolted up in a room she'd never seen.

It was real.

His sweat had dripped onto her face.

Bile filled Sara's throat, and she puked it out onto a bedspread as pale and pink as the walls around her. She saw a metal headboard painted white, curtains the color of turned cream. She closed her eyes, but couldn't unsee the room.

It was a bedroom.

She had no clothes.

She buried her face in a strange pillow; afraid to scream, afraid he would come.

Him.

He.

All she knew were the strong hands and the moon of his face, the open mouth and the teeth, like a child's teeth.

That's my girl, he'd said.

My good, good girl.

Sara screamed into the pillow; she had to. She wanted to be sick again, to make herself empty; but reality was the one thing she couldn't vomit out. When that fantasy passed, she went looking for her courage. To do it, she kept her eyes closed, and focused on her heartbeat, then on the breath in her lungs. She reminded herself of all that she'd survived in twenty-seven years: the bad boyfriends and the back-alley abortion, the fight with her parents and the year she'd lived rough in Haight-Ashbury.

When she thought she could, she opened her eyes. A wooden floor. Baseboards painted white. Risking more, she saw a wooden chest at the foot of the bed, a dresser with a lace doily, a vase of plastic daisies. Small rugs lay on the floor. There was a vanity, a mirror, framed photographs of people she'd never seen.

Covering herself with a blanket, she picked up one of the photographs, a black-and-white shot of a young family in front of a roller coaster and clapboarded buildings with signs advertising beer and popcorn and ocean bathing. A small boy held a bag of peanuts. Only the father was smiling.

Sara put the picture down.

No noise in the room.

There were curtains but no windows.

At the bedroom door, she listened but heard nothing.

He would be on the other side.

He had to be.

Moving quickly, Sara checked under the bed and beneath the vanity. The dresser drawers were filled with old-fashioned undergarments; the clothes in the closet were equally dated. Dressing numbly, she saw herself in the mirror, hollowed out and pale as soap, a strange woman in a pencil skirt and fitted blouse.

"Not me," she said. "Not like Tyra."

She opened the door, and stepped into a hallway with a pink bathroom on one side and a second bedroom on the other. The hallway ended at a kitchen.

Still, no windows.

Crying openly, she staggered into the next room, and stumbled against a rolltop desk. The room was small, but there was a door and an umbrella stand. That meant, *exit, outside, escape.* Sara ran for the door, and tore at the lock, metal giving as she jerked at the knob, and the chain snapped tight.

"Shit! Shit!"

She fumbled at the slide, tore skin. The chain dropped, and she heaved at the door. Beyond it was a second one made of steel. No handle or lock. Not even hinges.

"No! No! No!"

Sara pounded metal until her hands ached.

"No, please . . ."

She slid to the floor.

"Not like Tyra."

28

The guards came midmorning, this time Jordan and Kudravetz. They took Jason to the subbasement, and there was no question of X's intent. Stripped down to fighting shorts, he stood barefoot on swept stone, the glint in his eyes cold, critical, and eager.

When the guards left, X leveled those eyes at Jason. "I assume we still understand each other?"

"You made your point perfectly clear. Nothing has changed."

"Do you require time to prepare?"

But Jason was already in the cold place, the killing place. He raised his hands, and watched X circle, looking for the feint, the feint within the feint. Hands. Feet. The flick of an eye. Sometimes the feints were words designed to distract or disarm. It was a favorite strategy.

Unsettle the mind; destroy the balance.

Destroy the balance; obliterate the man.

But Jason was prepared for that, his shadow on the wall as they circled, X's feet a whisper on the stone, his hands up as Jason made the first move, a flurry of blows and kicks, a feint of his own before drawing first blood with a jab so fast and sharp it split skin like the rind of a melon.

X showed no sign of pain or surprise, the only change a single blink as blood dripped into an eye. "I understand your father came to visit you. Strange that he never did so before."

Jason said nothing.

Circling.

"Has he changed, do you suppose? Or does he sense some change in you, some reason for hope where none existed when last you were here?"

"Are we fighting or talking?"

"In the past, we've done both."

X's words were like a shrug, but what followed was the most perfect display of controlled violence that Jason had ever seen, an explosion of movement and contact that left him staggered and stunned. X drew blood twice, then backed away, looking displeased.

"Again," he said; and came for Jason with the same relentless speed. This time Jason did better, blocking a string of blows before landing four good jabs and a punch to the ribs brutal enough to drop most any man alive. X just grunted, and came again, hard strikes to the face, a kick that numbed Jason's leg from the hip down. He took a single step, and the leg folded.

"Enough!" X turned away, angry. "Did I imagine the man you were two months ago? Have I misremembered, somehow?" Jason spit blood, and X looked down his nose. "This is pitiful. Stand up."

Jason straightened slowly, but X came fast, knocking him down twice more, then spitting once, and showing his back to underscore the contempt. After that, his attacks were clinical, strategic, perfectly executed. But the more strikes he landed, the more frustrated he became, lashing out harder and faster until he'd backed Jason into a corner, words grating from his throat with every blow.

Never . . . been . . . so . . . disappointed . . .

But Jason was in the corner for a reason, absorbing the blows until X hit him a final time, still flush with disgust. "Stand up, for God's sake."

He lowered his guard, and that was all Jason needed, a quarter second to strike out backhanded, the knuckles of his fingers and palm making simultaneous strikes on a pressure point at the center of X's eyebrow and the facial nerve below his left cheekbone. Done perfectly, the blow would cause excruciating pain and a near-instant blackout. But X twitched at the last moment, just enough to stay on his feet. Still, he was stunned; and that, too, was all Jason needed. He struck out stiff-fingered, caught X in the throat, then followed with a blur of jabs and a right cross big enough to fold X at the knees. Jason met him on the way down, twisting through the hips with an uppercut that might have killed a lesser man. Even X seemed half-dead when he hit concrete, eyes down to slits as he coughed out blood and bits of teeth.

Jason straightened, breathing hard. It had been a near thing. Another minute, and he'd have had no fight left.

Destroy the balance.

Obliterate the man.

That was the midnight decision: to make X angry, to build the anger into rage, and the rage into disdain. It was the only path Jason had left, so he'd taken the hits, the pain, and done it for what?

A quarter second.

The blink of an eye.

Jason dragged out a chair, found a bottle of wine, and waited to see if X would drown in his own vomit before color rolled back into his eyes. He considered helping the man along—ten full seconds of *that fucking close.*

When X could focus, he found Jason in the chair, the bottle half-empty. "I knew it," he said. "I was right . . ."

"About what?"

But X didn't answer. He was too busy bleeding, and nodding, and weeping tears that looked like joy.

For Warden Wilson, the world had long ago ceased to make sense. His office? *What did it matter?* His responsibilities? The future? How long since his wife had touched his hand or smiled? Or since his sons had called him *father?*

Could X actually die?

Of course, he could be physically killed, but what provisions had he made? The man was insane, vicious, and richer than sin. He had lawyers, mercenaries, God alone knew what. And only God knew what would happen if X died prematurely.

"Excuse me, sir?" The warden's secretary appeared in the open door. "Visitor processing still needs an answer, and the doctor called again. I really think you should go."

"Very well."

The warden rose from the desk yet seemed to weigh a thousand pounds. His secretary had ideas about X—many did—but only a few understood the monster in the basement: those who'd paid the price, and lived afraid. Buttoning his coat, Warden Wilson made his way to the sub-basement under death row. Two guards stood at the bottom of the stairs. "Status?" he asked.

"He's with the doctor. He's alert."

"Mood?"

The same guard looked at the other, then shrugged. "I'd say he looks happy."

That made no sense to the warden. X had never lost a fight, not like this. "Stay here," he said. "No one in or out unless I say."

Three days until he dies . . .

It was little enough, but Bruce Wilson had never been a courageous man. When his wife had first been assaulted, he'd planned to flee with his family, and pray to God he never saw X again. He'd been careful about it, too, buying tickets with cash and in secrecy, prepared to abandon every-thing but the people he loved.

Yet somehow, X had known.

As I recall, he'd said, *you are from elsewhere in the South.*

Mississippi. The Delta.

And your family has been there for some time?

As far back as memory goes.

I assume, then, that you are familiar with the brutal and once-common practice of hobbling recaptured slaves?

You mean . . . ?

Broken ankles and shattered knees, severed tendons and amputated feet, all very gothic and antebellum . . .

I don't understand.

I feel certain that you do.

Then X had placed a copy of the warden's itinerary on the table.

Charlotte to Atlanta.

Atlanta to Sydney.

The warden remembered little after that but the hard run home and the sound of his smallest son screaming. They'd been in the kitchen—his entire family—and thinking back, he remembered the oddest things: the linoleum floor, curled in the corner, an open bottle of wine, and the smell of burning food. Try as he might, he could recall nothing of his wife's face or of his older son, though both had been there. What had broken his heart then, and haunted him to exhaustion every day since, was the sight of his baby boy, but really just his legs, the narrow limbs with the scabbed knees, and how they bent at such impossible angles.

Choking on the memory, Warden Wilson moved down the corridor to the cell where the prison doctor stood above a bed, bending low to stitch a cut above X's eye. Pretending calm, the warden asked, "How is he?"

The doctor grunted once, still working. "A mild concussion and maybe forty stitches. Go on, show him your teeth."

"Tie off the stitch and get out." If X was in pain, he didn't show it. Shifting on the bed, he rose against the pillow, and laced his fingers on his chest. "How's your family?"

The warden felt a wild panic, and tried to conceal it, pretending to watch the doctor as he gathered his things and left. "They're fine," he said.

"And your youngest?" X continued. "Trevor, I believe. How is young Trevor?"

The warden thought, *Three days, that's it*, but couldn't hide the anger. "The limp still troubles him. The pain is never distant."

"You think me needlessly cruel."

The warden straightened his spine, a moment of rare strength. "I do."

"And if I wished to express some feeling of gratitude or remorse? If I told you that, would you believe me?"

"I don't understand the question."

"I'm saying that in spite of our difficult start, you've been both fair and responsive. I'd like to reward that behavior." X kept his gaze impassive. "How about three million dollars each for you, your wife, and your oldest son? Plus another five for Trevor, to compensate for the limp."

The warden gaped; he couldn't help it. "Fourteen million dollars?"

"Let's make it twenty."

The idea of such wealth made the warden feel faint. It meant a fresh start for him and his wife, better therapy for Trevor . . .

"I will require one last thing," X said.

The warden swallowed the last morsels of pride and honor. "Tell me what you need."

X did just that. He was very specific. "I assume you can manage the details?"

The warden said he could, and why not? After all the things he'd broken, all the men and lives and laws . . .

"I almost forgot," he said. "Jason French has a visitor, his younger brother. Shall I turn him away?"

"Why would you do that?" X showed the broken teeth at last. "After all, there is nothing more important than family."

That had once been true for X. As a child, he'd adored his parents. Even the younger sister made a fond memory, with her plump, round face and the way she'd liked to giggle. Those early years were like a dream: the mansions and travel, the great yachts and the fine chefs. His family's special nature had been obvious from the beginning, clear in the respect men had for his father, the way they did as they were told, but stole glances at the beautiful, young wife. She would read stories to X of princes in faraway lands, and X was supposed to love those tales—he saw it in his mother's eyes—but none of those make-believe princes lived a better life than X. The world was a kingdom, his father a king.

When X was eight years old, he burned his finger on a birthday candle, and the fascination with fire began. At first, it was a small thing: matches and cardboard and melted plastic. By his next birthday, though, the dreams he had were not of candles but of conflagration. He used his father's gold lighter to start his first real fire, a blaze that took ten acres of woodland from the Charleston estate. The second fire was a neighbor's car. Fifty thousand dollars, they said, a collectible; and he'd done it with a single match.

Conflagration.

Control.

His third fire took a house and two dogs trapped inside. Someone saw him, though, so the cops came, and money changed hands, and X—instead of juvenile detention—went away for six months of intensive therapy, a half year of false remorse and deception while the doctors made notes and encouraging sounds, all while X hid his painful erections and his thoughts of the dogs, and how their screams, as they'd burned, had sounded almost human.

If X had learned one lesson from his time in therapy, it was that fires were messy and hard to conceal. Plus, his dreams were no longer of fire but of screaming dogs, and the animals that came next: first a mouse or two, then the rabbits and squirrels, until his dreams were filled with red meat, and his days with expectation. X spent those days with his traps and his secret places. And though his parents kept a wary distance, things changed for real on the day he used a garden hose to freeze his sister's cat to a winter tree. Afterward, his parents traveled more often, and when they did, they took the sister, only. On those rare occasions they came home, X's mother seemed less lovely each time, a near stranger who sent servants at night to tuck in the covers of her only son. Even X's father said, *Better a handshake than a hug,* and tried to make a joke of it.

X was thirteen when his father was given hard proof of tortured animals, first from a gamekeeper at the mountain preserve, a small, nimble man who'd discovered a mallard, still alive, with its wings nailed to a tree, and—days later—a young bobcat staked to the ground with both eyes removed and its stomach unzipped.

The looks from his parents grew more worried, but no one asked him about it.

No one said much of anything.

A month later, a foal disappeared from the stable of the equestrian estate in Wellington. It was a special foal, his sister's. X killed it quick and messy, and left it imminently *findable.* Why? Because anything was better than the whispers and suspicion, or the quiet, cotton silence that filled up a room each time he entered. Part of him thought that if they'd only confront him, he might stop. If someone would say, *Son, this is wrong.* Or, *Son, why do you have such emptiness in your soul?*

When no one spoke a word, he took another foal, and hobbled it, and left it alive to scream like the dogs had screamed. After that, they sent X away, first to other doctors, then to the most expensive boarding schools in Switzerland. He'd hated them for that, and nursed the hatred, feeding on it for five years of solitude and denial, of unanswered letters and canceled visits, a lifetime of aching to belong, and knowing he could not, and rocking himself to sleep in the dark of every single night. They were so *weak*! Too weak to accept or love or answer the phone on Christmas Eve. That was too much to accept, so X took a cab to the airport in Geneva, cleared customs on a forged passport, and made his way to the winter estate, where he used the holiday quiet to kill them all.

X could remember their deaths without emotion, though their weakness still disgusted him, the way they'd whimpered and writhed, and sworn their love for him had never died. Only their softness was unconditional. So different from Jason, X thought: Jason, who was capable and quick, but also profound of thought and strong and utterly unafraid of his own capacity for violence. Were X to make a list, it would require pages to describe all the things he admired about Jason French: his courage and conviction, his awareness of self. Even his recklessness was absolute, but only when he *chose* abandon. Of course, Jason had a streak of self-denial that X found mildly irritating. Beyond that, he was the one thing X had sought his whole life. He was an equal; he was worthy.

Maybe it was a short list, after all.

29

The waiting room at Lanesworth Prison smelled like old sweat and stale air. When the guard came for me, I left my friends on a hard bench, and followed him to a blank room with a table and two chairs. A minute later, Jason entered the room, shuffle stepping in full restraints. He eyed me unhappily. The stitches. The bruises. "What are you doing here? I told Dad to keep you away."

"I'm not really listening to Dad these days."

Jason sat, chains clattering. "It's dangerous for you to be here, to be *seen* here. Do you understand what I'm saying? People will hurt you to get to me."

"It looks as if they're getting to you just fine."

"My face? That's just prison. What's your excuse?"

"Hells Angels. The Carriage Room." I shrugged like it was nothing. "They didn't like the questions I was asking."

"Questions about me?"

"You. Tyra."

"Damn it . . ."

"You *did* have a fight there. It *did* have to do with Tyra."

"That was about guns."

"But she was part of it."

"Not so much it got her killed. I had a deal with the Pagans, protection and cash in exchange for exclusive access to military-grade weapons. Some, they kept. Some, we sold together. Tyra thought I should sell to the

Angels, too. She wanted a cut, and tried to broker a deal. It was business. The Angels never cared about Tyra."

"Business." I said it coldly, but Jason was unmoved.

"I've never pretended to be the good guy. I needed money, pure and simple. I told you my reasons."

"You must have some idea who killed her."

"Look, little brother, Tyra was fun, but had a closetful of demons. You saw how she was. The girl could drive a saint to murder."

"All I need is a place to start."

"I don't want you to start! That's the point! I don't want you near me or this prison, not near the Pagans, either, and definitely not the Angels."

"If they convict you, they'll execute you."

"Yeah, well. Prosecutors."

I leaned away, cold on the inside. "What kind of fatalistic, inmate bullshit is that?"

"Go home, kid. Go to school. Kiss the girl."

"I won't give up only to watch you die."

"That sounds like something Robert would say."

"Sara's gone." It was my last bullet, so I fired it point-blank. "Burklow thinks she was abducted, possibly by the same person who killed Tyra. That means it's not just about you anymore."

"Listen to me, kid. You're out of your depth. You don't understand what's happening here."

"Explain it to me."

"If I did, you wouldn't believe me; and if you believed me, you wouldn't accept it. What I will tell you is this." His restraints clattered as he leaned closer. "You watch your back out there. I mean it. Walking. Driving. Be aware of the people around you, of *everyone* around you. Don't talk to strangers. Don't open the door to strangers. Stay inside. Stay with friends. If you find yourself outside and alone, be especially careful of middle-aged men who look older than they should, doubly so if they're small and narrow, and not at all dangerous-looking. You see someone like that, you run, and I mean for your life."

"Why run? What man?"

"Let's just say that a prison like this does not forget, and there are people who want to control me, bad people who will hurt you to do it."

"People on the inside or the outside?"

Jason smiled, then, but with little warmth. "I understand you, little brother. I truly do. You want to help because we're family, and it feels like a noble cause. But we've not been family for a long time. You don't owe me a thing."

"I don't see it like that."

"The brother you remember is gone, kid, killed as dead by Vietnam as Robert ever was." Jason stood, his eyes a wasteland. "The sooner you accept that fact, the better off you'll be."

The guard who returned Jason to his cell was not on X's detail, so Jason had to wait, and it wasn't easy. He paced the cell; pounded on the door. "I want to talk to X! Now! I want to see him now!"

Gibby wouldn't back down.

That was the problem.

"Guard! Guard, goddamn it!"

When Jason finally made it to the subbasement, he found X with a paintbrush in one hand. "What kind of deranged game are you playing this time?"

"Game?" X didn't turn.

"The girl. The missing girl."

X dabbed a bit of paint onto the canvas. "I'd like your opinion on this painting."

"Answer the question."

"The painting first."

Driving down the impatience, Jason looked at the painting. It was only a start, but the gist of it was clear: one fighter down, the second standing above him. "That's you on the floor."

"*Unconscious* on the floor." X dabbed more paint. "The first time it's happened since I was a student."

He made the word sound casual, but there was nothing casual about X as a student of the martial arts. As a boy in Switzerland, he'd mastered Wing Chun and hapkido before getting away with the murder of his family, inheriting his parents' fortune, and devoting himself entirely to the study of Shotokan Karate-Do. He'd spent a small fortune to train with an Okinawan master named Gichin Funakoshi, who'd first brought the discipline from China to Japan in 1922. X had described the training, once, as something akin to divine suffering. At the moment, Jason didn't care. "Are you targeting my brother or not?"

The paintbrush stopped an inch off the canvas.

"He's a tough kid, but just a kid. He won't survive inside this place, so if that's the endgame—"

"There is no endgame with regard to your brother." X turned, at last. "My concern is with you, alone. I've made that very plain."

"Then why take the roommate?"

"Roommate?"

"Tyra's roommate has been abducted. With me here, the cops will look at my brother. He knew the girls. He knew both of them."

X put down the brush. "This roommate? She is blond?"

"You know her?"

"I know only *of* her."

"It's Reece, then."

"Or not Reece at all."

But that was bullshit, and Jason knew it. "My brother is out there right now looking for the roommate. What will Reece do if he finds her?"

"Reece would not hurt your brother without my permission."

"I need more than that. Blow the whistle. Call off your dog."

"I will handle Reece."

"How?" Jason demanded.

"Like the dog that he is." X allowed his lips to twist. "Shotokan may be a Japanese discipline, but it began in China."

"What does that mean?"

X gestured, and two guards took Jason by the arms.

"Wait, X . . ." Jason fought to stay in the cell, but they dragged him out. "I don't understand what that means!"

X watched him struggle, and left the rest of his thought unspoken.

That the Chinese have never been afraid to eat their dogs . . .

· · ·

After the prison, I said little to my friends until we were halfway back to the city. It was a tense ride with a lot of unanswered questions. Finally, I said, "He doesn't want me involved. He won't help me."

"Did you tell him about the Carriage Room?" Chance leaned forward, every bit as angry. "That you *are* involved?"

"I told him."

"And he still wouldn't help? Unbelievable."

"What next?" Becky asked.

"I don't know what else to do. Jason won't talk to me, and I know almost nothing about Tyra, not her friends or where she worked. I don't even know where she's from. Normally, I'd ask Sara . . ."

The words trailed off because that sentence spoke for itself. Chance leaned forward, his sunburned arms folded on the back of the seat. "Sara's gone, man, and that sucks. I don't even know her, and it sucks. But maybe the cops will see things differently now. Time, you know. Perspective. Two victims, like Burklow said, a different dynamic. Maybe if your father pushes . . ."

I watched him in the mirror, and then glanced at Becky. This part was going to hurt. "I think Jason knows who killed Tyra."

It was as if I'd said something perverse. Chance's face went slack. Becky's lips parted enough to form a perfect, silent O. But how much of my brother could I share? I'd seen his bleakness and resolve, what, at the very end, had seemed like the blackest kind of despair.

The brother you remember is gone, kid, killed as dead by Vietnam as Robert ever was . . .

That part was private.

The rest of it, though . . .

I gave it to them word for word: the warning, the risk, everything Jason had told me. Afterward, Chance parroted my words, seemingly in shock. *"There are people who want to control me, bad people who will hurt you to do it."*

"He's trying to scare me off," I said.

"Or protect you," Becky replied. "Though, I guess that's the same thing."

"Let's assume it's all true," Chance said. "We have to assume that, right? And if it *is* true, who was he talking about? What dangerous people?"

"All I know is what I told you."

"It's not much, man."

"Becky?"

She took her time, more thoughtful than Chance. "What does he mean by *middle-aged men who look older than they should*? That's oddly specific *and* nonspecific."

I answered with care because this part would sting, too. "I'm pretty sure I saw him." Chance's mouth opened—he looked horrified—and even Becky paled. "Twice," I continued. "Once, the day we were in court, and then again right after Tyra . . . you know."

"Right after she was hacked into a million pieces." Chance almost came over the seat. "Is that what you mean? Right *after* Tyra was killed, and right *before* Sara was abducted."

"Settle down, Chance."

"*You* settle down! Jesus!" He slammed a palm on the seat top, then dropped back into a cross-armed, clench-jawed silence.

"Are you sure it was him?" Becky asked it softly, as if to make the point that she and Chance were very different people.

"He matched the description, like he was forty but looked sixty. Small and narrow. Not particularly dangerous-looking. Just like Jason said."

"Where else did you see him?"

"On Tyra's street, parked in a car . . ."

"Oh, that's perfect," Chance said. "On her street."

"It might not have been him."

"But you believe it was?" Becky asked.

"It would be one hell of a coincidence, a man like that parked on her street so soon after Tyra's death. And it *is* an oddly particular description. Specific. Nonspecific. Like you said. And he's easy to miss, too; he just kind of fades. Had I not seen him in court, I wouldn't have noticed him the second time."

"But you *did* see him in court." Chance interrupted. "You *did* notice him the second time."

"He was watching me, too. Maybe thirty seconds as I walked to my car."

Becky was the first to see the bigger picture. "If Jason knows who killed Tyra, why won't he tell the police?"

This part bothered me, too. "Maybe he doesn't really know. Maybe he has no proof."

"No, I think he's definitely protecting you."

"Why are you so sure?"

"Because it's what you would do." Becky leaned close, like it was the two of us, alone in the world. "Think about it. He won't answer your questions or let you near the investigation. He's warned you about this horrible man. He all but begged you to stop asking questions. If he knows who killed Tyra, he would want to tell the police—any innocent man would—unless there's some powerful reason not to."

"He said we're barely family."

"Do you really think he believes that?"

"I'm not sure."

"Aren't you, though?"

I drove the car in silence.

I had no kind of answer.

It took twenty minutes more before the tall buildings of downtown Charlotte rose in the distance. At a stoplight outside the city line, Chance said, "Turn here, man. Take me home." He seemed frustrated and troubled, and at his house, oddly embarrassed. "I'd go with you if I could—wherever you're going. It's my mom, is all. She only has two hours between jobs. I told her I'd come home for lunch."

I said, "Hey, brother. All good." But I knew him well enough to understand his thoughts. *Things were getting real . . .*

"What will you do next?" he asked.

"I don't know."

"Maybe you should do nothing at all. How about that for a change? Go to class. Graduate."

"Yeah, maybe."

Chance looked at his house, still struggling. "That man you saw on Tyra's street . . . How close were you?"

"Ten feet, I guess."

"Just sitting in his car?"

"Watching the condo, I think."

Chance studied my face as if some kind of answer might be written there. "Call me later?"

"Sure. Course."

"All right, then. Bye, Becky."

We watched him into the house. "What now?" Becky asked.

"I don't know."

"Maybe you're looking at this wrong. The whole thing."

"How so?"

"So far, it's been about Tyra. That's been your focus. *Who did she make angry? What did she do that got her killed?*"

"Yeah, because she is, in fact, the one who got killed."

"How well do you know your brother?" Becky asked.

"I don't understand."

She took my hand, and shrugged sadly. "Maybe Tyra's murder is not about Tyra at all."

Becky's insight was blindingly bright, and simple enough to open the door to an entirely new line of thought. From the beginning, I'd considered little but Tyra's life and choices. It's why I'd gone to the Carriage Room and to Sara's condo. Becky's modest question turned all that on its head. I truly did not know Jason at all; he'd told me as much. Even so, I'd assumed that the distance between us was born of mere circumstance, of war and distance and time apart. On that first day at the quarry, he'd said a brother should know his brother. But what effort had he made? We'd spent one day out, one day with the girls.

I am not a good person . . .

He'd said that, too.

"Where are we going?" Becky spoke for the first time since I'd pulled into heavy traffic. Before that, she'd been patient, and I'd used the time to turn Jason like a plate: brother, soldier, convict. Beyond the memories of our shared childhood, I knew only that he could be cold, violent, and dismissive.

Swim away, little fish . . .

"There's a restaurant," I said. "Soul food and Korean."

The restaurant smelled exactly as I remembered: tobacco smoke and collards, the faint, familiar odor of barbecued beef and fermented vegetables. We took stools at the counter, and an old black man called out from the grill.

"Charlene! Customers!"

A round-faced, wide-hipped woman pushed through a swinging door, a smile on her mouth as she ambled along behind the counter. "Well, now, aren't you the cutest little white people?" Cracks appeared in the purplish lipstick, and a pen materialized from behind her ear. "What can I get you on this fine day?"

"Coffees," I said. "And a word with Mr. Washington."

I nodded toward the old man, and her smile faded, sudden suspicion in her eyes. "You know my Nathaniel?"

"We kind of met last week. I'm Jason French's brother."

"Oh, Lord, that one. I should have seen it, just from looking at you." The suspicion drained away. The smile returned.

"So you know him?" I asked.

"The good and the bad, though with him, the bad was not so bad, and the good was awfully good. Nathaniel!" She barked the cook's name, her eyes all over my face. "Come see what the cat dragged in." The old man mumbled something about burning the mush, and Charlene sighed in false exasperation. "That man . . ." She poured two coffees, and put the pot back on the burner. "You know, I don't believe what they say about your brother. Newspapers. Television." She made a sour face.

"Why do you say that?"

"Well, now, don't misunderstand. I don't know your brother enough to say I *know* him. He *did* have a prison spell, and *did* get into the drugs. But killing that girl?" She shook her head. "He sat at that counter too often, had dinner in my home a dozen times. Then there's what he did for my boy."

"Darzell," I said.

"Ah, you've heard of my Darzell." Her eyes lit up. "You want cream with that, sugar?" She pointed at Becky's mug, then slid along a tin creamer without waiting for an answer. "You know, your brother saved his life." I put down the coffee, and she said, "Mmm-hmm. They met on the bus to Parris Island, and were thick as thieves right off the bat. Same hometown, same streak of wild and ready. Parris Island is twelve weeks of hell, but they bunked together, trained together . . ."

"And he saved Darzell's life?"

"Fourth day of boot camp." Charlene cocked a round hip, and spread plump fingers on the counter. "They were three miles out on a six-mile run, twenty or thirty boys in full gear, half of 'em puking up their breakfast. Darzell and Jason were out front when it happened, but they were always out front. Competitive, you understand . . ." Her gaze got a little smoky, remembering something only she could see. "With all those boots pounding sand, I guess no one heard the snake rattle. And a canebrake *will* disappear into pine needles and sand; you can trust me on that. It could have been your brother who got bit—side by side like they were— but it was Darzell who stepped on the canebrake, and your brother who carried him back to base, three miles at a dead run." She smiled again, and it was like sunshine. "You've not met my Darzell, but he's six-two, two-twenty, and so hard you can't kill him with a tire iron. Not like this little one . . ."

She hooked a thumb at her husband, but I saw the love in her eyes.

"You kids like soul food? Jason loves it like Sunday morning."

"Actually, Mrs. Washington . . ." I met Becky's eyes, and she nodded. "What I'd really like to do is talk to your son."

Darzell's address was not far away, but we were nervous about going there. When Becky spoke, I heard it in her voice. "About what the old man said . . ."

I was driving in four-lane traffic, but risked a glance at her face. Not nervous, I decided.

Wary.

That was the right word, the right emotion. During our conversation with his pleasant, round-faced wife, Nathaniel Washington had barely looked our way. He'd tended the mush and the ribs; smoked a cigarette or two. But when Charlene told us where to find her son, he'd spun so quickly from the grill that dark grease flicked from the end of his spatula. *You're sending these white kids into Earle Village? Are you trying to get them killed? Or is there some kind of foolish in you I've not discovered in forty-two years of marriage?* He'd tried to talk us out of going, but I'd explained my reasons, and he'd listened with care, nodding several times. Afterward, he'd kissed his wife and picked up his keys. *I'd best trail along, then, see people stay on the right side of things . . .*

Charlotte wasn't Baltimore or Detroit or any of the other cities that burned after James Earl Ray gunned down Dr. King at the Lorraine Motel in Memphis, but riots on the coast had sparked bloodshed across the state, and tensions were still high. Desegregation and forced busing. Black Panthers and the KKK. It wasn't all about race, either. People were angry about Vietnam and inflation, communism and Watergate, crooked leaders and the price of gas. Resentment, though, burned hottest where people were poorest, and that was Earle Village. *Good people,* my father often said. *But so damn angry.*

Nathaniel Washington saw things the same way. In a truck almost as old as he was, he led us down the narrow streets; and when we reached public housing, he parked and met us on the curb. His face was seamed with deep, dark lines, and he couldn't hide the worry. "You still want to do this?"

"It's important."

He studied me with yellowed eyes. "And if my son can't help?"

I didn't answer because I had no answer. He frowned but nodded. "We don't see a lot of white folks in here unless they're cops, so be cool. There're good folks in the village, but they're not *all* good. If someone hassles us, let me do the talking. And maybe don't mention that your daddy's a cop."

He had a point about my father. Black Panthers and the Organization of Afro-American Unity both operated out of Earle Village. That meant surveillance, harassment, resentment. I understood the pattern.

"All right, then." A frown appeared on his leathery face. "Let's go find my Darzell."

He led us down a block of sidewalk, then into one of the public units. On the second level, he stopped at a blank door, and knocked. "Darzell. It's your father." The door opened to the length of its chain, and a dark, distrusting face appeared. "Relax, Russell. They're with me."

Nothing in the eyes changed. Pure hostility. "Darzell's at the Cue."

The Friendly Cue was a pool joint two blocks down. We caught a lot of unhappy stares on the walk there, but no one said a word. Inside the pool hall, it was smoky and dark, and Darzell stood alone at a table, a big man over green felt. We watched him run three balls off the table. When he missed the nine, he straightened and met his old man's eyes. "Middle of the day, Pops. Who's minding the grill?"

"Your mother's watching things."

"Sweet Lord, help us all."

Darzell had unflinching eyes, five-inch hair, and no smile for us as the old man made the introductions. "Good kids, son, and looking for help. They're here on account of Jason."

"Jason French? Is that right?"

"He's my brother."

"I don't doubt that. You look exactly like him. Come on. Let's sit. You, too, sweetness." He winked at Becky, and we followed him past the bar, and into a booth, Becky sitting beside me with Darzell and his father across the table. "You want to talk about Jason, huh? What is it you want to know?"

His eyes had the same cool dispassion I saw sometimes in Jason. Maybe it was a soldier thing or a war thing. "Your mother told us you and Jason trained together."

"We did."

"Have you stayed in touch?"

"Your brother's not really a *stay in touch* kind of guy." Darzell flashed four fingers at the bar, and the bartender nodded back.

"When was the last time you saw him?"

"After the 'Nam and before he went to prison. Three years, maybe."

"Nothing since?"

"Just what's in the news. I don't think he killed that girl, though. Don't get me wrong now. If Jason had cause, he could kill every man in this joint, kill him and him and him." Darzell stretched an arm across the back of the booth, pointing at random strangers. "But they'd be good, clean kills, and done for cause, nothing like what the papers are saying. Shit . . ." The big man shook his head, a difficult expression on his face. "Jason mother-effin' French . . ."

"You sound angry."

"Angry? Nah, life's too short. But the motherfucker should pick up a phone once in a while." The bartender came with a pitcher of beer and four glasses. Darzell took the pitcher, and started pouring. "Don't get me wrong, I still love the guy. Hell, *worship* the guy." Darzell lifted an eyebrow, and slid a glass of beer to Becky. "You know about the rattlesnake?"

"Your mother told us."

"Well, that's a story, and a story's just words." He filled two more glasses, passing them around. "You know how hard it is to carry a grown man for three miles, up all those hills and back down, half the time in deep sand? And not some little man, either, but one my size. Three full miles at a dead run. You think on that." He gave us a few seconds for his words to sink in. "Did my mother tell you why he did it? Because he was my friend, and those other grunts weren't. You want to understand my feelings for your brother, then you need to feel *that*."

He drained his glass, and poured another. "Why are you asking about Jason, anyway? He's your brother. You know him better than I do."

I shook my head. "Not since Vietnam."

"Hey, if Vietnam is the great divide, sign up for the war. It was still there last time I looked."

"You mentioned the girl in the papers."

"I did, yeah. And that was some cold, cruel shit."

"I think Jason knows who killed her. He won't tell the cops, though. I'm trying to understand why."

"You want to help him, is that it?" Darzell lit a cigarette, and snapped the lighter shut. "Ride in like the cavalry, all junior G-man and shit?"

"Something like that. I'd think you'd want the same thing."

"First of all, Jason French has never needed the cavalry, but let's say this time he does, and that you, little man, and you, sweetness"—he pointed a cigarette at Becky—"you're the ones on horseback riding to his rescue. What is it you need from me?"

I wasn't exactly sure what I needed. "To understand him, I guess. He won't go to the cops, and I can't get my head around that. I guess I want to know how he's changed, and why it happened. If I knew that, then maybe I could talk to him."

"You want his stories. I get it. You want to know about war, and what it does to a man. All right, let me break this down." Darzell pointed again with the cigarette. "War is personal, kid. You're surrounded by other soldiers, but you're fundamentally alone. Every combat soldier will tell you the same. You pull the trigger, and a man dies. You paint a tree with his brains or spill his guts out in the mud. The *how* of it don't signify, except in the nightmares, maybe, or what you see in the mirror first time you find the courage to look. 'Cause the truth of it is this: whether you're a good soldier or not, a coward or right as the rain, you own the bullet *and* the guts; and that's just the way of it: who you kill or don't kill, what buddy goes chickenshit and runs, or steps wrong and blows off his leg. *Stories,* motherfucker! That's what the people want—reporters and draft dodgers and rich, white college boys. And yeah, maybe I'd be talking about you if this weren't about your brother. But you got to be there. You dig? You got to be in the shit to understand the shit. 'Cause that was *my* friend, lost his leg, and me who carried the fucker out, choking on his blood, trying to keep him from bleeding out. You know how long it takes a busted femoral to squirt a body dry? *Stories,* man! That's the problem, because the stories are mine, and they're personal. Maybe I share them and maybe I don't, but that's on me, too. Now I have to ask myself if Jason's any different, if he wants me telling *his* stories?"

Darzell ground out the cigarette, and leaned close. "You're of a mind that Vietnam changed your brother, and you're right, it changed us all. If you want to understand how, then you go fight the fucking war. And if it's Jason's stories you want, then you should talk to him."

"Son, please . . ."

"Take it easy, Pops. We're just talking this through." His stare had grown hard, and his back was flat against the back of the booth.

"Listen, Darzell." Becky reached for his hand, and what I saw in her face was real understanding and true compassion, as if the war, for her, had never been made so personal. "We're trying to help. That's all."

"And you think he knows who killed this girl?"

"We do."

"And that there is your problem." Darzell withdrew his hand, but was gentle about it. "The man likes his secrets. That's not on me."

"It's on me," I said. "He's doing it for me."

"Why?"

"He's protecting me, I think. *Bad people,* he told me. Inside the prison, or outside, I don't know. He said they'd hurt me to get to him."

"You don't know much," Darzell said.

"I know the DA wants to execute the man who saved your life."

Becky said, "Please, Darzell."

But Darzell kept his eyes on mine.

"One brother died in the war," I told him. "Jason is all I have left. That means I *am* in the shit."

Unsmiling, Darzell drummed his fingers. Eventually, he looked at his father, who nodded. "It's the right thing, son."

"All right," Darzell said. "I'll tell you what I know. It'll take a while, and I need to do it in my own way. So don't interrupt. Don't ask questions. We can circle back later, but this isn't something I *want* to do." Darzell settled into the decision, not happy about it but willing enough to loosen up as he lit a second cigarette. "Jason is a hero, all right, and any marine that knows his story will tell you the same. Two full tours and most of a third. But it ended badly. Military prison, dishonorable discharge. That's all most people see, so I'm going to start there, and then we'll go back for the rest of it. Cool?"

"Very."

Darzell nodded, satisfied. "You ever hear of My Lai?"

"You mean the massacre?"

"The slaughter, yeah."

He looked at Becky, but she knew about My Lai, too. Most everyone did. In 1968, a company of U.S. soldiers murdered five hundred villagers in what, even now, was considered the worst atrocity of the war. There'd been no reason for the killings—they'd found no VC in the village, met no resistance—but over the course of that day, a company of U.S. soldiers systematically slaughtered innocent men, women, and children, blowing them up with grenades and rocket launchers, lining them in ditches and gunning them to death. Infants. Pregnant women. Anything that moved, breathed, or crawled. There'd been a massive cover-up followed by congressional hearings, a trial, national outrage . . .

Darzell had been clear about questions, but I couldn't help myself. "My Lai was U.S. Army. Jason was a marine."

"All very true, but Vietnam is a big, out-of-control, great, ugly mess of a war." Darzell blew smoke, and stared me down with those hard, brown, soldier eyes. "You think My Lai is the only place bad shit happened?"

30

Darzell was right about one thing. Telling the story took time, and in the warm sunlight of *after*, I felt disjointed, cold, and overawed. Thoughts of my brother, the things he'd done . . .

"How about I drive this time?"

Becky took the keys, and I looked back at the pool hall, squinting in the bright light. Darzell was still inside, but his father stood in the open door, giving me a long look and a somber wave before stepping back into the gloom.

"Come on, handsome."

Becky got me back to the car, and inside. Even behind the wheel, she left me alone; as if she understood the kind of processing I needed to do in order to understand the many pieces and all the complicated ways they fit.

"It's not fair," I finally said.

"No, it's not."

"I don't know him at all. I don't think anyone does."

"Do you want to talk about it?"

I ran the movie Darzell had put in my head, a silent reel of bodies in a blood-soaked river, of all the people dead, and all the ones *not* dead. "Why didn't Jason tell me? Jesus, Becky. Why didn't he tell any of us?"

"I don't know. I wish I did."

"It makes sense, though. The drugs. The way he is."

"Are you going to tell him?"

"That I know the truth? I don't know. I feel like my head is going to explode."

"Just breathe, okay? In and out, nice and deep."

I closed my eyes, and did as she asked. When I opened them again, I had no idea where we were. "Wait. Where are we going?"

"You trust me, right?"

"I do."

"So trust me."

She showed cool eyes and a slender smile, so I watched the city pass, thinking of cops, reporters, and prosecutors, thinking, *They don't know him, either, none of them do . . .*

Ten minutes later, I knew where we were. *The abandoned hardware store. A tumbledown and familiar house.* "We're going to your place?"

She flashed another slender smile, but drove past her street, turning at the next one, and pulling to the curb at an empty lot with old, small houses on either side. "Come with me."

She took me into the vacant lot, and we clambered through the foundations of a long-gone house, then out the other side, and down a steep bank, wading through waist-deep kudzu until trees appeared and the vines grew up and over. She pulled me deeper into the forest, and when we reached the creek, she turned along the bank, parting vines until the same pool of deep, clear water appeared.

"You remember our swim?" She slipped off her shoes, entirely serious. "How about a real one this time?"

When her shirt came off, the bra came with it. She blushed only a little, and I thought of all the times I'd seen her at the quarry, browned by the sun and sleek as a seal. She helped me out of my shirt, and kissed me. Her breasts flattened on my chest, and I felt them there, small and warm, a brush of skin before she stepped back and removed the rest of her clothes. The blush was still there, but she turned for the pool, crooked a finger, and tossed off a knowing smile. "Are you coming or not?"

I undressed and followed her into the pool, moving close until there were mere inches between us. "Why now?" I wanted to know.

"Because I was watching your face, and not Darzell's." She moved closer until we were touching. "Did you know that you were crying?"

"Only at the end."

"I thought it was beautiful."

"Why?"

"Because he made you believe in what you were doing."

"I already believed."

"But there's a difference between duty and love. You wanted to help Jason because he's your brother—that's the duty. Darzell made you love him."

It was true. She was right.

"Kiss me," she said, and that's what I did.

Softly.

Adoringly.

"Now, love me," she said, and I did that, too.

Later, with Becky stretched beside me on a bed of ferns and moss, I thought for the millionth time that the day was barely real: the touch of our bodies, the foundations of childhood we'd burned down together. Even now the lines of her were like forgings on my skin: one leg across my own, her fingers twined into mine.

"Regrets?" she asked. In response, I held her tighter. "Can we do it again, then?"

"Are you sure?" I asked.

It was becoming my favorite question.

Much later, we dressed self-consciously, the awkwardness passing only when Becky caught my eye, and grinned. "The clothes came *off* a lot easier."

After that, it was familiar and easy, her hand in mine as we made our way uphill through the old trees hung with ivy and kudzu. At the car, Becky pushed her hands into her pockets, shoulders rising as she measured me in a knowing, still-amused way. "Was that your first time?" I blushed furiously before she took pity. "It was pretty awesome."

"The second time was better," I said.

"Really? I thought, the third . . ."

She grinned again, and I kissed the curving lips, one hand on hot denim and the other on hot metal. Only the breeze was cool, and that's because it was getting dark.

"So . . . ?"

She broke the kiss as if dusk on the street ended more than the day. Sadly, I felt the same truth: that time may have stopped for a while, but only in the place we'd been. "This has been good," I said.

"Good, but real."

"Next-level stuff," I agreed.

"So . . . ?"

She said it again, but this time it was about Jason rather than us, the shadow of the day. "I'll go home, I suppose. Talk to my father."

"Will you tell him what we learned?"

"About Jason?"

"Maybe it will help."

I nodded, but had my doubts. I was still so angry.

Even if my father believed . . .

Or if he already knew . . .

Becky took me home in Dana's car, and the quiet between us was a comfortable one. We said goodbye at the bottom of my parents' driveway, and what I saw in her eyes was like a jewel to carry in my pocket, and take out if the night got long. After she left, I stayed outside to watch stars come alive as purple light was drawn off like a veil. The air was heavy with the perfume of my mother's garden, a blend of climbing rose and camellia, of Princess Blush and heliotrope, hibiscus and Plum Mist, hydrangea and dogwood and daffodil—a glut of plants and vine I was embarrassed to know as well as I did.

Turning, at last, I walked up the long drive and found my car parked near the garage. My father must have brought it from the impound lot. Inside the house, it seemed every light was burning, the rooms so bright I couldn't find a shadow if I tried. I closed the door gently, wary of hushed-voice sounds that carried from the kitchen. In the years since Robert's death, caution like that came to me as naturally as breathing. Fights. Tears. Hysteria. I'd walked in on every scene imaginable.

This time, it was quiet but tense, my mother looking wan as my father knelt at her side, speaking with the kind of calm assurance that had become, I'd often thought, the thread that held her together.

"He's fine, sweetheart. I promise."

"But we don't know . . . we haven't heard . . ."

"I'm sure he'll be home soon."

"But Chance said . . ."

"Chance said Gibby was fine, honey. He said not to worry."

"But that was hours ago . . ."

Damn. I could have called. I should have. "Uh . . . hi, guys."

They turned at the same time, and my mother swept up and across the room, her arms tight on my neck as she squeezed. I tried to disentangle the embrace, but she only squeezed harder, her face hot against my shirt before she pushed back, and let the anger out.

"Where the hell have you been? Do you know how I've worried? Do you have any idea?"

"I'm sorry, Mom. I'm okay."

She pulled me into a second embrace so desperate and maternal I could barely stand it.

"I said I'm okay. Okay?"

Thank God for my father.

"Sweetheart, please. He's home and safe." He drew her back, and guided her across the room. "Let me talk to him for a bit. You should rest. How about a hot bath and some tea?"

"Don't patronize me, William."

"He's not going anywhere. Gibson, tell her."

"I won't go anywhere."

I made it sincere, but she pulled away from my father, her eyes wide and dark with worry. "Did you have something to do with that girl? They say you've been sleeping with her."

I couldn't have been more surprised had she drawn a knife and stabbed me.

"Martinez and Smith," my father explained. "They've been here twice, trying to find you. They made some veiled allegations, asked some unpleasant questions. We'll talk about it in a bit. And *you*?" He turned my mother into the circle of his arms. "Don't let them rattle you. You're a cop's wife. You know how this works."

"I just hate it so much! What they said, what they implied . . ."

She cut her eyes my way, but my father caught her chin with a finger.

"He's home and safe. I won't let him leave." He kissed her forehead, and she relaxed against him. "Now, how about that bath?"

They left me alone with my thoughts, which in essence were, *What the hell?* When my father returned, he put the kettle on to boil, and offered a pinch-lipped, apologetic smile.

"You're not angry?" I asked.

"I am, but mostly at Martinez. He's running early and hot, and knows it, too, the uncaring little shit." He pulled two beers from the fridge, and handed one to me, a first. "As for your mother's concerns, it didn't help that you ditched school, skipped dinner, and told Chance you were coming straight home. She has imagined all kinds of horrible scenarios."

"What did Martinez say that made her so upset?"

"Oh, nothing much." My father sat across the table. "Only that you've been involved with an older woman of dubious morals, and that he found you, once, half-dressed in her home. That said woman is considered *missing,* possibly *abducted.* That you know more about Tyra than you're letting on, and more about Jason, too, that brothers are brothers, and genes will tell." My father sat across the table. "Martinez doesn't like me very much."

I had no idea what to say. I didn't even try.

"Let's talk about Sara." He gave a keen-eyed look I didn't much like.

"Burklow told you what happened?"

"That you entered Sara's home illegally? That you're the one who found her gone? You should have come to me, son. Are you really that angry with me?"

I stayed quiet again. I didn't want to answer.

"Listen, Martinez and Smith may be ahead of the curve on this, but they're not on the wrong road. Any cop would look at you sideways right now. That means you need to talk to me. I need to know everything you know. It's how I stay ahead of this. Son, look at me. Do you understand the stakes involved?"

"I didn't hurt anybody."

"That's childish thinking. Martinez can ruin your life without convicting you, or even charging you. He can hold you, interrogate you, destroy you in the press." He turned the beer bottle in his heavy fingers. "Chance said you dropped him off at two o'clock. That was seven hours ago. I want to know where you went afterward, who you were with, and what you were doing."

My time with Becky made an answer to that question impossible. "Ask a different question."

"Let's start with Sara, then. Have you been sexually active?"

"Is that your business?"

"Martinez will ask, so I need to know."

"No," I replied coldly. "No sex with Sara."

"But you've been in her condominium."

"Yes."

"Her bedroom?"

I looked away.

"Son, I need to know what you touched, when you were there, who saw you there. So let's try this again. Have you been in Sara's bedroom?"

"Yes."

"Why?"

"I was worried. I went upstairs to check on her."

"What did you touch? What did you see?"

I told him the same story I'd told his partner.

"What about Tyra Norris?" he asked. "Have you been in her bedroom?"

It went like that for ten minutes. An interrogation. Round and round. Backtracking. Checking for inconsistencies. "When you were with Sara, where would you go?"

"Her place. The car. We didn't spend that much time together."

"Were you ever alone with Tyra?"

"No."

"In her room?"

"I've already told you."

"What about her car?"

"No."

"Chance mentioned a girl named Becky Collins. Is that who you were with today?"

"What if I was?"

"Does she know you were involved with Sara?"

"No."

"Could she have guessed?"

I shrugged.

"Why did you go to Sara's condominium?"

"I wanted information on Tyra. I thought Sara could help."

"A moment ago, you said you went because you were worried."

"I guess it was a little bit of both."

"So this *is* about Jason?"

I shrugged again. He didn't like it.

"You said you were done trying to help your brother. This morning in your bedroom, that's what you said."

"I don't remember saying that."

"Are you done with this foolishness or not? Because you need to be. And you need to look at me, too. Look at me, and tell me that you're done trying to play detective. I want to hear it. No more bullshit for your brother. Tell me it's over."

I clenched my jaw, as stubborn as I'd ever been. "I went to see him at Lanesworth."

His eyes narrowed before he got control of his anger. "When?"

"This morning."

"Son, that was an incredibly stupid thing to do. You don't think Martinez can make hay with your visit? He's already thinking, *Conspiracy.* We need to worry about you, your future."

"What about Jason?" I asked.

"What about your mother?"

He raised his voice, probably from long habit. My mother was the lever that had always worked. "I'm not a kid anymore."

"From where I sit, you are."

"I understand that you feel that way. Let me tell you the problem from where *I* sit." I stared him down, as cold as the bottom of a cave. "From the time I could speak, what I heard from you was *family first.* Family first, and *then* faith and trust and love and everything else. Those were good years and good lessons."

I stood, and looked down, flush with all the things I wanted to say: that my father lived on the fence, and my mother on the wrong side of everything, that trust was *not* built into the bones of this house. There were other things to say, too, like Jason's warning about dangerous people, and what I'd learned about his time in Vietnam, that it explained *who* he was, and *why* he was. I wanted to say, too, that Jason knew who'd killed Tyra, that he was protecting me, and that he knew more than the cops, who thought they were so smart. I should have told my father all of those things, but did not.

He should have believed in Jason.

He should have believed from the very start.

In my room, I locked the door. The place was not that big, but I paced it, thinking of Vietnam, Jason, and my father, the thoughts like a dog chasing its tail. Throwing myself on the bed, I pictured Robert's dive from Devil's Ledge, the cross of his body nailed to that high, pale sky. He'd been too soft for war.

Jason, though . . .

His first year in Vietnam had been raw combat from day one: deep-cover recon, search and destroy, cross-border infiltration. In that first year, Jason won a field promotion, two Purple Hearts, and a Silver Star. Darzell's feelings about it had been pretty plain.

People talked about him even then . . .

We never heard a thing about it.

Jason must have impressed some important people, though, because when he re-upped for another tour, he was seconded to a Navy SEAL master chief and an ARVN colonel in command of three South Vietnamese rangers, the six of them tasked to run disguised gunboats into the DMZ to rescue downed aviators. In the first six months, they saved eleven Americans, including a marine lieutenant with a bullet in his lung, and two shattered legs. Under heavy fire, Jason dragged him from a crumpled jet, and carried him four miles through dense jungle, getting shot twice for the trouble. That earned him another Purple Heart and, this time, the Navy Cross. None of us knew about that, either, but Darzell had nursed the bitterness for a while.

Should have been the Medal of Honor.

Ask any marine.

No one could doubt my brother's willingness or courage. He'd won other commendations. Darzell had other stories.

But the rest of it . . .

What came last . . .

I rose from the bed, too keyed up to have my head on a pillow. The room was still a box, but I paced it, anyway.

What else could I do?

Seriously.

31

X had Jason brought to the subbasement, and his eyes were keen as the young man entered the cell. It was the last cell in the row, and the one he used to store his completed paintings. Dozens hung at eye level; hundreds more leaned in stacks against the walls.

"Ah, Jason. Good. I want to show you something." He took a canvas from a stack of others. It was a portrait of Jason, his eyes intent behind strands of dark hair, his face battered and bruised, but set in determined lines. "I call it *The Unconquerable Soul*. It's what I see in you when we fight."

Jason struggled with a sudden surge of unexpected emotion. The painting was . . . *intimate*.

"It's in the eyes," X said.

For Jason, looking into those painted eyes was like staring into something at once familiar, terrible, and strange, a part of himself he preferred to keep hidden and dark. That a man like X could capture it so perfectly . . .

"Put it away, please."

"You don't like it?"

"Please. If you would." X seemed surprised and hurt, but Jason didn't care about that. "When I finished my sentence, you said I was free, that you would stay out of my life."

"I did say that, yes." X propped the painting against the wall. "But I have so little time in the world."

"I don't understand what that has to do with me."

"Hours, Jason, a few days at the end of this life. Is it so hard to imagine that I'd wish to spend that time with a man I admire? There's no need to respond, of course. I see how angry I've made you—it *is* a selfish desire, but you should be flattered. I say *flattered* because what I see in you, I see in me. I'm a sociopath, of course, and you are not; but as the world forgets, *you* will remember."

"And that's what you want?"

"As epitaphs go, it's better than most."

"An epitaph." Jason could not conceal the anger.

X didn't care. "An epitaph. A marker." He shrugged languidly. "When the time comes, I want you there, an admirable man to bear witness. I've asked Warden Wilson to make the arrangements."

"You did all of this so I could bear witness?"

"I won't leave this world surrounded by sheep, alone. The last thing I wish to see is your face. As I said, you should be flattered."

X smiled as if the matter were settled, but that's not what Jason felt. Rage. Loss. He was a blind man. "I should have killed you when I had the chance."

"Perhaps you should have."

"I should kill you right now."

"As always, in this place . . ." X showed his palms, no smile left. "You are very welcome to try."

Twenty minutes later, guards dropped Jason onto a table under bright lights, leaving the room as a weary doctor snapped on latex gloves, and cut away Jason's clothing.

"Can you roll for me?" Jason shifted so the clothing could be removed and discarded. "Now back."

Jason could recall no conscious decision to *try*, but staring past the doctor's shoulder, he remembered X at the end, the last man standing but *almost* as bloody and *almost* as broken.

You must understand, Jason. It's not the dying that bothers me but the idea of doing it front of these people. I know you find me horrible, but tell me you see that . . .

He'd collapsed into a chair, almost begging.

Tell me you understand . . .

The troubling thing was that Jason did understand. In three years of war, he'd been shot, stabbed, and burned, and come back to fight so many times that even hardened marines thought him charmed or blessed. And maybe that was true. All Jason knew for sure was that strength mattered, and that he respected it.

Of course, X was insane . . .

Jason ground his teeth as the doctor worked his narrow fingers, probing and pushing.

"Well, you've looked worse." The old man's voice was thin as a reed, but his eyes were clear. "Cracked ribs—*again*—and at least one that's broken. Dislocation of the left shoulder. I can't count all the contusions, but he went easy on your face this time. Kidneys are the worst. You'll pee blood for a few days. Let me know if it lasts longer than that." He cocked an eyebrow over the sharp, right eye, looking down until Jason nodded, then continuing in the same reedy tone. "Two broken fingers, a dislocated thumb . . ."

Jason closed his eyes as the doctor droned on.

He'd been here before.

He knew the drill.

In his cell sometime later, he remembered something X had called him.

An admirable man . . .

But Jason knew the deeper truth: that if he were truly that admirable, he'd have killed X then and there, for Tyra's sake, if nothing else.

One more day and another night . . .

Jason shifted on the bunk, wary of the pain.

After that, the bastard dies . . .

32

In thirty years on the force, Bill French had faced a lifetime of short-cut lives and the disbelieving stares of those who'd somehow survived. What he'd learned in all that time was to watch the eyes, the eyes of the grieving child, the wife, the empty-handed lover. Some could accept the changes life had so cruelly wrought—roadside or blood-spattered, they gathered shards of hope as a child might gather shells. Others would never recover, and when that showed, it did so in the eyes, as well.

French didn't like what he'd seen in Gibby's eyes. They weren't the warm eyes he knew so well, nor were they the thoughtful, deep ones, and not the kind or steady ones, either. Five minutes ago, eyes like that might have peered out from his son's face, but not anymore. His eyes now were remorseless and unflinching.

Like Jason's eyes, he decided, *and not like Robert's at all.*

French was still at the table when headlights slashed through the window. He recognized the car; checked his watch. Outside, he found David Martin halfway across the driveway, looking haggard in the shadows. "Captain."

"You know why I'm here?"

"I have a suspicion."

"You're lucky it's not uniformed officers, cuffs out."

They met on the bottom step, and French stuck out a hand. "It's not exactly *great* to see you."

Captain Martin grunted in agreement, and they shook. "You're not on the top of my list, either."

"He's pressing charges?"

"Let's talk inside?"

"Yeah, sure." French led the captain into the kitchen. "Beer?"

"You have anything stronger?"

"You still like Macallan?"

"The twelve-year?"

"What honest cop can afford the eighteen?"

"You're the only one I know."

"Three hundred a bottle? No thanks. You think that's why Martinez hates me?"

"Rich wife? Fancy house? Nah, nobody wants that."

"Funny. Thanks."

"He does want your job, though. He pretty much asked me for it."

"Recently?"

"An hour ago."

French made his own throat noise, then poured three fingers of scotch into a pair of cut tumblers, and gave one to the captain. Martin took a sip and made all the right faces: appreciation, contemplation. That lasted about three seconds. "Did you have to hit him so hard?"

French sat, and sipped, and shrugged. "He made my wife cry."

"Martinez was right to come here, and was right to ask those questions. Gibby's whereabouts and movements need to be accounted for, if only to rule him out as a suspect. It's Cop 101."

"Yeah, well. He was being an asshole."

"Oh, an *asshole*?" The captain faked amazement. "No one told me that. Can you imagine the shock I'm feeling right now?"

"Now you're being an asshole."

"Only to make a point. Because I know you've pushed hard plenty of times, and suspect that what Martinez did was no different. Right or wrong, my friend, your son is in the thick of things."

"Only circumstantially."

"He knew Tyra *and* Sara. Your other son knew them, too, but that's not the point. Or, hell, maybe it is. The only thing clear to me is that Martinez was doing his job. You were out of line to interfere, let alone lay him out on your kitchen floor."

"Maybe." Another sip. "But you didn't see the pleasure he took in doing it."

"You shattered his nose."

"Worth it."

"You also broke off two veneers."

"That reminds me." French fished in his shirt pocket, pulled out bits of fake teeth, and dropped them on the table. The captain turned a little green. French threw a leg up on the table beside them. Blue jeans. Nice loafers. "Will he press charges?"

"So far, he's not . . . uh . . . amenable to letting you slide."

"You don't really believe Gibson has anything to do with this, do you?"

"Two days ago? No. Never. But now?" The captain spread his palms in a way French did not like at all. "Now, his brother's back in town, and dealing guns. Gibby's out all hours, and mixed up with another outlaw motorcycle club—"

"Just the Angels, and only the once."

"A naïve kid trying to help his big brother. Yeah, you told me. But it's not that simple anymore." The captain pushed his drink to the side, his features serious. "The night we arrested Jason on weapons violations, we picked up one of the Pagans he'd been selling to. Darius Simms, some kind of shot caller. You heard of him?"

"He says Jason shot him in the foot and leg. I read the report."

"Not all of it."

The tone of his voice was not a good sign. "You held back on me?"

"I'm sorry, Bill. I had to. Gibby was there when Jason shot Darius Simms. He was in the room, an accessory."

"Accessory to what?"

"Multiple assaults? Attempted murder? The DA has it under review, and is keeping his cards close. What we know for sure is that Gibby helped Jason carry off the guns and cash, and load it all in the van. And don't argue with me, Bill. His prints are on the guns."

"I don't believe it."

"It gets worse. He was seen at Sara's condominium. Today. This morning. Martinez found a witness."

"Who?"

"You know better than that, Bill."

"How solid is the ID?"

"Bulletproof. I'm sorry . . ."

"Who is this witness?"

"Come on, Bill. I'm over the line even being here. You know that." The captain reached for the drink, waiting for French to shake his head, and stare off into space. Seeing what?

His wife, when she heard?

The ruin this would cause?

"Is there anything else you can tell me?"

"Only that two others were with your son when he entered Sara's condominium, a young man we believe to be his friend Chance, and a young woman we've not yet identified. It's also possible that Ken Burklow made an appearance. I'm dragging my feet on that, but Martinez is foaming about it. I think Ken will be okay, though. The witness is barely twelve, and every white man over fifty looks more or less the same. The rest of it, though . . . The wheels have to turn."

"Those unfortunate wheels, yeah."

"Do you know where Gibby is now? You don't have to answer. I'm here as your friend. It's just that, well, I was there on the day of his christening."

"He's upstairs. Asleep, I hope."

"You might want to talk to him. Prep him for what's coming."

"I'll give him tonight. Best for both of us, I think."

"If Martinez asks . . ."

"You were never here."

"Well." Captain Martin offered an expression of unusual helplessness.

"Yeah." French patted him on the shoulder, and guided him to the front door. "That about sums it up."

33

Sara was awake, but afraid to open her eyes. If she did, it would be real: this place, the helplessness. But hours had passed. Her knuckles were bloody, her fingernails torn.

How long since she'd risen from that horrible, skinny, metal-railed bed?

Beyond hunger and thirst, she had no way to tell.

Where was he?

That was the worst.

What was this place? What did he want?

Him.

He.

Asshole motherfucker.

That was all she had, rage and fear, back and forth. Tears had fallen and dried, but that was over. She'd decided. She looked for more of that courage, and a sound escaped her lips, the smallest thing.

I will not be weak.

I will not die like Tyra.

Reece was behind the wall when she made that first sound. And the angle was perfect! The light on her face. Small darkness where one leg pressed against the other. It would happen soon, he thought.

She would stop pretending.

She would open her eyes.

When the moment came, Reece felt a pounding in his chest; and when she moved, he was behind the walls. She was not panicked as she'd been before, no tears or drama as she drifted from room to room touching the walls or opening drawers. In the kitchen, she filled a glass with water and drank it down. In the bathroom, she splashed water on her face, and he was there for that, too, behind the mirror, and close on the other side, watching as she stared at her reflection, bare inches between them. She would submit, in the end—they all did—but would she choose to do so? His was such a simple desire: to know as other men knew, to be drawn down, invited, to close his eyes and stab out the sorrows. He saw how it could be with Sara, the *yes* in her throat, and a needful rise, the velvet hinge of her un-scissored legs.

She was perfect.

She would be different.

He closed his eyes to imagine it better.

In the darkness beyond the walls of Reece's house, three men sat in the back of a windowless van. Zachary Byrd was in charge. He had the scars, the clients, the money. The other two were hired hands, good with knife or gun, and willing to kill anything for the right price. Wilkinson and Pugh charged five thousand apiece, and Byrd was happy to pay it. His contract with X was for a half-million dollars, plus a fifty thousand kicker if he made Reece beg, and got it on tape. Of course, Reece was supposed to be some kind of tough-nut killer. He worked for X, so maybe he was. Either way . . .

"Why can't we just shoot this guy?"

Wilkinson had small eyes and a wound of a mouth. Frowning at the question, Byrd said, "You know why."

"The client says *slow and bloody,* I get it. But why does he care?"

Byrd thumbed a knife's edge, and sheathed it. "I guess this Reece guy stepped on the wrong toes. What does it matter?"

"*The wrong toes.* Ha!"

That was Pugh, as thoughtful as a murdered cat, but good with locks and alarms. Byrd sheathed a second knife, frowning. "Listen up, and let me be clear. We do this like I said. Screw it up, and I'll peel your face like a potato."

Wilkinson was smart enough to nod, but Pugh was still grinning like his dick was a jack-in-the-box and Miss America was turning the crank.

Byrd scowled at them both, but on the inside was smiling.

One night's work . . .

Half a million plus . . .

Reece had always had a powerful imagination. He could look at a woman and know how they would be together, whether she wanted it or not. If the target was a man, he knew exactly how the man would scream, and what bribe or debasement he might offer up to make the pain stop. For Sara, he imagined the time she would need to adjust and accept. If it took weeks, that would be fine. Even months. It wasn't just her looks. It was the way she moved and smiled, something about the soul, and Reece had *never* cared about the soul. It would require patience, and for Reece that was hard.

For Sara, though . . .

He played it out: the carrot, the stick. Almost blissful, he opened his eyes.

Amber lights were flashing in the silence.

Someone was on the grounds!

In a sudden panic, Reece spun from the two-way glass, crabbing sideways in a mad dash for the security room. He took the next corner too fast, tore skin on a nail, ignored it. At the monitors, he bent over the controls.

He'd been so careful!

But the cameras didn't lie: three men over the wall, and moving fast, single file as they neared the house.

Not cops, though . . .

If cops knew about Reece, they'd have come in tactical squads.

Simple thieves?

He discarded the thought as soon as it surfaced. The house was lit up like Christmas, three cars in the driveway.

Private contractors, then.

A three-man crew.

Reece's first thought was X, but X didn't know about the girl. He couldn't.

Other enemies?

Reece did know violent men, but, like him, they ghosted in the cracks, and killed in quiet places. So maybe it *was* X. In the end, it didn't matter. This was Reece's home, and his home was a killing place. So he watched them come, three men, moving like pros, one directing the others. They drew down in a patch of cover, but there was no such thing as *cover*, not here. Every camera was night-capable, with intersecting lines of sight. Reece watched for another moment, then thumbed a switch, unbolting the side door.

Byrd was feeling cocky. An easy climb, up and over the wall. No dogs or automatic lights. When Wilkinson and Pugh settled into the darkness beside him, Byrd gestured with an open hand. "West-side corner."

He went first, and the others followed, crossing a final stretch of open ground, then settling into darkness beneath a pair of French windows. Pugh grinned in the gloom. "Walk in the park."

But Byrd had checked the windows, and knew better. "Polycarbonate windows. Steel frames and armored hinges."

"Bulletproof? Come on, man."

"Nothing has changed." Byrd cut off the complaint, but he saw the look that passed between the other men. Armored glass cost money, lots of it. Now they worried about other countermeasures, greater risk. "We knew he was rich when we took the job. I'm sure he has nice furniture, too. So stay cool. Do the work." He gestured north along the wall. "Side door. Forty feet." When they got there, he said, "Pugh."

Pugh examined the lock. "Four-ton dead bolts. Hardened steel cylinders. Drill plates, probably. Ball bearings . . ."

"Alarmed?"

"Nothing I can't handle."

"Do it."

Pugh unfolded a packet of picks and bypass circuits, then put pressure on the door handle, just in case. The handle turned, and Byrd shook his head, disbelieving.

Easiest half million ever . . .

Reece gave them five seconds to clear the door, then triggered a circuit to close and seal it.

No handle on the inside.

No access to the hinges.

Reece waited for that to sink in, then triggered the second door.

"Byrd, what the hell just happened?"

Byrd waved Pugh to silence, drawing a pistol as he did so. The floor was mortared flagstone, the walls concrete. Thirty feet down, a second door had just slammed shut, and it looked every bit as solid as the first.

"I don't see any nice furniture."

"Can it, Wilkinson." Byrd pointed at the second door. "Pugh, check it out."

The second door was solid steel, exactly like the first, nine feet tall, and faceless. "We're not getting through this," Pugh said.

"Talk to me."

"Hardened steel in a recessed frame. I'd need an oxyacetylene torch and at least thirty minutes."

"Jesus. You want a sandwich with that?"

"You see the cameras?"

Byrd did: one mounted high at each end of the hall.

Wilkinson said, "What do we do about this, boss man?"

Byrd studied the trap they'd sprung: thirty feet of concrete, stone, and steel. "I'll figure something out."

"I would love to believe that."

"I've been in worse places," Byrd said.

But he was wrong about that, too.

As soon as Reece got bored, he gassed them. The process wasn't pretty. Pumped into a confined space, most incapacitating aerosols caused vomiting, seizures, or death, sometimes all three. Reece used a mix of methyl propyl ether and bovine anesthesia, a concoction perfected by a Mennonite serial rapist who liked to creep about in the dark and spray it into open windows. Reece found it acceptable, but only if the odd death was not a problem. He'd never use it on Sara, for instance.

But for these guys . . .

When all three were down, Reece pumped out the gas, rolled in a

pallet dolly, and wheeled them outside to a concrete ramp, then down
to a basement room equipped with surgical lighting, trench drains, and
hydraulic tables. Metal shelving held the preferred tools of his trade, not
just the scalpels, scissors, and saws, but forceps and towel clamps and organ holders, bone mallets and chisels, curettes and skin hooks and rib
spreaders. Reece had trephines and Stryker saws, all kinds of retractors
and hemostats. Ironically, he'd never used the room. Like the space upstairs, it was intended for special occasions and special people.

But these men had come, intending harm.

That made them special enough.

When the screaming started, Sara was curled in a corner beside the bed.
She thought maybe it was a nightmare, but the sound went on and on, and
sounded like a soul being torn apart. She covered her ears, but nothing
helped. And when the first scream stopped, another one began.

A different scream, she could tell.

A different scream and a different soul.

For Reece, the first two were mostly mechanical. He took some time, but
not as much as he normally might.

The first one, he skinned alive.

The second took four tourniquets and a bone saw.

"Can I assume you'll answer my questions?"

Reece peered down at the last man living, naked as a newborn, and
sheeting sweat as he bucked against the restraints, frantically trying to
force words past the ball gag in his mouth.

"I beg your pardon." Reece leaned close, amused.

But the clock really *was* ticking.

He removed the gag, and the words poured out. "Anything! I'll tell
you anything you want! But please, please don't, not like them, dear God,
Jesus Christ, not like them . . ."

Reece waited for the tears and silence. Both came quickly. "I have
questions," he said. "If you answer them for me, you won't die like, you
know . . ." Reece tipped his head at the dead men on the other tables.

"Anything! Please!"

But Reece shushed him like a child. He already knew the answers. This was more about confirmation. "You came here to kill me?" The man dipped his chin, still sobbing. "X hired you?" Another nod. "Any special instructions?"

"F-fifty thousand. Fifty extra if we . . . if we . . ."

"It's okay," Reece said. "I asked the question. There is no wrong answer."

"Oh, Jesus . . ." Sweat sheeted the man's face, dripped into his eyes. "Fifty thousand if we made you beg."

"For my life?"

"For the pain to stop."

"Ah. I see." Reece pointed his chin at the dead men on the other tables. "Something like that?"

"He wanted it on film."

"That explains this." Reece picked up a video camera he'd found in one of the dead men's satchels. "How much was the contract?"

"Half a million."

"Plus the fifty?" Reece frowned deeply. It was insulting. Fiddling with the camera, he wedged it onto a shelf, making small adjustments.

From the table, the bound man said, "Nothing personal, right? You know X. You understand how he is. It's just business."

"I do know X, that's true." Reece spoke distractedly. Video cameras like this were new to the market. He had little experience with them.

"So we're good, yeah? Just business."

"Well, I don't know that we're *good* . . ." Still distracted. Reece checked the lighting, tweaked the angle of the camera. Satisfied, he rolled out a fresh tray of surgical gear.

"Whoa! Hey, man! Come on, now! We had a deal! You said you'd let me go!"

"Actually"—Reece pointed with a skin hook retractor—"I said I wouldn't kill you like *them*."

34

It took hours for Reece to dismember and bag the bodies, then bleach-clean the tables, floor, and instruments. It was grim work, but he needed that time to think about X. A voice inside argued that time alone would solve the problem, that X would, in fact, be executed very soon. As resolutions went, it was simplistic. X was the most vindictive man Reece had ever known, the proof of which now filled two chest freezers in the corner, each bit of body neatly bagged and taped and stacked. Of course, those three men were only the beginning. Reece had seven places he considered safe, and X could not have known he'd choose this one for the girl. He had to assume, then, that X had dispatched as many as seven teams. The specifics didn't matter. The implications did. X wanted Reece found, tortured, and killed; and cost was not an issue. That risk wouldn't simply disappear once X was executed. He had money, lawyers, access to dangerous men. He'd put a contract on Reece's life just to make a point.

A laugh escaped Reece's lips, but sounded more like a high-pitched, disbelieving titter. In X's world, there were unspoken rules and unforgivable sins. Reece was a dead man walking, and starting to feel that way. How much money *did* X have? Hundreds of millions? A billion? No one could escape that kind of reach. He'd spend his life afraid and running.

Sweet Jesus, he thought. *Is this how it feels?*

He couldn't simply run. X's people would find him, no question. Besides, Reece had too much pride for that. Too much faintheartedness, too—that was becoming sadly evident: the liquid insides, a certain weakness in his limbs. He had to get ahead of this, of X. Reece tried to think it through.

Why did X want him dead?

Because he'd taken the girl after X gave specific orders not to do it.

Why did X care if Reece took the girl?

Because if Sara died, reasonable minds might doubt that Jason French had killed Tyra Norris. Cops might look elsewhere.

But why did that matter?

Because X wanted Jason at Lanesworth.

Why?

Unknown. Unknowable.

What made Jason so important to a man like X?

Good question.

Just how important was he?

That was the rubber on the road.

An hour later, Reece was behind the wheel of a jet-black BMW, peering through darkened grounds at the house where Gibson French lived with his parents. The structure was set back from the road, but undoubtedly had a high-end security system. Plus, the father was a cop, and Reece hated cops.

Ticktock, motherfucker . . .

Reece was hard on himself, but things were moving fast, and he had to move faster.

How long until X learned that Reece was still breathing?

Not long.

For a moment more, Reece stared up at the big house, then U-turned across the road, heading for the poor side of things. That's where Gibson's friend lived.

He was the weak spot.

That's how it would happen.

Chance spent the night alone and wide awake, most of it cross-legged on an old blanket, huddled where the bedside lamp spilled yellow light in a broken circle. Magazines littered the blanket around him—more war porn—but Chance couldn't look past the photograph cupped in the palms of his hands.

"Fuck you, Martinez."

He blinked away a tear, but the photograph remained: *Tyra Norris, or what was left of her.* He could only see her in parts. The ruin of her body was so . . . *immediate.* It hadn't happened on a battlefield far away or in some distant, other city. Whoever did this to Tyra was in the here and now.

"Goddamn it."

Chance sniffed loudly, and scrubbed his face with a sleeve. Martinez had come to the house twice, and the first time, Chance had claimed to be a minor whose mother should be there for him to answer questions. The second time was different. Late at night, a shit-slick grin on his face.

You're eighteen, kid. I checked.

Then he'd started with the questions about Gibby, easy ones at first, things like places and timing, and when did Chance last see his best friend. Eventually, he'd asked about Gibby's brother, killed in the war.

Did Gibby view the body? How did that make him feel?

Does he blame the government?

Society?

Tell me about the funeral . . .

He had a real hard-on for Jason, though, and got there pretty quick.

Does he talk about him?

Admire him?

Does Gibby want to go to war like Jason?

How often do they speak? See each other?

I know he's been to Lanesworth . . .

Questions like that came hard and fast. Ten minutes' worth, at least. Then the questions got dark.

Does your friend like dirty movies?

Those flat, cop eyes.

Magazines, I bet. The really nasty ones.

Are girls afraid of him?

What about animals? Does he like to kill things?

Martinez went down so many twisty dark holes Chance decided he must be screwed in the head to *think* of those questions.

Is your friend into ropes and knots?

What about chains?

How about in the locker room? Does he pay a little too much attention in the shower?

Does he do drugs?

What about booze?

Let's go back to the pornography question . . .

Turned out they were still on the easy part. When Martinez finally lost his cool, he'd pulled out a picture of Tyra's murdered corpse, and made Chance look at it. *Closer,* he'd ordered, his hand on the back of Chance's neck. *Get up in there, good and close. You see that? You freaking taste that?*

It took the partner to pull him off.

When dawn came at last, it gathered like a fist, and Chance pulled himself into the shower, water beating down as he imagined mountain roads and a girl on the back of a brand-new motorcycle, maybe someone as pretty as Becky.

Why couldn't it happen like that?

He wasn't ugly.

He wasn't stupid.

Out of the shower, Chance twisted a towel around his waist, thinking he would never have that new motorcycle. His mother was pulling two-and-a-half shifts, all night and most of the day. She needed a new car. They were two months down on the rent, but she wouldn't let him work until the schooling was done . . .

Chance pulled on jeans, and got a comb through his hair before he heard music, a hint of it from down the hallway. He wasn't imagining it. His mother had come home early, he thought. A forgotten something. An unexpected shift change. Either way, it was all for the good. He'd make her breakfast, and put her to bed.

But that's not how it went down.

The man in the living room chair looked like Jason said he would:

narrow and seamed, with eyes too old for such a bland face. That was the first thing Chance saw. Second was the gun.

"This will be easier," the man said, "if you do not scream."

Chance closed his mouth; couldn't feel his fingers.

"Good boy. Sit down." He gestured with the gun, and Chance sank into a chair. "Tell me your name," he said.

Chance told him his name.

"There is no car in the driveway. Is there anyone else in the house? Mother? Father?"

"Mother. At work."

"Does she come home during the day?"

Chance couldn't answer. His mind had stopped working.

"Yes or no," the man said. "It's a simple question."

"One o'clock. She comes home at one."

"What about housekeepers? Friends?"

"Just me."

Grunting once, the man produced a pair of handcuffs, and held them out. "If you would, please. Behind your back."

Chance didn't move. His fingers were numb; he couldn't feel his arms or legs, either.

"Here, I'll help you."

The man stood, his eyes damp, flat and gray. He pressed the gun to Chance's neck, and manipulated the cuffs one-handed. One wrist. The second. He sat again, and the room tilted.

This can't be real . . .

But the man was right there, dry-skinned and pale, with those street-puddle eyes. "I need a favor," he said. "A phone call. You have a friend, Gibson French." Chance nodded; felt drool at the corner of his mouth. "Is it Gibby or Gibson?"

Chance blinked slowly. "Gibby."

"I'd like to meet him. Now. This morning. I'd like him to come here, and I want you to make that happen."

I heard my father's footsteps long before he knocked on the door. I'd not really slept. That kind of night.

"Gibson?"

Another knock would come—no stopping it. I could all but predict the timing.

Five, four, three . . .

"Come on in, Dad."

He looked as sleep-deprived as I felt. Same clothes as last night. Same red eyes and stubble. "Good morning. Did you sleep?"

"Like a baby," I said.

"Yeah, me, too."

That's how the day started, with a pair of matching lies. He sat on the bed, and had trouble with my eyes. His big hands looked useless, too. I didn't know what he wanted, but words gathered in my mouth, as if they had plans of their own. "I know why the Marine Corps kicked Jason out."

It's not what he'd expected to hear. His eyes narrowed in suspicion. "Have you been in my office?"

"I have not."

"Where did you get that information?"

"Does it really matter?" He said nothing, and the silence told me everything I needed to know. "You know the reasons, too, don't you? Why they sent him home with a dishonorable discharge?" He did; I could tell that, too. "Do you know about the medals?"

My father moved toward the window, looking as if he'd kicked over a box marked VENOMOUS REPTILES, and was in fear of whatever creature might crawl out first. "I do," he said.

"And the massacre?"

"Jesus Christ, son." He palmed his eyes, paler than usual. "That's classified information."

"They say that without Jason, it might have been another My Lai."

"You *did* break into my desk. You read the damn file, the DOD file on your brother."

"I wouldn't do that." But I had considered it. "I'm right, though. Aren't I?"

"It's not a fair comparison. American soldiers slaughtered five hundred villagers at My Lai, civilians, every one of them, women and children, even infants. This wasn't like that."

"It could have been, though. They say Jason saved an entire village."

"Few things in war are so black and white."

"This was. His actions were."

I saw in my father's eyes a deep and abiding pain, and understood why he might feel that way. In the church of Don't Be Like Your Brother, he was a high priest. But what I'd learned from Darzell changed everything I'd once believed about Jason. Three years after the massacre at My Lai, a platoon of U.S. Marines went as war-mad as Charlie Company had at that small village in the Sơn Tinh District of South Vietnam. The village was smaller than My Lai, little more than a clutch of huts gathered along a tributary of the Bến Hải River.

Darzell didn't know what triggered the slaughter, but Jason and his crew were five miles out of the DMZ when the first body appeared, faceup in the river: a young girl, according to Darzell, a tiny thing, shot four times through the chest. By the time Jason's gunboat arrived at the village, that platoon of marines had already spread thirty-three bodies along the muddy banks, or left them bobbing like corks in the reeds along the river's edge. The ARVN troops used the gunboat to carry off what survivors they could find, but for Jason and the master chief, that wasn't enough. Guns were still firing, people screaming; so they went in alone to stand down an entire platoon of red-eyed, raging marines. Jason took three bullets before the madness broke, and even then beat the commanding lieutenant within an inch of his life.

"We never listened to him," I said.

"What are you talking about, son?"

"He saved three hundred people that day . . ."

"A remarkable thing, I know."

"You didn't let me finish. He did that *remarkable* thing, and when he came home hurting, we never listened."

"Jason didn't want to talk about the war, not any of it."

"We didn't make it easy, though, did we? Mom, like an eggshell ready to break, and you so certain of right and wrong."

"We did some things wrong, yes. But your brother's no saint. You can trust me on that."

"You mean the drugs." I laughed harshly. "Of course you mean the drugs."

"Heroin is tearing the city apart. I see it every day. Whatever your brother did in Vietnam, he ended up a user, maybe even a dealer. I can't condone that. And I can't have you near it."

"Whatever your brother did in Vietnam." I threw the words back. "You talk about a DOD file. Did it include the terms of Jason's discharge?"

"Yes, son. It did. Right or wrong, your brother almost killed a superior officer. The military gave him the choice of ten years in Leavenworth, or a dishonorable discharge in conjunction with a signed nondisclosure agreement. It's a cover-up. I understand that. I don't approve of it, but after the My Lai fallout, I recognize the necessity. Support for the war is already weak. Another massacre. Another black eye for the country . . ."

"It's not about support for the war."

"It says so in the file."

"Does the file say who was in command of that platoon?"

"The name was redacted . . ."

"It's Laughtner, Lieutenant John G."

"Laughtner?" My father's mouth opened and closed twice before he could continue. "Isn't there a General Laughtner on Westmoreland's staff?"

"Second in command of ground operations."

"Related?"

"Father and son. And it gets worse." My father closed his eyes, but I didn't relent. "They needed time," I said. "How to spin the killings. What to do with Jason. They held him off books for seven weeks. Drugged. Morphine. If it weren't for the master chief, they'd have probably just killed him. But the master chief had friends in high places." I met my father's eyes, and dared him to blink. "They turned him into a junkie instead. They strung him out and sent him home."

"Who else knows about this?"

"About the drugs? I have no idea. The rest of it seems to be an open secret in the Marine Corps."

He showed me his back, and I wondered at his thoughts. Did he feel guilt or shame? Because I did. What about regret? None of us had been there for Jason. He'd come home from war strung out, quiet, and bitter. But did my father ever ask why? Wasn't that his job? Wasn't it my mother's? Or mine?

"Will you give me a few minutes?" he asked.

I said I would, and left him there.

Halfway to the kitchen, I heard the phone ring.

35

Warden Wilson rose early, showered, shaved, and dressed. It was a big day, with a bigger one coming.

"Twenty-four hours. Maybe a little more."

He spoke to the mirror as his fingers worked a dark tie into a Windsor knot. The suit was brown. So were the shoes. For color, he put a fresh rose in his lapel, cut in the darkness from a small garden he kept beside the house. By noon, the petals would begin to droop. Then they would curl and dry, and he would mark time with those petals, increasingly light-hearted as they withered, shrunk, and died. Thinking of X, he hummed quietly as he adjusted the flower just so.

"Perfect."

That's what his life would become. X would die, and the warden's family would find its heart again. They would travel; they would heal. Eventually, they would choose a place to start over, France or maybe Italy, some high, windswept place with views of the Mediterranean.

First, he had to manage the day.

"The last day."

He offered his reflection a solemn nod, then turned off the bathroom light, and moved quietly through the still-sleeping house. At the bedroom door, he peered in at his wife. She knew only that X would die the following day, nothing about the money or the new life it would afford them. He wanted to surprise her with the news, to make the grand gesture. Maybe she would look at him like she used to. Maybe her eyes would sparkle.

More determined than ever, he took his heavy heart into the light, sweet air of a perfect daybreak. The car started easily. The drive was thoughtful but pleasant. At the prison, he cleared security, and was ushered through an armored door, and into an underground parking garage beneath the administrative building. It was a small garage—eight spaces—and he only allowed a few others to use it. One of them was there and waiting.

"Warden."

The warden locked his car, frowning. "Captain Ripley. Is there some kind of problem?"

"Not necessarily a problem. Something you should know about, though."

"Walk with me."

So early in the morning, the subbasement corridors were empty, not that the warden worried about Ripley's discretion. They'd both endured too many hard lessons for that. It was no accident that X had contrived to live as he had for so many years. The warden, alone, could not guarantee the liberties X enjoyed. No warden could. But if a guard spoke out of turn, he paid a heavy price. Same with other prisoners. Even rumors were quashed without mercy, and the first time a reporter *had* come sniffing after a story of favoritism and graft, he'd disappeared as quietly as a setting sun. A second reporter showed up six months later, and died within the week. No one knew how many informants X had on the inside or how many enforcers worked for him beyond the walls. He knew so many things, *touched* so many things.

Ripley waited until they were in the corridor, then said, "X has had four visitors already."

"Four?" The warden stopped mid-stride.

"It makes me nervous."

It made the warden nervous, too. Surviving X was about understanding X. "He's never had so many in one day."

"And never so early."

"What's his mood?"

"Like he could eat a baked baby for breakfast."

"Explain."

"White-lipped. Agitated. I've never seen anything like it."

Ripley's concern made a lot of sense. X was the most disciplined man either of them had ever seen, so in control of thought and emotion that he rarely showed more than pursed lips or a lifted eyebrow. For those who understood the man, little more was ever needed.

"You have the names of his visitors?"

Ripley rattled off four names, and the warden recognized two of them. Enforcers. Killers. "Where are they now?"

"Off-grounds, and thank God for it. He's been asking about Byrd, though."

"What about *our* arrangements?" The warden started walking.

"Prisoner French will attend the execution. It's not the normal thing. We'll need an excuse."

"I'll come up with something. What about after?"

"Like we discussed."

"Good. Good." The elevator dinged, and the doors opened. "Did he, uh . . . Did X want to see me?"

"He didn't mention it."

Nodding in relief, the warden stepped into the elevator, and waited as it carried him to his office. This early, he was alone there, so he made the coffee, and stood at the east window, looking out across the prison as color bled into the world. He wanted peace of mind, but had so many concerns about the execution, so many demands on his time. The governor would attend, and that alone had caused a week of sleepless nights. He also expected two state senators, the U.S. attorney general, and twenty-nine family members of X's long-dead victims. And they all needed to be *handled*.

Then there was the media. He'd already denied forty-one petitions to attend the execution, some from outlets as influential as *The New York Times* and NBC News. Those outlets had powerful friends in the state of North Carolina, and pressure had come in every conceivable form, from long editorials to brute, political force. The execution had already been front-page news in *The Charlotte Observer* for four days straight: profiles of X's family and its fortune, details of the murders, more profiles on the victims. They'd delved into X's past, and run photographs of his early days, pictures of him with models, movie stars, and politicians. The drumbeat was incessant. But a decision on the media was entirely the warden's prerogative, which made it X's prerogative. And he'd been clear on that point, as well.

I've sold enough of their newspapers . . .

Of course, the newspapers would sell, regardless. So would the air-time. The warden had passed a dozen news vans at the front gate, and knew how things would play on the six o'clock news: *Lanesworth at dawn tomorrow, a time, at last, for justice . . .*

Or some such shit.

Removing the rose from the buttonhole in his lapel, the warden took a moment to study it from every angle. Like all of his roses, it was a lovely specimen, perhaps the loveliest he'd ever grown. Barefoot in the damp grass and darkness, he'd tried to pick the very best, silken-soft and fresh as the morning dew.

Just die, he thought, before smelling of it deeply.

Can't you pretty please, just hurry up and simply fucking die?

36

When my father came to the kitchen, I pretended it was a regular day, and that his eyes weren't bloodshot from crying. Raw emotion was not a thing I liked to see in my father, but I gave him a pass, since I was the one who'd drawn it like a thorn from his soul.

"Have you seen your mother?"

"No."

"Who was on the phone?"

"Chance. I'm going over."

"It's kind of early."

"He's had a rough few days; sounded a little strange. I'll give him a ride to school."

"I'd rather you not."

"I do it all the time."

"You misunderstand. I'd rather you not go to school." That got my attention. "Somebody saw you at Sara's on the day she disappeared. Martinez found a witness who saw you go inside."

"So what if I did?"

"Just stay away from Martinez and Smith. Avoid your usual routines and places. Don't make it easy for them. I need a day to figure this out."

I told him I would do as he asked. "Do you have my car keys?"

He pointed at a bowl on the counter, and watched me scoop out the keys. "About your brother," he said.

"Don't." I pulled a baseball cap from my back pocket, and tugged it down above my eyes. "At least, not now."

"I want to say one thing, and it's this. I've always tried to do right by you boys, by all of you boys. You're so different from each other, but I've loved you each with everything I have, all of my heart and hopes, everything inside. And I've tried to be even and fair, to not play favorites, to temper your mother when I can, hard as that can be, at times. I've done the best I could to give you boys the childhoods you deserve, to raise you to be strong and kind, to become good men. None of that happens overnight; it's the work of a lifetime, the *gift* of a lifetime.

"But no father is perfect, and if I've been wrong about Jason, if I've been harsh and unfair, I'll do what I can to fix it. I'll talk to him. I'll try. That's a promise. And if I've been hard on you, too much a shadow on your life, it's only because I lost Robert, and thought I'd lost Jason, and because you scare me, son. I won't lie. There's a fire in you I can't temper or control, and I worry about fires that burn too hot. I guess that's what I'm saying: that I worry more for you than I do for Jason, more than I ever did for Robert. And if that's made me a bad father, I'm sorry for that, too. If it's put this anger in you, if it's ruined what we've always had . . ."

He looked away, and I told him it was okay, that we were fine.

"Do you really believe that?" he asked.

"I'm trying to."

He wanted more, but that was all I had, those few words before I walked into the morning heat, started the Mustang, and pointed it at Chance's house.

For Reece, it felt like being pulled apart. He needed to be here, but wanted to be with the girl. He'd looked so long for the right girl; there'd been so many disappointments.

"Your friend is late."

He dropped the curtain and turned from the street. The kid couldn't help that his friend was slow, but X would be awake by now, and eager for information. If he knew that Byrd was missing, he'd have a location: Reece's home. And the girl was at Reece's home.

"Did he seem normal on the phone?"

"Yes."

"Nothing strange? No suspicions?"

"No."

Reece studied the kid, looking for the lie. He was slumped, the jaw slightly open. "If you're lying, you'll regret it."

"I already regret it."

It was the first *life* Reece had seen in the boy, and he felt unexpected sympathy. "If you hadn't made the call, I'd have killed you. You'll feel better once you accept that fact."

But the kid didn't understand. Or *wouldn't*.

Reece paced the room until a car sound took him back to the window. Not the French kid, but almost as good. The driver slowed to check the address, then did as Reece had asked, parking up the street, and then walking back to the house, a large duffel bag hanging from each shoulder. He moved quickly for such a tall and heavy man, wind rising off the street to stir his shaggy hair. Unlocking the door, Reece said, "You're late."

"Yeah, well." The big man shouldered past. "It's not the easiest address to find."

Reece had not seen Lonnie Ward since the night they'd taken Tyra Norris, but his eyes had the same eagerness, and his face the same misshapen cast. "Did you bring everything I asked?"

The big man shrugged the first bag off his shoulder. "Sony DXC-1600 Trinicon tube handheld color camera, paired with a Sony BVU-100 U-matic-S Professional Portapack VCR color videocassette system, state of the art and fully portable at four ounces under fifty-five pounds."

"And for editing? Splicing?"

"Second bag. Lighting, too."

"Good, good. Thank you."

"So?" Lonnie put down the second bag, his eyes on Chance. "We killing this kid?"

Reece said, "It's complicated."

But the big man was clearly puzzled. The boy was bound and silent; they had this quiet place. "So what are we doing here?"

"Waiting."

"For what?"

"Him, actually." A sound rose in the street, and Reece twitched the curtain, staying in the shadows as a second car pulled to the curb.

The big man peered over his shoulder as a teenager stepped onto the sidewalk. "Another kid?"

"Not just a kid," Reece said. "A lever long enough to move the world."

For Chance, it played out like a dream. He heard every word, but couldn't hold them in his head. He saw the men separate, but didn't understand the reasons. The small one stood behind him, and the other disappeared deeper into the house.

"Yo, Chance."

Gibby had said as much a thousand times in a dozen years. Chance wanted to call out, to say, *Run, damn it, run,* but the small man had a blade against his throat, his mouth so close to Chance's ear that his breath was damp and warm.

"Tell him to come in."

The blade was fire on Chance's skin.

"Go ahead, son. It's okay."

"I'm in here." Chance closed his eyes to wish it away. "The living room."

The front door closed with a click of steel. "Gibby in the house!"

He'd said that a thousand times, too. Three footsteps, and then six. By the time he reached the living room door, Chance was broken all the way through.

The line of fire . . .

This thing he'd done to his friend . . .

Gibby rounded into the room, and froze in disbelief, his eyes flicking from the blade to the man who held it, both hands fisting as his jaw tightened into a dogged line. One full second. That was the tick of the clock. Then the shaggy giant stepped near-silent from the hallway, and dropped Chance's best friend with a single blow.

Reece secured Gibby to a second chair as Lonnie went to work. For a man so inherently slow and shambolic, he managed the equipment with impressive dexterity, connecting the camera to the tripod and VCR, and the VCR to the editing deck, all of it done with minimal movement and a snake's nest of thin, black cable. There was, however, the matter of time and timing.

"It doesn't have to be perfect. Bare minimum is fine."

But the big man shook his head. "You've never asked me to do this before. I want it to be perfect."

He unpacked lights, reflectors, and diffusers, so filled with enthusiasm and pride that Reece felt a twinge of regret. Lonnie did love a good snuff film. "Um, we're not actually killing anyone."

"What?"

"It's like I told you. It's complicated."

The big man stood and glowered down, wheels turning as he processed the betrayal. "That one saw my face." He pointed at Chance. "The other one will, too, no doubt, and I don't take chances like that. You shouldn't ask me to."

"We'll figure something out."

"That's not good enough."

"Seven years," Reece said. "Have I ever let you down? All I'm asking for is a little faith."

Weighing what he'd heard, the big man glared at Chance, who stared back like a ghost. "For now, then. Okay. Why don't you show me what you have, and tell me what you need?"

Reece produced the camera he'd taken from Byrd and used to film his death. The big man turned it over in his hands. "Panasonic 3085. Not as good as mine, but not bad." He ejected the tape, and inspected it. "Tell me what you need."

Reece laid out what was on the tape, and what he wanted to add.

"Mind if I watch this first?" Without waiting for an answer, he pushed the tape into the VCR, speaking as he did. "This portable equipment can only run playback in black and white. On the right machine, you'll have full color."

"What about sound?" Reece asked.

"You tell me."

He started the tape, and as the screaming began, both men agreed that the sound was fine.

·　　·　　·

For Chance, the nightmare wouldn't end. It couldn't. It was real. Gibby was actually unconscious in the chair beside him. That was a real man being butchered on tape, with real killers nodding along and commenting as it played. At one point, the big one seemed to realize that Chance was still in the room.

"You want to watch?"

He turned the machine so Chance could see what a man looked like with his stomach opened up and his intestines looped like a tie around his neck. The horror on that man's face was like nothing Chance had ever seen, both eyes staring down as he screamed and screamed, and bloody hands dipped inside for another coil.

It came out in a matter of seconds.

Chance passed out in another ten.

When Chance woke, the first thing he saw was the camera, pointed at Gibby, and the big man dialing in focus. "How much do you need?"

"Not much. Fifteen seconds."

The small man crossed the room, and stood behind Gibby. "I'm out of the frame?"

"Visible from the neck down. The kid is front and center."

As if he understood, Gibby began to stir. "Chance? What's happening?"

His voice was so slurred Chance thought, *Concussion;* but that was a bottom-of-the-list worry.

"Okay. Filming."

A blade appeared at Gibby's neck, and he was alert enough to feel it. Chance closed his eyes, but heard the struggle. When he looked, he saw muscles twist as his friend rocked the chair, and the small man's fingers twined deep into his hair, holding his face to the camera, keeping the chair upright. Chance wanted to scream; he wanted to fight. After a lifetime, the big man said, "That's it. Fifteen seconds."

The blade came away from Gibby's skin, the fingers out of his hair. "Let me see."

Chance stared straight ahead as they played back the tape. Gibby was still confused, but he'd say Chance's name soon enough.

He'd say the name, and want to know why.

Chance conjured words so they'd be ready on his tongue: *I'm a coward and ashamed, and I want you to hate me.*

Chance closed his eyes, and spent some time in that place. He wanted to die. He wanted to live. When Gibby remembered what Chance had done, the world would never be the same. How could it be? How could it ever?

But it wasn't Gibby who changed the world.

Loud sounds drew Chance into the moment. There was an argument brewing, and it was serious. The big man towered over the other, his face such a deep, angry red that his eyes looked black. His shoulders were drawn up around his neck, his fingers hooked and stiff. "You promised a solution."

The small man held up his hands. "I did, yes. And we'll figure it out."

"They've seen my face."

"Mine as well."

"I'm not going to prison for something as small as a videotape."

"If you would just load the equipment—"

"Fuck the equipment!"

"Please don't push me on this."

"You do it or I do it. Those are the choices."

"And there's nothing I can do to change your mind?"

The big man stepped closer—a foot taller, twice as heavy. "If you'd told me the truth up front, I'd have never come. We have rules for a reason."

The small man glanced at Chance, but nodded sadly. "I did make you a promise."

He stepped aside, sweeping out an arm, as if inviting debate on which boy to kill first.

The big man dipped his head and grunted once, lumbering forward with an expression that Chance would not forget if he lived a thousand years. No heat in his face. No soul in his eyes. He closed his fists as if he would simply beat the boys to death, and then find someone else to kill for fun. But the small man had a different plan. He allowed his friend a single step more, then conjured a blade, and opened his neck like an envelope.

37

The warden's day quickly went from bad to worse. His secretary called in sick, he spilled coffee on his best shirt, and by eight thirty, he'd received two calls from the governor asking that he reconsider a media presence at the execution. It seemed images of Lanesworth Prison were already running on major affiliates up and down the East Coast, and the governor was unhappy.

I see your prison on every network program but Captain Goddamn Kangaroo!

That was the most polite part of the conversation.

The governor, it turned out, was not a forgiving soul.

"Alice." The warden stepped into the secretary's vestibule. "It is Alice, isn't it?"

"Yes, sir. From records." She frowned from behind the small desk, an iron-haired woman with enough spine for three men. "I *have* covered this desk before."

"Of course you have."

"December 3, 1968. Good Friday, the following year. Two days in March of '70 . . ."

"Yes, I remember. Thank you. May I ask you a question, Alice?" He did not wait for a response. "Do you watch the evening news? I mean the national news. I'm wondering if there's been much interest in tomorrow's execution."

"You don't watch the news?"

"But you do, I presume?"

"Walter Cronkite. *60 Minutes.* It can't just be *The Lawrence Welk Show,* now, can it?"

She sniffed in disapproval, which the warden ignored. "The execution?" he asked. "Much interest?"

"Oh yes." She nodded solemnly. "There's been tremendous interest, what with Juan Corona caught last year, and Mack Ray Edwards and that other one, I can't remember his name. Then there's the Gaffney Strangler, the Broomstick Killer. Only last month, four girls have gone missing in Seattle, and probably more we don't know about yet. I shouldn't be surprised, working where I do and knowing what evil dwells in a man's heart; but it seems there are always new depths yet to plumb. There's even a new term they're using. *Serial killer,* if you can believe such a thing. So yes, the news is talking, and people are listening; and I don't see how that's a bad thing. A good execution is exactly what this country needs."

"Umm, yes. Well. Thank you, Alice."

"Yes, sir, and God bless you for what you do."

Filled with righteous approval, she spoke as if he, himself, would drop the switch. He hesitated a moment, and she nodded a final time, her chin folding so firmly into her neck that the warden backed away, as if allergic to such utter conviction. He made his way to the northeast tower, which looked down on to the main gate and its approach. The guards nodded at his appearance, then melted into the corners to give him space. The warden mopped his face from the long climb, then looked down on to the dusty approach, and said, "Good God Almighty. How many?"

The nearest guard said, "Protesters or news vans?"

"Vans, I suppose."

"Thirty-seven, last I counted."

The other guard said, "Thirty-nine," and pointed off in the distance, where two more vehicles made bright spearheads on plumes of boiling dust. The warden shaded his eyes, and stared down at TV people in their fine clothes and blown hair. As for the protesters, he guessed there were at least a few hundred, with more certain to come. He counted seven buses from churches with names like Grace Baptist and Mount Zion Church of Christ. They'd parked haphazardly in the fields, and a few were still spilling parishioners out into the heat, most of them holding placards with slogans like ONLY GOD SHOULD TAKE A LIFE or BELIEVE IN THE RE-DEEMER. By midday, the merely curious would begin to arrive, as would those who supported the death penalty, and those darker souls who wished nothing more than to be nearby when a human being was cooked alive from the inside out.

One of the guards said, "We could push them out to the state road, if you want."

The warden took his time in responding. He watched the two news vans draw near; saw that another bus was trundling down the road behind them. "Let's leave 'em be," he said, and left the rest of it unspoken: that with all he had to do for X, a little chaos might not be a bad thing.

For the next ninety minutes, the warden worked in his office, trying to arrange seating for the family members who planned to attend the execution. It was an unpleasant job, but he wanted to do it right. That meant revisiting many of X's murders in an attempt to discern which families had suffered the most, and thus had the better claim for good seating. *The father who'd lost two sons, but quickly? Or the husband whose wife had endured a long week of brutal torture?* It was painful math, and the warden welcomed each interruption when it came.

The first was Ripley with an update on X. "Still agitated. Still asking about Byrd."

"Any more visitors?"

"Two of his lawyers. Actual lawyers, I mean."

"Any talk of last rites?"

"None."

Nor would there be. X would die as he'd lived, without apology or regret.

The second interruption came forty minutes later, and was entirely unexpected, unimagined, even. "Sir?" Alice spoke from the open door. "You have a call on line two. It's your wife."

"Thank you, Alice. Would you close the door?" She did as he asked, and the warden stared at the phone, almost afraid to touch it. His wife never called. "Sweetheart?" he said. "Everything okay?"

"I'm calling because I know how hard this day will be for you, and that tomorrow will be even harder, given your thoughts on execution." She spoke softly. "We've not been much use to each other these past years, but I am with you in this matter."

"Sweetheart, that is so very kind."

"At least until tomorrow," she said. "When you kill that horrible, wicked man, and send his soul to hell forever."

The line went dead, and left the warden staring at the receiver as if he'd never seen one. Slowly, he replaced it on the cradle. That's when Ripley came back to his office, and the world really went to shit.

Five miles down the state road, Reece was parked in the shade of an abandoned gas station whose windows were broken out and boarded over. The Coke machine was broken, too. So were the bathroom doors, the pumps, and the faded, plastic sign that, once upon a time, said ESSO. It was a grim place, remembered only by those who passed it by on the dusty two-lane. But the pay phone still functioned, and that's why Reece was there.

He checked his watch, and thought, *Soon.*

More worried than he cared to admit, he checked his fingernails for the third time, making sure he'd scrubbed off all traces of Lonnie's blood.

He had.

Of course he had.

"This waiting," he said. But it wasn't the wait.

It was X. It was the gamble.

Almost absentmindedly, he opened the trunk, and looked down into it. "You boys still breathing?" Neither could respond, taped up as they were, and jammed in so tightly. But they *were* still breathing, so Reece gave them a nod. "Stay quiet, and you might get out of this alive."

Reece closed the trunk, and shaded his eyes to peer up the road. A few buses had rattled past en route to the prison, but nothing much had come from the other way, just an old sedan, a timber truck, and a combine that rolled past at twenty miles an hour. A mile down, though, there was a wink of light where the road bent north to avoid the river.

"Here we go."

The shimmer hardened into a Buick sedan driven by a soft and balding middle-aged man who looked like every such man who'd ever lived.

The car slowed, and turned into the lot; and Reece walked out to meet it. "Any problems?"

Squeezed in behind the wheel, the driver squinted in the bright light, and shrugged. "Traffic was a little tight, going in. Protesters and such. The guards didn't want to talk to me, but I told 'em what you said I should, and that got this Ripley fella out there pretty quick."

"You put the package directly into Captain Ripley's hands?"

"Is that the name on the receipt?" The driver pushed a piece of paper through the window. Reece checked the signature, and nodded. "Then that's who I gave it to."

"Describe him." The driver did. A perfect match. "Go on, then." Reece produced a hundred-dollar bill, and watched it disappear.

When the car was back on the road, Reece checked his watch again, adding up the minutes. He knew the guards, the prison's ways. That told him about how long it would take.

The package sat untouched on the warden's desk, a rectangle wrapped in brown paper, and sealed with tape. Perched on the edge of his chair, the warden decided he'd be happier if Ripley had handed over the package, saying it contained nitroglycerin or body parts, anything that had nothing to do with X. "Tell me again what he said."

"He said, 'This is for X, and he'll want to see it. You tell Warden Wilson it's in his interests to make sure he does.'"

"He called me by name?"

"Yes, sir." Ripley nodded once, but looked a little green, too.

"Have you ever seen this man before?"

"No, sir. He said he was a paid messenger, and didn't know the name of the man who'd hired him. The man he described, though, sounds a lot like Reece."

The warden could easily believe it. Only Reece looked like Reece.

"You want me to go?" Ripley asked. "Privacy, I mean."

Ripley didn't have a family, but he did have a live-in girlfriend and three out of his original four dogs. The killing of that first dog had taught him early to take the carrot over the stick, and he'd been on X's payroll for years. The warden had never asked how much money Ripley had made off the relationship, but it would be a considerable amount. The warden shook his head. "If this package concerns X, it concerns you, too."

With no other choice, he drew the package across the desk, and slit the tape with a pocketknife. Inside, were a videotape cassette and a sealed envelope. Turning to the envelope, he read aloud what was written on its front. "To Warden Bruce Wilson, #2 Prison Farm Lane, husband to Gertrude, father to Thomas and Trevor."

"That's strangely specific."

"He's reminding me how vulnerable I am."

The warden used the same knife to open the envelope. Inside, was a phone number on an index card, and a single piece of paper folded neatly in half. The warden read what was written there, then handed it to Ripley, whose lips moved as he read it in silence.

> Dear Warden,
>
> The enclosed videotape is to be IMMEDIATELY viewed by our mutual friend in the subbasement, and I trust you to make the necessary arrangements. In case you find yourself squeamish, I've kept a second copy of the same tape, and will deliver it to our mutual friend's attorneys, if necessary. You can imagine our mutual friend's displeasure should he discover any malfeasance on your part. I, of course, would also be VERY UNHAPPY.
>
> With Warmest Regards to Your ENTIRE Family,
>
> R

Ripley met the warden's eyes, but there was little point in commiseration. They turned to the videocassette. The label on front had two words, in black ink.

Byrd Song

Ripley frowned. "X has been asking about Byrd all morning. You think it's related?"

"It has to be."

"What do you want me to do?"

"Lock that door, and let's get on with it."

Ripley locked the door, and they met at the television in the corner of the office. The warden pushed the tape into the player.

"No way this is good," Ripley said.

He was right about that.

The warden had no choice but to show it to X. He entered the subbasement carrying the tape as if it could still hurt him, largely because it could. He had no idea what X would do. Because of that, he stopped at the bottom of the steps. "Um, hello?"

Murmured conversation ceased, and X emerged from one of the cells. "Yes? Speak."

"Ummm . . ."

"I said *speak.*"

"It's about Byrd . . ." His arm rose with the tape. "This arrived with instructions I show it to you."

X took the tape, and examined it. "Instructions from whom?"

"The tape is, ah, self-explanatory."

"You've seen it?"

"Unfortunately, yes."

As he spoke, four guards appeared with a television, video player, and extension cord. While they worked, X summoned his lawyers from the cell. Legitimate attorneys, the warden knew, all of them from a top firm in New York. That would be about X's estate, his dying wishes. "Get started on what we discussed," X said. "But stay close. We have a lot of ground to cover."

They took the stairs up, burdened with briefcases full of God-alone-knew-what. When the machines were plugged in, the warden dismissed the guards, too. X watched them go, then turned with a stare so bottomless and black the warden felt a wet flutter where his heart would normally beat.

"Play it."

The cassette rattled against the player as the warden tried twice to insert it. "I'm sorry. Sorry." The machine welcomed the tape, at last, and the warden tried to walk away, eager to be anywhere else.

"Stay."

X caught his arm, and turned him like a child. As the first images appeared, the warden covered his mouth. He'd never cared for Byrd, but no man should die as he had, and no one else should be forced to watch it, let alone be forced to watch it twice. Byrd's torture did not faze X, of course, but he *was* affected. That was clear. But the warden had no idea how or why.

"It's Reece," X said. "You can't see his face, of course—that would be foolish of him, even knowing what he knows—but it's definitely Reece."

"What does he know?"

"That I would never allow the police to see this tape. That what exists between us is personal." X squatted in front of the television, his face only inches away from the screen. "How long does this last?"

"This part, umm, seven or eight minutes."

"This part?"

"Killing Byrd, I mean. Something else comes after."

"Show me."

The warden almost fell in his rush to clear the screen of Byrd's murder. He ran the tape forward, overshot the mark, and had to back up. "Here. Just here." He stepped back as the scene changed to show a young man bound to a chair, a blade at his throat as he struggled. "That's Jason French's little brother."

But X knew the boy; the warden could tell. It showed in the sudden, lock-jawed stillness, and in the flush of blood that made his face swell. It was pure rage, fury like nothing the warden had ever seen. Even his eyes looked hot enough to burn.

"Play it again."

But the warden didn't move. "There's more," he said.

The *more* was a blank wall, and an off-camera voice.

You shouldn't have sent Byrd to my home. All our time together, and it ends because of what? A girl. Because you couldn't allow me that one indulgence.

A soft exhalation could be heard on the tape.

Problem is, I know you too well. If you want me dead now, you'll want me dead until the day it happens. That won't change once they kill you.

More like Byrd will come, an unbroken chain, and all because I belittled your precious trust. Do you see how much I hate for it to end like this?

Another sigh, as good as a lament.

You know, I've never understood your feelings for Jason French, but I was around when they first appeared, so I know how strong they are. I could tell you it's pitiful, but I won't. And I can't pretend I'm not a little jealous. You did, at times, fill that fatherly place in my heart. But this is where we are, and here is what will happen. You will make assurances that our disagreement is behind us. In exchange, I will release Jason's brother unharmed. If things go the other way, the boy stars in his own production of How to Die on Videotape, *and I make sure Jason knows it's entirely your fault. I'm sure he would never forgive you.*

I don't want it to be like this, but I know the kind of man you are. If you say we have a deal, I'll believe you. Otherwise, I'll burn it all down, the kid and his friend, and Jason, too, but only after he learns the truth of why his little brother died. So that's it. That's the deal, the boy's life for mine. Think about it, and give me a call. The warden has the number.

The screen went blank, and X spoke with his eyes closed. "Is it true that you have a number?"

His voice was soft, but the warden was as afraid as he'd ever been. One had to know X to understand. "Yes, I have a number."

"Where is he?"

"With God as my witness, I do not know."

"The man who delivered the tape?"

"Gone. I'm sorry . . ."

"Stop." X divided his palms, his eyes still closed. "I need five minutes alone, and then I need a phone."

"Of course."

X breathed in through his mouth, and out through his nose. "Do your children ever disappoint you, Warden Wilson? Does your wife?"

"Disappointment is part of life."

"How do you punish them?"

"Um . . . ah . . . I don't."

"Because you love them?"

"Because they're all I have."

"And if you can help the ones who matter?"

"I'd do anything for them."

X nodded once, his eyes still closed. "Five minutes, please. Five minutes, and a phone."

38

Stifling, hot, and dark, that was the world. I didn't know where I was or what was happening. Chance's knees dug into my spine. Something like a rivet was gouging the top of my head. Whatever the bastard's name was, he'd wound enough duct tape around my arms and legs to immobilize someone twice as large. The tape was on my face, too. I was seriously fucking afraid, and Chance was no better off. He was sucking hard through his nose, trying to find enough air.

Three hours in the trunk?

Five?

At some point, time had simply stopped. I didn't blame Chance for crying. I remembered a jet of blood, hot and quick, from some big man's neck.

I could still smell it.

Why were we still alive?

That was the first question, and as questions went, it was pretty fucked up. I'd driven it around the block once or twice. It had something to do with Jason. That's all I could figure.

Why the trunk?

What were we waiting for?

I took those questions for a longer spin, but came up just as empty. I was in the dark, and cooking alive.

Hot air in.

Hot air out.

Nothing changed until the phone rang.

When Becky Collins woke that morning, she took particular care of her appearance: the low-rise jeans that flared just right, the white vinyl belt and the daisy-print top, a little makeup, but not too much. She wore the round sunglasses with purple lenses, and pulled her hair back into a ponytail. Most of the clothes were secondhand, but they fit right, and made her feel right. Even Dana White sensed the change. "Damn, girl. What's gotten into you?" She was leaning against a brick wall, smoking a cigarette ten minutes before first bell. "Go on, girl. *Swing* those hips."

Becky couldn't hide the blush, but didn't mind it, either. Life was different. She'd crossed over. "Give me one of those, yeah?" The cigarette gave her time to settle her thoughts: the shakeout and the light, the first, deep drag. She leaned against the same yellow brick, pushed out the same smoke, and shared the only thought that made this day different. "I'm looking for Gibby. Have you seen him?"

"It's 7:50 in the morning. Why would you want to see any boy at such an unholy hour?"

Becky tried to play it cool, but her lips twisted in a way that most young women would recognize. She didn't mean it to happen, but it did. And when it did, Dana came off the wall, her eyes widening into a knowing, almost suspicious look.

"Is that why you're so smoking hot today? Because of Gibby French?" Dana said it jokingly, but gawped as the blush in Becky's face spread like wildfire down her neck. "Wait. Is that it?" She looked Becky up and down, nothing *almost* about her suspicions. A wry smile twisted her face. "Did he get to second base?" One eyebrow went up, teasing her. "Third base?"

Becky turned away, dropping the cigarette at the same time, and grinding it beneath a boot.

"Oh my God." Dana was so excited, she was almost dancing. "You went all the way! Look at your face. You totally slept with Gibby! The most notorious virgins in the school . . ."

"Come on, Dana. Stop it." Becky played firm, but wasn't really angry.

She was too warm on the inside; too satisfied with the way her life had changed.

"I'm not going to stop anything. Are you kidding? Good God, girl. You've been talking about him since when?"

"First week of sophomore year."

"And you really . . . ?"

Becky had too much self-respect to share details, but she did slide the purple shades down her nose, and let Dana get a good look at her eyes.

"Oh my." A wicked grin spread on Dana's face. "So he was . . . um? I mean, was he pretty, um . . . ? Come on, you know what I mean."

Becky allowed herself the first real smile, teasing her friend in return. "I'm not at all sure that I do."

"Now, Becky Collins. Don't tease a girl."

"Let me put it this way." Becky put a finger on her lips, as if in deep thought. "If he asked me out again, I would say yes."

"Oh my God . . ."

"An immediate, eager, and most *definite* yes."

Dana had lost her virginity in ninth grade, so it took time for Becky to settle her down, and peel away into the morning crowd. Gibby was not in precalculus; she couldn't find him in the courtyard or the halls. By third period, Becky decided he wasn't in school at all. No one had seen Chance, either.

Becky used a pay phone to call his house. No answer, but that was nothing new. At lunchtime, she went looking for Dana, and found her leaning against the same wall, her earlier enthusiasms melted away, as if by the heat. Her eyes were half-closed, one foot braced against the brick. "School sucks this close to summer."

That was all the opportunity Becky needed. "Do you feel like ditching?"

"Yes. Please. God."

They waited until the end-of-lunch bell spilled a thousand students into the hallways, then used the confusion to slip away, across the baseball diamond and into student parking. Squatting by the car, Dana fumbled with her keys as Becky craned her neck to see if they'd been spotted or followed. "Come on, let's go."

"Keep your skirt on, woman." Dana found the right key, and unlocked the driver's door, climbing in to unlock the other side. "God, this heat." She started the car when Becky got in. "We're clear?"

"Right as the rain."

"Then we are *out*." She didn't bother with reverse, but thumped over the curb and onto the street, saying, "Yes! Thank you, Becky Collins!"

"Ah, it was nothing."

"Where are we going?"

"Gibby's house."

"Wait. That's why we're doing this?"

"He wouldn't ditch without a reason."

"Seriously?" Dana shook her head, half-smiling. "He's cute and all, but I *knew* there was a reason I didn't like that boy."

"Stop. I'm serious."

"I know you are." Dana grinned around the cigarette pinched between her perfect teeth, hair whipping out as she drove faster. "Sometimes a cowgirl needs a pony."

The rest of the drive went like that: Dana amused, and Becky tied into knots of worry. Gibby's car was not in the driveway when they got to his house, so Becky rang the doorbell. When no one came, she rang five more times.

"He's not home!" Dana yelled. "Let's go already!"

Becky got back in the car, and belted herself in. "Let's go to Chance's house."

"I hate that side of town."

"Just drive the car, Dana. Please."

They found Gibby's car in Chance's driveway, top down and glinting in the sun.

No response to the doorbell.

Dead silence in the house.

Dana made a shooing motion, and said, "Go on in!" But Becky was thinking of Tyra and Sara. Dark house. Dead quiet. Dana stuck her head through the car window, shouting, "Go on, cowgirl! Ride that pony!"

Becky put a finger against her lips.

"Put a *brand* on that pony!"

Dana could get in these moods, and Becky knew from hard experience that the best way to shut her up was to take away the target. So she opened the door, and stepped inside, half-blind.

"Hello? Anyone?"

Becky couldn't explain the fear she felt, but it grew by the second, a serious, no-bullshit kind of fear. Gibby should have been in school. His car was here.

And what was that smell?

Every curtain was drawn, and that felt wrong on such a sunny day, the kind of wrong that made Becky think of outside and people and fast fucking cars. Instead, she went to the living room, which was darkest. Something shapeless was on the floor. In the gloom, it could be a pile of laundry, but Becky knew better. She thought she saw a leg, that maybe those were fingers.

Don't do it, she thought.

But her fingers found the switch on the wall.

When the light exploded, she wanted to run—God, did she want to run! But those *were* fingers. And that *was* a leg. So Becky screamed. She screamed so loud and long that Dana tumbled from the car, and burst into the house, following the sound of those screams. She came at a dead run—a fine damn friend—and that's how she tripped on the body, and fell facedown on top of it. *Ride* that *pony,* Becky thought, but it was a mad thought, and a wild one, a where-the-hell-is-my-boyfriend thought.

39

Cops came like buzzards to a kill, the marked cars and dark sedans, the men in somber suits. Becky sat on the porch with an arm around Dana, who could not stop scrubbing at all the places she'd been stained by the dead man's blood.

"I need a shower. God, please. A bath. A washcloth."

Two cops approached, and one said, "We really do need to talk."

"Give her another minute," Becky replied.

"How about we question you separately. How about that." They weren't questions, and he wasn't pleasant.

Becky said, "It's Martinez, right?"

"*Detective* Martinez."

"I'm not leaving her, Detective, so give us another minute."

The cops actually did step back, and Becky used the time to get her head straight. Everything was crooked: the dead man on Chance's floor, Gibby's abandoned car. When the cops came back, she said, "You know we had nothing to do with this, right?"

The other cop said, "Of course, sweetheart. We do have questions, though." He gestured at the bustle around them. "We can go as slowly as you like."

"We just want to go home."

"We'll be quick." With an understanding nod, he lowered himself to sit on the step below them. "Do you know the man inside?"

"No."

"You've never seen him before?"

"Never."

"What about you?" He looked at Dana. It took her a moment, but she shook her head. "You girls are in the same class as Gibby and Chance?"

"Yes, sir."

"Why aren't you in school?"

"Gibby wasn't in class." Becky smoothed away a single tear. "I was worried."

"Kids do skip school. Is there any particular reason today was worrisome?"

There was no right way to answer that question. How much could Becky say? How much would Gibby want her to share? "I was worried." She kept it vague. "He's a good student. He doesn't skip school without good reason."

"So this is unusual behavior for him?"

"Or he had some good reason."

"Did he have one?" Martinez asked. "A good reason?"

"I don't know."

The nice cop waited a moment, and then tried a different angle. "Is there anything else unusual in your friend's life? Has Gibby been acting strangely? Has he spoken to you about anything odd that may have happened?"

"Just that his brother's in prison. You know."

Martinez said, "Ask her about the car."

"Ignore my partner," the nice cop said. "He tends to interrupt. How about you walk us through it in your own words. Tell us what happened. There's no wrong way to do it. I promise."

Becky did as he asked. She told them what time they got there, and what happened after she went inside. He wanted details, but the narrative wandered. She had to backtrack; start over. "I know I shouldn't have gone in someone else's house without permission, and it's horrible that Dana fell on the body—crime scene and all, evidence, I mean—but I was screaming, and she was trying to help, and I was just . . . It was just so . . ." She smoothed away another tear.

"Take your time, young lady. You're doing fine."

"Oh, for God's sake . . ."

"Hush, Martinez."

"Ask about the car."

The nice cop sighed, but nodded. "The Mustang belongs to your friend, right? We know it does. I'm sorry. That sounds like I'm trying to trick you somehow." He shook his head as if frustrated by his own questions. "Was the car here when you arrived?" Becky nodded. "And your friend? Did you see him at all?"

"No."

"What about Chance?"

Becky shook her head, increasingly suspicious of Martinez. He was too intent, the way he leaned forward and stared. "Why do you care about the car?" she asked.

"It's a routine question."

"It's just his car," Becky said. "He bought it last summer."

"That's fine. You're doing great. Did you see anyone when you arrived? On the street? Anywhere nearby?"

"I wasn't paying attention."

"If someone had left the house through the back door, do you think you would have seen them? As you arrived, or as you entered the house, did you hear anything? A door closing? Footsteps?"

"No."

"Any sense of movement inside the house?"

"You think he was still in the house? Whoever did this?"

"No, sweetheart. I doubt that very much."

But Becky thought he might be lying.

Martinez said, "Ask her about the keys."

The nice cop held up a hand, but did not respond to Martinez. "Look at me, sweetheart. Okay?" He lifted his eyebrows, an invitation for her to stop staring at Martinez, and focus. "A few more questions. Did you happen to notice if the keys were in your friend's car?"

Becky shook her head.

"How about in the house? Did you see the keys inside?"

"What do Gibby's keys have to do with someone killing that man?"

"It's just a question, sweetheart."

"Will you please stop calling me that?"

"Of course. I'm sorry. I have daughters. It's a habit."

Becky looked at Martinez. "And you, you're scaring my friend."

Martinez showed his palms, and moved back a step, an almost-apology. The nice cop smiled encouragingly. "The keys," he said again.

"The keys were beside the body." Dana looked up for the first time. "That's why they're asking. They think Gibby and Chance are involved."

"Hang on now, no one here thinks that." The nice cop tried to keep things calm.

"*He* does." Dana pointed at Martinez.

"Just questions," the nice cop said.

But he didn't seem so nice anymore.

For Bill French, the day was an exercise in bureaucratic futility. He'd gone to the station early, and Captain Martin had been there, waiting.

I'm sending you to Raleigh for a conference. You don't want to go, but I need you gone for the day.

French had argued back, but the captain was determined.

Gone for the day or suspended for a month. Your choice . . .

"So here I sit." French mumbled under his breath, shifting on the hard, plastic chair. "Goddamn it." He was in a conference room on the third-floor headquarters of the North Carolina State Bureau of Investigation, Capital District, one of a hundred city cops from across the state attending a seminar on cross-jurisdictional cooperation. An hour in, and he'd already slipped out three times to borrow a phone and call friends at the station back home. The desk sergeant. A junior detective who owed him a favor. They didn't know anything, or wouldn't tell him. He found Burklow on the third call. "Sit tight," he'd said. "If something breaks, I *will* track you down. In the meantime, have faith."

But faith was for rookies and civilians. French knew too much about bad cops, bias, sloppy work.

He looked at his watch.

Eighty-three minutes since he'd first sat down.

It had to be longer than that!

For another twenty minutes, he cooled his heels as some state plebe droned on about the architectural hierarchy of a multi-jurisdictional investigation as might be used in pursuit of a purely hypothetical, cross-county, serial rapist. "If you'll turn to the diagram on page twelve of your manual . . ."

"No. Just no."

He was in the wrong city, doing the wrong thing.

French left the conference room without looking right or left, his steps loud in the hall as he stalked past the outer offices of the Professional Standards Division, en route to the elevator bank. He was almost past the double doors before a young woman interrupted his thoughts. "Excuse me, Detective?"

It was the same pleasant young woman who'd allowed him to use the phone on her desk. "Yes, Agent . . . ?"

"Foil," she said. "You have a call."

At her desk, she handed him the phone, and moved away to give him privacy. Four agents stood at a conference table across the room; no one at the adjacent desk. Only Burklow had this number. "Ken?"

"What's the last thing I said to you?"

There were background sounds. Men in the squad room. Orders. Activity. French's hand tightened on the phone. The call would not have come without good reason. "You told me to have faith."

"Shit. No. What was the second-to-last thing I said?"

"That you'd track me down if something major broke."

"That's the one. So you give those state cops a nice thanks-for-your-time, then get your ass home, fastest. 'Cause I'm telling you, brother"—a rustle on the line as Burklow shifted the receiver from one ear to the next—"shit down here just went sideways."

Raleigh to Charlotte was all interstate and open highway, so French lit up the cherry, and put the pedal down. *Chapel Hill. Greensboro. Salisbury.* He counted cities, pulling 95 in traffic and 120 when the traffic thinned. Eighty-nine minutes after Burklow's call, he hit the Charlotte line. Two miles in, he braked hard, and rocked into the parking lot where Burklow wanted to meet. He was there, and waiting. "When you said *ninety minutes,* I didn't think you could actually do it."

"I think it took ninety-three. Any sign of Gibby?"

"Not yet. I'm sorry."

"Gabrielle?"

"She's still in the dark, and I convinced the captain to keep it that way, at least for now."

"Does he know you called me?"

"Suspects, maybe. He squawked twice, and left a message at the station."

"Saying what?"

"That you're in Raleigh for the day, and he wants you to stay there."

"What about the body?"

"Transported forty minutes ago. Lonnie Ward. White male, thirty-seven, and big as a house, six-eight, maybe, and about two-ninety."

"He has a sheet?"

"A few minor convictions: loitering, lewdness, solicitation. There was a Peeping Tom charge that went away back in '68 when the witness recanted. The DA was an associate then, but remembers the case; thought there might have been some intimidation. No family, far as I can tell. No word yet on occupation or known associates. He has an apartment near the university. Smith and Martinez are there."

"What about the girls?"

"Becky Collins and Dana White. Scared to death, but home with their parents. They don't know anything. Other developments since we spoke. They put Gibby's car on a flatbed, and hauled it out for full forensics. Can't imagine what they hope to find, but there it is. Still, no murder weapon or witnesses. Martinez and Smith interviewed Chance's mom, but she knows nothing of use. Never seen the dead guy. Has no idea where the boys could be."

"How's this playing with the captain?"

"Honestly? The man is lost. You know how he is, too decent to be a murder cop, and more *bureaucrat* than *street*. I don't think he's recovered yet from seeing Tyra Norris the way she was."

"What about the rank and file?"

Burklow rolled his heavy shoulders, almost fatalistic. "You're well-liked. You know that. Plus, a lot of these guys watched Gibby grow up.

There's respect, too, for how Robert died in the war. But then again, there's Jason, and he's a scary dude, even for cops. A few of the newer guys wonder if Gibby has some of those same qualities tucked away inside. The car keys are a problem. Martinez is on that like white on rice. If you're asking me to lay odds, though, I'd say most cops in the know think the boys got caught up in something they weren't looking for. Wrong place, wrong time. I'd call it 70 percent."

"And the other 30?"

Burklow shrugged, soulful and sad. "They think the boys are involved."

"With Jason?"

"Jason, yeah. Tyra, and Sara. Now the dead man in Chance's house. None of it feels random."

"Christ, it does look bad." French scraped dry palms across his face. "What do I do, Ken? How do I save my family?"

40

The warden brought the phone, but was nervous about it. There was too much intent in X's eyes, and too much stillness in his limbs.

"I said *five minutes*."

"I know. I'm sorry." The warden tried to swallow, his tongue so suddenly dry it cleaved to the roof of his mouth. "It took time to find a cord that was long enough to reach."

Nothing changed in how X stood or spoke, but the warden's entire body chilled. Predator. Prey. A viper tasting the air. He offered the phone, and X took it.

"Wait upstairs. This won't take long."

Reece was off by a few minutes, but the call came about the time he thought it would. He let it ring six times, then lifted the receiver, and spoke with ill-concealed satisfaction. "Hello, old friend."

"We are most assuredly *not* friends."

Reece squinted across the sun-scorched fields. He was afraid of X, but the thrill was real, too, a madness that felt like falling. "Can I assume from this call that we have an understanding?"

"Release Jason's brother unharmed, and I will cancel the contract on your head. I won't hire anyone new. I won't spend a dime."

"And after tomorrow?"

"Once I am dead, you have nothing to fear."

Reece closed his eyes as a wave of relief swept over him. "I have your word on that?"

"You can consider it a solemn promise."

"I appreciate your promise. To be safe, though, I'll keep Jason's brother until after the execution."

"So long as we have a deal."

"Once you're dead, I'll let the kid go."

"Unharmed."

"Yes."

"Swear it."

"I swear it," Reece said; but thought, *Maybe.*

X felt better after the phone call. Decisions had been made, events put into motion. He checked himself, though, afraid self-deception might wear a mirror for a face.

No, he was good.

Maybe better than good.

"Warden Wilson. Come down, please."

"Yes?"

"Send down the lawyers, but don't go far."

"Is everything okay?"

"Things are fine," X said. "But plans are changing."

When X summoned him back, hours had passed.

"Warden Wilson, if you would join us."

That from one of the lawyers, a tall, spare man who disappeared back into a cell, leaving the warden no choice but to trail along behind. Inside, X sat at a table lined with rows of documents, the second lawyer across the table, saying things like, *Sign here, thank you, now initial here . . .*

X said, "Warden Wilson. Just in time." He kept his head down, dashing off signatures on trust accounts, transfer documents, letters of incorporation. Numbers seemed to leap from the pages.

Ten million to the Bank of the Caymans.

Forty million to fund a revocable trust.

Two hundred million to Zurich Cantonal Bank.

The warden could barely process the numbers, and there were others, so many others.

X signed a final document, and one lawyer notarized it, adding it to a stack for the other attorney to sign as witness. That done, X held out a hand, saying, "Mr. Preston."

The attorney handed X a sheaf of papers, and X, in turn, offered them to the warden, who took them numbly. "What you'll find there," X said, "is an account at Mellon Bank in New York, established in your name, as well as transfer documents, a notice of verified funds from the transferring bank, and a letter of authorization signed by me, notarized and witnessed. You'll see that the transfer documents are dated for tomorrow."

"After your, uh . . ."

"Yes," X allowed. "After the scheduled execution."

Warden Wilson looked down at the documents, but words swam on the page. He tried again, but only one thing sprang into focus. "This is for twice the amount we discussed."

"Because I'm changing the terms of our arrangement. The numbers should reflect that."

Papers trembled in the warden's hand. "What changes?"

X smiled, but it was thin as a dime. "Gentlemen, a moment."

The lawyers rose, and left. When they were alone, X put a hand on the warden's shoulder in a manner so unexpected and intimate, it was absolutely terrifying. "I need something more from you," he said. "Something I never expected to ask for or want." X laid it out for the warden. What he wanted. When it should happen. He spoke slowly for the warden's sake, and repeated it twice. "I'll leave the *how* of it to you."

The warden stared dumbly. "The *how* of it?"

"Shall we go through it again?"

"No. No." The warden shook his head. Nausea. Cold sweat. "I'm not sure I can manage that."

"I'm giving you forty million dollars." X squeezed the shoulder until it hurt. "Of course you can."

"But tomorrow . . . I mean . . . the timing."

What he meant was, *I can't do it, I won't, I'm not fucking insane.*

X, though, had no patience for fools and their feelings. "We spoke recently of your youngest son, Trevor. We've never really talked about his older brother. Thomas, I believe."

"Thomas, yes." The warden nodded stupidly.

"He lives at home, I'm told."

"He helps his mother."

"He has a girlfriend? A job?"

"No. Neither."

"Physically, though . . ." X sat, and laced his fingers. "How is young Thomas?"

41

Nothing changed until the phone rang. After that, we drove for a long time, open roads at first, and then traffic sounds, starts and stops that felt like the city. By the time we stopped for real, Chance had been too quiet for too long, and I was half-dead from the heat. The car rocked when the driver got out, and it was another bad moment, because it felt so *final*.

I didn't die, though.

He left us in the trunk.

Ninety degrees on the outside, maybe one-forty in the darkness. Chance was as loose as a dead man.

Was he breathing or not?

I couldn't tell; I didn't know.

I thought maybe I was dying.

When the trunk opened, it was dusk, and I was still alive. I saw black trees and that purple sky, everything fuzzy at the edges. I couldn't move, and he knew it. Maybe that's why he'd left us in for so long. Or maybe he wanted us dead the easy way. It wouldn't take much more. He stood there for a few seconds, and then was gone; and I drank down cool air, lustful, lost, and drowning. When sound came, it was a slaughterhouse sound, like a pig squealing. He hauled me out and dropped me down, folding Chance like a blanket beside me, dead or alive, I still couldn't tell. His heat could be *trunk* heat, his movements involuntary as wheels squealed again, and he rolled us toward a house I'd never seen, then down a ramp to a room filled with tables, cages, and horrible things made of bright metal so they glittered in the light.

At the first cage, he rolled us inside, and then dragged us onto the floor. I hit hard, but couldn't feel it. Chance's head bounced. A knife appeared, but cut tape instead of skin. He didn't look at my face or say a word, just closed the cage, and locked it with a hunk of brass the size of my fist. I thought he would leave us then, but he ran a hose and sprayed us down with cold water, the shock of it like a slap as it hit my face and mouth, and choked me. It was water, though, and when he was gone, I sucked it off the floor.

I couldn't feel my arms or legs.

Chance never moved.

For French, the day was tough, but not impossible. He *did* have friends, and good friends would risk a lot. Late afternoon, he met one of those good friends in an alley two blocks from the station, a narcotics detective named James Monroe. *After the old, white dude,* he liked to say. A ten-year cop, he was dark-skinned and lean, with a hard face under gold-rimmed shades and eight inches of Afro.

"The APB went out ten minutes ago. Citywide. All departments."

French nodded grimly. "I heard it on the radio."

"It's worse, though. Captain Martin ordered it statewide. SBI, FBI, highway patrol. I'm sorry, brother. I hate to be the messenger."

French squinted into the bright light shining off the streets and buildings. Going statewide was an escalation. It meant Captain Martin considered his son a flight risk. The larger problem was that cops took statewide alerts seriously, and were much more likely to go in hot. "What about Burklow?"

"Still trailing Martinez and Smith. For a big guy, he can ghost along pretty good."

"And the ladies are still with us?"

"Come on, man." Monroe showed his teeth. "You know the ladies love you. More importantly, they love the kid."

That was the cornerstone of French's loose network: those who actually knew his son. The *ladies* included Captain Martin's assistant, two dispatch supervisors, and a desk sergeant named Irene Devine who used to bounce Gibby on her knee. Not much happened in the station that one or more of them didn't know about. The plan was simple: find Gibby before he got picked up, shot, or made things worse; keep Gabrielle in total ignorance for as long as possible. But the first part needed to happen fast, before the second part blew up in his face. He'd looked everywhere he knew to look, burned every possible bridge. "What aren't you telling me? Come on, Monroe. I see it in your face."

"All right, man. Shit." Monroe's frown deepened. He pulled off the shades, and showed some seriously unhappy eyes. "Captain Martin called a press conference for five fifteen. He's going live, man. He wants Gibby's face on the six o'clock news."

French's fingers tightened into a fist. He couldn't help it.

Monroe understood. "He thinks he's helping, all right, that a press conference is the best way to bring Gibby in and keep him safe."

But French didn't see it like that. A clean takedown required control, and a press conference ceded that control to a city full of fucking idiots. "Where's the press conference?"

"Usual."

That meant the station house media room. Thirty seats. Good lighting. The captain was very proud of it. The time was 4:37. Thirty-eight minutes before they opened the doors, and the news crews piled in. "Martinez and Smith will be there?"

"What do you think?"

French chewed on a fingernail, an old habit he'd abandoned in his twenties. He studied the street, the station house. Captain Martin would run the press conference, but Martinez would have face time. He'd paint a bad picture. Another escalation. "All right, buddy. Thanks for the information. You might want to make yourself scarce for a while."

"Are you planning something?"

French said no, but that was a lie, and both men knew it. "You go on and take off, okay? Have a drink at the Dunhill, and tell Mary to put it on my tab."

"I don't like this."

French didn't, either. His wife watched the six o'clock news. "Make it two drinks. Take a lady friend, if you like."

"Are you sure?"

"Go on. Get out of here."

"If that's how you want it." Detective Monroe slipped the dark glasses back over his eyes. "I do have a lady friend."

When he was gone, French went to his dark place, working out the steps and asking hard questions like how far was he willing to go.

Leaving the alley, he worked his car through the neighboring blocks until he found what he needed, a three-story building in mid-renovation, and partially gutted, a half-dozen trucks still on-site. The clock was ticking down, but French had yet to meet a construction crew willing to work more than a minute after the five o'clock bell. This crew was little different. At five, they started packing up. Seven minutes more, and they were gone.

French gave it a fifty count to make sure no one had forgotten a lunch pail or tool belt, then pulled in behind the building, and parked. The lot had been ripped up, too, and that meant red dirt under his tires, a row of trees with dusty leaves. There were other buildings, built close. People could see him if they looked; it wasn't impossible. He honestly didn't care. His wife liked to watch the news on WBTV, and he could see her on the sofa, unsuspecting.

Six minutes.

Quitting the car, he took the back steps, and shouldered the door without slowing down. It was a construction door, plywood and flimsy, and the screws tore right out. Inside, it was bare studs and gypsum dust, but the stairwell was intact.

Goddamn right.

Back at the car, he snatched a gun case from the trunk, and strode back to the building as if he owned it, moving faster inside, second floor, the third. A voice said, *This is not you,* but he told the voice that thirty years of cop meant fuck-all next to his wife and child. On the roof, he checked his lines of fire, then dropped to a knee, unzipping the case.

Three minutes.

Reporters would be lined up outside the pressroom door, techs inside checking mics and lighting, as cops got ready. French could see that, too: the captain with his cue cards, Martinez chewing his lip like it was made of bacon and butter.

The rifle was as familiar as an old friend, but nothing special, a Remington 760 in .308 with a Bausch & Lomb 4× scope. Not a sniper rifle, not even police issue. But .308 was the right cartridge.

French glanced over the parapet. The station was a block away, the first transformer half that distance, a gray, metal unit silhouetted at the top of a tall pole. Maybe it fed the station, and maybe not. There were options, though. A second transformer was twice as far and west, but still an easy shot. The third was on the *other* side of the station.

Two targets, then.

Maybe three.

French had no idea how many bullets it would take to short out a transformer. How thick was the steel casing? Was there one best place to hit?

Not enough time to worry about it.

French fed in cartridges, and chambered the first. *Second thoughts?* Not even close. He was running dark, and wanted the station the same way.

"For Gabrielle," he said.

The first shot took out four city blocks.

Reece was drowning in a wealth of riches. First, he'd beaten X. No, he thought gleefully, *broken* him. X might pretend to be aloof, but he hated losing to anyone not considered his equal or his better. How many times had Reece heard him blather on about respect and clarity and purity of purpose? It was exhausting. Admittedly, there'd been a time when Reece had wanted that respect—had craved it, in fact—but things had gone a different way.

Not my fault . . .

The sense of richness dimmed for a moment, in part, he knew, because some piece of him still craved that admiration. There was also a splinter of fear he didn't quite understand. X would never break his word, and he'd been very clear.

I won't spend a dime . . .

The execution was only hours away, and he'd been plain on that point, too.

Once I am dead, you have nothing to fear . . .

For a moment more, Reece worried at the splinter, but just for a moment. X was nothing special, after all. Maybe that's why Reece felt so out of sorts.

With a mental flourish, he returned to all the *good* he'd achieved. He had two boys in the cage, and he really *couldn't* let them live. Lonnie had been right about that. He'd keep them alive until tomorrow, of course.

But after the execution?

Reece poured a glass of his father's favorite bourbon.

Such a small word to mean so much: *execution.* For Reece, it meant a life without shadow or reason to feel small. He had money. He had the girl. What *couldn't* he do once X was out of the picture?

He sat on the sofa, and watched the television play in silence. He would be there, of course. Hundreds already were; they'd been all over the news, old Christians, young hippies, and other strange souls. Some called it a protest, others a vigil, a field full of headlights and campfires and lanterns. None of them really knew X, and that part did make Reece sad. X was a dinosaur and stiff as an old rope, but he *was* one of a kind. Reece could admit that much, at least. Raising his glass to the television, he watched shadows climb and dance on the prison walls. "The end of an era," he said, then drank the whiskey down, and went off to watch the girl.

Alone in his office, Warden Wilson watched the news coverage. WBTV aired an hour-long special at seven o'clock. WRAL aired a similar program at eight, but focused more on the victims, and less on X's childhood, family fortune, and long-ago string of famous acquaintances. After a time, he unlocked a desk drawer, removed an envelope, and spilled its contents onto the desk. *Passports. Travel documents. New identities.* According to X, the money would be wired *after.*

But only after . . .

What X had asked him to do was a horrible thing—a reprehensible, unforgivable, and horrible thing—but the warden had no choice.

"No choice at all," he said.

And then he called Ripley.

When he arrived, the warden said, "Come in. Lock the door." Ripley did and when the warden said, "Sit," he did that, too. They'd known each other for a long time, not a friendship—how could it be?—but they understood each other. "What's our status?"

"The lawyers are gone. X is eating."

Warden Wilson glanced at the clock on the wall. The execution was scheduled for 9:00 a.m., a civilized hour, and not dawn, as people tended to think. "What about Jason French?"

"He'll be front row, center. Like X wants."

"And after? Who are you using?"

"Jordan and Kudravetz."

They were good choices, mercenary as hell and just smart enough. Unlocking the desk, the warden opened the bottom drawer, and removed three buff envelopes, two the size of a large dictionary, the third even larger. With a felt-tip pen, he wrote a name on each one. *Ripley. Jordan. Kudravetz.* He pushed the largest across the desk. "Open it."

Ripley did as he was told, no expression on his face as he stacked bricks of cash in neat rows. "Three hundred and fifty thousand dollars," he finally said.

"And a quarter million for each of the others."

A moment's silence followed. A man could buy a good house for forty thousand, a sports car for five. Ripley laced his fingers, and leaned back in the chair. The wheels were invisible, but they were for-damn-sure turning. "All right," he finally said. "Who do we have to kill?"

42

For Reece, it seemed anything was possible, and he wondered if this was what Christians meant when they spoke of being reborn. He was behind the false wall, and the girl was taking off her clothes. Too soon for a long bath, he knew, or even a hot, quick shower; but clean clothing had proved too much a temptation.

A richer world . . .

He followed her to the kitchen, only a few feet away as she uncorked a bottle of wine, and flared her nostrils before taking a sip. She moved room to room, and he trailed along behind the mirrors and the walls. When she slept, she did so fully clothed, with her knees drawn up. He'd planned to watch like this for nights or weeks, but it was the dawn of a new world.

An hour after midnight, he went inside.

He wouldn't touch her yet, but wanted to smell her hair and her skin, to feel the heat of her neck on his face. He stood by the bed, looking down. She was on her side, her lips slightly parted. Leaning close, he studied the line of her nose, and of the lashes, dark on her skin. He breathed deeply, but her hair smelled unclean, and her breath was slightly sour. He would have frowned, but she woke unexpectedly: a shutter-snap of wide eyes and the shadow-pink of an open mouth. For the first time in his life, Reece froze, utterly panicked.

He was ruining it!

The stare held for half a second, then Reece turned and ran, the girl screaming loud enough to shatter every thought he'd ever had.

•   •   •

I heard the scream, muffled by the house, but definitely *in* the house. It went on so long that even Chance stirred, which was more than I'd been able to manage in all the long hours we'd been caged.

"Hey, buddy, are you with me?"

He rolled onto his side, coughing up a lung. "Don't touch me." He found his hands and knees, his forehead against the floor. "The hell is that sound?"

"We're not the only ones here."

"*Here?* What here?"

Chance sounded out of it. I thought he was. He crawled a foot or two, and got his back against the wall. Cracked lips. A heat-swollen tongue. He tried to focus, but the room was dim. He saw the cage, though, and the tables. "Take it easy," I told him. "You were locked in a hot trunk for most of a day."

I saw the memories when he got them back, a parade across his face, nothing pretty. He put his palms over his eyes, and pushed hard. "What is this place?"

"A house. I don't know. Isolated."

"I heard a woman."

"I know."

"She was screaming."

"You're all right, man. Take it easy."

He blinked at me, bloodshot. "Is there water?"

I shook my head.

"What's that about?"

He meant my fingertips, torn and bloodied. I pointed at the place where sharp-edged bolts secured steel mesh to the steel frame. "A tool kit might have been better."

There was blood on metal, dried black.

Chance stared for five good seconds, then closed his eyes for so long I thought he'd checked out or fallen back asleep. When he spoke, they were still closed. "I don't know what to say to you. How can you even look at me?"

"Just take it easy."

Chance shook his head. "I *called* you. He told me to do it, and that's what I did."

"How about we worry about this cage and all that scary shit out there. How about that?"

"He can kill me. I don't care."

"He had a knife at your neck. I'd have made the call, too."

"I don't believe that."

He said it softly, but was looking at me, at least. I slid across the cage, and leaned against the same wall. "So that's it? You're officially a pussy? Got a membership card and everything?"

"Don't joke."

His mouth was open, his eyes glazed. If he had reserves left, I couldn't see them. "Chance, buddy. Listen . . ."

I got no further than that. The outside door swung open, and our kidnapper stepped inside. He had a revolver in one hand, and a wild look on his face, red-eyed and swollen, like he might fly apart.

"Back the fuck up! Back up!" He pointed with the gun. "You! Come here! Not you. The little one." I started to rise. He thumbed the hammer. "I said back the fuck up! You! Now!"

He unlocked the cage, and Chance stepped out like he didn't care, or couldn't. His eyes were down, both hands at his sides. The little man locked the cage, and up close like that, I saw more of the crazy in his face. Something had changed. He was off the rails. He pushed the barrel into Chance's chest, backed him away from the cage.

"Hey!" I rattled the door. "Hey, asshole!"

"Shut up. It's ruined."

"The hell are you doing?"

"I don't want them!" He shoved with the gun. "Anger. Regret." He swung the barrel into Chance's face. The blow staggered him; he bled. "I don't deserve to feel those things! I don't want to carry them!"

He hit Chance again.

I said, "Shit! Shit!"

Chance fell to his knees, blood dripping. He climbed slowly to his feet, still no expression. *Heatstroke,* I thought. *Concussion.* The little man hit him again, twice with a fist and again with the gun. Chance fell into a shelf; metal clattered. The barrel swung in—back of the head—and Chance went all the way down, every cord cut. The little man kicked him in the ribs, the face, then went back with his other foot, kicking and grunting as all that regret and anger found a place to go. "Not! My! Fault!"

"Leave him alone!" I yelled. "Damn it! Leave him alone!"

"Shut up or you're next!"

"Chance!" I beat on the mesh, but nothing changed.

The guy had a lot of anger left.

A lot of regret, too.

Afterward, Reece stared into the mirror, sweat on his face, still breathing hard. There was a glitter in his eyes he'd never seen, a shiftiness that looked dangerous. He was moving too fast. That was the problem.

"Goddamn it, X."

Had he ruined the girl?

It was the only question that mattered. He'd risked everything for her. He'd looked for so many years, been so patient . . .

"What patience?"

He punched the wall, the look on his face a sarcastic, angry sneer. He was supposed to give her time to settle, months, if need be. He'd been ready to wait that long, or even longer.

It was X's fault.

X was in his head.

Reece pulled at his hair, then forced a deep breath.

Two sides.

Every coin.

Lonnie Ward was dead. No real loss; he'd been a convenience. And X would die in hours. Once he was gone, there'd be no one left alive who knew Reece or what he was or where he lived. The thought was like a breath of air. Reece had money. He was still young. Maybe a fresh start was the way to go. Kill the boys. Kill the girl.

A clean slate.

Reece closed his eyes, and tried to see the future. It was cloudy, and *cloudy* was frustrating. So he went to his secret place, and watched the girl. She'd crawled under the bed, and pulled the blanket with her. Reece couldn't see much. He chewed his lip until it bled. The taste of it surprised him.

He didn't like that she was under the bed; he couldn't see. How long would she stay there, and how would she be when she came out, ruined or resigned or something else?

Maybe she did not have to die.

Or maybe she did . . .

For me, it was all about Chance. I'd dragged him into the cage as the man who'd beaten him so badly stood by and watched, his chest heaving as sweat ran down his neck. He'd said nothing at all, just locked the cage, and left.

Son of a bitch.

Motherfucker.

I still didn't know if Chance was all right. He was on his side, arms folded to cushion the ribs, his eyes closed. He didn't speak, but his face was better than I'd thought. Blood, yeah, but none of the cuts were deep. I used my shirt to clean him up.

"Gibs." It was a whisper.

"Yeah, man. I'm here."

"That kind of sucked." His eyes stayed closed. His lips twitched.

"Dude, are you smiling?"

"I don't know. My face hurts too much to be sure."

"Why are you smiling?"

"I couldn't find a tool kit."

That made no sense. I thought again, *Concussion. Or shock.*

Then he opened his hand, and showed me what looked like a pair of scissors, curved at the tips, some kind of surgical clamp.

Chance's voice was very soft. "It's called a hemostat."

He seemed so certain and calm I thought maybe I was the one in shock. "How in the world do you know that?"

Another smile, very faint. "I saw it in a magazine once. Medics in Vietnam . . ."

"Chance, Jesus . . ."

"Much better than your fingers."

43

Jason waited for someone to take him to X, but no one came to his cell or even into the hall. The world was stillness, dark thoughts, and dead silence. Like most inmates unfortunate enough to be awake in the middle of this particular night, Jason was thinking of the execution. He knew enough to visualize the way it would go down. At eight o'clock, three corrections officers would remove X from his cell, walk him the length of death row, and down a short hall to the execution chamber, where thick, leather straps at the wrists and ankles would secure him to the chair as the final two straps crisscrossed his chest, shoulders to hips. One officer would shave his head as close to the skin as possible, as a second prepared the sponge and bucket of salt water, placing those items beside the chair. The third officer, the most senior, would adjust the headpiece to assure a proper fit and maximum conductivity. Every preliminary step was designed to further that end: the salt water and sponge, the bare skin and the cranial cap lined with copper mesh. Those steps wouldn't take long, maybe twenty minutes.

After that, X would have to wait.

At nine o'clock exactly, blinds would be raised at two different windows, one to the outside world, letting in the new day's light, and one to the observation room so that those present might witness the death. The warden, by then, would be in the execution chamber, and would offer X a chance for final words. Jason had no idea what X might say, only that he would be there to hear those words, and that to X, his presence would matter in powerful, complicated ways that Jason would as soon *not* consider. As for the other witnesses—the politicians and the families of the victims—Jason suspected that X would die as he had lived, contemptuous to the end.

After last words, the sponge would be soaked in salt water, placed on X's bare scalp, and secured there by the cranial cap. Water would stream down his face and into his eyes; it would darken his clothing at the collar. A power cable would be attached to the headpiece, as would a dark shroud designed to conceal his face in what Jason considered the final mercy of allowing a condemned man's last expressions of pain, fear, and despair to be his alone.

Jason had imagined the moment countless times: silence in the gathered crowd, black cloth stirring as X measured out his final breaths. When the moment arrived, 1,750 volts would pour into X's body, lifting it, and then dropping it. Fifteen seconds later, a second jolt would be delivered, followed by a mandatory five-minute wait and a declaration of time of death.

Assuming everything goes well.

When they came for Jason, they did so in the dark. Half-blinded by a flashlight, Jason still recognized Captain Ripley. The others he thought were Jordan and Kudravetz. The core of X's detail. Old-school. They pulled Jason to his feet, and every inch of the journey hurt.

"Get dressed."

They gave him civilian clothes, and Jason did as he was told. They took him into the hall. Cuffs only. No chains.

"This way."

Ripley set a fast pace, and they met no one as they moved down deserted hallways, and passed through checkpoints that would normally be guarded. That set off alarm bells, but when Jason slowed his pace, they yanked him hard by the arms. Outside, the sky was clear and dark.

Not dawn.

Not even close.

They drew him along a dim path, cellblock D emerging from the gloom.

No lights on the towers.

No movement.

With each turn, Jason ticked off places they *weren't* taking him.

Not the infirmary.

Not death row.

They weren't taking him to X, and that made the bells sing.

Ripley said, "Six minutes."

Jason felt the tension, the new tempo. They hustled him toward the admin building, where they passed two guards, down at the gate, and bleeding. Ripley got them through, and locked the gate behind them.

"Shift change in four minutes."

They rushed through the darkened building, found another guard down at the entrance, and two more on the inside. They moved Jason down zigzag stairs, and into a subbasement hallway that led to a concrete ramp lit by dim bulbs in rusted cages. The big guards urged him up the slope to a parking garage occupied by a single car and lots of dark corners. If Jason wanted to disappear a man, this would be a good way to do it, a quiet, clean kill, then in the trunk and gone. At the car, Ripley popped the trunk. Inside was a spare tire and a jack, a water bottle and a ratty blanket. "Get in."

"No."

"Get in the damn trunk."

"You'll have to kill me first," Jason said.

Something primal showed on Ripley's face. Jason might be injured, but he'd gone toe to toe with X more times than any man alive. Three guards or not, no one wanted to roll those dice. "Okay, tough guy. Back seat, but on the floor."

"Ripley, no . . ."

"Shut up, Kudravetz. Get him in. Cover him up."

Jason didn't give an inch.

"Get in the car," Ripley said.

"Where are you taking me?"

"We don't have time for this." Ripley drew a revolver Jason had not seen or suspected. Guards did not carry inside the walls. Not ever. "I'll say please if it makes things easier."

Jason let the fight bleed out of his limbs—no choice. They got him in the car, down deep in the shadows, beneath a blanket that smelled like mothballs and gasoline. Ripley and Jordan got in front, Ripley behind the wheel. Kudravetz took the back seat, and his face pale white as he stared down in the gloom. "Fuck this up, and you'll kill us all."

Ripley turned the key. The engine caught.

"Cover your face."

Jason did, but kept enough of a gap to see a slice of concrete ceiling. The car lurched into motion, turned a tight radius, and angled up a second ramp. When it stopped, he heard steel rumble as a metal door rolled on heavy-gauge tracks. Then they were outside.

"One minute. We're cutting this close."

The main gate was brightly lit. Ripley spoke to a guard, and the gate ground open, so massive that Jason felt the vibration. The car rolled forward, and they were through. Jason saw treetops and firelight, then heard the rumble of the crowd. Jordan said, "Jesus, there must be a thousand of them by now."

In seconds, bodies crowded the car, signs stabbing up and down as people yelled at the car and at each other, a wash of angry faces. Ripley intimidated with the big engine. Short lurches. Hard stops. Some backed off. Others beat on the car. When they were through, the sky opened up, and so did Ripley.

"Pursuit?"

"No."

"Alarms?"

"Nothing yet."

They hit the tree line, and blew through it in a boil of gravel and dust. "Kudravetz, let him up."

Jason got off the floorboards, and held on for dear life. Too much car and not enough traction. When they reached the state road, Ripley pumped the brakes and turned left, rear end drifting until the tires caught pavement. Then it was forty miles an hour, racing fast to sixty-five and ninety. The car looked old, but had the goods where it counted: rock steady on the shocks, engine still eager as they broke a hundred, and reached out for one-ten. Kudravetz was watching him closely, and so was

Jordan, both of them wary and ready for anything. Jason thought, *Pagans, payback, Darius Simms*. Simms was the kind to want his payback in person, to look Jason in the eyes, and say something stupid like, *You shot me twice, motherfucker, and nobody does that to Darius Simms . . .*

"How about now you tell me where we're going?"

Ripley's eyes flashed in the rearview. "A farmhouse. Not far."

Wind poured through open windows, and Jason watched the dark fields and distant woods. More places to disappear a man. He ran scenarios, but none looked good. The speedometer was pegged at one-ten, and Ripley still carried that .38.

"Ten minutes." Ripley's eyes, again in the mirror. "Please don't do anything stupid."

Nothing marked the turn but a battered mailbox with catseye reflectors that glowed yellow from a hundred yards out. Ripley slowed the car, and turned onto a dirt road in an abandoned field. A hundred feet in, two four-wheel-drive vehicles were angled in to block the drive. "Take it easy, people. No surprises here."

Where the vehicles blocked the road, two men stood on the hard, red dirt, M16s carried at the low-ready. Maybe ex-military, definitely trained. When Ripley stopped the car, one maintained his position center road as the other came to the driver's-side window, and shone a light into the car. "Names?"

Ripley shielded his eyes, pointing in turn. "Ripley. Jordan. Kudravetz. That's Jason French behind me."

The light stayed on Ripley's face for five full seconds, then swept the other faces a second time. "Any weapons in the vehicle?"

Ripley handed over the .38.

Slowly, Jason noted.

"Wait for us to move the vehicles, then proceed to the house at no more than fifteen miles an hour." He straightened, and keyed his radio. "One car, inbound. Four men."

He got into a Bronco, and the second man got into a Jeep, rocking the vehicles through the ditch line and off the road. Ripley drove them through the gap, and the vehicles rolled back out of the fields, blocking the drive behind them.

Not Pagans, Jason thought.

Not unless they contracted out top-dollar private security.

For a moment, he thought military brass might have sent private contractors to make sure the Bến Hải River massacre stayed well and deeply buried, that General Laughtner's fear of exposure meant no loose threads could be left to dangle. And Jason felt very much like that loose thread. The dirt track stretched into blackness and scrub, no sign of any house. Maybe the general thought it wasn't enough to string him out on morphine, then send him home disgraced and shot full of heroin. But that didn't feel right, either.

Why send him home at all?

Why not have these guards kill him in a quiet, dark corner of the prison?

Ripley kept the car at fifteen miles an hour, rolled onto a low hill, and began to climb. At the top, they leveled out, and then began a shallow descent on the other side, a cluster of lights gleaming in the near distance. Closer, the scene resolved into an abandoned farmhouse lit by temporary floods and the lights of five vehicles arranged in a loose circle. The house was decrepit, abandoned. Jason spotted armed men at the corners, and in the dimness beyond the cars. Ripley pulled into the circle of headlights, and turned off the engine. "My advice," he said, "is to move slowly."

He tipped his head to mean, *Out of the car.* And Jason was fine with that. If it was a fight, he'd fight. And if it came to dying . . .

He opened the door, stepped out, and turned a slow circle. He'd missed the sniper on the roof, the shapes of people in some of the cars. He looked at the faces of the nearest armed men. Not one face showed a flicker. "Shoot me or talk to me."

He wanted answers. He didn't know a damn thing. Then suddenly he did.

A car door opened, and a man got out. "Hello, Jason."

Jason kept a calm face, but felt something different on the inside.

Dear God, he's out.

In the cone of bright lights, X did not look particularly dangerous, but neither would a coral snake. He seemed pleased with himself, too, still bruised and broken-toothed, but smiling modestly in a seersucker suit with calfskin loafers and a snowy shirt, open at the collar.

"May we talk?"

It sounded like a question, but it really wasn't. Jason counted eight armed men, plus the two at the entrance.

"Please." X gestured at the car behind him, something large, long, and brand-new. "Warden Wilson made arrangements to delay the alarm at your escape, but it *will* sound."

Again, Jason ran scenarios. Four armed men were watching his every move, no fingers on the triggers, but close. The other men were turned outward, covering the drive and the cross-country approaches. No escape in any direction.

Jason got in the car. Soft leather. New-car smell. X slid in beside him, and someone else closed the door.

"Cuffs?" X showed a small key, and Jason lifted his wrists so the cuffs could be removed. When X spoke again, his voice was low and the smile was in his eyes. "I told you before that Lanesworth would not be your life."

Jason could no longer pretend to be unfazed. "How did you do this?"

"Plans were in place to release you after the execution. I had to change those plans, so here we are together." X gestured at a dark van, not far away. "The warden is just there, if you wish to thank him."

Jason saw cutouts of people, more than one.

"His family," X explained. "Unhappy, but together. They'll disappear, as will the guards who brought you here."

"Disappear, *dead*?"

"No, not disappear dead."

The car was cool and quiet, the air conditioner running. Jason should be angry, but wasn't. He wasn't even afraid. Life on the run would be no day at the lake, but twelve years on gun charges would be pretty shitty, too. "Is there some kind of plan here?"

"You and I will speak. After that, we all leave."

"You'll just let me go?"

"I actually brought you a car."

He pointed, but Jason wasn't ready to go there. So *many* thoughts! His past, the future, all his hours in the subbasement. "You could have done this at any time?"

"Escape? Yes."

"Why now? Why not years ago?"

X seemed suddenly uncomfortable, smoothing the front of his coat, and coughing lightly, as if to clear his throat. "Have you ever been bored, Jason, not for hours or days but so jaded and weary, so uninterested in life that you'd consider dying if only to try something new? It's a horrible feeling, that emptiness, like a silence. I remember a time I could not conceive of such a barren existence, except as an affliction of the aged and infirm. It was simply . . . *unimaginable.*" He met Jason's eyes, and shrugged. "It's amazing the way life changes."

"You're telling me you got bored?"

"*Jaded. Weary. Barren.* I chose those words with care. Life was worse than bland. It was a drain. Food had no taste. Money didn't matter. I had no reason to wake up, no desire to go to sleep. Nothing *mattered.*"

"What about the people you murdered?"

"They helped for a while."

He sounded wistful. Jason wanted to kill him.

X turned so he could face Jason more directly. "You asked, once, how the police caught me. There was news coverage, as you know, and reporters did their best, I suppose. Most would say I made a series of ever-larger mistakes, that I grew arrogant or careless, or that time is the great leveler. None of those things are true."

"You wanted it," Jason said.

"Wanted it, facilitated it. Frankly, I was ready to die. That's a truth I've never shared. It's been the great secret, the last of my shame. It's a relief to speak of it aloud."

"You murdered sixty-nine people. You don't deserve relief."

"Not even one as small as this?"

"You should have pulled the trigger yourself."

"Come, Jason, how often have we spoken of weakness? Suicide was never a possibility."

"But suicide by cop was?" Jason scoffed. "Or suicide by electric chair?"

"They seemed the only options, though I have, at times, hoped you might do the honor." Jason's jaw dropped. X shrugged again. "It would have been a good death."

"So why this?" He meant *outside, escape.* "You don't want to die anymore?"

"Yesterday, I did. Then I found reasons to live: one man to love, another to hate, good reasons, and unexpected."

Jason pinched the bridge of his nose. His head ached. "Why are you telling me this?"

"Because some things *haven't* changed. Dead or alive, the good of me or the bad, I still want an admirable man to bear witness, one who can see past the headlines and the fury. A man who knows me, and whose soul I know in return. It's not so much to ask, is it, to be thought of on occasion, to be known and remembered?"

"I'm not your friend or your priest."

"Nor am I in search of absolution. But you do understand me better than anyone alive, my thoughts and the things I've done."

"I'm sorry. No. No way. I don't want this. I can't."

Jason needed out of the car, needed to move. He opened the door, but X stopped him with four simple words.

"Reece has your brother."

Half out of the car, Jason froze.

X slid across the seat, peering upward. "Reece did something to make me angry. I'm very upset, and he knows it. He took your brother to hold me off. It's why we're here, why all of us are here."

"Get out of the car," Jason said.

"Let me help you."

"I said *get out of the fucking car.*"

"Very well." X swung out his legs, and folded at the waist. Jason hit him before he was off the seat. It was all he had, and it felt *good*!

For about half a second.

He took a rifle butt in the head, another in the kidneys. He bent, but didn't go down. X said, "Enough! That's enough!" Armed men stepped away, fingers on the triggers. X took Jason by the arm, and straightened him up. "I can help you, but time is short. Are you able to focus? Good."

X led Jason past the men who'd struck him down. The car was a Mustang, but not like Gibby's. A hardtop. "The keys are in it." X handed Jason an envelope. "Reece's address. His floor plans and alarm codes, plus a full set of security schematics. That's where you'll find your brother."

Jason opened the envelope, and flipped pages. Numbers. Diagrams. Sight lines. "How did you get this so fast?"

"I'm a paranoid billionaire. I bought Reece's security consultant the day after the system was installed. The system is good, but not perfect. You can get inside."

"Why are you doing this for me?"

X ignored the question. "Reece won't hurt your brother until he knows I'm dead. The boy's an insurance policy. It's not personal." He looked at his watch. "It's almost four. You can be at Reece's house in eighty minutes. Don't drive fast enough to get pulled over. If your name's not out yet, it will be. You'll find weapons in the trunk. Reece will want to be at the execution. He'll need that. He's planned for it. I can promise that. If you can bear to wait, the house will be yours, and you can get your brother out, easy. If you can't wait, you can't. I know the boy matters." X paused for a beat. "I'm sorry about this, Jason. I truly am. I did not foresee this behavior from Reece."

An armed guard approached. "Sir, we don't have much time."

X gave Jason a searching look. "You should go."

Jason got in the car, his thoughts running hot. He started the engine; turned on the headlights.

"I do have one request." X stooped at the window. "Don't kill Reece unless you have to. Protect yourself, save your brother. But Reece has become . . . meaningful to me."

"In what way?"

"The kind he will not like."

Jason stared into the night, jaw clenched. "I can't make you that promise."

"And I could have left you in prison."

That was the X Jason knew—hard edges and expectation. Jason's fingers tightened on the wheel. The big engine was talking. "Tell me why it matters."

X tilted his head, black-eyed and not quite smiling. "Do you remember Christmas as a child? Well, this is very much like the night before, like Christmas morning is right around the corner, and you just know there's something special under the tree."

If Jason lived to be a hundred, he'd never forget the expression on X's face, that glint-eyed half smile of childish anticipation. But Jason couldn't make the promise. He would kill Reece without thinking twice. He'd kill anything or anyone that got between him and his brother. If that made X a problem, then it was tomorrow's problem. The whole situation was X's fault. He'd brought Jason back to Lanesworth. He'd put Reece on Gibby.

At least Jason was out.

That was real, too. No walls, but no future, either. He had no money, and he grieved for the only thing he'd ever wanted for himself: a few acres of rocky coast, and an old boat with a new engine. But that was out of the question now. He had to run fast and far, but only after he found his brother, and murdered the shit out of Reece.

Or not.

He gave X a small nod, then put the car in gear, and got the hell out, over the hill and down, all along that dirt road. At the end of it, the blocking cars made way, and Jason hit pavement like he lived for the drive. He couldn't see the city, but felt it out there, like a moon rising. His look at the schematics had been brief, but he'd seen enough to worry. He had bad ribs and busted fingers, blurred vision, and blood in his piss.

He couldn't do it alone.

He needed help.

Jason ran options as the world flicked past, still and silent, as if respectful of the man and the cause. Jason had been in this place before, fast-moving in deep jungle, or church-quiet on the back of some starlit river. Three years out, and it was still an old friend, the dark charge of war.

When city lights rose in the distance, Jason turned into an empty gas station, and parked beneath one of its lights. The place was closed. No traffic. X wanted Jason to wait for Reece to leave the house, a fine plan if it wasn't your brother inside. Reece was unstable enough to do anything at any time, so Jason needed another plan. He studied the schematics until he knew them by heart, then opened the trunk, and found what X had promised: an M16A1, a Colt .45, and a half-dozen loaded magazines. Jason checked the actions.

Clean.

Crisp.

Also in the trunk was a hard-sided suitcase with his name written on it in black marker. It was heavy. Jason dragged it out, and popped the clasps.

Cash.

Lots of it.

There was a note, too. Jason read it in the gas station light.

You think me evil, I know, but the money is clean. Burn it if you
wish, or give it away if that makes you feel better. Nor, is this a
gift—you would decline on principle. See how well I know you?
I hope you will consider it compensation, and use it accordingly.
                                                Respectfully, X

PS—I don't plan to kill people, now that I'm out. Boring.

PPS—Except for Reece, of course. Not boring.

Jason read the note three times, then pulled two bills from the suitcase, and locked everything back in the trunk. He crossed the parking lot, looking sideways as he passed the pay phone.

A couple million in cash, and all he really needed was a pair of dimes.

At the gas station, he picked up a cinder block, tossed it through a window, and let himself in. The place was old and dusty, with shelves of oil and oil filters, headache powders and cigarettes and licorice gum. In the back was a beat-up desk covered with loose papers, ash, and moisture stains. Jason slipped two hundred dollars under the ashtray, and picked up the phone. He needed to make a call, and hated having to do it.

44

When the girl crawled out from beneath the bed, Reece tried to read the future in her face. She was afraid. *Obviously.* And cautious. She sat on the bed, clutching the blanket.

Wide eyes.

Beautiful eyes.

Reece chewed on the pad of his thumb.

If only she would settle in. Prepare a meal or open a bottle of wine. Maybe hum something. If she hummed a song, he might recognize it. He could find the record, maybe. And maybe leave it for her as a gift. It could be an opening, he thought, a shared love of the same song, this thing between them. The song would play, and she would smile. He imagined it on her face, the rose-petal lips and those straight, white teeth. He could hear the music; see the sway of her slender frame. The more she moved, the more she relaxed. She swayed, too, as she cooked. And they ate dinner together, and afterward, they danced, and her fingers were soft on his cheek, those lips slightly parted. When she took his palm, she pressed it on her breast; and the sway moved into her hips; and her legs were warm on his, and her breath was warm, and her lips were warm . . .

"Ow . . . damn it."

He'd bitten through the skin. His thumb was bleeding.

"Hello?"

Suddenly, the girl was on her feet. Reece held his breath, but she dropped the blanket. Reece did not like what he saw.

Nothing soft.

Not anywhere.

"I'm not insane," she said. "I did *not* imagine that."

She took three steps in his direction, and Reece flinched away, so quick and clumsy he struck a wall stud, and made enough noise to freeze the girl where she stood. That was the tableau. Two seconds. Then she came straight for the place he hid. Reece wanted to run. He couldn't stop watching. She smoothed a palm along the wall, then pressed her ear against it. He could see a bit of hair, the curve of her forehead. A foot to the left and she might find the hole he'd drilled into the base of a wall sconce.

So close!

If he held still . . .

If he was patient . . .

"Hey!"

Her palm struck the wall, and a sound escaped Reece's mouth, something like, *Yeep.* She fell backward, said *in the walls,* then picked up a chair, and flung it. It hit like a bomb; crashed to the floor. Reece wanted to calm her down, wanted her to breathe, so they might one day dance.

It's not too late.

It doesn't have to be.

He watched in horror as she picked up the chair, and beat it to pieces on the wall that stood between them.

In the basement cage, Gibby tilted his head.

"Chance, do you hear that?"

A distant pounding. Hollow. Rhythmic.

"I hear it."

Chance tried to sit up straight. He was stiff and hurting, though the bleeding had stopped.

"That way, I think."

Gibby gestured toward the corner of the room, and both boys stared through the mesh, up at the floor joists. Not directly above them, but, *Yeah, that way,* and like the screaming, inside the house.

Gibby said, "Whatever that is, I don't like it."

Chance agreed. "Come on, man. Get us out of here."

"Damn right."

Gibby went back to work. It wasn't easy. The clamp was small, and tended to slip. Half the bolts were rusted in place. He had five out, and needed to strip out three more along the bottom. He figured four more up the side and he could beat the corner into an opening.

"Let's go. Let's go. Let's make this happen."

Gibby needed no convincing. He broke a bolt loose; twisted it out, and went back for the next. "Six more."

That's when the pounding stopped, and the screaming started.

For French, the night was a tribulation of body and soul. He was exhausted, desperate, and half-blind from the glare of a million headlights. He'd crossed the city a dozen times, lied to his wife on six occasions, and humiliated himself in front of Captain Martin's entire family: midnight on the porch, and begging for information. But he was prepared to lie, steal, or cheat, to beat an informant half to death if he thought the guy was holding back.

Would he kill someone?

He was too tired to answer the question, and wouldn't trust an answer if it fell out of his mouth. He was down to random streets and places: a park they'd gone to when Gibby was a kid, the dead man's neighborhood, his neighbors, the crash pad of a dealer who'd grown up on Chance's side of town, just on the chance he might have heard something.

Nobody knew a thing. That was the problem. They had an ID on the dead man in Chance's house, and that gave them an address and a rap sheet, but that was it. The captain had sworn it: even the cops were dry.

How long until dawn?

Two hours?

"David 218."

The radio squawked, and French keyed the mic. "David 218, go ahead, Dispatch."

"Detective Burklow requests you call a private line. Stand by for the number."

"Go ahead, Dispatch." He found a pencil; jotted down the number.

"David 218, be advised the matter is urgent."

French was on a four-lane, west side of town, and the last pay phone he'd seen was two clicks back. No traffic this late, so he cut the wheel hard, and left an arc of smoking rubber. When the Food Town appeared, it was across the street, so he left another black arc, and hit the parking lot entrance so fast he grounded out the shocks.

Burklow picked up a half second into the first ring. "This is complicated, so I need you calm. Are you calm?"

French squeezed the phone until he thought his hand would break. "Yes, I'm calm. Where are you?"

"Pay phone eight blocks from your house. Before you ask, your wife tracked me down an hour back, saying things like *you were lying to her and she knew it, and it had to be about Gibby, and why would you lie about her last good son.* She was on the ledge. I went over to talk her down. That's when we got the call from Jason. He's out. He's looking for you."

"How is that possible?"

"I don't have the answers. He had little time and a lot of things to say, and that wasn't part of it."

French ground his teeth, trying hard to fight off the confusion and disappointment. "You said this was urgent. I thought it was about Gibby."

"That's the thing. Jason claims to know where he is."

"Say that again."

"Where he is, who has him, and how to get him out. He said the kid's in serious danger, that the guy who took him is a killer, the worst kind."

"Give me the address."

"Bill, he says it's the guy who killed Tyra Norris."

French realized something ten seconds after he left the lot: his tires did not have enough rubber for the way he wanted to drive. If he could break the laws of physics, he would. Burn the sky. Shake the ground. None of it was about choice.

But that was not exactly true.

Jason wanted Gibby safe and clear, but needed Burklow and his father to get it done. Just them, though, the three of them. But French believed in *bigger* help, and that meant manpower, control, the overwhelming force of the state. It was simple math. Roll heavy, and lock shit down. Resolution might take longer, but it was usually the better resolution. The hostage lived. No cops died.

That's where Jason became a problem.

If he was out, he'd escaped, and that meant people would be looking. French's people. There'd been nothing on the radio, but he couldn't exactly call in a request, either.

Dispatch, could you please confirm that my son has escaped from prison?

No. Couldn't do it.

And if Jason was right? If the man who'd butchered that poor young woman was the same who had Gibby?

The thought was unbearable.

So was the next.

Roll heavy or go light, whatever decision he made in the next few minutes would put one son in greater danger. If he called in reinforcements, Gibby would have a better chance of getting out alive. Tactical teams. Snipers. Trained negotiators. French believed that to the bottom of his shoes. It was instinct, faith, thirty years of cop. But Jason was a wanted man, a suspected killer; and there were cops in the city that would take him down without thinking twice, oil and fucking water. And Jason was very likely to give them a reason. He'd go hot; resist arrest. If French could do it, he'd tell Jason to leave, go now, let us handle it. But Jason had no trust for cops. *They'll get my brother killed . . .* He'd told Burklow as much.

French rolled down the window, but it didn't help.

There was this house, and in it, a killer . . .

Was this really the question he faced?

One son or the other?

It wasn't fair, but what was? French had gone to war, and killed, and lost one son already; he'd seen victims and unspeakable crime, spent years in the pursuit of evil men. In a good life, there'd been bad moments, but this was the worst, wind screaming in the car as he did the same in the silence of a breaking heart. One or the other, he had to choose.

French reached for the mic.

He made the call.

Finding the house was not a problem. The neighborhood was new money, but big money. Lots of gates and walls. Garages the size of a workingman's house. French got there first, did a slow drive-by, and then parked where he could see the gate, the roofline, the glow of lights beyond the wall. Burklow rolled in five minutes later, and it was a long five minutes.

"You okay?"

They met on the sidewalk, low-voiced as Burklow did a hard-target search of French's face. Whatever he saw there made him happy enough. He didn't repeat the question.

"Where's Jason?"

"I don't know. He said he'd be here."

The street was empty. They settled more deeply into the shadows cast by a streetlight two houses down. "Tell me everything he said."

Burklow glanced at the house. To save time, they'd decided to do the full rundown in person. "Jason knows a lot about the property. The structure is fortified with polycarbonate, armored glass and steel-core doors in hardened frames. The security system is state of the art. Eighteen cameras on the grounds. Another dozen inside. Motion sensors and infrared. Pressure plates at the main and rear gates."

"How does he know that?"

"How does he know any of it?"

"Do you believe him?"

"Do you?"

French thought, *Yeah, I do.* "Did he give you a name?"

"*Reece,* but he thinks it's fictitious. There's no Reece listed at this address. We can check property records after." An unhappy moment passed between them. "I think he might be injured."

"Jason? Why?"

"Something in his voice, his breathing, the fact he called us at all. I've never known him to ask for help."

That was true. Not even as a kid.

Burklow shifted uneasily, looking down from all his great height. They'd been together a long time, thick and thin. French didn't have to see his face to know his thoughts or the unanswered question that still hung between them. He nodded once, glad for the shadows, and how they hid his face. "Yeah," he said. "I made the call."

"I'm sorry, Bill."

"Yeah, me, too."

"How soon?"

"Not long." French did not trust his voice to say more. The first wave was already rolling: everyone on duty, and close enough to get there fast. Behind them, other cops were being called up, body armor issued, the armory broached. They had no warrant; they barely had probable cause. But no cop in the city had ever seen anything like what had been done to Tyra Norris, and every one of those cops wanted the guy who'd done it, proper procedure or not. French had slipped the chain, and it was coming, no stopping it.

Where was Jason?

Why wasn't he here?

Misunderstanding the expression on his partner's face, Burklow said, "Brother, you made the right choice."

French believed that, too.

It didn't help in the slightest.

45

Inside the bedroom, Sara rode emotion like the crest of an impossible wave. It lifted her, took her, and tossed her. She'd never been the angry person, the forceful personality. She'd gone along to get along. The easy friend. The laid-back neighbor. Only twice in her life had she lost complete control of her emotions, once on the day her parents kicked her out, and then again on the foggy, back-alley night she'd had the abortion. That was it, two times lost and out of control. This was the third, and after so much helplessness and fear, she stepped joyfully into the fire of pure, blind rage, screaming wordlessly as she tried to beat down the prison, the man, the wall she hated. When one chair came apart, she picked up another. Every chunk of drywall was pure adrenaline, the haze of dust like a drug.

Him. He. Whoever.

The rat in the walls.

The second chair shattered, and she could feel it out there, the tail end of her madness. Sheeted in sweat and fine, white dust, she picked up a length of jagged wood, thinking, *Fuck this place, and fuck this guy.* The screams were gone, but she stabbed at the Sheetrock, hoping the hard, sharp point would find something soft behind the wall.

Reece had no idea what to do. He'd chosen the girl for many reasons, one of which had been the easy compliance he'd seen in her approach to the world. He knew from bitter experience that women so lovely could be prone to disdain for men who looked and thought as Reece did. Sara had every quality he admired in a woman, the way she looked and moved, the soulful eyes and easy laugh. He'd followed her long enough to make sure, and everything he'd seen confirmed that first assessment.

She was compliant.

She could be taught.

Reece had never been so wrong in his life, and had no idea what to do with this rage machine tearing down his house. There was no *saving* this. His mind was already in transition. It wouldn't be the first time he'd cut losses.

The question was how.

She'd broken through the drywall and was attacking the plywood underneath it. Given enough time, she might actually punch through.

He'd have to shoot her, he decided. No fun in that, but he had no desire to be stabbed, either.

With a strange shock, Reece realized that he was feeling something close to actual fear. He lived for control, and had none. She was pounding on the plywood, and if anything, the pounding was getting louder and harder.

Get the gun; kill the girl.

Yet his paralysis was total.

Boom.

She hit the plywood.

Boom.

It gave a little more.

A high-pitched laugh found its way past Reece's lips, another disbelieving titter. Could it be any worse?

No, he thought. *Not possible.*

Two seconds later the alarm went off.

Schematics or not, the security system was too good for Jason to chance on his own. He had a fine memory and knack for tactical thinking, so keeping track of sensors and sight lines was far from impossible. But he didn't like the odds of running half speed on unfamiliar ground, not against a man like Reece.

So he did need help.

What he'd said to Burklow was not an actual lie.

Jason arrived ten minutes before his father, and parked one street over, slinging his weapons, and working through a strip of forest where Reece's property touched a neighbor's. He made a quick recon along the perimeter wall, located the rear gate first, and then a good access point to scale the wall, and watch the front approach. Lying flat, and invisible in the darkness, he was there when his father arrived. He watched Burklow arrive, too; saw them huddle in the gloom between streetlamps.

Jason studied the sky in the east. Paling, at last. Barely perceptible. He turned his attention to the house and grounds, confirming his opinions on sight lines and sensors, then marking doors and windows, looking for problems and the most likely places for opportunity to arise. More light in the east, false dawn, a time Jason knew well. *Soon,* he thought; and then it happened: sirens in the morning stillness, a cavalry call, the sound of his father's choice.

The alarm broke Reece's paralysis, his thoughts suddenly quick and sharp. The girl wasn't going anywhere, not for a while, at least. Somewhere was a larger threat. Reece hit the security monitors at full stride, eyes on the screens. It was a nightmare. Cameras at the gate showed a swarm of cops. Ten cars. A dozen. Three more rolled in as he watched.

Byrd, he thought. *He'd told someone about the job, given someone the address in case he didn't make it out. Now, Byrd was in the freezer with his two friends.* Reece's thoughts rolled over, logical and mechanical. The house was lost. Unfortunate, but not irretrievably so. Ownership was held by carefully layered corporate entities, none of which would trace back to Reece. Same with the cars, the utilities. He stored his financial information off-site for exactly this kind of circumstance. They'd collect his prints, of course, but Reece was not his real name, and he'd never been printed.

"Damn it!"

His control slipped, and he beat his fists on the console. The girl would live; he didn't have time to kill her now. Guns were in the main house. There and back would take time. What about the boys? That required thought, but he had to think fast. If the cops were smart, they'd circle the entire block. Reece didn't need to go through the front gate, but if they shut down the surrounding streets . . .

A terrible thought struck like a jolt of electricity. Cops on the street would not trigger the alarm. Reece scanned the screens.

Camera 1? Nothing.

Camera 2?

A flicker of movement drew his attention to camera 9, a slash of something dark, there for an instant and then gone.

Reece pulled at his hair.

Nothing!

No, wait . . .

Camera 12 caught another hint of movement. Someone was on the grounds. Cops? Something else? It didn't matter.

"Time to go."

Reece twisted through the secret corridors, and sprinted from the north wing, his thoughts touching again on the boys. Could X be responsible for this? He'd given his word: no contract on Reece's head. And X would never call the cops, not if his own life depended on it.

"Think!"

He'd planned for this. He had time.

But what if X *was* responsible?

Reece burst into the main house, snatching up cash and a gun, running numbers in his head. His escape route was through the side door, then across the rear grounds and through the small gate at the back. He owned the property on the other side, a second house with a second garage, bought years ago for contingencies like this. He'd timed it out before. He could clear the gate in sixty seconds. Another forty, and he could be in a car and on the road. What about the boys? Kill them? Take them? Kill the little one and take the other? He ran those numbers, too. Ten seconds to get out of the house. Five more to reach the basement door.

He made the decision on instinct. X was not involved. He'd been *specific.* It had to be Byrd. Or Reece had made a mistake with Tyra, or with Lonnie Ward, some bread crumb of a clue that brought the cops, at last, to his door. Smart move was to go, and do it fast.

But he did hate Jason French.

Handsome Jason.

Favorite Jason.

In the dark outside, the thought only grew. He couldn't get to Jason, and even if he could, he couldn't beat him. He'd seen what the bastard could do; those qualities X admired so much. A dark desire built as Reece hugged the shrub line, moving quickly, no sign of cops or intruder. He wanted to make Jason hurt, and for Jason to know it was he who'd taken, and he who'd destroyed. It would be easy, too. The boys were caged; the basement door was right there. How long could it take?

Pop, pop.

Two seconds, and gone.

46

When the last bolt dropped, Gibby bent the mesh as quietly as he could. It took time; it was harder than it looked. "You first."

He pulled the mesh as high as he could off the floor, and Chance slipped through like a greased ferret.

"Here, take this."

Chance took the pressure, and Gibby forced himself into the gap. He was larger, but made it through with only a few cuts and scrapes. Dusting himself off, he said, "I'll never look at a dog pound the same way."

"Whatever, man, I'm calling you *Houdini* from now on."

"Not yet. That door's locked from the outside."

Chance checked to make sure. It was solid steel, and seriously locked. "So what do we do?"

"A lot of dangerous stuff in here. I guess we find something sharp, and kill the bastard."

Chance waited for the punch line.

It never came.

"You check over there." Gibby picked up a scalpel, gripped it like a knife, and then put it down when he found a larger one. "Anything?"

Chance opened a few cabinets. "I found bleach."

"Check that big chest."

"It's a freezer."

"Check it, anyway."

The freezer door went up. "Um, Gibby."

"Yeah?"

"No. Seriously."

Chance's face should have been warning enough. It wasn't. Gibby crossed the room, and stared down. "Oh, Jesus."

"That's somebody's leg."

Gibby closed his eyes, but the image wouldn't go. Plastic, frost, those things that were beneath . . .

"Oh shit," Chance said. "I think that one is somebody's head."

"Close it, please."

Chance did that, too.

Behind them, a key grated in the lock.

For a moment, time stopped, then Gibby charged the door. It opened, and framed the small man—same gun in his hand—and there was a moment of pure comic genius: his face when he saw what was about to happen. Because Gibby was big and fast, and not about to slow down. He tucked his shoulder, and hit chest-high, one hundred and ninety pounds of pissed-off, shit-scared, eighteen-year-old with a very strong desire to live. He drove the little man back through the door, and they went down in a tangle, Gibby on top, and trying hard to stab a man somewhere it actually mattered. He had little luck, and no time at all. The gun went off, maybe into the dirt. Gibby rolled right, and the world exploded again, powder grit and fire as the gun lit off ten inches from his face.

Still alive, though.

Chance must have been close behind, because the next three shots went into the basement, then the little bastard was up and running. Gibby tried to stop him, but couldn't. He was half-deaf, half-blind.

"Chance?" He stumbled back into the basement. "Chance? You alive?"

"Yeah, believe it or not." Chance straightened as he stood, ten feet from the door and big as life. "That dude cannot shoot for shit."

Jason's plan had always been a simple one: distract Reece, then get in quickly and quietly, but *very* quickly and *very* quietly. Reece was a predator, and even predators could panic. Usually, that meant a hard run in a straight line, but Reece was the crazy kind of predator; and crazy was hard to predict. So Jason kept one eye on the house, and the other on the cops. His father was agitated and uncertain; they all were.

Right now, that was good.

The more the better.

And the cops were coming faster, too. Not a car here or there, but three or four at a time, light bars strobing. Jason waited for critical mass, then rolled left, and dropped over the wall. Best he could tell, the camera angles were almost perfect, but not quite. There were blind spots, and he used them, quick but smooth, stopping if he thought he needed to. He couldn't go straight at the house, and remain unseen. It was more like, *Twenty feet due north, then ten more at a diagonal.* He stopped more than once to get his bearings. It made for slow going, but the house was close, tall and massive, with multiple wings. That was the tricky part—not just getting inside but finding his brother, and getting back out before the cops worked up sufficient nerve to storm the gate.

He was counting on the time.

And the alarm codes.

If the codes were bullshit, he'd have to improvise, but he was good at that. Violence, speed, sudden changes to whatever plan had blown up in his face. It was a skill set he'd honed in three years of war, the difference between living and dying, going home empty, or getting the job done. In all those hard years, Jason had learned to not expect much from the world, but sometimes it could be a giving place.

Kind of.

When the shots came, they were close, two quick blasts, followed by three more. Jason took off at a dead run. No pain, no thoughts of pain. He had a location, but knew these things, too: it was doubtful Gibby had the gun, and the cops would for damn sure be coming in. Jason weighed his options in terms of seconds, not minutes. He went hot on the M16.

Five seconds, straight ahead.

Left at the corner.

He made the turn, weapon up, and saw Reece in full flight for the back wall, a perfect silhouette twenty yards out and running in a straight line. Jason could put one in his skull, count *one Mississippi,* and still have time to put another in his heart, all before he hit the ground. He didn't do it, though, and that hesitation surprised him. Maybe it was because he was tired of killing, or because there were a million cops beyond the gate. Maybe it was for X, or because Reece deserved something more than a clean, quick death. Whatever the cause, Jason's finger came off the trigger. When he lowered the gun, he saw his brother, standing with Chance outside a basement door.

"Jason? What are you doing here?"

"Kid, it's a long story."

"What's that noise?"

"That would be Dad and about a hundred cops. I suspect they're taking down the front gate. Either of you hurt? Either of you shot?"

Gibby blinked.

And Chance blinked.

Jason had seen it before in raw recruits. "You're in shock. You're going to be okay, but I have to move, and you have a choice to make."

"I still don't understand."

"It's this simple, little brother. Wait for Dad or come with me. There's no wrong answer, but you need to decide right now."

"Where are you going?"

"Not far and not for long."

"I'll come with you." No hesitation.

"Chance?"

"I go where he goes."

"All right, then." Jason slung his rifle as the gate came down. "Let's get the hell out of here."

47

The gate crashed to the earth in a cloud of splinters and dust, and the cops needed no more invitation.

Shots fired.

A blank check.

Tactical teams led the assault, but French cared for nothing but Gibby. He wanted to search the house at a dead run, but it was enormous, and Burklow was a very steady friend. "Just be still. Wait here. We have a lot of boots on the ground, and suspended or not, you're still the ranking detective. Information will come to you first."

Fear was the only reason he'd agreed: fear that he would find the remains of his son. He'd never felt anything like it. Nakedness. Raw terror. Those fears were only compounded when officers discovered a girl locked in the north wing. Burklow broke the news. "Tyra's friend Sara."

"Still no sign?"

"No sign is a good thing. Keep the faith."

Easier said than done. The girl was distraught, but dry-eyed. She continued to repeat the same thing: "He was in the walls, I heard him in the walls." They watched as she was led to a police car, and then to an ambulance.

"Something good," French said. But he was more concerned about the body parts in the basement freezer. *Eighteen-year-old parts or something else?* No one could tell him. He stood at the front door. Twenty minutes since the gate came down. "Any word from the medical examiner?"

"Five minutes out. Can I get you a coffee?"

French didn't want coffee. He wanted to know who fired the shots, who they were fired at and why. Dispatch had delivered three different messages from his wife. She wanted news. Where was her son?

"He has to be here." French tried to scrape the sleeplessness from his eyes. "And where the hell is Jason?"

"Oh, man."

"What? Ken? What?"

"Something Jason said. Bill, I'm sorry. With all that's happened, I forgot. It made so little sense when he said it. I had no context. Had no idea we'd find this."

He dipped his chin toward the house, and French squared up on his best friend of thirty years. Anger. Need. He could hide none of it. "Said what, exactly?"

Burklow lowered his voice. "He asked me to tell you that if things went sideways, he'd be at the quarry. You can see why I'd blank on that. It was four in the morning. I had no idea any of this was coming. The quarry? Seriously."

French raised a finger, too tired to conjure any real force. "You deal with this." He meant the house, all of it. "And please don't talk to my wife."

At the quarry, French parked beside the only car there. Jason stood alone at the water's edge, the morning light thin on his face. In spite of all that had transpired, the sun was still low, not a hand's breadth above the trees. French wasted no time; couldn't hide the distress. "Is he okay?"

"Gibby is fine. He was in shock for a while, but he's better. No physical harm." Jason kept his eyes on the water, but lifted his chin toward the cliff. "He's up there with Chance. Processing, I think. I told him I'd stay down here and wait for you. I wasn't sure you'd come."

French let his eyes move up the cliff's face. He saw them there, and almost broke. Now that he knew. Now that he could breathe. "He was at the house?"

"He was."

"Son, I don't understand any of this. Why was he there? How did you know he was there? How did you get him out?"

"Me? I was never there."

"Son, please."

Jason sighed, and it came from a deep place. "It's a long story, and I'm tired. As far as the cops are concerned, Gibby can tell you everything you need to know."

"The cops, yeah." French said it reluctantly. "Why did you call us? Burklow said you needed help."

"All I needed was the distraction."

French felt that one in his chest. "You knew I'd call it in."

"I believed you when you told me that Gibby was young and needed protection. I don't take it personally."

"What if you'd gotten him killed?"

"What if *you* had?" That bought a moment between them. Father. Son. Nothing quiet between them. "Like I said, I don't want to talk about it. He's alive. You're here."

"Just like that?"

"Pretty much."

"Do you really hate me so much?"

"Hate?" Jason looked his way for the first time. "Dad, I'll never hate you."

"But the rest of it?"

He meant family, the future. Jason raised his shoulders, and let them settle. "Too much water, I guess. Besides, it looks like I'm rocking this outlaw thing now. And, well . . ." He made a motion with his hand, like he was shaving down a piece of wood. "The open road is calling."

French wanted to say something to get his son back, to make up for the mistakes he'd made. "Would an apology help?"

"Not now, no." Jason's head moved. "In time, maybe."

French lifted his eyes to the cliff's edge. They were so small, the boys. "I know what you did at Bến Hải. How you saved that village. And I know what General Laughtner did to you, afterward, the way he tried to cover it up, the drugs and the dishonorable discharge. I wish I'd known sooner. I wish I could go back."

Jason raised an eyebrow, but showed no emotion at all.

French took that one in the chest, too. "Will you say goodbye to your mother?"

"She doesn't want to see me. You know that."

"Where will you go?"

"Are you asking as an officer of the law or as my father?"

"Enough, Jason. Please. As your father. Always, your father."

Jason took a deep breath, as if to fill himself up, then stooped for a rock, and skimmed it. "You feel like a walk?"

The trail was a quarter mile long, but felt longer. French still had things to say; and still had no idea how to say them. Each step was a moment lost, a steady dwindle. As they neared the top, Jason broke the silence. "He was only trying to help me, you know. Whatever he did to make you angry or make Mom worry . . . He's a good kid, and a lot like Robert."

French shook his head. "Once upon a time, maybe. The older he gets, the more I see of you."

Jason stopped for a moment. Birds were calling. Light slanted through the trees. "Do you really believe that?"

"Like you could be twins."

"Is that right?"

There was a note of surprise in Jason's voice. A smile came, too, and the sight of it broke French in half.

At the cliff's edge, he gave Gibby a hug, but not the fierce one he felt in his heart. It might have crushed the boy to death. He held him at arm's length, and studied his face. "Jason tells me you're okay."

"I am, yeah."

He kept his hands on Gibby's shoulders, but looked left. "Chance?"

Chance nodded, but kept his eyes down.

"I'm just glad you're okay, the both of you." French squeezed his son's shoulders, a final touch, an assurance. "We can talk about it later, okay? There are things I need to understand, but those things can wait, so long as you're okay. Tell me one more time. Not hurt? Not traumatized?"

"I'm good. We're good."

The worst of French's tension subsided. He looked across the quarry, thinking of his sons, of *all* his sons. A quiet moment passed. "This is where Robert dove, isn't it?"

"Right there. Jason did it, too."

French leaned out, looking down in disbelief. "Is that right?"

"It was just a thing." Jason shrugged as if the vacuum of that fall wasn't trying to suck them all down. "Do you guys mind if I have a moment alone with Gibby?"

My father led Chance to the trailhead, and they sat at the forest's edge, a hundred yards of stone between us. Jason looked from them to me, and when he smiled, I was surprised. It was not the normal smile; nor did it last. It was an eye blink of a smile, and it said a million things. "Let's talk about the dive," he said.

"What about it?"

He pointed. "That's your spot, right?"

"More or less."

He stepped to that spot. The stone was smooth, the cliff's edge sharp. Jason leaned out and looked down. "How long have you been working up the nerve?"

"Two years, I guess."

He dropped a rock, and watched it fall. "The world record is only fifteen feet higher. Did you know that?"

"You care about stuff like that?"

"I heard about it after I made the dive, but yeah. It's pretty cool." Jason stepped from the edge, his eyes very bright. "You know that *cool* is not enough reason to make this dive. You know that, right?"

"I guess."

"You guess? Really? It's four seconds, top to bottom. Hit wrong, and it may as well be concrete." He was quiet, but intent. "You need a reason to make a dive like this. Robert, for instance. Robert was going to Vietnam, and wanted to believe he couldn't die. He needed that. It's why he dove, and for him, that reason was good enough."

"I hear what you're saying, but come on, Jason. You did it on a wager. You did it for a day out drinking beer."

"Do you really believe that?"

"It's what you said."

"*What I said.*" He scoffed at the words, then looked away for long seconds. "Maybe I did it for a day out with my brother, for a chance to know the only one I have left. Did you ever consider that?"

I shook my head, wordless.

"Or maybe I'm the opposite of Robert," he continued. "He needed to believe he couldn't die. Maybe I needed to believe I was still alive, that my heart had room for something more than war and prison and regret. Maybe I *had* to make that dive." He made a fist, and tapped me on the chest. "You feel me, little brother? You feel what I'm saying?"

I offered up a solemn nod.

"It's the same with Vietnam," he said. "Don't go because I went, or Robert went. There's no glory, no honor. You have nothing to prove to anyone but yourself. That mirror can get cloudy at times—you're eighteen, I get it—but trust me when I tell you that war is no place to prove anything. Be a friend. Love the girl."

I looked at Chance. I thought of Becky.

He tapped my chest again, and said, "Trust me on this."

I told him I did trust him, and that I'd think about everything he'd said. When he turned to look across the quarry, I stood beside him, and we could see the forest and the water and the far, pale sun.

"I have to leave, you know."

"Cops. I get it."

"The Tyra thing—that'll go away now. The guns, though?" He shrugged. "There's only one thing here I'm sad to leave."

The emotion was real.

I could feel it between us.

"Take this, all right?" He handed me a piece of paper. There was an address there. "Nova Scotia," he said. "A little house on a black-pebble beach. I won't be there for a while—a year, at least—but when I get there, I plan to stay. Maybe you'll come see me sometime. It's a good place, I think. It belongs to a guy I ran rivers with in the DMZ. His grandparents left it to him, but he has no interest. Stone walls, though. A fireplace. He tells me the ocean is black at sunrise and hazel at lunch, that the surf is loud and the wind is like a woman's breath."

"Sounds . . . poetic."

"Yeah, well. My friend is a bit of a drinker." Jason smiled, and it was a good one. "Will you come see me sometime?"

"I will."

"Is that a promise?"

"It is."

48

Chance watched from the tree line, and felt more distance than the hundred yards between them. *Brothers,* he thought. *What could be closer?* They would smile at times, and looked normal when *nothing* was normal. Jason. Detective French. It didn't matter. People asked Chance if he was okay, and each time, he did the same thing. He nodded and said yes; but the sun was rising, and he was in the dark.

When Gibby and Jason returned to the trailhead, Chance stood quickly and awkwardly. "Um, does anybody mind if I stay up here for a few more minutes?"

"Here? Why?"

"I don't know, Gibs. The view. The quiet." Some of that darkness came out in his voice, so he dialed it down the best he could. "Look, it's been a rough couple days and one hell of a night. Can you give me a minute?"

Gibby's dad nodded as if he understood. "We all have things to think about. Take your time. We'll wait at the car."

"I'll be right behind you."

Chance watched them file down the trail, and disappear into the trees. When he was alone, he stepped to the edge of the cliff, and looked down. Wind rose up the stone, cool on the sweat of his face. How many times had he stood here? Not at the very edge, not like this . . .

Chance hung his toes over the drop, and leaned out to *that . . . exact . . . point.*

He'd always been so afraid of the cliff, even when it was Gibby at the edge. Each time he talked of diving. When he tried to find the will to do it.

Chance was tired of being afraid.

Last night, he'd been afraid, but not all the time. He'd helped them escape, and had been a few steps back when Gibby charged the gun.

Maybe it could be more like that.

Or had he followed Gibby on instinct? That was the pattern of his life, and the thought that wouldn't die.

Was he a follower?

A coward?

Chance stared across the water, and then down, a young man at the top of the world. He felt a hundred different fears: the fear of war and mutilation, of falling now, just now, or of diving wrong, and breaking. He feared his friend might not forgive him, that the wound would fester and that the cracks ran all the way through. Most of all, he feared whatever life waited at the bottom of the trail, the future if he walked instead of dove, the man he might become. That was the devil inside, a demon with a face as familiar-soft as Chance's own. Maybe it was fate that brought him to this place, or fate that people called it the Devil's Ledge.

Four seconds to the water.

Four seconds to know.

Chance spread his arms and counted to three.

He bent at the knees.

He rose.

49

Reece was bitter, and unable to deny that truth. He was cut and bleeding. That damn kid was still alive. He'd really wanted to hurt Jason in a very personal way.

At least he'd put that pretty boy in prison.

At least X was about to die.

That was the thought that made everything better. Even bleeding in the back seat with a bottle of hydrogen peroxide in one hand and a wad of bloody gauze on the floor, he could at least feel *that* joy. He had money and the whole world. And X had, what? Thirty-seven minutes?

Reece finished cleaning and dressing the places he'd been cut. Some were deep, none fatal. His shoulder. His ribs. He'd bought supplies at a drugstore, and stolen a shirt off the line as he'd worked out of the city and into scrub country where cops were thin on the ground.

Laying the last bandage, he taped it, and climbed out into the morning heat, where he'd parked at the end of a dirt road, oak trees grown tall on both sides of a farm gate, their shadows like ink on the ground.

Twenty minutes to Lanesworth.

Five or six if he had wings.

Reece flexed a bit, testing the tape. When everything held, he scooped up bloody gauze and his ruined shirt, and dumped it all in the high weeds beyond the gate. The stolen shirt was small, but would do the job. No bloodstains. No signs of injury. Not even the guards would look twice.

Starting the car, Reece planned his future as he drove. New name. New city.

Los Angeles, maybe.

Or maybe Miami.

Checking the time, Reece drove faster.

He really wanted to be there when X died.

Nearing the prison, he pulled on a cap and dark glasses; parked for an easy out. He knew better than to get hung up in the buses and news vans. The fields were packed with people, but people had never been a problem. *Keep your eyes down. Kill anyone you have to.* Simple rules for a simple man. He didn't need to be up front, either. Let the Bible thumpers handle the crush and the heat and the noise. Reece just needed to be there on the grounds, to know the moment he was gone. He'd take the memory with him, and wear it like a medal on his chest.

Five minutes.

He felt giddy.

Reece counted down the time, but nine o'clock came and went, and nothing changed. He'd expected an announcement when it was done, or to feel some shift as X left the world. The crowd seemed to feel the same frustration. He noted the strange looks that passed between people, the perplexed expressions of those newscasters he could see. That's where the ripple began. The news crews sprang to life. Cameras rolled tape, and the pretty people straightened up. But the expressions Reece saw were more shocked now than perplexed.

"Excuse me, sir?"

The voice was female and severe. Someone tugged on Reece's sleeve, and when he turned he found an iron-haired woman with heavy glasses and a thick neck. "Whoever you're looking for, it's not me."

"Are you Mr. Reece?"

The whole world seemed to stop. Noise died. No breath in his lungs. He said, "No."

Her disbelief showed in the frown and sharp glance. "I was given a very specific description of you, Mr. Reece, of your appearance and of five possible cars you might drive, including the one you parked just there. I was told you'd wear dark glasses and a hat of some sort, and that you'd stand at the rear of the crowd. I have a letter for you."

Reece shook his head, still struggling. "Who are you?"

"I work for the warden, if that makes a difference." She offered a sealed envelope. "Will you accept the letter or not?"

He took it with numb fingers, and she left with a final glance of disapproval. The envelope was thick, creamy, and expensive. It terrified him. Reece broke the seal, and removed a single page. He tried to focus, but the crowd was growing restless and very loud. Near the front, people began to push and shove, to actually shout. The noise spread like a wave. It rose, crashed, and spilled, in seconds, to the place Reece stood.

There would be no execution.

The prisoner was gone.

Rumor? News? Reece couldn't know, but he stumbled back, as if from an imminent, physical threat. He found a place between two cars, but the chaos only grew. People were pushing and fighting. Others stood in stunned disbelief. Reece tried to read what he'd been given, but his hands were shaking so hard he had to crouch between the cars, and put the letter on the ground.

He read it twice as a dark stain spread in his lap.

Epilogue

May 18, 1972

My Dear Reece,

    Or should I call you Teddy? That is your name, isn't it? Theodore Small, born forty-two years ago in Fairhope, Alabama? It was your mother, I believe, who liked to call you Teddy. And curl your hair, I've been told. And dress you in lace.

    But I digress . . .

    The point I wish to make is achingly simple. I have broken no promise—I never would. It was Jason French who came for you, and he did it gratis.

    But I digress again. Strange how that happens once there are so many thoughts to fill the mind . . .

    Specifically, Teddy, my thoughts are of you, and of what might happen when next we meet. They are such deep and lovely thoughts, an endless parade. And I must thank you from the bottom of this bottomless heart. Before you made me so angry, I had little reason to feel or care or live. Now I burst with purpose . . .

    I imagine this is disconcerting to you, but do take comfort from my other solemn vow. Once I am dead, you are perfectly safe.

    Until such time, I remain yours,

X